Who am I?

I waved my right hand. Chest-high flames sprung up around the nightwalker, completely encircling her. Her blue eyes widened, losing their unnatural glow. Her eyes were locked on the fire. I gave her a rough shake, and she finally met my gaze.

"Who am I?" I snarled, tightening my grip. Her eyes stared at me, confused and terrified. There was blood on her face. She too had fed on poor, chained Tristan—she deserved to die, consumed in the flames that surrounded her. And she knew it.

"You are the Fire Starter," she whimpered in a strangled voice.

"Tell them what I have done," I commanded in a low, grating whisper. "Tell them that if anyone touches what belongs to me, I shall hunt them down and collect their hearts for display in my domain. Remind them of who I am . . ."

By Jocelynn Drake

The Dark Days Novels
NIGHTWALKER
DAYHUNTER

daybunter

THE SECOND DARK DAYS NOVEL

JOCELYNN DRAKE

An Imprint of HarperCollinsPublishers

This is a work of fiction. Names, characters, places, and incidents are drawn from the author's imagination or are used fictitiously and are not to be construed as real. Any resemblance to actual events, locales, organizations, or persons, living or dead, is entirely coincidental.

EOS
An Imprint of HarperCollins*Publishers*
10 East 53rd Street
New York, New York 10022-5299

Copyright © 2009 by Jocelynn Drake
Cover art by Don Sipley
ISBN 978-0-06-154283-1
www.eosbooks.com

First Eos paperback printing: May 2009

HarperCollins® and Eos® are registered trademarks of Harper-Collins Publishers.

Printed in the U.S.A.

10 9 8 7 6 5 4 3 2 1

To Nate
Thanks for all the laughs

Acknowledgments

A special thanks to my editor, Diana Gill, for making me a better writer, and to my agent, Jennifer Schober, for working so hard to keep me sane.

dayhunter

ONE

We needed to feed.

Tristan's hunger seared my senses, burning through me in a hot, angry wave, until I was pressed against the rough brick wall that lined the alley. My nails dug into the palms of my hands, leaving bloody crescent moons as I hung onto the last tendrils of control over myself and the young nightwalker. Slowly, the consuming desire for blood subsided as the vampire struggled against the red haze. The wave pulled back, dragging across my bare flesh like a bouquet of stinging nettles.

Leaning back, I closed my eyes and drew in a steadying breath in an attempt to get a better grip on myself, but instantly regretted it. The narrow alley was filled with stale, fetid air, laced with rotting meat, mold, and what I could only guess was the smell of a decaying rat or two. Gagging, I lost my hold on Tristan's mind and the next wave of hunger swamped us both, knocking me to my knees.

Across the dingy expanse, Tristan's blue eyes glowed with a light that had nothing to do with heaven or the glory of God. His long fingers were like claws and his nails were dug into the wall behind him as if in one final, desperate attempt to keep himself from attacking the first creature to cross his path. There was little left to him that was human beyond the slender frame that held him. His beautiful features were drawn and lean; a fierce collection of bone and muscle possessed with the need for blood.

Mira.

Tristan's mind reached out and touched my own, but it wasn't his usual soft voice. It was deep, rough, and darkly seductive; matching the rumble that echoed against the ragged remains of my soul. The same monster lived inside of me, craving blood, longing for the feel of my fangs slipping into flesh. It was the monster that demanded I drink so deep I felt the soul of my prey brush against the back of my throat.

The voice in my brain faded, replaced by the cacophony of man. Sweet London, teaming with humans and the thunderous pound of their hearts. The night was so young and fresh, like a fragile girl on her way to her first ball. Tristan and I had escaped to a dark, seedy corner of the old city that overflowed with life calling out in a steady drum beat.

We both needed to feed, desperately. The battle had gone badly, leaving Tristan and me wounded and drained of the very substance that had sustained our existence well beyond what should have been our natural end. We needed blood and we knew I was the only thing keeping him from killing his prey when he finally sank his teeth in. He wouldn't mean to; we didn't need to kill. But there was no moral fiber guiding his decisions any longer. There was only the red wave of blood lust and the need to survive.

At the other end of the block a man with graying brown hair shuffled out of the night and paused at the corner. Cupping his hands before his face, he lit a cigarette and looked around, his heavily lined visage apparent in the lamplight. He gazed up and down the street, the hand holding the cigarette trembling, the little bud of fire twitching in the darkness.

A low growl rose from Tristan's throat as his eyes locked on this prey. I launched myself across the tiny alley and crushed him against the wall. The young vampire snarled at me, fangs bared and blue eyes reduced to narrow slits. He no longer saw me or cared that I could rip him apart without straining myself. I was older and stronger, but he needed blood and nothing was going to stand in his way.

"Wait," I ordered between clenched teeth, my fingers biting into his muscular arms. His clothes were ripped and splattered with blood from our struggle with the naturi earlier in the evening. My thoughts stumbled as the smell of Tristan's blood and that of the naturi mingled in my nose, conjuring up images I didn't want to recall just yet. The battle had been a success only in the sense that we both survived and had the energy to hunt, a failure in that my beloved bodyguard Michael lay cold and dead back at the Themis Compound.

With a grunt, I turned my attention to the man standing on the distant street corner. I had to exert only a little effort to touch his drug-addled brain and draw him over with the misconception that a potential customer had beckoned him, interested in viewing his wares. When the man was standing within the shadows of the narrow alley, I released Tristan and slipped silently back to the opposite wall.

"Don't kill him," I whispered as the nightwalker lunged.

Tristan's prey heard my words and managed a half step backward, his fear spiking so I could feel it cut through the dark alley and the haze of blood lust, but it was too late. I stepped back, pressing against the brick wall as the night-walker wrapped his arms around the man like a pair of steel bands. I couldn't tear my eyes away and found myself sliding to my knees as Tristan fell to his.

Slipping into the nightwalker's mind, a wave of sensations washed over me, pulling me under. Tristan drank deeply, sucking the intoxicatingly warm blood into his cold body. I could hear his throat muscles convulsively working, sending the thick liquid down into his stomach. To make the feast that much sweeter, he left the man conscious. The drug dealer's heart was pounding in his chest, a single piston hammering away but getting him nowhere. His fear filled the narrow alley, overwhelming the scent of rotting garbage and damp mold, dragging a soft moan across my parted lips. Kneeling on the ground with my hands clenched into fists, I listened to the man's heartbeat start to slow. He had passed out.

"Release him," I said in a hoarse voice. Tristan hesitated but did as I commanded. Laying the man against the wall, he turned to look at me, balanced on the balls of his feet. His blue eyes glittered and danced, rare gems in the darkness.

For the first time since I had met him, Tristan seemed truly alive. At the nightclub with Thorne, he had been on the run, hiding from Sadira, his personality muted by the constant fear of discovery. But now, something within him finally pulsed with new life. It was my promise to help him gain his freedom from our maker. A promise he knew I would do my best to keep.

The scrape and shuffle of footsteps intruded into our dark, blood-splattered corner of the world. Both of us froze, waiting to see who approached. From the moment Tristan sank his fangs into his meal, I had been cloaking our presence; a natural reflex at this point in my existence rather than a conscious thought. The veil protected us from the sight of any and all nonmagic users. In other words, normal, everyday humans.

At the steady cadence of footsteps, the young nightwalker had thrown up his own protective veil, which was instantly interwoven with my own. He felt stronger now and his thoughts were sharp and clear. I could sense the nervousness that worried the frayed edges of his mind, but he remained as still as stone, and I was confident that he would follow my lead.

A man with short brown hair started past the alley. His walk was brisk and confident. He turned his head toward the alley and his eyes quickly swept the narrow expanse. Tristan and I remained unmoving, waiting. For a moment I felt as if I was somehow both predator and prey. Yet the man's gait never faltered and his gaze returned to the street before him. He didn't see us.

But the witch and werewolf did. Following two steps behind the man with the square jaw was a witch in worn jeans and a lycanthrope in khakis. Her easy walk skidded to a rough halt and her shoulder-length brown hair swung forward to crowd her narrow face. The lycan stopped beside her and frowned, causing heavy lines to furrow his hard face.

"Shit!" The explosive whisper escaped her as she stared at us.

Tristan and I remained frozen, waiting for the intruders to make the first move. Tristan's dinner was still unconscious and mostly hidden behind the young nightwalker. However, we were both covered in blood and our clothes were torn from our fight earlier in the evening. Not one of our most attractive moments. Of course, when it came to the other races, we had all developed a kind of "to each his own" attitude. So we waited. If the witch and lycan resumed walking, we would all pretend we didn't see each other.

We weren't that lucky. The human spun on his heel at the witch's exclamation, grabbing a gun from the small of his back. It had been hidden beneath his loose-fitting, button-up shirt with a garish dragon print. His eyes and gun swept the alley again, but he still did not see us.

The witch reached over and laid her right hand on his broad shoulder. She whispered, *"Specto,"* and I felt a small ripple of power move through the air. The spell could have been performed by nearly any novice with a basic knowledge of Latin, but it was enough. The man blinked once and instantly paled as his grip tightened on the gun. Now he saw us.

"Keep walking," I said in a low voice. I couldn't risk a fight. The need to feed was nearly overwhelming, and if I was forced to fight, there was a very good chance that someone would end up dead. The monster inside me roared and hammered against the inside of my chest like a frantic heartbeat, demanding blood.

Tristan turned his head to look at me, waiting for my direction. Unfortunately, our new friend was trigger-happy. Jerking the gun over to point at the young nightwalker, he squeezed the trigger. With the soft click of the firing pin, Tristan and I were already in motion. The young vampire fell to the ground, but the bullet slashed across his upper right arm.

Darting across the alley, I grabbed the man's hand as he swung around to point the gun at me. Stupid humans. Even if he shot me in the heart, he wouldn't have succeeded in killing me. Guns couldn't kill a nightwalker. Shotguns could be troublesome, but then the shooter had to get lucky as well. With fangs bared, I slammed his hand into the nearby brick wall, crushing bones. The man screamed as the gun fell from his limp fingers and clattered to the ground. Still holding his hand, I tossed him like a bag of trash over my shoulder into the alley. He hit the wall and crumpled to the ground unconscious.

"Watch him," I growled to Tristan as I turned my attention to the witch and the lycan.

There was no chance to slow down and talk it out. And in truth, I was no longer in the mood for polite conversation. With an ugly snarl, the werewolf launched himself at me, his eyes glowing copper red. He slammed me into the brick wall, pinning my arms between our bodies, but his arms were free. His right first slammed into my left side, cracking at least two ribs. The shock wave of pain that rippled through me cut through the haze of blood lust and fatigue. His left fist followed, hammering my right side, bruising organs still tender from my earlier fight with the naturi.

Grunting under the pain, I jerked my head forward. The top of my forehead connected with his nose, breaking it. He fell back a step and I lifted my knee, slamming it into his groin. The lycanthrope howled in pain, stumbling away. His hands moved from his broken nose to his groin, holding himself as if it would ease the pain. The scent of his blood instantly hit the air.

Any thought of restraint evaporated. I was on him before he could draw a breath. My fangs sank into his throat, tearing the flesh. The blood rushed into me and sweet relief swept through my entire body. It was thick and warm and carried with it the lycan's strength. He fought me, pushing, punching, kicking, and clawing desperately, but I could not be removed. With each swallow, he grew weaker and I grew stronger, slowly draining his life away.

"Mira!" Tristan shouted, finally causing me to lift my head. I let the lycanthrope fall unconscious at my feet. Tristan rushed forward to stand between me and the witch in an attempt to protect me, but she must have assumed he was coming after her.

"No!" she screamed, her small, narrow face a ghostly white. She hadn't moved during my brief scuffle with her companion. I doubt she even breathed. Her wide brown eyes skipped from me to Tristan.

Raising her right hand, she began murmuring an incantation under her breath. I had taken a single step toward her, trying to get in front of Tristan, when her right hand was engulfed in a ball of yellow and orange flames. I paused, a tiny smile toying with my lips. She was smart. Normally, the sight of fire in the hands of a witch would send any nightwalker running for shelter. However, I wasn't just any night-walker, I was the Fire Starter. Controlling fire had been both my gift and curse since I was a human child. Poor witch.

With a grunt, she hurled the fireball, aiming for Tristan. Reaching out with my right hand, the fire curved toward me and settled in the palm of my open hand. Smiling broadly, I closed my fingers and extinguished the flame, plunging the narrow alley back into darkness.

The witch frowned, confusion clearly written across her pale face. Refusing to admit defeat, she lifted both hands and repeated the spell. This time I could feel the pull of energy in the air. She was putting everything she had into this one. I stepped in front of Tristan as she threw a pair of large fireballs at me.

My eyelids drifted nearly closed and time slowed. The smell of the rotting garbage and the sounds of the people within the city ceased to exist. There was only the fire as it roared at me. With my palm out, I waved my left hand before my body. The flames once again followed my pale hand. They gathered around it for a moment, then slithered up my arm and down my chest like a well-fed python. I could not be burned.

Yet something was off. While my focus was on the fire, I could hear the monster inside me screaming, but it wasn't the roar of hunger I had listened to for more than six centuries. It was a shriek of anger and pain. Suddenly confused and fearful, I redirected the flames to wash down my legs like water. However, the second the fire touched the ground, my senses exploded. The earth was consumed in a blinding white light, scorching my brain. Beneath my feet I could feel an enormous well of power flowing like a river, and the fire was returning to it.

And then nothing. The fire was gone and cold silence crowded around me. The new connection had snapped off before I could even begin to guess at what I'd tapped into. The white light faded. Even the growling hunger inside of me had gone still, possibly with the same wary confusion.

The telltale scrape of a shoe across concrete drew my attention back to the witch. Her arms were tightly wrapped around her middle and she was slowly shaking her head. "Oh, God," she moaned in a hoarse voice. "The Fire Starter. Here."

Before I could take another step toward her, the woman reached into the front pocket of her jeans as she took a step backward and disappeared.

"Damn it," I whispered, fighting back the chill that swept up my spine. She knew who I was. It was one thing for a nightwalker to recognize me on sight. Fear was useful when it came to controlling those who would try to control you. But I didn't like it when the other races discovered my presence. There was no telling who was pissed at me at any given time.

Now the questions became: Where did she go, and was she reporting my presence to someone stronger and meaner? Judging from her age, spell choice, and amount of power used, she wasn't a particularly experienced witch. Furthermore, transportation spells like that were extremely advanced. When she'd reached into her pocket, she must have touched a locator charm, probably created by someone much more powerful.

Frowning, I bit back a curse. This was all idle speculation. I knew a fair amount regarding magic because I had suffered through enough run-ins with witches and warlocks to learn a few things. I needed to talk to Ryan and get his thoughts. Unfortunately, the white-haired warlock was his own bundle of trouble, and I was in no hurry to deal with him again just yet. I would have to manage with the witch's unconscious companions for now.

Turning to approach Tristan, my knees buckled and then I found myself kneeling on the ground. I blinked once to clear the growing fog from around my thoughts. Using fire had sapped the last of my strength, and my body was demanding that I feed again and rest. What strength I had gained from feeding off the werewolf was gone.

The young vampire appeared at my side, a firm hand resting beneath my elbow. I gazed up at him, a worried expression twisting his handsome face. "Has she done something to you?" he inquired. For the first time since meeting him, I heard a soft accent in his speech. French maybe, but different. A remnant of his human life. Slowly, he guided me back to sit on the ground, my back pressed to the brick wall.

"No," I replied with a weary smile. "Just tired. I need to rest a minute." I jerked my head toward the human who had pulled the gun. "Is he still alive?"

"For now," Tristan grumbled, the hand on my elbow tightening as his eyes drifted over to the body of our gunman.

Laying my left hand beneath his chin, I forced him to look at me. "And he'll stay that way. I need you to discover the identity of our attackers without killing him."

Frowning, Tristan rose and returned to the man's side. He stood over the man, his fists on his hips. I couldn't tell whether the nightwalker was stalling out of distaste for the task or if he had begun rummaging through the man's mind. Some nightwalkers had to physically touch their prey to enter his or her mind, especially if the person was unconscious.

"David Perry," Tristan suddenly said, a faintly far-off quality to his voice. His mind was half with me, half with the human. "Thirty-six. Ex-marine. From Birmingham, Alabama. He's—" His words were broken off with a harsh hiss and his eyes glowed pale blue when he looked over at me. "He's a member of the Daylight Coalition."

"Tristan!" I barked, lurching to my feet as the nightwalker

started to reach for the unconscious man. He halted, but still growled in the back of his throat, and I couldn't blame him. I would have been happy to rip the human's throat out at that second too.

The Daylight Coalition was a group of humans within the United States who knew of the existence of nightwalkers and sought our total extermination. Humanity believed them to be a cult of insane fanatics and didn't take them seriously. Of course, that didn't erase the fact that members of the Coalition had staked a number of nightwalkers during the daylight hours. Regardless of whether you resided in the United States, all nightwalkers knew of the Coalition. We all feared they were the future we faced if we came "out of the coffin," so to speak.

But for now my concern was not the little zealot at my feet, but the witch and lycan he traveled with. All our information said that the Daylight Coalition was exclusively human, wisely avoided by the other races. In fact it was against our law to work with the Coalition. One turncoat could result in all out war. This was not a good development when we already had a war brewing with the naturi.

"Focus," I snapped, standing beside Tristan. "Who was the woman?"

Tristan stared down at the man, radiating a lethal mix of anger and fear. "Caroline . . . Caroline Buckberry, but he wondered if it was her real name . . . " The anger started to ebb as his focus tightened on the man's thoughts, causing his eyes to drift closed. "He didn't know her. He was sent by the Houston branch to fetch the woman and the man. Harold Finchley. That's all." Tristan opened his eyes again and looked up at me. "He was told to go to London and bring them back to Houston. I don't think he even knew what they were."

"He didn't have to know," I murmured. "Perry is just a foot soldier. He follows the orders he's given."

"Do you think they were to be plants by the witches and lycans?" Tristan inquired. I didn't miss the hopeful note in his voice.

"No," I replied with a slight shake of my head. "The witches and warlocks have no business with the Coalition. Either one of them could have said something to explain their association with the human. But instead they attacked because they know the law."

"But—"

"Forget what you saw," I said, cutting off his next comment. "We have bigger problems."

"The naturi." His hands curled into fists and the muscles in his jaw tightened.

Yes, the naturi were coming and they would destroy us all, human and nightwalker, if given half a chance. In comparison, the Daylight Coalition was nothing; a fly on a rhino's ass.

Standing, I propped my right shoulder against the alley wall and let my eyes drift shut for a moment. I hardly recognized my world anymore. A few nights ago I had been standing in my own domain back in my beloved Savannah, the warm summer air filled with the scent of honeysuckle and lilacs. It had been five hundred years since that night on Machu Picchu. The naturi were a distant memory, a dark nightmare from my past that could no longer touch me. The Daylight Coalition was just a fringe group with no contact with the others. But now both were threatening. My world was crumbling at an alarming rate and it all started with the hunter, Danaus. But there was no need to kill the messenger . . . yet.

Thoughts of him brought a faint smile to my lips as I pushed off the wall and opened my eyes. Tristan was watching me intently, waiting. He needed me alive to fulfill my promise to him. There was still time.

Briefly, I looked around the alley until I located the gun the human had used. There was no hesitation. There was no gray area in this law. Standing close, I fired a single bullet into the head of the lycanthrope. He had betrayed not only his own kind, but all the other races. He endangered our secret. And now he paid the cost with his life.

But his death didn't dissolve the cold knot in my stomach. The Daylight Coalition's main target had always been night-walkers, but we were all confident they would attack any nonhumans eventually. Had Harold Finchley been a wolf acting alone, or was he part of a larger movement against nightwalkers?

"Wipe the memories of both men," I said, motioning toward the drug dealer Tristan had fed from only minutes ago. Walking over to the Coalition member, I wiped the gun off on his shirt and dropped it by his body. "Then return to my hotel room." Danaus would already be waiting there for us. From the hotel, we would head to the airport and grab my jet to Venice. If we were to have any hope of stopping the naturi and the coming war, we would need to first go to Venice and meet with the nightwalker Coven. They would know the best way to deal with the growing threat. They were the only ones who could summon an army.

"Where are you going?" Tristan asked.

A broad smile lifted my lips, revealing a pair of long white fangs. "To hunt."

Two

I ran several blocks, merging with the shadows until I was nearly a mile from Tristan. A horrible trembling had started in my limbs and began to vibrate through my entire body. I throbbed and ached with a mixture of fresh wounds sustained during the past few hours and old wounds not completely healed from the night before. The world was an angry swirl of pain and noise and glaring lights. Pushing it all aside, my focus narrowed to a single pinpoint of finding prey.

Hunting had been a solitary act almost from the moment I was reborn. For me, it was a personal moment. Most nights I was particular about my prey, choosing him or her based on history or personal philosophy. I would listen to my prey's thoughts until something finally enticed me to move. And then there were nights like tonight, where I grabbed the first poor fool to cross my path.

She was nineteen, and for a second she thought I was a rapist. Grabbing a handful of her dark brown hair, I jerked her into the deep shadows of a doorway. She pushed against me, tears gathering in her wide hazel eyes. I sunk my fangs into her throat as a scream rose to her lips. Out of some latent kindness, I pushed her thoughts down into a deep sleep as

I drank. Swallowing her blood, I let its warmth and life fill me, and I drank until my memory of the night grew blurry and distant. The monster in my chest, hiding behind the remnants of my soul, was briefly appeased by the offering.

Reluctantly, I released her as her heart slowed to a lethargic beat. Holding her in my arms, I stared down at her smooth young face. I didn't know her. She could have been a college student or a young mother on her way home. I hadn't taken the time to sift around in her thoughts, learn her hopes or her fears. I didn't know her dreams for the future and I felt cheated. Hunting and feeding were more than a power rush. It was my last contact with humanity, the last thing that kept me bound to a race I had once been a part of. While I felt rejuvenated, a more subtle ache had started in my chest. A type of weariness that might have worried me if I allowed myself to dwell on it, but there simply wasn't time.

I gently sat her against the doorjamb and healed the wound on her neck. It was a gift of evolution, I think. We could heal the puncture wound caused by our fangs so we could remain hidden. Unfortunately, I couldn't heal knife or bullet wounds, forcing me to watch more than one injured human companion die in my arms.

Before leaving, I wiped her memory clean. It was better that my kind not be remembered just yet. But it was more than a need for our own protection. She didn't need to recall the momentary horror of being held in my arms.

On my way back to the hotel I fed twice more, using the same care as with the young woman. While I never bother to learn their names, they would never remember that they had been stopped. I walked down the winding London streets, angling back toward the river as I slipped through the crowd of people. Those few remaining on the lamplit streets were oblivious to my presence. My bloodstained appearance would have caused a panic.

The night air was thick with moisture, as if the skies were preparing to open up in a late night summer shower. A slim mist hovered just above the ground and wound its way around the occasional tree. Thin and wispy, it seemed little more than a ghost, or maybe the forgotten soul of this old town.

Wandering the streets, I let the warm summer air dance around me as I thought of my home in Savannah and walking along River Street. After a night of entertainment at the bars in the area, I would stroll through one park after another that dotted the neat little city, heading back toward Forsyth Park. I would smile at the scantily clad young people as they hurried to and from the row of bars, restaurants, and nightclubs, oblivious to me even if I wasn't using an enchantment. Their laughter and voices lowered to rough, giggly whispers skipped about me like leaves caught up in a breeze, bringing a twinkle of amusement to my eyes.

At Forsyth Park, I would pause at the enormous fountain bathed in yellow lights. Seated on the edge, I'd close my eyes and listen to the steady hum of traffic as it swirled around me. The leaves would rattle and the Spanish moss sway in the breeze, whispering to me old tales of love and death and loneliness. From there I could feel the pulse of the people in my city.

But trudging along the streets of London, covered in dried naturi blood, I couldn't hear my city or the soft murmur of laughter from her people. For the first time in a very long time, I was homesick. I missed my city's streets, dotted with old oak trees and tidy little parks. I missed her fountains and the river that caressed her banks. I would have liked to see her one last time; to stroll along the historic district and gaze up at row after row of vintage homes restored to their pre–Civil War beauty. To enjoy just one last dance at the Docks, where the music pounded in loud, angry beats and the air was thick with the scent of sweat and blood.

Just days ago I had been queen of my little mountain, or as we preferred to say: Keeper of my domain. Then Danaus waltzed in and destroyed my world. The vampire hunter brought news that the naturi were threatening to escape their bindings and enter our world for the first time in centuries. While Danaus obviously held no love for nightwalkers, he at least understood that the naturi were worse.

Guardians of the earth for centuries, the naturi had finally decided that the only way to truly protect the earth was to destroy all of mankind. So a war was waged over countless years, resulting in the deaths of hundreds of naturi, humans, and nightwalkers. We finally succeeded in locking most of the naturi in another world, separate from earth but forever linked. But it was temporary. With naturi on both sides of the seal working to open the doorway, we knew it would be a constant struggle to keep them contained. A triad of nightwalkers kept the seal protected, but all went strangely quiet for roughly five centuries, and despite our long memories, we forgot to pass along information to the fledglings we created.

The end result was a series of deaths that should have never occurred. After nights of struggling to reform the nightwalker triad that sealed the naturi host away, I not only failed to protect Thorne, who was to join the triad, but also lost my precious bodyguard. Michael, my guardian angel with golden locks. Adding to my worries, I discovered that I was to be the weapon wielded by the triad, which now included a vampire hunter.

With a sigh, I looked up and found myself standing in front of the Savoy. It was time to return to the task of saving the world. I was tempted to say the hell with it all, but I would be losing my beloved city as well. And if I didn't protect it, who would?

Smiling grimly, I slipped inside the hotel and rode the

elevator up to my room, where Tristan and Danaus were patiently waiting for me. Well, one more patiently than the other.

When I opened the door, Tristan was lounging on the sofa, hands behind his head, ankles crossed. His cheeks were flushed and he radiated blissful satisfaction. He had fed again after I left him and was obviously feeling quite pleased. It also probably helped that he'd showered and was clean of all the blood that once covered him. He was still wearing his bloodstained clothes, but I knew he couldn't care less. There was something about having a full stomach that made a nightwalker much more tolerant and amiable. It also didn't hurt that Sadira, our controlling maker, was already in Venice, giving him an extended break from her.

The vampire hunter, on the other hand, was standing at the window, arms folded across his chest. He was still in his torn, bloodstained clothes, but like Tristan, the blood had been washed from his skin. His dirty hair was pulled back from his face, revealing high, strong cheekbones and vibrant eyes of deep cerulean blue. His chin and jaw were covered in a shadow of dark stubble, giving him an even grimmer appearance than usual. I imagine he wasn't used to patiently waiting around for anyone, much less a nightwalker.

Shaking my head at him, I wordlessly darted through the suite to the bathroom. I quickly stripped out of my clothes and turned on the hot water. I had just stepped under the spray when I heard the bathroom door open.

"We have to leave," Danaus said irritably.

"I'm not traveling like this," I shouted over the noise of the falling water. "Five minutes."

Danaus grunted, leaving me to assume that he accepted my decision and was going to wait "patiently" in the other room. The hunter was a puzzle I was positively itching to work on, particularly with his informative, monosyllabic replies guiding me. Yet, for all his irritation and threats, I was becoming accustomed to his presence.

"Wait!" I called out when I heard him turn the door handle to leave. With my left hand, I grabbed a handful of the mauve shower curtain and pulled it back just enough to poke my head out. I cracked one eye as water ran down my face. Danaus stood half turned toward me, with the bathroom door partially open so he could beat a quick retreat if he needed to.

"What do you know about the Daylight Coalition?" I asked, running my right hand over my face to get some of the water out of my eyes.

Danaus released the door handle and gave the door a little push shut. Folding his arms across his broad chest, he leaned his hip against the white marble sink. "Just humans hunting vampires. Sounds like a good cause to me." His hard face was expressionless but his sharp eyes were intent upon my face.

Throwing one last scowl at him, I jerked the shower curtain closed and moved back under the water. As I grabbed the washcloth to resume scrubbing, Danaus laughed. Actually, the hunter didn't make a sound, but I could feel him laughing on the inside. He was teasing me, trying to get under my skin.

Earlier in the evening he had touched my hand and sent his powers through me. Our connection was still strong when we were in close proximity. We had killed the naturi and survived, but we were still working out all of the repercussions. I couldn't quite make out his thoughts, but his emotions flowed easily to me. And I had a feeling he could just as easily pick out my emotions.

"Bastard," I grumbled, scrubbing my right forearm. I did not doubt that he heard me over the water. I didn't know what Danaus was, but he wasn't human. At least, not all of him. He felt human, but his hearing appeared to be as keen as any nightwalker's. He had the speed and agility of a lycanthrope, but not their strength. He couldn't cast spells like a warlock, but had a dark ability that allowed him to boil a creature's blood within its skin. At the very least, this combination had taught me to be wary of him.

"They're fanatics," Danaus said after a moment. His voice sounded tired, worn down to a smooth murmur. "They've killed as many humans as they have actual vampires. Why?"

"Tristan and I encountered a trio tonight," I said. I soaped up the washcloth again and ran it over my stomach, relieved to find the hideous gash I received that night was completely healed. "No, that's wrong. We encountered a member of the Coalition, a lycan, and a witch."

"Traveling together?"

"Yes. The man had been sent to fetch the witch and lycan."

"Did you kill them?"

"Danaus!" I shouted, my fist tightening around the wet washcloth.

"Did you?"

Throwing down the washcloth, I turned and pulled back the shower curtain again so I could look at him. "Does it matter that they attacked us first and they were trying to kill us?" I snapped.

"No." While his face and voice were calm when he replied, I felt the flutter of something else in his chest. A flash of anger and frustration. Maybe a bit of fear. But he had his emotions back under tight wrap before I could clearly identify any of the swirling maelstroms within his mind.

"The human is still alive," I said between clenched teeth, jerking the curtain back into place, the metal rings holding up the divider letting out a little squeal. "I broke the man's hand and knocked him out. The witch disappeared after trying to flambé Tristan and me."

"And the werewolf?"

"The lycan is dead," I bit out. Werewolves can heal from a lot of things, but a bullet in the head while you're low on blood isn't something you come back from. "He broke our law. If I hadn't, he might have told the Coalition about us all." I said the words and believed the rationale, but something knotted in my stomach for a second time. It was my complete lack of remorse. The fact that I hadn't even hesitated in my decision to kill him. Knox, my assistant in Savannah, once called me a mindless killing machine. The description had been kind.

I stood under the hot water, trying to wash away the memory of the encounter and Danaus's words. Our occasional teasing and joking meant nothing to him. My respect for his skill and his sense of honor were worthless. In the end he wanted all of my kind dead. He wanted me dead because he saw me only as a killer

"Damn it, you're missing the point," I said into the water.

"No, I'm not." His words were softer than they had been. "A witch and a lycan were traveling with a member of the Daylight Coalition. I'll call Ryan and see if he knows anything. Do you know the name of the witch?"

"Caroline Buckberry," I sighed. "That might be an alias, but I'd wager she's a local. Or at least, her mentor is."

"Why?"

"I think she used a charm to disappear, and judging by the amount of power I felt in the air, I'd guess she didn't travel far. She's a novice."

"I'll check with Themis. Ryan might know something."

"Thank you," I whispered, not caring if he heard me over the water.

"I understand why you did it, Mira," he said. I hadn't heard him move, but he sounded closer, as if he were just on the other side of the shower curtain. "You did it to protect us all. I understand it, but I don't have to like it."

I listened to the sound of the door opening and closing, a frown pulling at my lips. Bracing both of my hands against the wall in front of me, I closed my eyes and put my face into the water, wishing it could drown out my thoughts.

But I couldn't. It was the "us" that caught my attention. It was the first time I had ever heard Danaus include himself with the other races, admitting for a brief moment that we were linked in some strange way. The knot in my stomach eased.

With a sigh, I returned to the task of washing off a layer of dried blood from the earlier battle at Themis and Stonehenge.

In the grand scheme of things, the Daylight Coalition was a minor annoyance. For now, I would leave it to Ryan and his people at Themis to investigate—that was what they did. Themis was a bunch of gray-haired librarians who studied all the races that were different from humans and wrote down their findings in thick, leather-bound volumes.

Of course, Themis also had its group of hunters; trained assassins dispatched for the sole purpose of killing my kind and anyone else who stepped out of line. Ryan had smiled at me and said that it was all in the interest of maintaining the secret, protecting mankind from the knowledge that vampires and werewolves were real. But I trusted the warlock about as far as I could throw him. Probably less.

With a frustrated groan, I turned off the water and quickly dried off. Rubbing my hair to dry as much of the water as possible, I stepped out of the bathroom and into the master bedroom, where I pulled open my bag. Clean clothes. Sometimes it's the little things in this life that can pick up a person's mood. I had worn my last outfit through my meeting with James Parker at the Themis town house, Thorne's death, my fight with Jabari, my fight with the naturi, and the naturi encounter at Stonehenge. I tossed the pants and shirt into the trash can, resisting the urge to set them on fire. Burning the clothes wouldn't purge the memory of the past two nights.

Quickly, I pulled on semiclean clothes and shouldered my bag. Dawn was only a few hours away and we had to be in Venice before the sun rose. The Coven was demanding we make an appearance. And the ruling nightwalker body would not be denied anything it wanted.

Three

I hesitated at the bottom of the stairs leading up to my little jet. Instead of winging me back across the ocean toward home, it was carrying me into the dark heart of the night-walker empire, the Coven. Jabari would claim it was for my own protection; I had no doubt that the Elders had some other dark scheme in mind. Of course, I had no say in the matter. Running would only make it worse. And I still had to figure out a way to protect Danaus and Tristan.

With a grimace, I climbed on and came face-to-face with the young nightwalker. Tristan stood in the middle of the plane, his hands resting on his slender hips as he looked around the pristine white interior. His eyes settled on me after a moment, with one brow arched in question.

"White?" he inquired, amusement cavorting through his voice. I swept past him, ignoring his comment. What could I say? I thought the black clothes were enough of a stereotype.

"Contact Sadira," I snapped, noticing the way his smile slipped at the mention of our maker. Neither of us was in any great hurry to see her again. I had escaped her "tender care" nearly five centuries ago only to find myself faced with the controlling vampire once again. Tristan had recently escaped, but was recaptured by me as I'd been unwittingly manipulated by her.

"Tell her to have a taxi waiting when we arrive," I ordered as I dropped my bag on the floor. "We're going to be cutting it that close." Lounging on one of the long benches that lined the interior of the plane, I tried to keep up the appearance of being completely unconcerned with the fact that we were flying to Venice, with sunrise only four hours away.

"Anything else, Mistress?" he asked with an elegant bow. I frowned at the nightwalker. Get him away from Sadira and he turns into a sarcastic ass, I thought. Just what I needed. I already had my hands full with Danaus, the Coven, and the naturi; I didn't need to worry about a young nightwalker now that he was away from his master. But I also had a sickening feeling in my stomach that he was confident I would find a way to free him from Sadira's grasp. Desperation made me promise to help him. At the time, I'd been sure that one of us wouldn't survive the encounter. I was wrong, and now I was stuck.

"Go to the back and take a nap," I grumbled.

I watched him as he took a couple steps toward the back of the jet, where a tiny bedroom lay behind a door. But he paused before reaching the door, seeming to hesitate.

"Go ahead," I called. "Say it."

"Why go?" Tristan's voice was barely over a whisper when he finally spoke, as if fearful of some kind of punishment for questioning me. He turned and his eyes held that same haunted look they had just a couple nights ago in that London alley. Fearful. Hopeless. "We've got a jet. Let's go west. As far from the Coven as we can get."

"And spend an eternity running from the Coven? From the naturi?" I rose to my feet and slowly approached him. His narrow shoulders curled inward, his body tensing for an expected blow. "There is nowhere to run. Jabari will hunt us down. The naturi will hunt us down. If we go to the Coven now, they can raise an army and we can finally stop the naturi from freeing their queen."

"What about the Coven?"

I smiled at him and brushed the tips of my fingers along the side of his face. "Others have survived facing the Coven. It just takes a little finesse."

"The Coven needs you alive."

"And I promised to keep to you," I said with a shrug. "So, if I live, you live."

A cynical smile twisted on Tristan's lips, failing to lift any of the doubt from his eyes. But he nodded once before turning and disappearing in the tiny back bedroom. He knew there was no escaping our destination. We would go before the Coven. If we were to defeat the naturi, we would need their assistance.

I bit back a sigh as I returned to the bench I had been sitting on. It wasn't a great plan, but at least it was something. As I stretched out my legs and tried to relax, Danaus stepped onto the jet.

A surprised smile tweaked the corners of my mouth as he sat on the bench across from me. It was only a few days ago since we boarded the jet together for the first time. He had been tense and uneasy as we headed off to search for clues as to how the naturi were attempting to break free of their cage. Now he seemed almost relaxed. I was no longer a threat. At this point we both had darker things to worry about than what we could do to each other.

"What?" he asked in a wary, near growl.

"You're still here," I replied. His blue eyes narrowed. I waved one hand at him, brushing off his dark look. "I didn't mean it quite like that. I thought we would have parted ways by now, whether through your death or not."

One thick dark brow quirked at me. "I've thought the same."

I think he was taunting me. It was hard to tell. His thoughts and emotions had grown distant and hazy again, while his expression retreated to its usual unreadable stone. The link we had established through our combined powers had faded to almost nothingness. My awareness of him was now obscured by the cloak of energy that wrapped around him.

"So I've heard. Ryan said you've been itching to cut my heart out. Do you plan to keep it as a trophy?" That finally earned me a frown while my own smile widened. "Regardless of your plans for my various body parts, we'll have to keep working together if we hope to survive the next few nights. Trust me, I'm not pleased. You're giving me a bad reputation."

Danaus chuckled quietly, and for a brief moment his features softened. Through that slim window of time, I glimpsed sight of a beautiful man. His weariness and shadow of worry melted away. Normally, with his glares and frowns, he was a virile creature exuding strength and power. Yet when he smiled and laughed, his humanity shone through a break in the clouds. It was a strange combination. Danaus had somehow found a way to be human without all the usual human frailty.

And then I realized I no longer wanted to kill him. Lurching to my feet with none of my usual grace, I paced to the back of the jet, a curse on the tip of my tongue. Was I going soft? Had I lost my edge?

But just because I didn't want to kill him didn't automatically mean I saw him as a comrade in arms. He was a strong fighter, and it was nice having someone at my back who could take care of himself. Danaus wasn't as frail as my beloved angels, but he also didn't have their warmth and compassion.

Stretching my arms above my head as best as I could in the jet, I shook off the strange realization. Danaus was probably still in my head, mucking up my thoughts. It would pass, I tried to reassure myself. So he wasn't on my to-kill list anymore. That could change easily enough, and probably would during our stay in Venice.

"Can he hear us?" Danaus suddenly inquired, motioning with his head toward the closed door at the opposite end of the jet.

I paused as I paced back toward the bench opposite him, my brows bunched over the bridge of my nose in confusion. "Why?"

"We need to talk." Those ominous words rumbled in his chest before finally finding an exit from his lips. I could guess at what he wanted to talk about and I was in no rush, but it had to be done. Mentally reaching out, I brushed Tristan's mind and found him stretched out on the bed in the back of the jet. With a little shove, I pushed him deeper into sleep, where he would stay until the jet landed.

"Tristan is asleep. He can't hear us," I said, sitting on the bench across from Danaus. I stretched out my legs and crossed them at the ankle, trying my best to affect a relaxed posture when all the muscles in my body seemed to be tense and waiting. "What is it that we're keeping quiet?"

"What happened. Have you ever done that before?"

I didn't have to ask what he was talking about. Hours ago Danaus, Tristan, Jabari, Sadira, and I had been at the Themis Compound, surrounded by naturi. It seemed that we were dead. There was no escape, nothing to swoop in and save us. In a last desperate attempt, Danaus and I agreed to use our powers: boiling blood and fire. If we survived, we'd be exhausted and at the mercy of our "comrades." Instead Danaus somehow pushed his powers into me, his deep voice echoing through my brain as I destroyed them all. And not just the ones at Themis. I had killed every member of the naturi within several miles of the Compound.

"Incinerated someone? Yes," I said, purposefully vague. I wanted to hear him say the words. I needed to know that I wasn't alone in what I felt.

"That's not what happened and you know it," Danaus snarled. He flinched at the loudness of his voice as if afraid he would wake Tristan. He couldn't, but I wasn't about to disillusion him. I didn't need him yelling at me. I had enough on my mind without an irate vampire hunter to worry about. "We destroyed their souls," he continued in a low, heavy voice.

I remained silent. Was there anything I could say that wouldn't sound lame? Not really. Maybe a part of me was hoping I'd been wrong. But I wasn't. Danaus had felt the same thing.

"I'm assuming you couldn't do that before," I finally said.

"No!" he shouted, lurching to his feet. His hands opened and closed restlessly at his sides twice before he finally returned to his seat, his emotions once again under control. "No, I haven't. I can't do that. I've never heard of any creature doing that." His voice was a little calmer than before, but it was a forced calm. Panicking would solve nothing, not that I wouldn't have enjoyed the brief luxury.

"Then why did you force me to do it?" My own voice turned even harder and colder than I meant it to. I hated the naturi with every ounce of my being, but even so, destroying another creature's soul? It . . . it was an unspeakable act, something that smacked of true evil.

"I didn't force you to do anything!" he said, jerking his eyes back to my face.

"I heard your voice in my head. You told me to kill them. You told me to kill them all."

"Not like that."

"I tried to crush their hearts or set them on fire but you

wouldn't let me." I shifted uncomfortably, placing both of my feet flat on the floor as I moved to the edge of my seat.

"I didn't stop you from doing anything." Danaus shoved one hand through his thick black hair, pushing some strands away from his exquisite blue eyes. I could almost sense the frustration humming through his muscular frame, building in him as he recalled events from earlier in the evening. "The moment I touched your hand, it felt like my powers had been amplified. Considering we were outnumbered and about to die, I didn't think this was a bad thing."

"And that's all?" I asked, failing to keep the skepticism from my voice.

Danaus took another deep breath and held it for a moment. "I could hear your thoughts," he finally admitted, his voice near a whisper. His eyes moved away from my face, dropping down to his hands, which rested half open on his thighs. "You were scared and in pain. I just kept thinking, 'kill them. Kill them and the pain will stop.'" He paused and I could feel his anger starting to ebb. The faint smell of the sea filled the cabin, seeming to cleanse the air. Danaus's unique scent. My eyes drifted closed, letting his voice brush against my cheek. "I didn't tell you to destroy their souls. I didn't think such a thing was possible and I would never have asked that."

"I didn't think so, but this is all new to me. I wanted to be sure." My head fell back against the bench. I didn't want to think about this anymore. There were no answers for what had happened or for what I knew would happen again.

Danaus let a deep, heavy silence slip back into the little jet, holding us together in the gathering darkness. It was several minutes later before he bothered to speak again. Neither of us wanted to think about this anymore, but certain questions had to be answered before we reached Venice and the Coven.

"How is it that I can . . . "

"Control me?" I finished the statement that seemed to get stuck in his throat; whether because he had a sudden concern for my feelings or just a distaste for the ability, I didn't know. Despite my own carefully crafted facade, I couldn't keep the bitterness from my tone. Jabari could control me. Sadira could. While he lived, so could Tabor. The original three members of the triad, and my makers. And now Danaus.

"I've been around enough vampires throughout my life. What I felt when I touched you . . . " Again his voice died, and I let the sentence wither away before I spoke.

"I can answer only part of that question. Jabari and Sadira and potentially other nightwalkers can control me because I was . . . made differently." I paused, nearly choking on the word. This story was not supposed to go this way. All the popular tales told of a chosen one, a child born under a particular star that was supposed to rise up and lead the downtrodden to redemption and victory. Well, this so-called "chosen one" was a tool, a weapon, a nightmare that could just as easily destroy my kind as lead them to salvation, and I hated it.

Frowning, my eyes darted around the interior of the plane as I tried to frame my explanation. "There are two ways to make a nightwalker. The first is quick, easy, obviously the most common. A nightwalker drains a human of his blood and replaces it with the nightwalker's blood at the exact second of death. The next night the human rises a nightwalker. It takes a few centuries for these vampires to gain any significant powers. These humans are reborn as nightwalkers to serve as a form of entertainment for their master. They're not expected to live long existences and rarely outlast their masters."

"Why?"

A grim smile skipped unchecked across my face, causing the hunter to stiffen. "Because many of our entertainments are lethal, even for nightwalkers. Among my kind, these quickly made nightwalkers are commonly referred to as chum."

"Is Tristan . . . chum?" Danaus asked, the term falling from his lips like something distasteful.

"Yes, but I wouldn't call him that to his face."

"I guessed as much," he murmured under his breath.

"Most nightwalkers are made this way. It takes little effort and dedication to the task."

"Have you ever . . . ?"

"No." My hands gripped the edge of my seat for a moment as I sat straight up. "I have never made a nightwalker, nor will I." With a shake of my head, I relaxed again and sat back. There were enough of us roaming the earth.

Closing my eyes, I listened to the steady rhythm of Danaus's heartbeat, the sound barely rising about the dulled roar of the jet engine. The beat was soothing, wiping away my momentary anxiety. I didn't create nightwalkers.

"But I wasn't made that way, and up until a couple nights ago I thought that Sadira was my only creator." I paused again, licking my lips as I searched for the words. "There are three stages of death. The first is that the body stops breathing, then the heart stops, and then finally the soul leaves the body. When I was made, the transformation was started before my soul had left my body. Sadira worked slowly and carefully to make sure my soul never escaped from my body.

"The process takes years—sometimes decades—to complete, but when the nightwalker finally awakens, he is stronger and more powerful than those newly born chum. Some believe that by retaining the soul throughout the whole process, the nightwalker attains a higher level of power. In general, those made this way are stronger, more powerful, and harder to kill. They are called First Bloods."

"So Tristan doesn't have a soul?"

"He does," I growled, lurching to my feet. I didn't like to hear those words uttered. It was a very old myth that vampires were soulless creatures, a myth that many humans still believed. And they would use that archaic belief to hunt us down when they discovered we existed.

Staring down at a tired Danaus, I forced myself to relax. He had meant nothing by the question and I knew I'd overreacted. My nerves were growing rawer the closer we got to Venice. Flopping back down, I bit off a sigh. "When the body is reanimated with the vampire blood, the soul is called back to the body. But when the sun rises, he dies again and the soul leaves. Of course, this is all theory."

"And you?"

"They speculate that I don't technically die like the rest at sunrise. Sadira thinks it's why I'm able to dream when the others cannot," I said with a shake of my head.

"Why did she make you like that?"

"If she is to be believed, it was what Jabari wanted," I replied. "I was kidnapped centuries ago because of my ability to control fire. When they feared the plague would take my human life, they decided to make me a nightwalker. However, Jabari wanted to see if I could retain my ability, and the best chance of that was to make me a First Blood."

"Jabari's blood is in your veins."

"And Sadira's. And Tabor's. The original members of the triad." And two of the four members of the Coven. Some of the most powerful nightwalkers in existence, then and now. "They believe they and some of their progeny can control me because their blood is a part of me."

"But I'm not a nightwalker. Never have been, never will be," Danaus said.

I bit back a comment about how there was still time. There was nothing to be gained by antagonizing him right now. He had enough problems in the form of the Coven and every vampire in Venice wanting a piece of his nightwalker-hunting hide. "You? I have no idea. Since you refuse to tell me what you are, I can only guess you're a freak of nature like me and that must give you some kind of strange edge."

"Do the others know what really happened?" Danaus demanded, deftly changing the subject. He wasn't going to tell me yet, but I liked to think I would have the truth out of him before his last breath.

"I don't think so," I said with a sigh on my lips. "If they had, I don't think we would have made it out of Themis alive; naturi or not. It would be best if we kept the full extent of what we can do to ourselves. We are about to head into the heart of the nightwalker hierarchy. It might be a good idea not to give them any more reasons to crush us into the dirt."

"You don't think they will when we arrive in Venice?"

"At the moment, they might be kind enough to wait until after we stop the naturi," I said with a frail chuckle, lifting my head to look at him.

"Lucky us," Danaus grimly said. "You expect to survive the next few nights?"

"Not really." A carefree shrug lifted my slim shoulders. "But that doesn't mean I'm not going to try."

"Then you have a plan for when we hit Venice," he prodded.

I smiled back at him, extending my legs out in front of me with my ankles crossed. The leather seat crinkled and crackled beneath me. "I have some ideas, but no specific plan. I work better off the cuff," I said, causing his expression to grow even darker. I couldn't blame him. We were in yet another situation in which he would have to trust me to protect him from my kind. Not a comfortable position, considering he had killed many of us during his extremely long career as a hunter.

"You're going to try to talk your way out of death?" Danaus guessed, sounding incredulous as he sat forward on the edge of the bench.

"I plan to bluff, cajole, grandstand, and outright lie if necessary to save my skin," I said, and laughed, throwing open my arms. One of the most powerful nightwalkers in existence wanted me dead. I had nothing to lose any longer.

"And sacrifice me when the opportunity presents itself," Danaus finished, shoving to his feet. I rose as well and stepped closer so only a couple of feet of empty space were separating us. It felt odd being that close without weapons drawn.

"I bear the Elders no love," I said. "Jabari was the only one who once resided in my heart and he crushed that before departing Themis. "On the other hand, you've saved my life on more than one occasion. I don't know your rationale behind it and at the moment I don't care," I quickly finished, holding up my hand before he could interject any of his reasons for prolonging my life, which I'm sure were on the tip of his tongue. It didn't look good for a hunter of his caliber to go around saving nightwalkers. "We will walk into Venice together and we will walk out together, I promise." I held out my hand to him. Danaus stared into my eyes for a long time, weighing my words before he finally took my hand and shook it, sealing the bargain.

"And after?" he demanded, his hand still tightly gripping mine.

"After Venice? Assuming we both actually survive, we get back to the business of trying to kill each other like nature intended," I mocked, releasing his rough, callused hand. A half smile briefly lifted one corner of his mouth as he sat back down.

"All I ask is that you keep your mouth shut and trust me," I said, looking down at him. "It's not an impossible task.

You're a hunter. I have no doubt that you've slaughtered countless nightwalkers. You're not exactly winning over many friends."

"It's not my goal in life," he said, sounding grumpy.

"I believe that," I muttered as I returned to my seat. Draping my body over the bench, I listened to the roar of the engines. Even if I did live long enough to finally gain the ability to fly, I would still use my pretty little jet. Besides the obvious comfort, I liked listening to the moan of the air rushing past the windows and the roar of the engine.

As the plane carried us closer to Italy, Danaus bent down and started digging around in the large black duffel bag near his feet. I could hear the clang and ping of metal striking metal as he sifted around in his trusty bag of weapons. I was sorry that I'd left the sword I used at Themis behind, but my hands were full of Tristan at the time. My mind hadn't been on proper weaponry for our trip to Venice. Lucky for me, Danaus remembered to grab his bag of tricks from the hotel. He might have even made a pit stop for extra toys at the Themis town house where we met James Parker.

After a moment he sat back with a gun in his hand. He quickly checked the magazine before standing and walking over to me. My eyes briefly flit from the gun he was holding out to me and back to his face questioningly.

"Guns seem to be effective against the naturi," he said when I had yet to move. I stared at the gun for a second, frowning. I didn't like guns. They were so impersonal. They were also ineffective when dealing with nightwalkers. Being shot just pissed vampires off and didn't slow them down much. We also hadn't fought the naturi on a regular basis in several centuries, so most of us never bothered to learn how to use a gun.

With a frown, I finally took the weapon from him, holding the grip between two fingers away from my body like a piece of rotting garbage. Growling in frustration, Danaus took the gun back and sat down next to me. "It's a Browning Hi-Power loaded with 9mm bullets," he explained, letting it rest in the palm of his hand. "The magazine holds fifteen bullets." With a couple of deft motions with his fingers, he showed me how to load the magazine and turn off the safety. My knowledge of guns didn't extend much further than pointing and squeezing the trigger. I had no desire to learn any more than that, but if I was faced with another naturi, the Browning was going to feel a whole lot better in my hand than a knife.

"I'm guessing you can manage that," Danaus taunted, trying to get a rise out of me.

"I'll manage," I almost growled, the two words squeezing between my clenched teeth. "Holster?"

He returned to the opposite bench and pulled a leather double shoulder holster out of his bag. He tossed it across the jet and I caught it with my empty hand. It was made of a supple, dark brown leather and was adjustable so I didn't have to worry about it being too bulky. Unfortunately I wasn't wearing a belt so I wouldn't be able to use the belt-securing ties. While I was strapping on the shoulder holster, Danaus brought over a second gun.

"It's a Glock 17 with 9mm rounds," he said as I accepted the gun and placed it in the right holster. The Browning went in the left. I looked down at myself and frowned. A nightwalker carrying guns. It seemed almost sacrilegious, if that was possible. We were graceful creatures from the Old World. When we killed, it was either with our bare hands or a blade.

"Is it wrong that the refrain from 'Janie's Got a Gun' keeps running through my head?" I moaned. Danaus made a noise in the back of his throat as he quickly looked away, but not before I saw his lips quirk in a half smile. "What? You don't like Aerosmith?" I asked.

"No! I—" He halted and shook his head, no longer fighting the smile. "Aerosmith is fine. I was thinking of another song."

"Which one?"

When he looked up at me, his smile was gone, but laughter danced in his eyes. "'Sympathy for the Devil,'" he answered.

"Ha ha. Real funny, hunter," I said snidely. "At least it's the Stones."

"Nope. Guns N' Roses," he corrected, one corner of his mouth quirked in a grin. I snorted in disgust but couldn't stop the smile that settled on my lips. However, when I looked back down at the guns hugging my frame, a sigh escaped my lips and the smile disintegrated.

"It's not that bad," Danaus said, interrupting my thoughts.

I just glared at him. He had no idea how bad it was.

His weary sigh seemed more show than exasperation as he returned to his bag one last time and quickly withdrew a long sword and scabbard. With a deep chuckle, I snatched the weapon from his hand and clutched it against my chest. The hilt and grip were of simple design, with an onion pommel and slightly curved cross guard with a flat ricasso. I pulled it out of the scabbard a little and discovered that it was a double-edged broadsword in exquisite condition. Actually, it was a sort of hybrid, with an elongated hilt common to a hand-and-a-half sword. The strap on the scabbard was designed so I could secure it across my chest and draw the sword from over my shoulder. I looked up to find him shaking his head, a smiling haunting his lips.

"I'm not the only one who prefers the old ways." A smirk twisted my mouth and I raised both eyebrows at him. Danaus rarely used a gun, and the way he held a sword made me think he'd been born with one in his hand.

"But to survive, you learn to adapt," he said grimly.

"True," I whispered, looking back down at the pistols resting on either side of my chest. I didn't like them, but they would stop a member of the naturi faster than I could cut them into pieces with my sword. "Thanks."

Danaus grunted and returned to the white leather bench. I carefully removed the shoulder holster and laid it on one of the empty seats with the sword. I stretched out on the leather sofa again, grateful to be rid of the guns.

A deep silence settled in the jet. Only the sound of the screaming wind could be heard. I relaxed against the upholstery with my eyes closed, both of us lost in our own worlds. I blotted out thoughts of my wounded Gabriel, reassuring myself that he was safe with Ryan and James. I tried not to think about the Coven, Jabari, or the naturi. I tried not to think about the fact that I had lived with Jabari in Egypt for nearly a century. For almost one hundred years he ran his little experiments, letting other nightwalkers try to control me, and I couldn't remember a moment of it. The years were a blur, but they weren't a gaping black hole in my past. I remembered nights in Jabari's home near Karnak where we would sit talking about the things we had seen. We discussed what it meant to be a nightwalker and others who had come before both of us. The Ancient nightwalker had given me a sense of history and a philosophy. He'd been a mentor and guide in the night.

I pushed those thoughts away, plunging deeper into the blackness of my mind, only to have images of Michael swim to the surface. His soft, golden locks rose up before me, and I ached to touch the smoothness of his skin as it stretched over miles of thick muscle. I remembered his wonderful smile and how it was always unsure and crooked when he struggled to read my moods. Yet tainting those good memories was the feel of his body in my arms as he died, a lead weight pressing down on my legs and awkward in my arms.

The brush of his soul still chilled my skin. It beat against his chest, battling for freedom when I desperately wanted him to stay. I left him when consciousness abandoned him at last, unable to bear the final moments when his soul broke free and left me forever.

Leaning my head back, I rested one elbow on the back of the bench and threaded my fingers through my hair. A lump rose in my throat and my eyes burned with tears fighting to slip down my cool cheeks. I had killed Michael as surely as if I plunged the blade in his back myself. I had seen him slowly sliding deeper into my world, slipping further away from his own kind. The descent was slow and I had convinced myself that he could handle it. Gabriel had, after all. My remaining angel had served me as a bodyguard for more than a decade with no ill effects.

But Gabriel was always careful to maintain a normal life away from me. I had dipped into his mind on numerous occasions and saw the things he enjoyed. Gabriel looked forward to watching football on Sunday and drinking with friends at a local bar. He dated and kept lovers. I never saw such things in Michael's mind. There had been only me.

Humans did not last when they became involved with my kind. For a while it was fun, but after a time there were only two paths for their fragile minds and bodies: death or rebirth. I could have saved my guardian angel at any time from his fate, but I could not bring myself to release him. A naturi may have wielded the blade that freed Michael's soul, but I had set the trap and baited it with myself.

FOUR

Venice. Europe's ultimate tourist trap, with its clichéd gondola drivers and pigeon-filled piazzas. Venice was like watching a grand dame of society slowly wither and die. She was filled with chatty, boisterous tour groups and their little clicking cameras as they crowded San Marco Piazza and oohed at the basilica. Then it was down to the Rialto and the open air market. Did any of them bother to cross the Guidecca Canal or wander through the quiet beauty of Campo Santa Margherita? Or even venture into some of the finest restaurants in San Polo?

When I'd traveled with Jabari, I spent many nights wandering the narrow streets of La Serenissima. I loved the vibrant nightlife in Dorsoduro, populated with its college students from the nearby universities. I loved the thickly populated island of Burano with its vibrantly painted little buildings. But my favorite was taking a water taxi to Torcello in the northern part of the Lagoon. This was where Venice had been born centuries ago, but now it was little more than a ghost town, its inhabitants shrinking from twenty thousand to fewer than thirty. Torcello's streets were only dirt and broken cobblestone, while most of her buildings had been torn down so the materials could be used elsewhere. However, those fragmented shells and the desolate, overgrown land offered up a quiet respite from my world. I had even lingered on this nearly forgotten island during the daylight hours, sleeping in a dark, quiet corner of an empty building.

But I doubted I'd be able to wander along her ancient sidewalks this time. When we stepped off the plane, an escort was already waiting to greet us. Tall and lean, the nightwalker stood not far from where our jet had taxied to a private section of Marco Polo Airport. I had seen him on my last few trips to Venice. The vampire was picking pieces of lint from his dark Armani suit, looking supremely bored with the task at hand. I knew better. A toady of the Coven was a tenuous position, one that you were careful not to screw up.

Climbing off the jet, I glanced nervously at the sky. Dawn was less than two hours away and we still had to deal with the formalities of landing in Venice, *the* nightwalker playground. If not for the time constraints, I would have been happy to wait until sunset tomorrow to leave for Venice.

The nightwalker in Armani gracefully strolled over as Danaus came to stand beside me. I had given him the guns and sword. I'd take back the Browning and Glock if forced to hunt the naturi again. For now, I didn't have a clue about the Coven's plans, but I knew that Rowe wouldn't give up on his plan to break the seal just because I had thwarted him once. The naturi was going to try again, and I suspected the Coven would "request" that I be the one to stop him again.

Tristan descended the stairs last, carrying both of our bags with ease. He was lowest on the totem pole so he got to play the part of pack mule. It wasn't fair, but we were protecting him and that task was more easily done without a bag on your shoulder.

"Benevenuto a Venezia," the vampire greeted in flawless Italian, bowing deeply to me. *"Il mio nome è Roberto."*

"Mira," I said, biting out my name through clenched teeth, fighting the urge to use Italian as well. "Danaus. Tristan." I completed the rest of the introductions with a quick wave of my hand toward my companions.

Roberto smiled at me, his eyes flickering with amusement. "The Elders are glad that you have arrived safely," he replied, slipping into heavily accented English.

A snide comment nearly tumbled from my lips, but I bit off the words at the last minute. No reason to start a fight just yet. There would be plenty of opportunities for that later.

"We are losing moonlight. Shall we go?" I stiffly said in quick, sharp Italian. The language came easy for me. Sadira had insisted that I learn it even before I was reborn, and it was all Jabari had spoken while attempting to teach me Arabic. But I didn't want to speak Italian; each syllable carried with it an echo of grim memories and dark pleasures I had left behind.

"Do you have any other baggage?" Roberto asked, his eyes darting to the jet.

"No. I assumed the Coven would see to my needs," I said.

"Naturalmente." With a wave of his hand, he turned sharply and started walking toward the canals. He had been inquiring about my customized coffin. The five-and-a-half-foot box with interior locks was my sanctuary from the sun. I'd left it in London with instructions to ship it to the States. It had become too impractical to keep moving the coffin around with me, but I hated traveling without it, though it could be done. If necessary, I could sleep in the Lagoon. Nightwalkers didn't breathe, and the silt and algae made the water murky enough to block the sun. Now, I'm not saying the experience was enjoyable—there are few things more repulsive than waking covered in dirt and algae—but at least you wake up again.

Our little trio followed Roberto to a waiting boat. Once we were seated, the nightwalker deftly maneuvered the sleek speedboat from the dock and across the Lagoon. Yet, something seemed off. Instead of heading toward the southeast side of Murano, Roberto passed the southwest side of the island and soon entered the winding canals of Venice. This didn't make any sense. Typically, we traveled southeast toward the Lido before heading back north to the remote island that housed the Coven. This way would take longer, as we would be forced to travel at a slower speed while within the narrow confines of the Venice canals. There wouldn't be much time if we were to appear before the Elders before sunrise.

After a few moments darting down one narrow canal after another, Danaus touched my arm, drawing my eyes to his face. Silently, he held up three fingers and then tilted his head toward the rooftops. We were being watched, which wasn't surprising. I had felt them as we stepped onto the tarmac at the airport. However, the hunter had miscounted. With a wink and a smile, I chuckled deeply, catching Roberto's attention.

"What has amused you?" he inquired, glancing over his shoulder at me.

"The hunter is honored by the Coven's thoughtfulness to send an escort of four nightwalkers," I replied. Danaus's expression remained unreadable, but I'm sure those were not the words he would have used.

"He can sense them?" Roberto asked, his eyes briefly shifting to Danaus. His hand swept over his slicked-back, dark brown hair.

"Naturalmente," I purred.

Roberto looked over at Danaus one last time, the tip of his tongue nervously flicking across his lips before he turned his attention back to the canal. "The Coven is eager to meet him," he softly said, his voice barely carrying over the rumble of the boat's motor and the splash of the waves.

I was sure they were, but I wisely kept my comments to myself. Instead I watched the passing buildings and the shimmer of lamplight reflecting in the waters in the canal. We had briefly cut across the Grand Canal and were now moving down the Guidecca Canal. The nightwalkers watching us kept their distance and did nothing to provoke the passengers of the speedboat. They were there to make sure we didn't attempt anything stupid, though I'm not sure exactly what the Coven thought we might try.

After about thirty minutes Roberto slowed the boat and carefully docked in a beautiful landing on the Guidecca side of Venice. I frowned, my gaze and powers sweeping the immediate area. This wasn't where the Coven held court. That was still another ten minutes away on a lonely island in the Lagoon.

"Are we not going before the Coven?" I asked Roberto when he turned off the motor.

"Because of the late hour, the Elders have graciously decided to allow you to rest first. You are expected to appear in court an hour after sunset tomorrow," he explained.

"Alone?" I stood, my legs braced apart against the rocking of the boat. I doubted it, but it was always good to know exactly where you stood when you went before the Elders.

"All are to come," Roberto announced, his eyes sweeping over Tristan and Danaus before returning to my face.

I looked over at Tristan, who was still sitting. His expression was blank, but his knuckles were growing white from the death grip he had on my bag. After living with Sadira for more than a century, I was confident that he was as well versed in the romance languages as I was. "Have you appeared in court before?" I demanded, switching back to English.

"No," Tristan said with a shake of his head, peering up at me with wide eyes. A wave of fear from the young nightwalker rippled through me, skimming along my arms like a cold chill. The court of the Coven was a place of horrors and nightmares, particularly for the weak. It was there that the term "chum" had been coined.

I turned my gaze back to Roberto, who was watching Tristan like a predator sizing up his prey. "Relay a request to the Elders for me," I said, my words falling gracefully back into Italian. "Tell them I humbly request to be allowed to leave Tristan behind. He knows nothing of the matter we have come to discuss and will only waste valuable time."

Roberto smiled at my delicate choice of words. I had never been humble about anything I did. "He has come into their domain. He has to show proper respect," he reminded me, his dark gaze sliding back to my face.

"They've already given their approval for the day's rest. If they refuse, I can still send him back to London after the sun sets. No harm done."

"I'll relay your request," Roberto said stiffly, his lean face twisting with his displeasure.

"*Grazie*," I said, smiling at him wide enough to expose my fangs. It wasn't a threat; more of a friendly nudge not to cross me. Coven toady or not, I'd ripped apart stronger vampires than him for less, and he knew it. Besides, the noose was already around my neck, so what did I have to lose?

We climbed out of the boat and walked up to the hotel. I paused and watched Roberto pull from the dock and drive out into the Lagoon. He was headed for the Coven. The other nightwalkers remained around the hotel, watching. They'd hold for a little while longer but would have to find a suitable resting spot as the night crumbled around us. As I turned to continue into the luxurious hotel, I found Tristan standing before me, a look of gratitude on his face.

"Why?" he whispered, his voice seeming to catch on something in his throat.

"You wouldn't survive the night," I grumbled, stepping around him and striding toward the hotel. The look on his face, a sickening combination of gratitude and awe, was making me uncomfortable. It was the same look I had seen on his face when we first met in London at that punk bar. To Tristan, I was a legend and a beacon of hope—I had "escaped" our maker and gone on to live my own life away from her. And when he saw me for the first time, he assumed that I would help him do the same. Unfortunately for him, I wasn't the type to come rushing to the aid of a weaker nightwalker. In fact, I was frequently an exterminator of fledglings when they endangered our secret.

"Sadira won't let anything happen to me," Tristan argued, following on my heels.

"I will try to get Danaus to smuggle you back onto the jet before sunset tonight," I said, ignoring his comment. "You can be back in London or in the States before they awaken."

He grabbed my arm, stopping me. "What if they summon me and I'm not in Venice?"

"I'll tell them I shipped you away without your knowledge." It was a considerable risk. I had never defied the Coven before, but then I'd never had a reason to try.

"No," he firmly said with a shake of his head. "I'm staying." He repositioned our bags on his shoulders, completely at ease with their awkward weight. My brow furrowed as I stared at him. Earlier that evening he had wanted to run, to flee the Coven.

"I thought you wanted to be free of Sadira," I snapped. Exhaustion and fear ate away at the last of my patience. There wasn't time for this discussion.

"We both know shipping me to another country or continent won't free me from Sadira's grasp." Tristan stepped forward and placed a hand on my shoulder. He leaned in and our cheeks nearly brushed as we spoke. "Sending me away will only antagonize the Coven and Sadira. And while you may be the great Fire Starter, I don't think you are strong enough to take them both on and succeed."

My own words come back to haunt me. And he was right.

I stepped back so I could look him in the eye. "Very well." He was young, but determined. For now, he would stand by his mistress and endure the gaze of the Coven. If he were lucky, they would be so preoccupied with Danaus and me that he would be overlooked.

With a nod, I led my two companions into the opulent Hotel Cipriani. When I'd scanned the area upon our landing, I sensed Sadira on one of the upper floors waiting for us. Neither Tristan nor I had any desire to see the manipulative old nightmare again, but we were running out of time and I had something to accomplish before the night drew its final breath. As we neared the private suite, Sadira threw open the white double doors, smiling at her young ward.

"At last," she said, sounding deeply relieved. There was a slight flush to her pale cheeks, revealing that she had fed recently. She was wearing a pale pink shirt and long black skirt. The night's battle had been erased from her appearance, except for the lines of nervous worry that still clawed at the corners of her eyes. Stepping around the two night-walkers as they held each other, I rolled my eyes in disgust. I knew Tristan was obediently relaying the night's events to his mistress through his thoughts. I didn't care to review what had happened since we parted ways. For now, I turned my attention to our accommodations. I'd deal with Sadira later.

The main sitting area was coldly elegant, decorated in smoky gray and black marble with creamy white walls. The furniture was covered in an interesting black and gray fabric and perfectly coordinated with the large area rug in the center of the room. The area oozed luxury, offering an enticing mix of beauty and comfort. Yet, the windows troubled me. The far wall was comprised of a massive bank of windows looking out at the canal. Frowning, I quickly peeked into both bedrooms to find large windows spanning the far walls. Even the bathroom looked out onto the canal. At night the view was stunning. By day it would be a death trap as the sun slowly crept through the room, searching us out.

"How are we supposed to meet them tomorrow if we burn up during the day?" My voice exploded in the suite as I stalked back out into the living room.

"The curtains are thick in the master bedroom," Sadira said. "It will be enough to block the sun." Her seemingly eternal calm was unshaken by my lack of emotional restraint. The night had been too long already, with bitter revelations nagging at me from both my beloved Jabari and my enemy Rowe. There had been no time to sit alone and think over what I'd learned, to formulate my next plan for survival. Always moving forward, toward the next destination, closer to the next creature that wanted to control me or kill me.

I wanted my metal box with its double locks on the interior. I wanted my one sanctuary in this world that was unraveling faster than love after betrayal. Traveling without the box was insane. I hadn't taken any trips outside of my domain without it in centuries. It had saved me on more than one occasion. Unfortunately, I currently needed to travel light and fast. I had to find other options. Hell, for half a second I actually thought about sleeping in the Lagoon, but quickly pushed the idea aside. The Elders were having a little fun. If they wanted to kill us, they would have done something far more creative and painful. This was just a joke; a death trap draped in exquisite luxury.

The panic ebbed and I redirected my thoughts toward my primary concern as I felt the nightwalkers move away from the hotel. It was less than an hour from dawn, and they were seeking their own resting place. They assumed I wouldn't be up to any trouble this close to sunrise. Furthermore, their human guardians wouldn't be in place to keep an eye on Danaus for another hour or two. They would have to be sure their vampire masters were safely stowed for the day before leaving. It was a window of opportunity, albeit a very small one, and I wouldn't have a second chance.

"Come with me," I commanded, pointing at Danaus as I headed for the doors.

"You're leaving?" Sadira gasped, horrified that I was heading outside when dawn was already beginning to lighten the sky.

I threw open the doors and stepped back to let Danaus precede me. "I have a question that needs answering before tomorrow's meeting."

"But the sun—"

"Don't wait up," I said, and laughed, following Danaus out of the room.

We jogged down the hall and through the hotel as silent as the wind. I might have been laughing, but I could feel the night struggling as it entered the final throes of death. No matter how hard I clenched my fist, the sand was slipping through my fingers. I was going to cut this one close, but I had to know. Rushing back outside, I hurried down to the dock, the rubber soles of my boots silent along the worn stone sidewalk. I untied one of the speedboats resting there, fighting the urge to glance up at the sky.

"Can you hotwire it?" I called as Danaus jumped onto the boat.

Wordlessly, he walked over to the wheel and knelt before it. I was stepping onto the boat when I heard the sound of breaking plastic as he ripped the panel off. He fiddled with the wires for a moment, causing the motor to sputter and cough. I was skilled with some mechanical items, but had yet to learn the fine art of hotwiring a vehicle. When I needed to go somewhere, I usually hijacked a driver as well, saving myself the trouble. Unfortunately, most people were still asleep at this hour and I didn't want to try to track down a private taxi driver.

An impatient remark nearly leapt from my tongue before the motor suddenly roared to life. Danaus rose to his feet and shifted the boat into reverse. As he dropped it into drive, I pointed toward the Lagoon and he launched us into the darkness, moving me away from the safety of a resting place for the daylight hours.

"Where are we going?" he asked after a couple minutes. We had left the Guidecca Canal and entered the Lagoon. The dark waters opened around us, the gentle waves rising and falling in a hypnotic dance. Lights danced in all directions, cold and distant, as if taunting me with promises of protection from the sun that was rising closer to the horizon. The immediate area was a thick, inky blackness, a swamp of night created by the waters—a sanctuary that was chosen only as a last resort.

"Head for that island, San Clemente," I said, pointing toward a swath of land another ten minutes away. A large hotel rose up out of the darkness, a handful of its windows glowing against the slate-gray sky. A neat row of lamps lined the sidewalks, wrapping around the island. "That's where the Coven resides most of the year. It started as a monastery but was converted into a hotel in the past century. There are other buildings on the island, including the main hall for the court."

"Why are we going there now?" Danaus asked, turning the boat and putting on more speed. His eyes jumped up to the sky for a second, possibly judging the time left until the sun officially rose.

"We're not," I replied, forcing back a smile. "Turn off the engine."

His head jerked toward me, his brow furrowed in confusion, but he also wordlessly slowed the boat to a stop before killing the engine.

Standing next to him, I spread my legs as wave after wave rocked the small craft, lapping at its sides. "I want you to scan the area for naturi."

"Now?" he demanded in surprise. His eyes darted again to the sky, which was growing lighter by the minute.

I gripped the seat in front of me, my nails biting into the plastic. "Yes, now. Just do it. We don't have time for a debate."

With a frown, Danaus stared out at the Lagoon. His powers surged out from his body, ripping through me as if made of nothing more than smoke. I flinched but didn't move. Its warmth wrapped around me in a snug cocoon, holding me tightly, but it lasted only a few seconds before it dissipated.

"I can't search all of the city," he said at last. "That island is cloaked in some kind of magic. Everywhere else is clear, but I can't verify the island."

"I suspected as much," I murmured. I could sense the creatures through the barrier. Even without using much of my powers, I could tell there were more than two dozen nightwalkers on San Clemente, not to mention the nearly three hundred humans. However, I couldn't sense the naturi. No nightwalker could, as far as I knew.

But I could with help from Danaus. I had been able to sense them briefly when we combined our powers at the Themis Compound. This was stupid and extremely dangerous, but I had to know. I had to know what we were walking into tomorrow.

"I need your help," I slowly said in a low voice that barely reached above the sound of the breaking waves. "I have to know if there is a member of the naturi on that island. When we were linked in England, I could sense the naturi. We have to do that again. I'm the only one who can push through their protective barrier."

Danaus nodded and held out his hand to me. Hesitantly, I lifted my hand, but I still didn't take his.

"We can't kill anyone on the island. We can't even try. Don't think it, Danaus, or I swear I will destroy us both," I warned. "Let's just take it slow."

It took a great deal of effort to force myself to take his hand. The pain for our last joining was still fresh in my mind, and while I had recovered, I was in no rush to experience it again.

Lucky for me, it was different this time. The power didn't run screaming into my body, but slowly flowed in like a small woodland stream. It trickled up my arm and into my chest. The warmth seeped into my bones, filling my body. But then it changed. The power expanded in my bones until I thought they would splinter and break.

"Too much," I whimpered, struggling to keep to my feet. I tightened my grip on the chair before me but could no longer feel it. There was only Danaus's hand and the steadily increasing pain.

"I can't slow it any more. Focus," he said. His voice sounded distant, as if he were on the other side of the Lagoon. The sound of the water hitting the side of the boat had faded.

Focus on the island.

This time the words came as a command in my head. Thoughts about the pain starting to rip through my limbs ebbed and my mind focused on the island that bobbed ahead of us. It took only a moment, but I found what I was looking for. A member of the naturi lay sleeping on the island. By the size, I was willing to guess that it was probably a female, maybe of the light or wind clan. I made one quick scan of the buildings but knew I wouldn't find another. It didn't matter. One was enough for me.

"Stop," I said in a hoarse voice, struggling to release his hand.

I felt Danaus hesitate, his hand still tightly gripping mine. His thoughts were a jumble, but I understood the feeling. Frustration. One order from him and I would torch every nightwalker on the island. He wouldn't get another opportunity like this one.

"Stop!" I cried, my voice cracking. I jerked my hand but couldn't break Danaus's grip. I was fighting the power burning in my body, trying to halt its progress as it raged through me.

Angrily, Danaus released my hand and I dropped to my knees. He was breathing heavily, leaning on the steering wheel, but he looked to be in better shape than during our first attempt at this little trick.

My bones ached and my muscles burned and throbbed with a pain that I was becoming well acquainted with. Yet it wasn't as bad as earlier in the evening. I'd recover soon enough.

"You would have been tempted too," he breathlessly said, struggling to straighten.

"But I wouldn't do it," I croaked, leaning against one of the seats in the boat. "We made a bargain." I put my head down on the seat and closed my eyes, listening to the sound of the water hitting the side of the boat. "Don't worry. You'll get another shot at them, I promise."

Something had died inside of me, leaving a small, heavy corpse curled up in the pit of my stomach. I never had much respect for the Coven, but I'd always believed their ultimate goal was to protect my kind. I believed they would protect us all.

Countless centuries ago the Coven had been created by Our Liege to help establish some kind of control over the growing number of nightwalkers that were filling the earth; to establish order in the chaos. Four ancient vampires were handpicked by Our Liege to hold court and pass judgment when Our Liege chose to be absent. During the centuries, Elders were killed in power struggles and evil schemes, but the feel of the court never changed. It was a place of horrors and dark fantasies. The Coven was about power and control.

But in the end I also believed it was about the protection of our kind. The Coven was created to protect all nightwalkers as much as it was to protect humans. The naturi had slaughtered nightwalkers through history like animals. For nearly countless ages they hunted down and destroyed thousands of humans and vampires, believing both races to be a pestilence on the earth. Nightwalkers had sealed the naturi from this world, and we have protected that seal. Why would the Coven suddenly turn its back on that history?

Danaus stared down at me, a look of surprise filling his blue eyes. "Let's get out of here," I whispered. "I'm running out of time."

With a nod, he started the speedboat again and turned us back toward Cipriani. I pulled myself up into the seat and stared up at the pale gray sky. Dawn was close. The night was drawing in its last gasping breaths, its weight pressing down on me as it if were my job to support its lifeless frame.

"There's a very specific reason why we chose Venice for the seat of the Coven," I slowly began. "There are no naturi here. There never have been. Members of the water clan won't even lurk in the canals. They call it the Dead City. I'm not sure why. I think one of their gods supposedly died here. They've never set foot in the city."

"Until now," Danaus interjected.

"Not only is a naturi deep in nightwalker territory, but it had to have been invited. All magically inclined creatures have to be invited onto the island."

"How do you know it's not a prisoner?"

"Because it wasn't afraid or in pain," I said. My bitterness left a nasty taste in the back of my throat. I didn't know how I was sure of that fact. Something in me just knew it. When I sensed other creatures, I could get an emotional imprint. Something in me said I would have known if that naturi had been tortured or afraid for her life.

I'd suspected that my kind had been betrayed somehow. During my travels the past few days, the naturi remained one step ahead of us, always knowing exactly where to find me. The only way they could have managed such a feat was if someone were informing them. I'd suspected it, but I didn't believe I would actually be proven correct.

Silence settled back between us as we entered Guidecca Canal and drew close to the hotel. The area was still empty of nightwalkers, and most humans nearby were sleeping. The only ones who were awake were members of the hotel staff—not that they couldn't be servants of the Coven as well. I wasn't worried. The Elders knew I had been out in the Lagoon, but they couldn't know why.

By the time Danaus was tying up the boat, I was struggling to keep my eyes open. I climbed onto the dock, lacking my usual grace. I was hanging onto consciousness by a thread. My body was sore, fighting every movement. Danaus tried to pick me up, but I growled at him, lurching away from his touch. I had enough strength left to drag myself into the hotel.

"Promise me you won't go near San Clemente during the day," I mumbled as I entered the elevator. I leaned heavily against the wall, fighting to keep my eyes open. "They'll know. You'll put us all in danger. Just wait until sunset."

"But I—"

"Just promise," I snapped. "We're in their domain. We have to play by their rules."

"I promise," he grudgingly said, obviously less than thrilled with my request.

"Wait. Wait for me. We'll get them," I whispered.

The elevator doors slid open with a soft hiss and I lurched forward, hurrying into the suite. The sun was nearly up. I wasn't going to be awake much longer, and if I wasn't hidden, I'd be fried to a crisp. Throwing open the door to the master bedroom, I stumbled inside and slammed the door shut behind me. I didn't bother to lock it. If Danaus or someone else wanted in while we slept, they would find a way in. The room was pitch-black, as the heavy curtains had been pulled across the windows. Sadira and Tristan lay stretched out on the bed, his arms wrapped around her. I tripped across the room and slid onto the king-size bed next to Tristan. Exhausted, I was drifting off to sleep when I felt Tristan roll over and wrap his arms around my waist. He snuggled close, his long body curving against mine. And then there was nothing.

Five

The fog lifted from my thoughts the next night and I returned to consciousness to find Tristan stretched out beside me on the bed. He was leaning on his elbow, his brown hair hanging down around his eyes as he watched me. A faint smile played on his pale pink lips, but his blue eyes were worried. He was afraid, and for good reason. We had survived the day but still had to face the Elders.

Tristan lifted his hand to touch my cheek, but I jerked away from his fingertips and frowned. "I thought you might enjoy some company," he said gently. His open hand remained hovering in the air near my cheek, waiting for my permission to resume its descent. For a second I honestly wished I could accept his proposition. The curtains were still drawn and the room was quiet as a marble mausoleum in February. But a few stolen moments of bliss in his arms wouldn't chase away our fears regarding the Coven.

"No," I replied, though the word lay between us like a dead fish.

Lowering his hand, he wrapped his long fingers around my wrist when I sat up. "I wanted to thank you . . . for what you said yesterday." His words were hesitant. I understood what it cost him to say them. I remembered what it was like to be young and weak. You never wanted to feel as if you owed anyone anything. It gave them power over you, a little bit of leverage saved up for a special occasion.

"I don't want your thanks," I grumbled. Rolling to my feet, I ran my fingers through my hair, pushing the long red locks from my face. I didn't want his gratitude when we had yet to escape Venice. "Return to your mistress."

"She said that I am to see to your needs," he said, lounging across the bed. I turned to look at him, but what I saw only deepened my frown. He lay bare-chested, a smile haunting his handsome features. His lower half was in a pair of leather pants, while his feet remained bare. Tristan was an enticing mix, naughty with just a dash of nice. He extended one hand toward me, his gaze softening. He was hot, but I felt no real temptation. I was standing in Venice and was about to see the Coven, which had a naturi in their midst. There was no escape this time no matter how much I longed for it.

"Get out of here, Tristan," I sighed. "Tell the others I will be out in a few minutes."

I didn't wait for him to rise, but grabbed my bag and stalked into the bathroom, slamming the door behind me. After a quick shower, I dug through my bag for some clean clothes, only to discover I was running low. I hadn't thought to pack for more than a few days. I thought I would be handing this matter off to someone else not long after arriving in Egypt, not globe-hopping while I ran from the naturi.

With a grimace, I finally settled on a black halter top. I pulled the black leather pants I had worn the previous day back on, but chose the leather boots with the three-inch heels. They weren't great for fighting in, but the height would add to my presence. I was hoping to do more bluffing than actual fighting tonight.

I brushed out my damp hair and piled it on the back of my head, holding it in place with a pair of silver clips. By pulling it back, it opened my peripheral vision and still gave me the appearance of sophistication and class. With one last look in the mirror, I stifled a sigh. I looked good, but I didn't feel the confidence I needed to pull off this farce.

Leaning forward, I gripped the cold black marble sink with both hands. How the hell was I supposed to do this? A naturi was waltzing around the home of the Coven, Jabari could control me like some weapon sent from Hell, and somehow I was slowly building a contingent of creatures dependent upon me to save their collective hides. Not only had I promised a vampire hunter that I would get him out of Venice alive, but it was also becoming clear that both Sadira and Tristan were expecting the same.

I couldn't beat the Coven. While I might be able to last a little bit, Jabari would pummel me into bloody paste eventually. My odds against Macaire or Elizabeth weren't any better. How could I have been so careless as to promise to protect these poor creatures when I could barely protect myself?

But the Coven had to be stopped. My fears in London had been confirmed with the appearance of the naturi in the Coven. Too often the naturi knew exactly where to find me. They knew how to track me when only the Coven should have known my ultimate destination. Someone within the Coven was trying to kill me, and that person was using the naturi as the assassin.

A knock at the bathroom door shook me from my dark thoughts. I forced my fingers to release their grip on the sink and I straightened. "Come in." My voice was firm and steady, though I didn't feel it.

The door swung open to reveal Danaus standing on the other side, his expression even darker than usual. He was back in his typical black shirt and black pants, but gone were his wrist guards, assortment of knives, and sword strapped to his back. In fact, he was completely unarmed. Of course, he could destroy us all without even lifting a finger, but there's nothing like the feel of a trusted weapon in your hand.

"Ready?" he inquired.

"Would it make any difference if I said no?"

"No."

"Then, yes, I'm ready. Can't wait!" I said brightly, pasting an extremely fake-looking smile on my mouth.

A sharp bark of laughter jumped from Danaus's throat, surprising us both. I think the tension was getting to us. We were starting to crack. With a shake of my head and a wobbly smile, I stepped around him and started to walk through the bedroom when I felt a sudden sharp shift in his mood. In fact, the jump to violent anger and horror was so extreme that my fingers curled into claws and my lips pulled back, exposing sharp fangs. I twisted around, searching for our would-be attacker, but I found myself still alone with Danaus.

"What?" I demanded, my gaze still scouring the room for the enemy that had retreated to the shadows. The curtains had been pulled back to reveal the glittering expanse of the Lagoon and the glow of San Marco Piazza against the night sky.

"Your back," he replied, his voice harsh and almost breathless. I straightened, relaxing instantly. I had forgotten he had never seen the scars on my back. I'd worn that shirt for the exact purpose of showing them off, but they hadn't crossed my mind when I walked in front of the hunter.

Turning back around so he could see them, I remained standing in the center of the room. "I thought Nerian told you," I said. The name twisted briefly on my lips as an image of the naturi flit through my thoughts. My old tormentor was dead now, but memories of him still had the power to haunt me.

I heard Danaus edge closer, his movements slow and cautious, as if he was afraid I would lunge at him. "He did, but I didn't think vampires could scar. I thought you healed from everything," he said, his voice dropping to near a whisper.

Danaus had held Nerian captive for a week before I finally destroyed the naturi. It was ample time for the hunter to pull all kinds of interesting information from my enemy. The idea set me ill at ease around Danaus, fearful of the things he knew about me during my weakest moment. I was flaunting the scarring, but the rest of the painful and degrading things I endured over those two weeks were something I wanted no one to know about.

"If we don't feed soon enough after being injured by a naturi weapon, our bodies cannot heal completely," I said stiffly, trying to push back the flood of memories. "I wanted to remind the Coven of what they were dealing with."

His fingertips lightly grazed my back, tracing some of the marks. I flinched at his touch but didn't move. His anger brushed across my bare skin like a warm breath, and it was almost soothing despite our topic of conversation. "Some of these are symbols," he said in surprise. "They wrote on your back."

"I never learned what it said. Nothing good, I'm sure."

Danaus was silent a moment, his emotions a jumble as the anger started to ebb. He was studying the designs, his thoughts churning as he tried to place the symbols with matching words. "Kick me."

I twisted around, my mouth falling open in wordless shock. The hunter stared at me, the corners of his mouth twitching. Laughter, for one brief crystalline moment, shimmied through his cobalt eyes. Dear heaven, the dark vampire hunter was developing a sense of humor.

I laughed, letting the sound well up from my toes and soar through my chest. Shaking my head, I wrapped my arms around my stomach as the sound filled the room. Danaus chuckled softly too, the sound bouncing off me like a drunken monk trying to right himself in a swaying room. It was more than a minute later before I was able to finally stand straight and stifle the last of the giggles.

"Why is there a naturi within the Coven building?" Danaus asked, killing the last of our laughter. There was no harsh accusation or censure in his voice. I could almost hear the unspoken question, "What are we going to do?" in his tone.

"The Coven had struck some kind of bargain. I think it's the reason why the naturi have been able to track us so easily," I said, sitting down on the edge of the bed.

"Maybe. But they haven't gotten us yet."

"Rowe grabbed me the last time," I reminded him, trying to keep the bitterness out of my tone. Rowe had swept me away to Stonehenge to witness the sacrifice to break the seal, and offered me a chance to change sides. I didn't, and at the time I thought I had made the right choice. Yet, with the appearance of the naturi at the Coven Great Hall, I now had my doubts.

"Each time they attack, we get closer to stopping Rowe," Danaus countered.

"He always has the element of surprise."

"He's lost it." Danaus stood before me, forcing me to sit up straight so I could look up at him. "We know now that the naturi are after you specifically. We can watch out for them. Even if the naturi have struck a bargain with the Coven, their numbers are going to be limited here. We're safer here than anywhere else."

It was on the tip on my tongue to remind him that we were due before the Coven. We weren't safer. We just faced a different kind of danger.

Danaus knelt before me, wrapping one of his large strong hands around my thin wrist. "I will not let Rowe touch you. He will not kidnap you again. The naturi cannot have you," he vowed, bringing a shaky smile to my lips. Seated in a dirty London alley, covered in naturi blood and glass, he had made a similar promise to me. I could feel his anger now as he held my arm. He blamed himself for me being grabbed at the Compound. He felt angry and ashamed of his failure to keep his promise to me. But I didn't blame him. No one could have stopped Rowe at that moment.

With my free hand, I cupped his cheek, rubbing my thumb across his strong cheekbone. His pain and frustration beat at me, weakening the smile I was forcing onto my lips. How had we come to this point? Protecting each other from the threats that crowded us on all sides when we were supposed to be killing each other.

"Danaus, I don't expect you to keep such a promise. You would have to be close to me at all times. It's a step in our relationship I'm not ready to take," I teased, trying to lighten the weight in his chest. To my surprise, he didn't move. Usually when I teased him, the hunter would growl at me and stomp off. Danaus simply squeezed the wrist he was holding and shook his head slightly, his lips gently grazing the palm of my hand.

"I stand by my promise. The naturi will not have you."

"Thank you," I murmured, dropping my hand back into my lap. No one had ever anyone vocally sworn to protect me. Others had physically, but then it had the feeling of a piece of property being protected rather than a living creature.

Danaus pushed back to his feet and took a step back. "We should get going," he said, extending his hand to help me rise.

"Do you think other races know about the deal?" I asked as I slipped my cool hand into his warm one. The appearance of the witch and the lycan with the Daylight Coalition member seemed to take on a whole new frightening meaning.

"Let's hope not," he said, pulling me to my feet. "I can only fight one war at a time."

And I could already guess at which side he would fall on if the races went to war against the nightwalkers.

Six

When Danaus and I entered the main living room, we found Roberto lounging against the wall near the doors, hands shoved in the pockets of his trousers. Dressed in another black suit, he looked like a careless Italian play-boy out for an evening of reckless pleasure. The deep red shirt he wore was open at the throat, his dark brown hair perfectly slicked back. Roberto was a few centuries old; closer to my age than Tristan's, but still far from being an Ancient. My encounters with the Coven flunkies were few and far between. My patience was thin and I had a tendency to burn through them. My orders had always come directly from Jabari, and occasionally from Tabor.

Tristan stood expressionless behind a seated Sadira. He'd pulled on a deep blue shirt, but had yet to button it. They were all awaiting my arrival. How nice.

"The Elders are waiting for you," Roberto said.

"And Tristan?" I asked him, stopping the nightwalker as he turned toward the doors. Roberto turned back, his eyes sliding over to the young vampire as a dark smile lifted his red lips.

"He may stay behind. He has not been invited to court."

I looked from Roberto over to Tristan, who was watching

me with a desperate look in his eyes. Had I just put him in even greater danger? The Coven had granted my wish, but they never were so generous without a specific reason. If Tristan remained behind, he would be unprotected, vulnerable to any other nightwalker lurking in the city. Of course, he would have been in the same danger if he was coming with the rest of us. But someone feared that I might interfere with tonight's planned entertainment if I was around, so I was effectively removed from the equation. If I was with the Coven, I couldn't protect Tristan here.

I cursed myself and my stupidity. I had tried to outmaneuver the Coven in an attempt to protect the young nightwalker and only made an even bigger mess. He wouldn't survive an encounter with the court, but I also doubted he would make it through the evening alone in the hotel room.

While I was never an official member of the court, I had seen what it was capable of, played a part in its games as both prey and predator. Nightwalkers were resilient creatures who could survive all manner of physical torture for hours on end. But it was more than the physical pain that left a creature curled in a pool of its own blood, spewing an endless litany of pleas and prayers for mercy or death. They played with their prey until its mind shattered like a stained-glass window, so there was nothing left. No sense of self or reality.

My eyes jerked to Sadira as she stood and walked over to us while Tristan remained standing by her empty chair, one hand tightly gripping the back as if it were his last lifeline of safety.

"Say it," I growled at Sadira. My narrowed eyes followed her as she slipped by me and stood near the double doors.

"I don't know what you're talking about," she said, but she wouldn't meet my gaze nor would she look back at Tristan.

"Say it! Do what you would never do for me," I shouted, pointing at the young nightwalker. But she didn't look at him. She didn't speak. She lifted her chin slightly and continued to stare at the wall.

Against my better judgment, my eyes fell back on Tristan. I could still remember his smell from when he lay in bed with me, the sweet mix of heather and blood. The feel of his smooth skin pressed to mine and the memory of how he spooned me last night filled my brain.

I kept telling myself that he was just chum, entertainment was his purpose for being, but the words were bile in the back of my throat. A couple of nights earlier he had gone into the woods with me and attacked the naturi. He had fought beside me when we were outnumbered and destined to die horrible deaths at the hand of our enemies. He had stood beside me because he believed I would keep my word and save him from our maker. He had faith in my sense of honor.

Rage pumped through my veins, pushing aside the blood. I hated him. I hated myself. I hated the fates that had bought us to this precipice. There was no escaping the promise I had made nor living with myself if I even tried to.

Ignoring Sadira and the rest of the occupants of the room, I marched over to Tristan. Roughly grabbing a fistful of his hair, I pulled him toward me. "No!" Sadira's desperate scream echoed through the silent room. She had suddenly realized what I'd been about to do.

I had enough time to release Tristan's hair before she crashed into me, crushing me into the wall while knocking Tristan out of my reach. I tried to shove her off me but her nails were digging into my bare arms and I couldn't get a solid hold on her.

"You can't have him," she snarled.

"You're giving him up to the court," I countered, finally getting a grip of her thin bony shoulders.

"For a night of entertainment."

"They'll kill him!" I shouted, pushing her away. She immediately came at me, but I backhanded her, snapping her head around as the blow sent her to the floor.

"You don't know that," she argued.

"I do. And so do you."

Tristan is my child. The statement came as an insidious whisper across my brain, causing me to flinch as if Sadira had struck me. *Just like you will always be my child, my Mira. You can't have him.*

"I claim him," I snarled, balling my hands into fists as I tried to fight her claim on my will. Every fiber of my being screamed to obey her. Everything within me demanded that I kneel down and crawl into her waiting arms. But I couldn't. I had promised Tristan.

To my surprise, I was able to lift my arm to Tristan, beckoning him over. Sadira had the ability to manipulate my thoughts and emotions, but she wasn't as strong as Jabari. She couldn't control me physically like a puppet on a string.

Again I roughly grabbed a handful of Tristan's hair and pulled him close. Sadira increased her presence in my brain until the pain was positively excruciating. Tears streaked my cheeks, escaping from my clenched eyes. Not caring about the pain I was causing Tristan, I sank my fangs into his throat and drank deeply. It didn't require much, only a couple of swallows. The blood also seemed to wash Sadira's presence from my brain.

In those few seconds, I pulled all of Tristan's history and emotions into my brain. In a flash I saw his childhood home in Geneva, the beautiful face of his dead wife, the promise of a daughter who never survived, and a horrific slide show of events that comprised his years with Sadira.

Lifting my mouth from his neck, I pushed him down to his knees in front of me. "You belong to me now. You are mine until I choose to free you," I said in a shaky voice, my narrowed gaze capturing his wide blue eyes. Releasing him, I turned back to the others who were closely watching me and focused my attention on Roberto. "He is mine," I declared. Those three words hung like a worn hangman's noose in the center of the room for several seconds, daring anyone to argue with my decision. "Anyone touches him and I will know. Harm him and they will answer to me."

"But the Elders have already promised—" Roberto began, but I didn't let him finish that statement.

"No one touches him," I warned, my voice dropping to a low growl. "Tell the others."

Roberto nodded stiffly, his anger trickling through the room. The Coven might have granted the right to play with Tristan, but anyone who came near the young nightwalker would have to deal with my wrath. A vampire then had to decide if he thought the Coven would protect him from me, and there were no promises to be found there.

My gaze drifted over to Danaus, to find him frowning darkly at me, his brow seemingly furrowed in confusion. I could sense his disgust for what I had done. In his mind, I'd taken a slave. There was nothing redeeming in the ownership of another sentient creature. However, sometimes you had to do distasteful things to protect those weaker than you. If I were lucky, I had extended Tristan's life, if only by a few hours.

Unfortunately, it meant that I'd done the one thing I vowed I would never do—I had started a family. Tristan was mine for as long as I claimed him. He was mine to guide and protect. In my domain of Savannah, I was the Keeper, but that meant I preserved the peace and protected our secret. No nightwalker belonged to me or based his or her daily decisions on my wants and desires. Knox and Amanda acted as my assistants, but they were free to leave Savannah and pursue their own lives at any time. Tristan could not. And I could not leave without Tristan.

Anger bubbled in my chest, and I had yet to leave the confines of our hotel room. This was not going to go well. At least Tristan was a little better protected than he had been a couple minutes ago. But I'd crossed a major line, and stolen Sadira's plaything from her while she watched. It happened occasionally among nightwalkers, but never had the child of a vampire stolen another one of her maker's children. It reflected very poorly on Sadira. If she was going to save face at all, she would have to challenge me for Tristan.

And at the moment, I welcomed the chance to tear into her. Beyond our own dark history, she had been willing to leave Tristan to the tender mercies of the nightwalkers who hung around the Coven. She had done the same to me years ago, and my strength and ability to control fire were the only things that kept me alive. Tristan would not have lived to see the sunrise if I hadn't stepped up. He still might not, but at least he now had a fighting chance.

"Let's go," I said, glaring briefly at Sadira as I swept past where she still half lay on the floor and out of the room. Hatred burned in her eyes and her fingers hooked into claws. We would have words later, I had no doubt, but now we had other things to worry about. Silently, we filed down to the waiting speedboat, while Tristan remained alone in the hotel room.

Around us, people crowded the canals and sped across the Lagoon, headed out for an evening of entertainment or returning home from a long day of work. A warm summer breeze caressed my bare skin, holding me in its embrace. The air was laced with the salty scent of the Adriatic Sea. Ahead of us, the island of San Clemente loomed, its large hotel bobbing as the boat bounced and cut through the waves created by some of the larger shuttle boats. It took less than fifteen minutes to cross the Lagoon and dock at the island. It was both the longest and shortest fifteen minutes of my existence.

As I stood to disembark, I glanced over at Danaus, who had sat beside me on the trip over. His eyes briefly darted to my back and then back to my face. He silently mouthed the words *Kick me,* bringing a reluctant smile to my lips. That's pretty much what it all felt like, but for this ugly moment in time, he was with me in this endeavor.

"I assume you know the way," Roberto said, his lips curling with distaste. It was somewhat amusing. Where he had been gracious yesterday, he was equally snobbish and critical today. I had obviously put a crimp in the night's planned entertainment. Fine, let him take it up with the management. I already had a few choice words for them.

"I know it. Have fun tonight," I mocked, wagging my fingers at him as I stepped onto the dock. The nightwalker said nothing as he put the boat into reverse and backed away from the landing. I almost pitied his next meal.

Frowning, I led the way down the dock to a path that wound past the hotel and deeper into the island. Even if I hadn't been to the court before, I would have been able to find my way. Power throbbed from deep within the tiny island, and the concentration of nightwalkers grew thicker the farther we walked.

I stayed in front as we strolled down the path, Danaus behind my left shoulder while Sadira hung back on my right. Tension jumped and crackled through my frame. The fine hairs on my arms and on the back of my neck suddenly stood on end when I sensed one of the nightwalkers break off from the rest of the hidden pack and start to approach. I couldn't see him yet but I could feel him.

"Remain calm," I murmured to Danaus, but I think I needed to hear the words as well. My stomach twisted with anticipation like a snake winding itself into a tight coil. My focus had been completely on facing the Elders. I had not anticipated the long walk to the main hall. Every time I'd traveled to the island since leaving Sadira, I was under Jabari's protective wing, removed from the rigors of the horde of flunkies and courtiers who hung on the various Elders.

I stopped walking when the nightwalker stepped into the glow of a nearby street lamp. Valerio. We had traveled together for a time years ago. He was older than I was, but not yet an Ancient. He was close, though. Too close to that thousand-year mark for me to feel any kind of comfort.

"Did you leave Vienna for me?" I inquired, keeping my tone light and playful. "I'm flattered." I slipped my hands into the back pockets of my pants as Valerio strolled to the edge of the light.

He bowed graciously to me, his arms thrown open wide. It must have been a signal because I felt several other nightwalkers move closer, but they remained hidden in the shadows cast by the trees that dotted the island, creating a tiny forest.

"I come to court occasionally for a bit of entertainment," he said with a slight shrug of his right shoulder. "When I heard you would be appearing, I thought I'd pop in so we could catch up."

Valerio was the typical handsome vampire, with his blond-streaked brown hair and lovely dark brown eyes. He had a dreamy, movie-star kind of look about him. More of a romantic but sadly misunderstood lead, rather than the dark villain. His heritage was something of a Spanish-Italian hybrid.

"How thoughtful!" I laughed. I was trying my best to keep my posture relaxed, but it wasn't an easy task with so many hostile nightwalkers edging closer. Tension hummed in my frame, tightening the muscles in my shoulders.

"But I've heard that you've taken away some of our entertainment for the night."

"I see Roberto has been kind enough to spread the sad

news." Ahh, the vampire grapevine strikes again. Telepathy among my own kind had its benefits as well as drawbacks. This once it might work to my benefit, not that I was particularly counting on it. "Yes, Tristan has been removed from the menu. He's too young to be of any interest for this group."

"Fortunately for us, that young one was not the main course," purred a female voice from the shadows. A curvy brunette slunk out of the darkness to my left. At just over five feet, the vampire was an attractive creature in her breezy skirt with its soft, floral pattern and pale rose shirt that left her slender shoulders bare. While we had never been formally introduced, I knew she was called Gwen. She wasn't particularly nice. I could guess who the main course was, and so could Danaus, because the tension in his body ramped up considerably when she started to slink closer.

"The great Mira has returned to us," Gwen mocked. "And not only can she command fire, but she has tamed the hunter."

My eyes slid briefly to Danaus, but his gaze never wavered from the female nightwalker. "Tamed" was hardly the word I'd use, but now was not the time to quibble over semantics. I was sure Danaus would have something to say about this if we survived.

"I look forward to tasting him," she continued. Gwen reached up to touch his face, but I caught her wrist in a flash of movement and shoved her backward a few steps. Her eyes glowed with outrage but she managed to keep from hissing. She was a toady for Elizabeth and long used to having her way. We were close in age, but she had been reborn chum, giving me an advantage. Of course, challenging her directly would be seen as a challenge to Elizabeth, and I was trying to cut back on the number of fights I picked with Coven Elders.

Around us, more nightwalkers closed in. They were now leaning against the trees that lined the sidewalk and lounging in the grass. A quick count revealed sixteen vampires of varying age; more than the usual welcoming committee.

"He belongs to me," I said in a low voice, though I'm sure they all heard me.

"You've gotten greedy, Mira. First Tristan and now the hunter," Gwen said, taking a couple slow, cautious steps toward me again. "You've been away for too long. Forgotten your place. We've been promised a taste of the hunter."

"I don't share." My soft voice was filled with enough lurid menace to give her pause in her steady approach.

"You will if the Coven commands it," Gwen replied with a smug smile. The nightwalker was attractive enough, but her mouth bothered me. It was a large, shapeless thing, as if it were simply a giant slash across her face. And every time she spoke, an ugly wound reopened, marring her lovely features.

"Consider yourself warned," I said, matching her smile with one of my own. "Touch him or Tristan and you will face me. There will be no hiding behind the skirts of your mistress."

A haunting glow returned to her hazel eyes and her fangs glinted briefly in the lamplight. "You wouldn't dare." There seemed to be something hesitant and unsure in her expression, but she couldn't back down with everyone watching.

"No?"

I dropped my hands to my sides with my palms open. Out of the ground sprang two dozen snakes made of bright orange fire. The horde slithered around us once then shot out along the ground in all directions, chasing away the nightwalkers. No one was caught by my fiery serpents, and I extinguished the flames when the other nightwalkers were a comfortable distance away. Only Valerio remained behind. He had jumped onto the street lamp, with his feet braced against the pole while one hand clasped the top. Fury contorted his handsome features and the light reflected in his eyes.

"You're forbidden to use fire here!" he shouted. A fire snake slowly slithered around the pole, waiting for its prey to descend. I extended my right leg so that only the tip of my boot touched the ground. The snake instantly changed directions and came back to me. It wriggled up my leg and wrapped around my waist once before disappearing.

"We've been betrayed. All bets are off," I replied in a hard, cold voice.

"Yes, we have," he said, his dark gaze locking on Danaus. His words cut through me. I knew it looked like I was betraying our kind to the one who had hunted us for centuries. I could have told him that Danaus had protected Sadira, Tristan, and even Jabari in England, but I would have been wasting my words. Actions were the only thing these creatures believed. Words were just neatly packaged lies.

"When the day comes that you have to choose a side, ask yourself who will be willing to protect you," I called back, drawing his grim gaze back to my face. Tonight alone, I had sworn to protect not only another vampire, but a human, from the Coven. Any protection offered by the Coven was a flighty, mercurial thing at best, which seemed to change each time the sun set. I still hadn't been forgiven by Valerio, but at least I'd given him something to think about. It was a start.

We traveled the rest of the way to the main hall unmolested. That's not to say we weren't surrounded by a sizable group of very pissed-off nightwalkers. At the moment, however, they were content to let the Elders work me over first.

SEVEN

The Great Hall of the Coven was near the opposite side of the island from where we docked but still a distance from the shore, so that any one landing would be forced to walk at least a few dozen yards before reaching the main doors. The large three-story building was made entirely of dark gray stone and resembled an old fort with its long, slender windows reflecting the pale moonlight. It rose up from the interior of the island like a cold, silent guard refused eternity's rest. There were no lights leading up to the building, nothing to welcome the curious if someone happened to be on a leisurely stroll around the island.

Walking up the main stairs, a pair of heavily muscled men pulled open the massive wood and steel doors. There were other humans about the large building, a collection of servants and pets. And when the need called for it, food readily on hand. It was better than worrying about grabbing a bite from the nearby hotel when dawn drew close.

The two doormen barely earned a glance as I strode past them and down the long, dim hall to another set of doors. A heavy pounding echoed through the entryway as the front doors were closed, the sound bouncing off the walls as it flew up to hammer against the high ceiling. A chill skittered along my spine but I said nothing as I suppressed the old memories that attempted to crawl into the forefront of my mind. Clenching my fists at my side, I forced myself to take a step through the open doorway leading into the main throne room. I didn't let myself look back at Danaus for any kind of encouragement, though I wanted it. I just kept moving, my eyes never wavering from the trio sitting on the slightly raised dais at the other end of the room.

The cold, uneven stone that comprised every inch of the entryway gave way to jaw-dropping opulence in the main hall. Shiny black marble floors gleamed in the candlelight as if a lake of liquid night stretched out before us. The three-story ceilings disappeared in the darkness, as the flickering candlelight could not penetrate the inky blackness overhead. The Coven had found a way to cage the night itself, but had yet to find a way to stop the passage of time.

There were no windows in this room, making it a safe hiding place from the dawn if necessary, but the main sleeping chamber was several meters below ground. The walls were covered in exquisite paintings, tapestries, and flags—a collection of art almost as old as man. From the ceilings hung gold and crystal chandeliers that flickered and twinkled with candlelight. Yet as beautiful as it was, it was also cold and silent. The room somehow managed to have the feel of both an elegant ballroom and a dusty mausoleum.

At the end of the hall, three small steps led to a raised platform that held four intricately carved gold-leaf chairs. In the middle sat Jabari and Macaire, while Elizabeth rest in the chair to the far left. The chair on the far right next to Jabari remained empty. It had belonged to Tabor. That vacancy seemed all the more ominous now that I'd walked in with a nightwalker hunter. While no one on the Coven had said anything to confirm it, some believed that Tabor was killed by Danaus, while others believed he was killed by another

Ancient who refused to step forward, fearful of crossing Jabari. I'd begun to wonder if the slaying had been completed by the naturi. What better way to ensure that we couldn't protect the seal than to destroy the triad that had created it? Yet now, with the presence of the naturi in the main hall, an even darker theory began to take shape in my mind.

Behind the set of four chairs was another set of three stairs and a smaller dais. On this platform rested just one chair, made of wrought iron with a red velvet cushion. That chair belonged to Our Liege. It was empty as well. I stared at that empty spot for several seconds before finally dragging my eyes down to the Elders. I had yet to meet Our Liege, and while I wasn't particularly comforted by the fact that he was missing now, I was glad that I would not meet him for the first time under the current circumstances.

At the center of the room, I stopped walking and bowed my head to the Coven. It was polite but not overly subservient. I was treading on thin ice already. Jabari was more than a little pissed at me if he was looking to create my replacement, and I had never gotten around to playing nice with Macaire or Elizabeth, so there was no help to be found there. My goal was to not slit my own throat in the first five minutes, while I tried to keep the others around me alive. Danaus wisely remained a step behind my left shoulder and did not move. In fact, I wasn't even sure he was still breathing. However, by remaining behind me, I felt reassured that he was willing to follow my lead in this intricate tango. Well, at least for now.

Sadira, on the other hand, came around to stand next to me on my right. She was willing to stand with me, but her placement opened the door for her to jump ship if things got too ugly.

Macaire shifted in his chair, reclining while stretching out his left leg. His eyes paused over each of us before he finally drew a breath to speak. "*Benvenuto,* Sadira. It has been a long time since you were last in Venice." His Italian was smooth and flawless, as if he were a native.

"Grazie," she murmured as she bowed to the trio. "It is rare that I leave my home, but it is always good to look on the loveliness of Venice." Despite the anxiety I could feel washing off her in small waves, her tone remained its usual calm, as if nothing could disturb her tranquility.

I thought I was going to gag, but I kept my mouth shut and my face blank.

"Please, come sit near us. It seems we have much to catch up on." The silver-haired Elder motioned with a careless wave of his right hand for her to take a seat on the stairs before him.

Macaire was not the leader of the Elders, not even the strongest of the three. That was and always would be Jabari. However, Macaire loved to play with his prey. He liked to toy with their minds, break their spirits before he broke their bodies. It was a trait Sadira shared with him, one many nightwalkers shared.

"I am honored, but I would like to remain beside my daughter," she said, lifting her chin slightly. I raised one eyebrow in surprise before I could catch it. Macaire had given her an easy out, an extremely generous opportunity to save her own skin. She wouldn't get a second chance.

"Yes," he hissed. Macaire's eyes slid over to me and his gaze narrowed. "Mira. It has been a long time."

"Not since that last little job in Nepal," I said with a pleasant smile. It was a little nudge, a friendly reminder that I had fulfilled the requests of the Coven in the past. One of the Coven toadies had contacted me several years ago to eliminate a vampire who was causing some problems in a small village in Nepal. He was leaving behind a large trail of bodies. It was raising too many questions, and a major media organization was starting to look into it. I destroyed the nightwalker and it was covered up as a rare disease sweeping through the remote area. After the job, I stopped by Venice as a way of politely checking in before returning home. At the time, only Elizabeth had been in residence on the island.

"Yes. Well, it seems you were quite busy in England recently." I opened my mouth to argue, taking a step forward, but Macaire raised a silencing hand. "Jabari told us of how you were attacked by a horde of naturi not far from London. Nasty business." Macaire shook his head, while resting his elbows on the arms of the chair. He folded his hands over his stomach and watched me for a moment as if thinking. "We are grateful that you saved the lives of Sadira and our Jabari. It would have been a dreadful loss." He paused for half a second, and I thought I saw something in his eyes, but he quickly pushed on. "But it seems your little display has caused some problems that need dealing with."

"What problems?" I flinched, the muscles in my shoulders tensing. What new horror was I opening myself up to? I took a small step forward, wishing I could push Danaus and Sadira behind me a little better, but I could offer only so much protection.

"I'll let our visitor explain," Macaire blandly said.

At the same time, a door to the left of the dais opened and a woman walked out. She was African American, with rich black hair that poured past her shoulders and large, lovely brown eyes. She walked across the room with a natural ease and seductive grace that could bring men to their knees. I'd seen her do it. Her name was Alexandra Brooks and she was a werewolf. I'd known her for nearly five years, but I doubted that the Coven was aware of it. During the long centuries, lycans and nightwalkers had learned to tolerate each other. On rare occasions, nightwalkers and shapeshifters would team up for some mutual fun, but the peace never seemed to last long.

We had held a contest once. It was Valerio's idea. We grabbed a poet and made him decide which race was more alluring: vampires or lycans. Poor fool. It really was a no-win situation for him, but we found it entertaining. After more than two weeks of allowing his senses to feast on a handful of vampires and a choice selection of weres, he made some interesting comments. For this poet, vampires could be extraordinarily sexy just standing still, quietly occupying space like the white, slender beauty of the Venus de Milo. On the other hand, lycans seemed to come alive with sexual allure the moment they moved. Their energy flared and filled the room, brushing against its occupants; an exquisite blending of animal and man.

To my surprise, we released the poet after he made his comments. Both sides seemed content with the assessment, and Valerio's interest had wandered elsewhere. I later heard that the man committed suicide a few months after escaping our collective clutches.

Behind Alexandra, a prime specimen of male beauty strolled in. At well over six feet, he looked as if he were built of pure muscle with a hint of granite. A seeming child of the sun, the stranger possessed thick blond hair and bronze skin. His features were soft, with full lips and small cleft in his determined chin. He was also a lycanthrope. His movement was too liquid to be human, and with him came the scent of nature. Not the same as you would smell when the naturi were near, but definitely woodsy with a musky hint of man.

If the circumstances had been different, I would have happily taken the time to get to know the shifter. Unfortunately, my main concern then was making sure Alexandra didn't say anything to reveal our friendship.

I smiled coldly at the woman, my fangs peeking out. "I never thought I'd see the day when the Coven let a mongrel loose in the main hall."

Alexandra sharply halted and glared at me, but said nothing. She and the male lycan were outnumbered in the court of nightwalkers. As an emissary, she expected a level of protection from the Elders, but that didn't mean the members of the court couldn't mock her in an attempt to get her to attack. If she attacked, a nightwalker had every right to defend herself.

I walked over, drawing closer with each circle I closed around her. The sharp click of my heels on the marble was the only sound in the enormous room. The blond man stiffened when I slipped between him and Alexandra, but he didn't move, didn't even change his even breathing pattern. "Tell me, Alexandra, are you still an Omega or did a Beta finally have pity on you and make you his bitch?"

Alexandra growled low in the back of her throat at me, and I saw a subtle shift in her eyes for a second. Her brown eyes had faded to liquid copper as the wolf in her fought for control on the swell of anger. Lucky for us both, she caught it in time. She wouldn't risk changing here—it was too dangerous with this many vampires hanging about; she wouldn't survive the night.

Of course, after my last comment, I was asking for her to rip my throat out. There were three grades to the werewolf pack. There was the Alpha male and female; leaders of the pack. Everyone else generally filtered down to the Beta class. And then there were the Omegas hanging on the periphery of the pack, not exactly a part or accepted, just barely tolerated. They were permitted the scraps of the kill after everyone else had eaten, and they served as the whipping boy for the family. The only thing lower than an Omega was dead.

"*Arresto,* Mira," Macaire said mildly with a vague wave of his hand. There was no censure in his voice, only a note of boredom and maybe a hint of amusement. "It seems you have already met our Ms. Brooks," he continued, switching to English for Alexandra's benefit.

"She came sniffing around my domain a couple years ago. I sent her on her way," I said, turning my back on the lycan as I walked back over to Danaus and Sadira.

"How nice," he said with a false grin. "That does not matter. She's brought word from her people in England."

"It seems you have made quite a mess, Fire Starter," Alex said, smiling broadly at me. It was now her turn to make me twist, and I had a feeling she was going to come out of this meeting looking a lot better than me. "All throughout the southwestern territories of the U.K. people have found heaps of ashes accompanied by items like knives, swords, bits of clothing. The humans are smart enough to figure out that these ashes were from living creatures. They are going to automatically assume they were humans. Some very uncomfortable questions are being asked, and there is only so much we can suppress."

"Get our press out there," I argued, looking over at Macaire. "Start feeding the tabloids tales of aliens or solar flares at night." Shoving my fingers into the front pockets of my pants, I tried to affect a look of indifference, though that was a horrible lie. This was a turn I had not considered or anticipated.

When Danaus and I used our powers to destroy the naturi, we hadn't limited ourselves to those at the Themis Compound. We destroyed the naturi in all directions for several miles. I was just grateful to have them gone and my life intact. I hadn't thought about what the humans would find. My focus was so entirely centered on the naturi and stopping them from breaking the seal that I had not thought about protecting our secret. Hell, what was the point? If the naturi were free, we'd have bigger things to worry about than a few people discovering that nightwalkers existed.

"Some of the Wiccans have already mobilized and are posting items on the Internet. They're claiming that the creatures were once members of the naturi and that they were killed as part of ongoing war between them and vampires."

"And we're concerned about that? Don't you realize how ridiculous this sounds?" I said incredulously, pinning the lycan with my narrowed gaze. Sure, it was the truth, but no one believed the truth anymore. "Most humans don't know what a naturi is. They've never heard of them."

"Your lack of control has thrown off our timetable," Alexandra snapped, pointing one slender finger at me as she lurched forward a couple steps. However, she quickly came to a stop when she realized the sudden movement could be seen as an act of aggression. "The Great Awakening isn't supposed to be for another fifty years at the earliest."

"And what about Rowe? Don't you think he could throw off the precious timetable?" I replied, my gaze darting back to the Elders. I didn't know how much the lycans knew of the current naturi threat, which was growing with each passing night, but I didn't care anymore. I wasn't going to be the only one in the fire. It was time to up the ante.

"That is already being considered, Mira," Elizabeth said in a calm, placating voice. She was telling me to shut up. I took the hint.

"Thank you for your valuable information, Ms. Brooks," Macaire said. "We will not need to speak with you again." Alex bowed slightly to the three Elders, then left the main hall without looking back at me. The silent blond man followed close on her heels, but I could feel his dark eyes on me before he disappeared through the side door.

I waited until after the door on the left was closed before I opened my mouth again. It was time to take the gloves off and get messy. I had been purposefully dressed down by someone the Coven saw as an inferior regarding something that was supremely trivial at this point, considering the problems that loomed and their own betrayal. I'd had enough.

"Shall we bring out your other guest?" I demanded, taking another couple steps forward so the Coven's focus would be completely on me. My hands fell from my pockets and hung limp at my sides, but I was ready for any kind of an attack.

"Other guest?" Macaire repeated, tilting his head to the side. A nice act, but it wasn't all that convincing. The other two Elders hadn't moved, didn't even blink at the question. In fact, Jabari hadn't moved a muscle since I entered the room. We still had other issues that went beyond the Coven.

"The naturi," I supplied in a voice that could have frozen the Lagoon. Macaire smiled at me in his usual condescending manner and opened his mouth to say something, but I cut off his words. "Don't insult me! There was a naturi sleeping here last night less than an hour before dawn. Bring her out."

Macaire blinked at me once in surprise and then looked over at Elizabeth, who was regarding me with new interest. The Elder turned his cold gaze back at me, a calculating look crossing his face as frostbite sank its teeth into the marrow of my bones. *"Impressionate,"* he slowly said as he slipped back into Italian. However, this time an old accent flavored the single word before he could catch it. Something of who he truly was snuck past his defenses while he was distracted with a new thought. "We were wondering what you and the hunter were doing out in the Lagoon so close to dawn. We knew he could sense the naturi, but we didn't think he would be able to sense them through our web of spells."

"He couldn't, but *we* could," I corrected. Macaire's eyebrows jumped at that bit of information, and even Jabari cracked. Actually, it was just a twitch of one corner of his mouth, but it was something.

"Molto impressionante. It explains how you were able to incinerate the naturi far from your location. It was my understanding that you could only burn that which you could

see," Macaire said. The fingers of his right hand restlessly moved on the arm of his chair, and he was now sitting up a little straighter.

"Yes, well this is all very new to me considering that my memory was wiped," I sneered. My fingers balled into fists and it was all I could do to keep from lighting the tapestries hanging about the room on fire. "I thought the Coven would know exactly what I was capable of, considering it spent nearly a century experimenting on me." My words dripped with sarcasm so acidic I feared they would soon eat through the marble floor.

"That was Jabari's realm," Macaire said with a dismissive wave of his hand, but the motion was stiffer this time and there was something that flickered in his eyes again. There had always been a certain amount of tension between Macaire and Jabari. While they never openly attacked each other, they had no problems pitting their various flunkies and followers against one another. I would have been willing to wager that either Macaire couldn't control me or had never been given the opportunity to try.

Again the door on the left swung open, halting the conversation. Into the room stepped a female naturi. She wore a simple homespun dress and her long blond hair was braided down her back. There were five clans of naturi—earth, wind, water, light, and animal. She was too slender and willowy to be a member of the animal clan, which were typically dark, swarthy creatures rippling with muscles. A water clan member couldn't be out of water, and her coloring was all wrong for what I had seen of the earth clan, as their hair and skin pigment had the same variety as a summer flower garden. So that left only wind and light. If she was a light clan member, I was in trouble if I attacked, as she would be able to use fire as easily as me. But I couldn't imagine the Coven allowing a light clan member in their midst. Of course, I would never have imagined seeing a naturi walking free in the Great Hall.

With her hands folded in front of her like a nun going to prayer, she walked quietly into the room. Keeping her eyes on the Elders, she bowed her head to them, but ignored our trio completely.

"What is she doing here?" I demanded, each word struggling up my throat and past my lips. My whole body was clenched with rage. I had thought my reaction to seeing Sadira for the first time in five centuries was bad. This was infinitely worse. The sight of the slender creature with her sharp features instantly made me want to rip her apart with my bare hands. I wanted to hear her scream and plead for her life. And then I wanted to hear her plead for me to kill her.

Nightmarish memories of my two-week captivity at Machu Picchu centuries ago came screaming back with a flawless clarity. She reminded me of the starvation and the pain that flooded all of my senses so that there was no escape. The naturi had captured and tortured me in hopes of breaking my mind. They wanted me to use my powers to destroy my own kind. As I stared at her now, the scars on my back burned anew.

Danaus stepped forward so he was standing beside me. His right hand reflexively reached for a weapon that wasn't there. Frustrated, his hand fell back to his side, clenched in a fist.

"You asked to see her," Macaire said with laughter in his voice.

"Why is she on the island?" My voice cracked across them like a whip snapping at the air.

Macaire stiffened and moved to sit on the edge of his chair. "We have business together," he briskly replied.

"The only business we have with their kind is their total extermination!" I took a couple slow steps toward the naturi, my hands before me with my fingers curled into claws. I didn't have any weapons, but I would happily have killed her with my bare hands. The naturi turned frightened eyes on me and stumbled a couple of steps back, edging closer to the raised dais and the Elders.

"Macaire!" she cried in her soft lilting voice.

"Stop, Mira!" Macaire shouted, jumping to his feet. "She has the protection of the Coven."

Those words stopped me cold. My body froze as if my mind had suddenly lost the ability to command it, had forgotten how to work my limbs. With infinite slowness I turned my head to look at the Elders. "What?" The word barely made it past the lump in my throat.

"Stop," Macaire commanded.

I ignored him and dragged my eyes to Jabari's face, who sat watching me. "Say it," I snarled, my voice harsh and rough.

Jabari rose from his chair, his head held high. "She has the protection of the Coven," he said loud and clear. His words reverberated through my chest until I was sure I would shatter into a million jagged shards.

Wrapping my arms around my waist, I nearly doubled over in horror. "How could you betray us?" I moaned. "They killed hundreds of our kind."

"The same could be said about the man that stands beside you," Jabari replied. A cold smile slithered across his broad lips, stretching his dark skin to accentuate his hard cheekbones. I reached back one hand, unconsciously trying to move the hunter behind me as if it would better protect him from the Coven.

"They tortured me for two weeks in hopes of using me as a weapon." I flung the words at him, even though some part of me knew not one of them cared about the pain I had endured to protect my own kind. "They slaughtered nightwalkers in my domain."

"Looking for you," Elizabeth coolly interjected.

"They killed Thorne in London," I said, but my voice had lost some of its earlier strength and venom. I didn't like where this was going.

"In an effort to get to you," Elizabeth replied. Her lovely face was blank of expression but her blue eyes seemed to sparkle and dance in the candlelight. "Our Jabari and Sadira were attacked, all in an effort to get to you."

"Times have changed, Mira," Macaire stated, drawing my wide-eyed gaze to his aged face. "It would seem as if the naturi would have no business with nightwalkers if you were not around."

"The naturi don't change. Not ever," I snarled, straightening from my wounded stance. *They would not pin this on me.* But even that bitter declaration seemed to carry with it a whimper of pain. I wasn't the reason so many of my fellow nightwalkers had been slaughtered. I wasn't the reason the naturi hunted and killed both humans and nightwalkers. This war started long before I was ever reborn, and I was sure it would continue long after my bones had been reduced to dust. *I would not be the Coven's scapegoat.*

"Unfortunately, we cannot rid ourselves of Mira as of yet," Jabari announced in a weary voice, as if reluctantly granting me a pardon.

I snapped. There was no more clear thought, just raw, horrible rage. The Coven was protecting our greatest enemy and threatening my life when I had done everything within my power to protect my own kind from the naturi.

Stretching my arms out on either side of my body, I started calling up great amounts of energy. Without making the conscious decision, I summoned enormous waves of power to me, pulling energy from every living creature within the region. I could feel it coming to me not just from San Clemente, but from all around Venice. At the same time, grim images of

Michael's and Thorne's mangled remains crowded in my brain. Memories of my horrific nights with Nerian swamped me, threatening to weigh me down and deter me from my path. The Coven had to be destroyed. It didn't matter that they were the Elders, or even if I had the ability to do it.

Overhead, the candles in the chandelier flared, awakening the shadows lounging in the far corners of the hall. The shadows lunged forward and back, reaching out from under the dais chairs and crawling up the cold stone walls. The flags and tapestries waved and rippled as if a fresh breeze had rushed in through an open window.

You can't destroy me, desert flower. Jabari's dark voice whispered through my brain, threatening to shatter my concentration. *If you attempt this thing, you must be able to kill them both. Destroy the Coven, Mira. Destroy them both.*

The command was little more than a faint whisper among hundreds of fragmented thoughts and painful memories. I tried to weigh the command in that second. It's what I wanted, but now I was forced to wonder if I wanted the same thing that Jabari wanted after all his lies, betrayal, and manipulation. But I couldn't afford to pause.

Before the thought was completely formed in my head, I was stopped by the last person I thought would ever do such a thing. Danaus came up behind me and wrapped his strong arms around me, locking my arms against my body.

"No!" I screamed, my ragged voice bouncing off the high stone walls. I already felt his power swamping me, struggling to form a cocoon around me before seeping into my skin. He was stealing away my ability to choose. Jabari hadn't been forcing me. It was almost a test to see what I was capable of.

"Calm," Danaus whispered, his hot breath brushing against my ear. I also heard the word repeated in my brain like a thought, blanketing my rage, suffocating the fire. He was trying to use our connection in reverse. Instead of commanding me to draw in the power and destroy, he was using his own powers to control and calm me.

"No!" I screamed again, but even my voice had begun to weaken. The power I had drawn in was seeping from my body back into the air. I wasn't sure if he could hear me, but I tried to push my own thoughts into his brain. *Help me, Danaus. Together we can crush them like we defeated the naturi. Together we can destroy them.*

But all I heard was silence. I could still feel him in my brain, his will sapping my strength. "They have betrayed us; betrayed my kind," I whimpered pathetically, feeling as if the remains of my soul were shattering into sharp shards of glass.

"How dare you say that while you stand there in the embrace of a vampire hunter!" Jabari raged, his calm finally cracking. But I knew now it was an act after his attempt to have me destroy the other Coven members.

"He saved you in England!" I shouted, my eyes locking on his twisted face. "He protected you and Sadira when the naturi attacked. He protected you."

"He's protecting us even now," Elizabeth proclaimed, gracefully rising from her seat. There was a look of open surprise on her pale heart-shaped face. "Look. She was trying to kill us all, but he stopped her." Her voice was haunting, like a half-remembered dream drifting through my brain.

All three Elders were now standing and staring at us with a mixture of wonder and confusion. Something strange had happened, and everyone was individually working on the implications. A renowned vampire hunter who had killed countless other nightwalkers had potentially saved the lives of the Coven. Not exactly something that happened every day.

"Send the naturi away," Danaus barked, his arms still locked around me.

Macaire wasn't happy with the order, but he could see the wisdom in it. I obviously couldn't control myself when she was around. The Elder nodded, and the terrified female naturi ran from the room and slammed the door behind her. With her gone, Danaus released me. He had effectively sapped all my strength, and I fell to my hands and knees. I glared wordlessly up at the Coven. I hated them. You didn't do business with the naturi. You didn't talk to them. You didn't make deals with them. You killed them.

Jabari and Elizabeth had returned to their seats, lost in thought, but Macaire remained standing, his sharp eyes never leaving my face. I could almost hear the cold, steel wheels in his mind churning away, examining each angle of what had happened.

"That is enough for today," he suddenly announced, his voice taking on a weary tone. "You may go now. We will talk more tomorrow."

"What about the seal? And the triad?" I cried, slapping my hand angrily against the marble floor. Nothing had been discussed and yet he was calling an end to court for the night.

"We have much to think about," Macaire said, returning to his seat. "We will talk more tomorrow."

I was about to argue again. I had obviously lost all common sense the second the naturi entered the room. A smart person would have picked herself off the ground and left, grateful that she was still alive. But I got off lucky. The moment I was about to speak, I heard Macaire's voice in my head. *We will speak again later.* I got the point. Macaire wanted a private meeting. So be it. The scheming had begun anew.

Eight

Danaus tried to help me off the ground, but I jerked out of his grasp and less than gracefully pushed to my feet. I was livid with him and the Coven. Had he done the right thing? Had he saved our lives because I lacked the ability to control my temper? Had he pulled me away from whatever game Jabari was playing? Yes, but I was still angry. In the boat the night before I chose our joining, let him control me. But minutes ago he'd taken away my choices and forced me. I didn't give a damn right now if it was for our own good.

I wanted to tear his throat out, to see him crumpled and bleeding at my feet. My body had been used and abused, first by my own brethren and now by my enemy. I felt dirty down to my very core. I had become a thing worse than chum. I couldn't even fight my fate, only obey.

To twist the knife even further, I couldn't lash out at Danaus. The Coven and its dedicated court were watching closely. If I were to strike out at him, any one of them might take it as a green light to have some fun, and I was too weak to fend them off. And I'd made a promise to get him out of Venice alive. For now, we were one big happy family.

Silently, our little group—Danaus, Sadira, and I—trooped out of the main hall and across the island back to the dock.

The other nightwalkers kept their distance, but were closely watching our progress. I had no doubt they'd sensed my display of power. I was sure that creatures all over Italy had felt it. You don't create waves like that and not draw attention.

"Out of the boat," I snapped at Roberto, who stood behind the wheel. He frowned at me but said nothing as he stepped on the docks. We jumped on the little speed boat and I threw it into reverse. I had some business to take care of and I didn't want to have a nightwalker following me. The Coven would give me a little space for now. I had a bit of interesting information, but it wasn't going to do me much good at the moment. No one would believe me if I said the Coven was plotting something *with* the naturi. Not only was it ridiculous, but it would also be coming from a nightwalker traveling with a vampire hunter.

"What's going on?" Sadira softly asked when we were halfway across the Lagoon.

"I don't know yet," I said, refusing to look at her. I directed the boat down the Guidecca Canal, narrowly dodging a shuttle bus as it trudged across the narrow waterway, sending up a spray of water on some of the passengers. The driver's curses barely rose above the rumble of the boat's engine. "But I'll know before we leave here."

"There was a naturi, Mira!" Sadira said, her voice jumping in pitch. The sight of the naturi had left her shaken, crushing the last of her composure. "A naturi in the Great Hall!"

"I noticed." I shifted the boat into neutral and let it glide into the hotel landing. I looked up at the large, elegant Hotel Cipriani. Tristan was pacing in front of the windows, waiting for our return. No one had bothered him, but that had not lessened his anxiety. Since marking him, his thoughts came clearly to me when I wanted them. I would have known instantly if a vampire had laid a hand on him. But it also worked in reverse. He could feel my own concerns and anxiety, though my exact thoughts were shrouded.

"Go up to the suite and calm Tristan," I ordered, gripping the steering wheel. I needed to be away from her. I needed some space from Sadira, the Coven, and this whole damned situation so I could think clearly. "But do not harm him in any way. You know that none of this is his fault. It's between you and me."

"And what are your plans for him?" she inquired from her seat, her voice hardening to rusty steel. After our encounter in the room and with the Coven, she had once again grown wary of me. During our last years together, Sadira had been a constant shadow in my brain, fearing my powers. The fear had left her a hollow shell, resulting in the death of many of her other pets.

I spun on my heels, my fists clenched as I looked down at her. A loose tendril of hair fell against my cheek, tickling my neck. "I have no plans for him! I don't want him. He's your pet, and you should have taken care of him. You know they would have torn him apart tonight."

"He has to learn to protect himself," she said in such a matter-of-fact tone that I longed to smack her. "You were younger than he when you first appeared before the court."

"I was also ten times stronger, and even then I barely survived." I took another step closer to her, clenching my fists so tight my nails began to cut into the palms of my hands. "You only let him go because you are too much of a coward to stand up to the court."

"How dare you call me a coward after I stood with you before the Elders!" she said, surging to her feet. Her sudden movement caused the little boat to rock and lurch in the water.

"You stood with me because you were confident that I would protect you. That is beginning to wear thin."

She smiled back at me, her usual beatific smile of peace and supreme confidence. "I'm your mother, my Mira. You will always protect me."

"Get out of here," I growled, pulling back my lips to expose my fangs. Her smile never wavered as she alighted from the boat and walked gracefully up the landing into the hotel. She sacrificed Tristan to save her own skin, and she knew that I would step forward and protect both of them from the Coven. I wanted to scream. My decisions weren't wrong. I needed the triad intact, which meant protecting Sadira, though I longed to rip her throat out. It was insane to fight her, because winning would be finally killing her, and I couldn't.

Jerking the boat into reverse, I backed it into the waterway again. Shifting roughly into first, I headed to the Grand Canal. It was a short trip, but I wasn't in the mood to bother with water taxis or shuttles. I docked in an opening on the island of Dorsoduro, almost directly across from Piazza San Marco.

Danaus jumped to the ground right behind me as I secured the boat. I almost forgot he was there, having become so accustomed to having the dark rain cloud on my heels. Of course, I was also a little preoccupied with thoughts of the Coven and their special guest.

"Mira—"

"Don't talk to me yet, I'm still angry with you," I bit out as we walked down the winding streets, slipping past the locals on their way to the bars and restaurants for a few drinks and light conversation.

"You left me with no choice." His deep voice slipped around me like a pair of strong arms.

"You could have let me kill them."

"Could you?"

I didn't say anything, but marched down the street, my

teeth clenched. I didn't know. Maybe, but it was doubtful. The past few days had been strange, and I wasn't sure what I was capable of anymore. Of course, *we* could have most likely destroyed them, but he had hesitated. Last night when we were alone on the boat, I knew he thought about killing every nightwalker on the island. But today when we stood before the Coven, the opportunity spread out before us, and he stopped.

"That's what I thought," Danaus said grimly.

"You don't understand!" I shouted, whirling around to face him. "I've worked all my life to not have to answer to another creature—human or vampire. And then one night I wake up and find I'm wearing a choke chain and an untold number of people have the ability to jerk me to heel." I stepped closer, until he was backed against one of the buildings lining the sidewalk, and rose up on the tips of my toes so I could look him in the eyes. "To make matters worse, my enemy can do the same. I've become a threat to every thing on this planet. Do you have any clue as to what that feels like?"

We stared at each other in silence for several seconds. His face was unreadable, but I could feel the turmoil in his chest. Our connection was still strong from that night's brief contact. I could feel sadness, but it was cluttered with something else. I couldn't tell if it was sympathy, regret, or maybe even pity. For a second I was afraid we had more in common than I wanted there to be. He seemed to understand too well.

I softly growled in the back of my throat as I turned away from him. The sound was a strange mix of anger and frustration. It wasn't all his fault, no matter how hard I tried to pin it on him. Danaus just kept getting in the way. "You owe me," I muttered as I walked down the street.

"What?"

"I haven't decided yet. You owe me something. I'll get back to you."

"I'm on pins and needles," he said in a voice so dry I expected to see a puff of dust. I smiled despite my struggles to remain angry at him. It was becoming annoying that he could snap me out of my grim moods. Of course, dark ruminations were more of his forte than mine.

"That can be arranged," I said irritably, but he knew better. If I could sense his emotions, then he knew I was no longer angry. Frustrated and irritated, but not necessarily pissed.

Nine

We stopped at a small square flanked by some cozy restaurants and narrow shops. It was a quaint neighborhood that generally escaped the crowds of tourists, even during the high season. At night the area twinkled with guttering candles and little white lights. The air was layered with the tangy scent of spices and rich sauces with a hint of melted cheese. It almost made me miss the taste of food, but not quite.

"What are we doing here?" Danaus inquired as we came to stand in the center of the square. He turned and looked at the fountain at the opposite end, its falling water dancing in the faint yellow lights that flowed along the stone structure.

"Meeting a friend," I replied as Alex stepped out of the entrance of one of the small bars. There was an almost hypnotic sway to her hips as she closed the distance between us, her lithe body dancing to its own natural rhythm.

The lycanthrope was strong and independent, chasing after those things she wanted most in life. She cherished her existence as a werewolf, seeing her enhanced abilities as a gift rather than a curse, like so many of her kind. But even if she hadn't been a lycan, I think she would have reveled in all of her natural abilities as a normal human being. Life for her was a drink to be gulped, sipped, and always savored.

Alex had helped me escape myself and my past when my thoughts grew too dark. In return, I did everything within my power to foster amiable relations between her kind and mine. Not the easiest of tasks.

Her powers brushed briefly past me as she scanned the area. She was making sure we were alone. I had already checked. The closest nightwalker was stalking a tourist on the other side of the canal in San Marco. We had time. Besides, since dropping off Sadira on Guidecca, I had been cloaking Danaus and myself. We would need the privacy.

I opened my arms and was about to greet her when her fist connected with my jaw, snapping my head around. One of the benefits of being a werewolf was speed. The other was strength. I stumbled backward a step into Danaus, who tensed. I had seen her swing half a second before she hit me but was so surprised that I didn't try to dodge it.

"Bitch!" she spat at me.

"What are you doing? We're alone," I said, pushing off of Danaus. But even as I said it, I noticed the second lycanthrope stepping from the entrance of the bar. His broad shoulders briefly blocked the square of golden light pouring from the open doorway. He was either a member of her pack or assigned to her as backup should she run into any problems when dealing with my kind. Either way, I wasn't overly concerned. He was of her race and thus would protect her.

"That was for what you said," Alex told me, giving my shoulder a little shove with her index finger. Her narrowed eyes glittered in the faint light from a nearby pub but otherwise remained brown. "That Omega comment was a low blow and you know it."

I shrugged. "It had to be convincing. I'm not particularly

popular at the moment and I didn't want any backlash to hit you if they thought we were friends."

"Yeah, you always had a way with people," Alex said. Her full lips eased from a hard, angry slash to a reluctant smile. "Who's this?" she asked, jerking her chin toward my dark shadow. I turned and put an arm around her slim shoulders.

"Alexandra Brooks, this is Danaus, the hunter," I said, introducing her. She twisted out of my grasp so she could look up at me, her eyes widening to the point I thought I would have to catch them when they fell from their sockets.

"Are you crazy, girl?" she gasped. She looked over at Danaus then back at me. "There've been some rumors, but I didn't believe them. What's going on?"

"I'll explain soon," I said with a slight shake of my head. "Who's your golden companion? Pack member?"

Alex looked at me strangely, her brows drawn together over her pert nose. "I thought you knew," she softly said. "He belongs to Jabari."

"What?" I gasped. "No." The growl of frustration rumbled in my throat a second before I started moving, but my nails never made it into the lycan's bronze throat. Danaus quickly wrapped a strong arm around my waist and held me close, keeping me from ripping the man's throat out before a crowd of humans.

"Not here," Danaus snapped, tightening his arm around my waist, nearly cracking a rib.

"He's going to tell Jabari that I spoke with Alex. He'll know . . . he'll know we're friends," I said. Both my hands gripped the arm around my waist but I'd stopped struggling, my eyes never wavering from the lycan's face. He stared at me with a look of such sympathy and compassion that I could almost believe he cared for my plight.

"I don't understand," Alex interjected, drawing my gaze

back to her troubled features. "I thought you and Jabari . . . Well, you've never made any secret of your—"

"Jabari wants me dead," I said in a rush. "He wants my head on a pike and my heart on his mantel." Saying the words out loud suddenly made me feel very tired. My body went extremely still, as if I were made of stone, and I leaned back into Danaus, letting his warmth seep into me, calm my mind. Jabari had been my beloved mentor and guide through the night for nearly five centuries. He had been a companion when the emptiness threatened to consume me. And now he accused me of betrayal while he stank of it. I had been his puppet, his toy, his own personal assassin and servant. I had believed he would protect nightwalkers and that he would do what was right for our race.

But I'd been wrong about him; about a lot of things. Unfortunately, my blindness and ignorance were getting people killed. It couldn't continue.

"I won't say anything to the Coven about your meeting with Ms. Brooks," the man said, his deep voice like a distant drum beat waking me from my growing lethargy. "I may belong to the vampire, but my loyalty will always be to my own kind."

"Thank you . . . "

"Nico," he supplied.

"Nico?" I repeated, crinkling my nose at him. He definitely didn't look like a Nico. He was more like a John or Bruce. Maybe even Adonis, but that was guessing he looked as delicious naked as he did standing there in his cotton slacks and soft, hunter green button-up shirt. The sleeves of his shirt were rolled up past his elbows, revealing strong tanned arms covered in light blond hairs. I was willing to bet naked was better.

"Nicolai Gromenko," he replied, crushing the name with his clenched teeth.

"You're not Russian," I snapped, sounding equally irritated.

"Fourth generation. Nicolai is a family name. I'm from Phoenix. Anything else? Shoe size? Boxers versus briefs?"

"Don't worry," I purred, a grin slinking across my mouth. "There's always time to find out." The comment instantly erased the irritation from Nicolai's expression, causing a surprised smile to brighten his handsome features.

Danaus suddenly released me, a snort of disgust escaping him while Alexandra laughed. My attention snapped back to my companions and I winked at my old friend. I couldn't help myself.

"Lord! You had me worried for a minute," Alex said as she gave me a quick hug. "Between the hunter and Jabari, I seriously thought you were losing it."

"She has," Danaus grumbled.

My eyes darted from Danaus back to my friend, who noticed the smile that was crumbling from my face. "We have to talk," I said. Threading a loose strand of hair behind my ear, I swept my gaze over the area. This was going to take a while, but it would be worth it. "Hungry?" I asked, my eyes snagging on a pleasant-looking restaurant with a scattering of tables on the rim of the square.

"Starved," Alex said with a half sigh. She tilted her head toward Danaus while plopping her hands on her hips. "He need babysitting while you hunt?"

"She's eaten already," Danaus interjected, oozing disapproval.

Alex arched one eyebrow at me and threw a "What's his problem?" look my way. She had long ago adjusted to the fact that I drank of the blood of humans and thought nothing of the hunt.

Threading my arm through hers, I guided her over to the restaurant, with Danaus and Nicolai following close behind.

I motioned to the maître d' that we would be taking one of the tables in the courtyard. He nodded, then disappeared inside the building to find a server.

When we were all comfortably seated and our drink order taken, I relaxed in my chair, staring out across the quiet square. A pair of lovers walked arm in arm, whispering to each other. Three young children chased pigeons, their squeals of laughter skipping ahead of them. From inside the restaurant, loud boisterous Italian tumbled into the plaza. It was all pleasant and blissfully normal.

"Let's start with something simple," Alex announced as she scanned the menu. "Was that you I felt earlier?"

"I lost my temper," I murmured, my eyes falling to the tabletop. It had been stupid and irresponsible. Now that I was calm, I could admit as much. My actions had been careless and irresponsible, just like when I convinced Tristan to help me attack the naturi in England. We had been outnumbered and outgunned. I knew that when we spotted them, but I went ahead anyway. As a result, I barely escaped with my life, endangering Danaus and Tristan unnecessarily.

I knew better than to take these stupid risks and risk the lives of those I had sworn to protect. Shame and guilt burned away in my stomach. Fear of the naturi was driving me to make one bad decision after another, and it couldn't go on. I had already lost Michael. I refused to lose anyone else in my life because of my stupidity.

Drawing in a steadying breath, I lifted my eyes from the glass tabletop to look over at Danaus, who sat to my right with his arms folded over his chest. "Do you eat?"

"Yes," he said, frowning at me.

"Then find something to eat," I said, tapping his untouched menu with the index finger of my right hand. "Order something big. I'm putting it on the Coven gold card."

"That's petty," he chided, but he still picked up his menu.

"I regret to say that I'm feeling very petty right now," I said with a dramatic sigh, relaxing in my chair. Alex chuckled, shaking her head behind her menu. Her dark hair cascaded over one shoulder, caressing her cheek.

We let the conversation die while Alex, Nicolai, and Danaus perused their menus. I contented myself with twirling the stem of my glass of red wine. After what had happened to Thorne, I wasn't going to even sip it. Ingesting anything other than human blood had effectively lost its appeal. After the server returned and the others placed their orders, I reopened the conversation.

"How did you get stuck with Coven duty? Piss off one of the big dogs?" I teased, looking at Alex. She was frowning at me but there was no real anger in her eyes.

"Just rotten luck, I guess," she confessed with a shrug. "I had been in London on business for the past week. When news hit of the strange piles of ashes, phones calls were made and e-mails were flying. I was sent to a small town outside of London to check it out. I swear, Mira, the second I saw it I thought of you, but I've never seen you do anything like that. Their bodies were reduced to ash, but the ground around them was completely untouched. Some are talking warlocks and spontaneous combustion, but there are still too many holes in the theories."

"They'll cover it up," I said indifferently. "In a few days they'll think of some very simple explanation and blast it across all the news agencies. It may have holes, but people will buy it because they want to. They need everything to make sense."

"You think?" she said skeptically. She stared down at her short but perfectly manicured nails. "I wish I had your confidence."

I shook my head, not liking to see her so shaken. Alex exuded confidence and strength in her own pack or when on her own, but when faced with issues outside her own control, her confidence and strength wilted like a flower with too little water. "Don't get me wrong," I said. "You were right when you said this moves up the timetable. Too many things have been happening lately, and science has gotten too far too fast to keep hiding."

"Damn it, Mira!" she suddenly exploded, shattering her mien of calm. "Fifty years was a nice number. I was hoping to be dead and buried before the Great Awakening. It's going to be ugly, and I don't want to be around for it." She leaned her forehead on her hands, her frame tense and her teeth clenched.

"It'll be fun!" I laughed, trying to cheer her up. "Just think of all the groupies we'll gain. These people are completely enamored of the idea of the occult."

"What about the Daylight Coalition?" she demanded. "What about him?" She jerked her thumb at Danaus.

"I'm not saying it'll be easy, but I don't think it will be that bad either. We've been preparing these people for a few centuries. It's not like it's going to come as a complete shock."

"Preparing? What's this Great Awakening you mentioned?" Danaus interrupted.

My gaze jerked over to the hunter and it was all I could do to keep from saying something incredibly rude, but I held back. Frowning, I shoved one hand through my hair, pushing it back from where it had fallen about my face. "You can't stay with them," I said in a low voice. I knew the others could hear me, but the comment was directed solely at Danaus. "Ryan should have told you a long time ago."

I wasn't the only one being kept in the dark by those I trusted and needed to trust. Themis was supposed to be a great society that studied the various other races, but they remained bogged down by archaic ideas and old myths that had no basis in reality. To make matter worse, the group was led by Ryan, an extremely powerful warlock who refused to set his flock straight, even if it meant the lives of my kind and the lives of members of the other races.

Danaus refused to meet my gaze, his dark blue eyes focused on the fountain at the edge of the square. But he didn't have to say anything. I could feel his frustration bubbling below his unmovable exterior of indifference. His time with me had proven on more than one occasion that he'd been operating under some false assumptions, and Ryan—the man he relied on for correct information—hadn't done anything to see that Danaus knew the truth.

"A few centuries ago, the various groups got together—"

"What groups?" Danaus demanded.

"Warlocks, witches, nightwalkers, lycanthropes, and a few other heavy hitters," Alex supplied, counting off each group on her fingers.

"The naturi?"

"No!" we both shouted. I held up my hand before Alex could continue to berate him for what I'm sure Danaus thought was a valid question. After what we saw at the main hall, it was actually a valid question, but Alex didn't know that yet.

"No," I repeated calmly. "The leaders of the various groups met and came to the agreement that mankind isn't as stupid as we would hope. One day, people are going to figure out that this whole other world exists. So in an attempt to control the chaos, the various groups agreed that mankind would come to this realization on our terms. A timetable was designed, with a date set for what is being called the Great Awakening—the day mankind wakes up and realizes that it's not alone on this planet."

"Along the timetable there are several stages where we try to prepare man for the idea that vampires and lycans are real," Nicolai interjected. "Things have picked up in the past hundred years with stories in the tabloids, major motion pictures, books, and now a large number of Web sites."

"Propaganda?" Danaus asked, sounding absolutely horrified by the thought.

"Of course," I laughed. I stretched out my legs and crossed them at the ankles as I relaxed in my seat. "Nightwalkers own three major publishing companies and half a dozen small press companies. We also own more than a dozen movie production firms around the world. We are constantly churning out positive propaganda for the cause."

Frowning, he shifted in his chair, sitting on the edge of his seat. "Promoting vampires." Such a thing would not make his job of hunting us any easier if we succeeded in winning the support of a large portion of humans when the Great Awakening finally arrived.

"Not just nightwalkers," Alex quickly said, drawing his glare to her. "The various groups agreed that anything put out by one of our companies would not intentionally cast another race in a negative light. We're in this together. If one goes down, we all fall."

But then, even that lovely idea had fallen into question following the appearance of a lycan and a witch with a member of the Daylight Coalition.

Our conversation ground to an uneasy halt as the server arrived with several plates of food. Alexandra had ordered a medley of shrimp and linguine in red sauce, while Danaus settled on manicotti and an order of veal parmesan. Nicolai ordered some kind of seafood concoction that I couldn't identify. But that wasn't surprising. I hadn't eaten real food in more than six hundred years. After that long, it all started to look the same. Sometimes the smells would tantalize, but the actual appearance of food had become unappealing. It frequently reminded me of the aftermath of some of my more gruesome and bloody battles.

As my companions dug into their meals, I stared across the plaza, which had begun to empty. The night grew darker and deeper, but much of the inky blackness was held at bay by the warm glow of lamplights scattered about the square. The pigeons had left to find a roost for the night, the air filled with the bubbling murmur of conversation and the faint hint of a melancholy tune plucked on an acoustic guitar somewhere nearby.

"When is the big day?" Danaus asked between bites.

"There's no exact date," Alex said, cutting her food into delicate little bites. It was almost amusing. She was such a lady in public, but I'd seen her hunt. Nothing ladylike about running down and tearing the throat out of a twelve-point buck.

"It's tentatively set for sometime in 2055," I said, twirling my glass again. "Every once in a while a few of the groups get together and reevaluate the timetable." It had been a while since I'd sat this long out in the open with so many people. I was continually scanning the area for anything, but we were alone. "Sometimes science or technology jumps a little faster than we anticipated and stages have to be moved up. It's always a very liquid process with room for change, but there's no denying that it's coming."

Danaus went still beside me, drawing my gaze back to his solemn face. "Were you counting on Rowe?" he asked.

"No," I softly said, looking down at the deep red liquid in my glass. I laid my hand flat on the table, suddenly fearful I would unintentionally shatter the stem. The dark naturi with the leather eye patch was determined to free his queen and the rest of the naturi horde waiting on the other side of the seal. He was also determined to accomplish this feat with my help.

"Why do I get this horrible chill whenever someone mentions that word?" Alex said, laying a forkful of linguine back on her plate. "What's Rowe? Does it have something to do with the reappearance of the naturi?"

With a faint sigh my gaze drifted away from my friend and back out to the plaza as I mentally sorted through the events of the past several days, even the events that had taken place more than five hundred years ago. What to tell her? So much of it would horrify her, but I also knew that keeping secrets at this stage wouldn't protect her.

Reluctantly, I launched into the tale of the naturi, sparing her of as many of the grizzly details as possible. I stretched back to what little I knew of that horrible night more than five centuries ago and mentioned tidbits of what had happened to us during the past several days. I told her of the sacrifice at Konark and the failed sacrifice at Stonehenge. I mentioned the symbols we had found in the trees as the naturi sought to break the seal that bound them. I described the attack in Aswan, Thorne's pain-filled death, and holding Michael in my arms as his soul fought for freedom during the final seconds of his life.

Alex sat back in her chair and blinked a few times when I spoke of my lost angel. She had met Michael a couple of times and liked his easygoing manner. I appreciated her teary eyes . . . I had yet to shed my own tears for the young man. There was no time, as the naturi hounded us and I attempted to outmaneuver whatever plans Jabari and the Coven were apparently cooking up for the demise of my race.

However, I purposely omitted the fact that I was not actually a member of the triad that protected the seal, but its weapon. Nor did I voice the fact that the hunter who sat beside me could wield my abilities like a sword. While Alex and I were friends, her loyalty would always be to the pack, and anything I told her could eventually fall on their ears. I was already skating on thin ice by telling her about Rowe and his attempts to free the naturi. The handling of the naturi had always fallen to the nightwalkers, and it had become a tightly kept secret. But if we failed, I didn't want her to be blindsided.

Nicolai remained silent during my tale. I wasn't overly fond of the idea of this outsider hearing all of these details. But I was forced to trust him since Alexandra and the lycanthropes had to know what they were facing before it was too late.

The female naturi in the main hall was also omitted from my tale. If Alex and Nicolai didn't sense her, then it was better that they didn't know about it. I didn't know what was going on yet, and wasn't about to start a panic among the other races. If the lycans thought the nightwalkers had aligned with the naturi, a horrible war would sweep across the globe before the naturi ever managed to escape their prison.

When I was finished with my tale, Alex pushed her half-eaten meal away. "I've lost my appetite," she said weakly. She actually looked like she was going to be sick, her eyes taking on a glassy appearance as the scent of fear drifted from her to my nose.

"Finish eating," I prodded, pushing her plate toward her again. "How often do you get to eat real Italian? I mean, outside of a full moon, of course."

"That's not funny," she snapped. No, Alex didn't hunt humans, though a select few of her kind did. Even in animal form there was enough of Alexandra the human left behind to restrain her from attacking humans. She hunted only animals, and even then, only on the rare occasion when she gave in to the urge. "How can you make jokes? Don't you realize what could happen if they enter our world?"

"Trust me, Alexandra, I understand better than most," I said in a low, even voice, my eyes narrowing as I looked anywhere but at my companions. Alex didn't know about my captivity by the naturi—I'd left that out while recounting the events in Machu Picchu earlier—but she knew there was something dark and ugly in my past that left behind some deep emotional and physical scars. She took the hint. "There are a number of things going on that I don't understand, but I will soon. Panicking right now isn't going to help."

"It gets worse." Alex's usually strong voice dropped down to an unexpected whisper, drawing my gaze back to her lovely face. Shadows danced across her features, thrown up by the candle flickering in the hurricane glass in the center of the table.

A part of me wanted to ask her how it could possibly be any worse. The vampires were meeting with the naturi in secret. The witches and werewolves were meeting with the Daylight Coalition. Ancient enemies were suddenly allies, and old alliances with the lycans and witches were crumbling before us.

"They've starting calling us," she said.

"When?" I demanded, barely able to push the word from my constricted throat.

"About a week ago, but after last night I've heard that it has gotten worse. Most of the leaders have managed to hold their packs together, but a few here and there have gone missing. Most of them are younger, newer to lycanthropy. It seems like the call is worse the farther west you head," she explained.

I looked back over at Nicolai, who was staring straight ahead, his full lips pressed tight into a hard, unyielding line. "What about your pack?"

"I don't know. I've been out of contact with them for more than a month," he said stiffly, his eyes refusing to meet mine. I left the comment alone. A member of a pack was never out of contact from its members for long. Lycanthropes also never "belonged" to a vampire. Something dark was going on and I was willing to bet that it was rather painful and horrible for Nicolai. It would explain why Alex did nothing to even acknowledge the man's presence. She didn't look at him, didn't talk to him.

I frowned, turning this new bit of information over in my head. There were four different ancient holy sites in North and South America that the naturi could potentially use for their next sacrifice attempt: Old Faithful at Yellowstone Park, Mesa Verde in Colorado, Easter Island, and Machu Picchu in Peru. Would they dare to return to Machu Picchu after their horrible defeat there centuries ago? If it meant freeing Aurora, yes, without a doubt.

Turning my focus back to Alexandra, I struggled to keep my sympathy for her plight from showing on my face. It wouldn't help her when faced with the threat of suddenly becoming servants for a vicious race bent on the total extermination of humanity.

There were a couple theories as to how lycanthropy started. Some thought it was the result of a spell or curse woven by an old Native American god. Yet, some thought the root of shapeshifters was older than that. However, the darkest of the theories was that lycans were created by the naturi as a type of servant and soldier. Because of a lycan's close tie to nature, the naturi could call to a lycanthrope, summoning him or her across vast distances to do their bidding. Most viewed that as the future of man if the naturi entered this world—extermination or lycanthropy.

"So we'll be faced with both the naturi and lycans if the next sacrifice is to be held in the West," Danaus said grimly.

"Maybe even an assortment of Wiccans," I said. It was becoming a real party, and it appeared everyone was invited.

I turned my attention back to one of my few friends. Alex was nearly fifty, though she could still easily have passed for someone in her mid-twenties. Lycanthropy gave a person an amazing ability to heal from nearly every injury, except for those caused by silver. Particularly silver bullets and knives. Her "curse" also slowed down the aging process, usually doubling or tripling a human's average life span. I liked Alex. She had a good sense of humor and philosophy on life. I didn't want this future for her.

"When is your flight home?" I asked, battling to keep a frown from tugging on the corners of my mouth.

"Tomorrow morning." There was no mistaking the anxiety that crowded those two words. She lived in Portland, on the lovely West Coast. She was in danger of succumbing to the call and she knew it.

"Go back to London and stay until after the new moon," I ordered, sitting on the edge of my chair. My eyes jumped over to Danaus, who was watching the exchange with a worried look. "Could Themis protect her?"

"Mira," he softly said, his voice deep and weary. "Themis isn't an organization of bodyguards. We can't—"

"Damn it, Danaus!" I cried, hitting the heel of my palm on the table, rattling the nearly empty dishes. It was a struggle to bring my voice back under control, but I finally managed it before I continued. "I'm not asking your people to protect a pack of rabid vampires. Alex is still human—the race you're so desperate to protect. Call Ryan. Talk to him."

Alex shook her head, pressing her lips into a thin line. "I can't. My pack needs me. I have to go back."

"You have to take care of yourself. Go back to London. Your pack will manage."

"I have to go," she said, her smile as fragile as a cracked eggshell. "I'm an Alpha now."

My brows furrowed at this announcement and I sat back in my chair. "And you're still in Portland?"

"You don't need to sound so surprised." She stabbed her

food with her fork, using enough force to cause the tines to scrape loudly across the ceramic plate.

"Forgive me," I said with a little bow of my head as I pressed my right hand to my heart. "Congratulations on your new position." It was quite an accomplishment. The Portland pack was large, with about forty members, last I'd heard. The packs out West were larger and there were more of them than on the East Coast in the States. Across Europe and throughout Asia, the packs had only twelve or fewer members and stuck to the rural areas.

With a shake of my head, I raised my left hand high in the air and snapped my fingers while my right hand dropped back to the arm of my chair. A server instantly appeared and placed the bill in my hand. I scratched out the name of an account on the bill and handed it back. It was the name of the Coven account and was known to all business operators across Venice. The bill would be sent to that account and immediately taken care of. I'd learned that trick when I started doing little odd jobs for the group not long after leaving Jabari. If you were going to do the dirty work of the Coven, they were willing to supply some basic perks while you were staying in Venice.

"With that said," I continued when the server walked away, "I still believe you should go to London for the next few days."

"You know I can't, Mira," she said, standing at the same time as Danaus and I.

I grabbed her elbow and squeezed it. "Don't go to them, Alex," I warned, dropping my voice so it was low and firm. The tone would leave my words burrowed into her brain like a swarm of ticks. I wanted those words to resonate within her mind during the coming months, hoping they would protect her against the siren song of the naturi. "I've enjoyed our friendship, but I won't hesitate."

Alex looked up at me with sad eyes. She knew that if she stood between me and the naturi, I wouldn't hesitate to kill her. Once she answered to the call of the naturi, she would be under their complete control.

"Just promise to make it quick," she said, a halfhearted smile lifting one corner of her mouth. "I don't want to think about being under the control of those bastards."

"I understand," I whispered, and pressed a kiss to her temple. "When it's over, come to Savannah and we'll go hunting."

Pausing beside the table, I looked down at Nicolai, still lounging in his chair, his glass of wine in his hand. We would meet again. Jabari might order the lycanthrope to kill me before I left Venice, and Nicolai would do it. Not because he bore any hatred for me and my kind, but because Jabari was holding something over him.

"It's been a pleasure," I said with a little smirk. Nicolai smiled in return and raised his glass to me. We both knew that we would meet again. It was a shame that it would be on opposite ends of the battlefield.

"Good luck, Mira," Alex whispered, grabbing my cool hand in both of her warm hands and squeezing it tightly.

I chuckled as I walked away, my hand slowly slipping from her grasp. "I don't need luck," I called, turning and walking backward so I could look at her as I departed. "I'm the Fire Starter."

I just wished I had a plan.

Ten

Danaus and I wandered down the dark streets in silence, slowly heading back to the speedboat. The sound of water lapping at the stone sides of the canal followed us throughout the winding city. The night was still in its infancy and I wasn't particularly eager to go back to the hotel suite where Sadira and Tristan were most likely cuddled. I paused on the sidewalk next to our boat and stared across the canal at the lights of the Doge's Palace and Piazza San Marco. The air was cluttered with the various thoughts and emotions of the people out enjoying the warm summer night.

"When was the last time you were in Venice?" I asked, looking over my shoulder at Danaus. He was also watching the lights reflect off the undulating waves.

"I've never been to Venice," he said. It was on the tip of my tongue to demand how that was even possible. He was Italian, or at least Roman, and more than a thousand years old. How could he have not visited the canals? But I knew I wasn't going to get an answer. He was still stingy about personal information regardless of the fact that he had popped into my thoughts on more than one occasion.

"Come on," I said, jumping onto the boat we had borrowed from Roberto. "I want to show you something." With a somewhat skeptical look, he climbed onto the boat and sat down while I started the engine. I rushed back out into the Lagoon, away from the bright lights and crowded canals. We cruised away from the tourist hot spots and the quaint neighborhoods, as I took him across the Lagoon and between the islands of Burano and Murano to the tiny island of Torcello.

I slowed the boat as I carefully maneuvered us past the swamps that surrounded the island. Navigating the *laguna morta* would have been treacherous at best during the middle of the day, let alone during the black of night when the moon had waned to a slender sliver in the sky. But I knew these waters and marshes. Torcello was my hidden sanctuary within the dark heart of the nightwalker world.

We glided down the main canal and pulled up near one of the few bridges that spanned the waterway. Danaus rose and tied the boat to an empty pole while I killed the engine. The only sound disrupting the silence was the break of the waves brushing against the side of the boat as we settled at the landing. In all of Venice, the island of San Michele would have been the only place more peaceful, but despite some of the popular myths about vampires, I didn't get any particular kicks wandering around a crumbling, mold-infested graveyard at night. The living were generally more interesting than the dead.

"Where are we?" he asked as we left the boat and wandered down the disintegrating *fondamenta* along the canal, toward the only cluster of buildings rising up in the darkness.

"The birthplace of Venice," I said. My voice hovered at a whisper, as if anything loud would break the spell. Lights began to appear as we reached the edge of the *campo* that was now more dirt and gravel than the original stonework. Grass crowded close to the road and weeds pushed their way between the cracks in the remaining paving. The main square was overgrown, with only a few bits of broken column and statues left to adorn the area like tombstone markers for the city that once was.

"The island is nearly deserted, but they say that this is where the Venetians first settled in either the fourth or fifth century," I said, running my hand over one of the stone columns. All its original marks were worn away, leaving what appeared to be a pale white, bonelike pillar rising up without the rest of the skeleton. "I've always liked it here. I love the island's sense of history and its peace."

"It's nice," he whispered. Danaus wandered over and stood before an odd chunk of white stone that resembled a chair. The locals referred to it as the throne of Attila the Hun, but no one actually believed he had ever sat on that hunk of rock. A light breeze stirred the leaves in some nearby trees, sending up their soft song into the night. Not far from the square, lights from the only restaurant on the island glowed in golden patches, but even they were beginning to dim under the lateness of the hour. The few inhabitants of the island were slipping off to bed, leaving Danaus and me alone.

"This city is almost as old as you, Danaus. Its memory is nearly as long as yours," I teased.

A faint smile lifted his features as he looked around the empty plaza. "A lot of Europe is," he reminded me. His voice was gentle, losing its usual gruff, angry edge. It was as if he had forgotten for a brief moment that I was a nightwalker; the enemy.

"True." I nodded, clinging to my smile though it was starting to fade. "I think it's one of the drawbacks to living in the New World; too new."

"No sense of history or identity," he murmured.

"Come on," I said. "I've got something else to show you."

I led him across the square and past the external colonnade to the front door of the church of Santa Fosca. The small structure was a mix of classical Byzantine and Greek. It took me only a moment to pick the lock and push open the dark wood doors. Pale slivers of moonlight shone through the open windows, revealing the high arching ceiling and wooden beams that crossed overhead. The forlorn coos of pigeons echoed off the walls as the birds settled in their roosts for the night. The interior was made of white bricks and a handful of white marble columns. There were no statues at the altar of the Blessed Mother, and only a single crucifix hung on the back wall. Tall white candles dotted the altar and filled the wall sconces that lined the walls. The center aisle was wide, but the intricate mosaic floor was cracked and broken, with a layer of dust veiling its former beauty. Only the old wooden pews still gleamed in the faint light, as if someone took the time to carefully wax each one at least once a week.

"Isn't it beautiful?" I said, spinning to look at my companion. "It's visited by only tourists now and hasn't been used as a church for a couple centuries. It's a shame. The architecture is as lovely as any of the churches in San Croce or even San Marco."

"How?" he asked breathlessly.

"How what?"

"How is it that you can be here? Has God abandoned this place?" I watched Danaus. His whole body was tensed, looking as if he expected one of us to be struck by lightning at any second. A faint sheen of perspiration glistened on his forehead in the moonlight.

"The magic is gone from this place," I replied. "It's not God, Danaus, but the faith of the people who go to a church that keeps me out. Faith is just another form of magic. If a human believes God will protect him, then he has cast a spell. And when people stop going to a church, the magic eventually fades."

Walking over to the pews to my right, I extended my hand, slowly moving it through the air. I could feel a light residue of energy. Someone had sat there during the day and whispered a prayer, a near-silent plea for hope or help, or maybe thanks or protection. There were other pockets in the air around me, thin and faint like a ghost, fading with the passage of time.

"I—I don't understand," he said, his voice faltering. I could taste his fear and horror in the air, but there was nothing enticing about it. From him, it was unnerving and even a little sickening, like a slow-working poison. It was as if the world was crumbling away beneath his feet and I was the cause.

"For some people, a cross doesn't work against night-walkers." I lowered my hand back to my side and turned to face my companion. "These people believe that something about the shape of the metal keeps my kind at bay. They have faith in the cross, but not in the idea of a protective God, and that's never as strong. Your heart and soul aren't involved in that kind of faith, just your mind."

"I don't believe you," he said, his face hardening. If he had been armed, I think he would have drawn his sword to protect himself against my words. But instead he stood in the darkness of the church glaring at me.

"I'm not asking you to," I said with an indifferent shrug. "I'm just telling you what I've learned from experience. But you have to consider, I am standing in what has been a Christian church at one time."

Danaus remained quiet as I walked toward the altar. He was still uneasy, his emotions verging on frustration and anger. I stopped at the two small steps that led up to the remains of a marble altar. Behind it hung the tortured image of Jesus Christ still pinned to the wooden cross. His face and body was streaked and stained from time and water damage. His benevolent face appeared as if he had been crying tears, mourning the state of his home, or maybe just the state of man.

"Why did you do it, Mira?" Danaus asked, his voice strangely gentle.

"Do what?" I replied, trying to sound only mildly interested. Something twisted in my stomach; this was going to take an ugly turn.

"Why did you abandon God?"

"What?" My voice jumped above a whisper for the first time since we landed on Torcello, shattering the silence that had become suffocating. I spun on my right heel to gaze with confusion at my dark companion. His whole body was tensed, his hands balled into tight fists at his sides.

"Why did you abandon God?" he repeated. "Why did you choose to become a vampire?"

Plopping down on the two little stairs leading to the altar, I laughed. I tried to tell myself that it was an amusing point of view, but even I heard the thick layer of caustic bitterness in my voice. Danaus had been born centuries ago, long before Christianity took hold as the dominant religion in Europe, but he had obviously learned and clung to its teaching during his long years. I, on the other hand, had taken a slightly different route.

"Abandon God?" I repeated, pushing back to my feet. "I didn't abandon God; He abandoned me. Take a good look at me, Danaus. This isn't vampire enchantment—I was born looking this way." A ball of fire suddenly hovered beside my face as I walked toward him. "Red hair and violet eyes. I was born on the island of Crete in a small fishing village during the fourteenth century. Everyone had either brown or black hair and brown eyes. Do you know what they said when I was born? I was the spawn of Satan.

"I spent the first sixteen years of my life on my knees, begging God to forgive me for being born. And do you know what His reply was? This!" I held both of my hands out to my sides and they instantly became engulfed in flames. "A group of men from my village tried to rape me one night as I walked back home from church. In my terror, I accidentally set two of them on fire. Before that day, I had never harmed a single human being, but that night I killed two men."

"It was an accident," Danaus firmly said.

"Was it? How could it be an accident if that's what I was born to do?" I extinguished the flames I had created, letting the darkness flood the church again as I walked back toward the altar. My heels hitting the broken stone floor echoed through the heavy silence. The night moved close again, wrapping me in its cold arms, holding me, protecting me against Danaus's questions and memories I desperately wanted to forget.

"Choosing to be a nightwalker wasn't about abandoning God," I continued, the hard angry edge disappearing from my voice. "I lost my faith that night when those men died. Becoming a nightwalker was about power and gaining control of my life."

"You traded power for eternal damnation when you died." Hard accusation filled his voice. His footsteps scraped against the gritty dirt floor as he moved a few feet closer to me.

"Why do you cling to these archaic ideas?" I shouted, sending several of the pigeons overhead nervously into the air. Their wings beat against the wind as they darted out the open window in search of a quieter location to spend the night. "Not in all my six centuries have I run across this Satan that you are so confident I have sold my soul to. No one has ever spoken of him. Not the Coven, nor Sadira."

"You kill."

"I have yet to meet a race that didn't kill. The naturi, humans, lycans, witches, even God's precious angels kill. Why is my race suddenly different?"

"You drink blood."

"So what! I feed on the life of others. I take their blood, and under most circumstances, leave the life behind. Most carnivores can't claim that."

"It's not right!" he shouted at me. There was an underlying tremble in his voice, as if something small and frightened within him had finally lashed out at me. His ragged breathing filled the quiet of the church, and I could easily make out the frantic beat of his heart.

"Says who? Your religious leaders up in their ivory towers? I don't know whether there is truly a Heaven and Hell, but I believe you earn either place based on the choices that you make."

"And you chose to become a vampire," he hurled back at me.

"I also chose to save more lives in the past few days at the risk of my own than I care to count." I took a couple steps up the aisle toward him, barely suppressing the urge to create a fireball in defense against his callous comments. "I'm no innocent, but I'm not the embodiment of all evil that you want me to be. You want to kill me because you think I'm evil. Fine. Just make sure it's because of the things I've done and not because of what I am."

"Is that why you're doing this?" His whole demeanor suddenly changed. The tension that had pulled the shoulder muscles taut eased and his fists loosened so that his fingers now hung open at his sides. "Because you're trying to earn salvation?" he asked, his tone losing its harshness.

"Fuck Heaven!" I spat, my hands balled into fists so tight my knuckles had begun to ache. "I'm doing this because it's the right thing to do. If I don't, my people will die. If I don't, everything beautiful in this world will die."

I paced down the aisle again, stopping at the two little stairs, willing myself to calm. I couldn't fathom why this was still a sore topic with me. For more than six hundred years I had turned over ideas of God, Heaven, Hell, and the devil in my mind. I came up with theories for why my kind existed and our place in the great scheme of things. Sometimes my theories proved to be wrong and I threw them out for new ones. I didn't have many answers, but my mind was open to possibilities.

When I finally spoke again, I was surprised at how tired my voice sounded. As if the long centuries had been condensed into a single sound. "You've walked this earth for more than a millennium. How can you still cling to the idea that concepts like these are black and white?" I turned to look at him. He still stood near the head of the aisle, as if afraid to enter this place. "Good and evil are not black and white. Human doesn't automatically equal good and vampire doesn't equal evil. You've spent a lifetime slaughtering my people. Have you never paused for half a second to wonder if we really are what you want us to represent?"

"Once." His voice was little more than a summer breeze through a maple tree, soft and soothing.

"When?" He didn't answer me, but I knew when as soon as I asked the question. It had been the first night we met. He hesitated that night when we fought. I'd believed it was because of Nerian and the naturi, but there had been something else brewing in the back of his mind. "And what did you decide?"

"I don't have an answer. I don't know! For some reason, you throw everything into confusion. You make me question all the answers I thought I had," he raged, taking an angry step toward me. His powers surged out from him, hitting me in the chest with enough force to make me take a steadying step backward.

"There's nothing wrong with asking questions," I said with a half smile. The anger and frustration I felt earlier had dissipated, leaving only a fine trembling in my muscles.

"But these questions take away hope," he said. I could feel the anger draining out of him, to be replaced by a bone-deep despair that threatened to crush us both. For just this brief moment in time he looked lost, and it was my fault. Before meeting me, he had purpose and direction, he had a light to sail by, but I had destroyed that. I didn't like him killing, but I also didn't believe in taking away another creature's hope.

"I want to call in my debt," I announced after a heavy silence had filled the air.

"What do you want?"

"Tell me what you are." He turned and started to walk out of the church without a word. "Stop, Danaus. I've thought about this since I first laid eyes on you. You're at least part human, that can't be mistaken, but you're not a warlock or a lycan. I've mentally gone through the laundry list of every creature I've encountered and nothing seems to fit. What is it that you are so desperate to hide?"

"Let's go," he said. The hunter stopped walking but was still facing the entrance.

"Not until you tell me. What's so horrible? Can it top the fact that I am a monster among my own kind? Or that I can be used as a weapon by my enemy to destroy both naturi and nightwalkers? This secret is destroying you and my kind. You have to tell someone." I was grasping at straws but knew that his twisted outlook on the world had to be rooted some- where. After more centuries that I cared to count, Danaus's mind and identity were still mostly human, but the secret of his existence was tearing him apart and destroying far too many of my own kind in the process. It also left him vulner- able to creatures such as Ryan, who were all too happy to use Danaus's desperation and confusion to their advantage.

"Why you?" he asked, glancing over his shoulder at me.

"Because us freaks got to stick together," I replied, flash- ing him a wicked grin.

He made a strange noise, almost like a strangled laugh, and shook his head. "Bitch," he muttered under his breath, but in the quiet church it was like he had shouted it.

"I pray you're not just figuring that out," I said blandly, but then quickly turned serious again. "What is this burden on your shoulders?"

Danaus turned around, resting one hand against the doorjamb as if to steady himself. When he finally spoke, his voice was low and rough, making me wonder how many times he had spoken these words aloud. "My mother was a witch. Before I was born, she made a deal with a demon to gain more power."

"And the price?" Those three words escaped my lips in a rough and ragged whisper. I already knew the answer. There was always a price for more power. I knew that personally. For my amazing abilities, I traded in my ability to be awake during the day and gained a complete dependence on blood for survival.

"Me."

My knees buckled and I landed on my butt on the edge of one of the marble steps leading up to the altar. Panic screamed in my brain as I struggled to comprehend the words he had uttered. A fierce shaking started in my hands and a sharp, biting chill swept through my body. There were no such thing as demons—not as humans comprehended them—but back in the beginning, when the world was young, there were two guardian races, the naturi who watched over the earth and the bori who watched over all souls.

The bori were an immensely powerful race that had come to represent both angels and demons in human mythology. And while the naturi had the ability to force all lycanthropes to do their bidding, the bori could easily subjugate the entire nightwalker race. The naturi wanted to destroy us, but the bori wanted to rule us. It was why both races had been banished from this world. Yet, something was off. While we all knew some naturi were left on earth after the seal had been made, supposedly none of the bori remained. All the bori had been locked away for centuries. Had Danaus's mother found a way to partially summon a bori back to earth?

I couldn't raise my gaze to look at him, not when I knew my horror was clearly written across my face. My world was crumbling around me at an alarming rate. Jabari could control me, Rowe wanted to use me to permanently free Aurora, and Danaus, with his link to the bori, could use me to destroy both the naturi and the nightwalkers.

Closing my eyes, I drew in a deep breath as I pushed down the rising wave of panic filling my chest. I needed to think clearly. "You're a demon?" I finally said, lifting my gaze to look down the long aisle at the creature that had saved me on more than one occasion.

Danaus narrowed his beautiful blues, closely examining my face for my reaction to the news. "Half. Like you said, part of me is still human."

But it wasn't that simple. The bori weren't demons, and I had never heard of anyone being half bori. There was no cross-breeding with humans. The closest mix between a human and a bori was a nightwalker, and I knew without a doubt that Danaus was not one of us.

It sounded as if the bori that made the deal was more of a parasite attached to Danaus's soul, lending him power as the bori bided his time. And while the naturi clung to twelve wells of power from the earth, Danaus had potentially become a walking doorway for the entire bori race. They just had to figure out how to unlock him.

And yet, Danaus had never used the term bori. He didn't know, didn't understand, their long history. He was just clinging to the ancient definition of what a demon was and making his decisions based on that. He had no idea what he was.

"So you're trying to save your human half by ridding the world of evil, namely vampires," I said, trying to quell my rising panic before he sensed it. What could I tell him? That it wasn't a demon that owned a part of his soul, but something nastier and more complicated? I didn't have any answers for him. And what information I could give him would only make it worse. I needed time and more information before I opened my mouth.

"I have no desire to spend eternity in Hell because of my mother's need for revenge," he coldly said, taking a few steps toward me.

I ran a shaking hand through my hair, pushing it away from my eyes. "How do you know that is your destination?"

"It is the destination of all demons," he simply said. He stopped when he was a couple feet away from me, his eyes on the ground.

"Maybe. Maybe not. I've not seen any proof to sway me one way or the other."

"Have you known any demons?"

I could only smile weakly at my companion. There was nothing I could say that would help him. I hadn't had any personal encounters with the bori. My experiences in this lifetime had been limited to battling the naturi, which had always been more than enough for me.

"They're evil," he continued when I remained silent.

"Most probably are," I conceded, rubbing my hands together to brush off some dirt. "But every creature that slinks across this earth is given a choice. You've chosen not to be evil. You're also part human. That has to throw something into your favor."

Danaus slowly lifted his gaze, staring deep into my violet eyes, searching for something. He wanted to believe me. He truly wanted to grab onto the lifeline I was tossing him as he struggled out in the dark abyss, but he was also fighting centuries of religious theory and conditioning. He wasn't about to toss aside his faith so easily because it eased his mind and conscience.

"I'm not asking you to believe everything I've said. Just think about it. These ideas you've clung to are man-made ideas. They're narrow-minded and flawed. Earlier tonight we were discussing the Great Awakening. Mankind's concepts of God and redemption didn't take our kind into consideration," I said, threading a lock of hair that had come loose behind my left ear. "If you survive this nightmare, go talk to Ryan. I have a feeling you're willing to believe him a little more than me."

"You've lived longer. How could he know more?" he countered.

I didn't trust Ryan, but the white-haired warlock was a potential source of information. He represented a starting point for Danaus. And if I survived this mess as well, I hoped to do a little digging around myself. "Ryan's spent his life studying the other races and religions. I've picked up what I can along the way. A lot of it is myth and rumor. You sift through it as best you can and keep an open mind."

"And then what?"

"Nothing," I said with a shrug. I rose to my feet in my boneless manner. "You keep moving. Let's go."

I stepped around him and strolled down the aisle in my usual breezy, happy-go-lucky way, but my mind was churning. A bori. Well, a half bori sort of. That was not something I had expected. I had thought maybe he was a strange half warlock, half lycan mix that couldn't shift. No, Danaus was a half bori that had the ability to control me. It was enough to send shivers down my back, but somehow I had to bury my terror deep inside my chest. Of course, if I had lost it in front of my dark companion, Danaus would have been out the door.

"Mira . . . " he slowly called, sounding hesitant.

"Yeah, I know. It's a deep, dark Danaus secret," I said, spinning around so I could look at him as he walked up the aisle behind me.

"So you can read my mind now?"

"Not quite. It's the type of thing I would request. Beside, it's not like I want you bragging to your little cult about your nifty new Mira marionette."

"It seems we're on equal ground," he said, extending his hand to me.

"Always have been," I replied, slipping my hand into his. I was surprised that I didn't hesitate to take his strong hand in mine after the last three times we had touched. There was no rush of power pushing to enter my body this time, no thoughts that didn't belong to me. Just his usual warmth washing over my skin, soaking in and heating me like the sun. Despite what he was and the heritage that haunted him, Danaus still had a choice and still had his honor.

Standing in the silence of the church holding his hand, a dark thought flitted through my brain before I could stop it. Had I promised to protect something more dangerous to my kind than the entire naturi horde? Wasn't death better than an eternity of slavery? For a reason I had yet to understand, the Coven had struck a pact with the naturi, offering up some type of protection. I'd brought Danaus into the center of our civilization, a creature that was part bori and a vampire hunter. Despite my best intentions, had I betrayed my kind in the same way?

"Of course, you realize that this conversation won't stop me from hunting vampires," he coldly said, releasing my hand.

I forced myself to laugh as I turned to leave the church. "I wouldn't dream of stopping you," I replied, pushing open the heavy wood door. "I just want you to think about why."

There was no forcing Danaus to do anything he didn't believe in. However, with enough time and knowledge, I believed he would choose to stop hunting nightwalkers.

We casually strolled back through the weed-infested main *campo*. Looking out across the Lagoon toward the glow of Murano and Burano, I could sense the other nightwalkers going about the usual nightly activities. They were hunting and feeding and laughing. Despite their dead bodies, they were as alive as the humans that surrounded them. I couldn't believe we were evil. Or more specifically, that I was evil. Would I still be mourning the loss of my angel if I was evil? Would I still cherish my sweet Calla and the life I once had if I was evil? In the gathering darkness with Danaus at my side, those questions were all I had left to cling to.

Eleven

A slow hiss slipped between my clenched teeth as I paused at the edge of the grassy courtyard. Jabari was playing a game. First, he demanded I come to Venice, where I was almost guaranteed to discover the Coven's plot with the naturi, and now this. We were no longer alone. My focus had been so completely locked on Danaus and our conversation that I didn't notice Nicolai until he stood watching us from the second floor window of a vacant building.

He was early. I hadn't expected Jabari to send his assassin at least until after the next sacrifice. Of course, this meant that the Ancient had broken his promise that he wouldn't send one of the court flunkies to see to my demise. But I knew Jabari's goal wasn't to kill me there. I was too old and experienced to be taken out by a lycanthrope. He wanted something else. Nicolai was simply a pawn that had been moved into play. Unfortunately, I wasn't the opponent Jabari was playing against; I was just another one of his game pieces. What was I supposed to accomplish in fighting Nicolai? Did Jabari expect me to kill the werewolf? Was he more important than I knew? I wanted to scream. Second-guessing myself and trying to predict Jabari's next move was going to get me killed.

Standing in the deep shadow thrown down by the building the werewolf occupied, I shoved my hand into my pocket and withdrew the silver ring that held the key to the boat. The little slip of metal jingled before I closed my fingers around it. "Take the boat back to the hotel," I murmured, not looking over at Danaus as he came to stand beside me.

"How will you get back?" he inquired, not yet reaching for the key.

"I'll swim." I extended my left hand and turned it over, waiting for him to put his open hand beneath mine so he could catch the key, but the hunter refused to budge.

"What's going on?" Tension tightened his words into hard little syllables that could barely squeeze past his clenched teeth. Before I had a chance to murmur *Nothing,* a wave of power swept away from his body and washed over the tiny island. I didn't know if he could sense werewolves as well as he could nightwalkers, but I was going to find out in a couple of seconds. There were only a couple dozen humans on the whole island, all of them older in age. Probably born on the island and determined to die there like so many of their ancestors.

"It's none of your business, hunter," I said sharply. "Get out of here."

"What does the lycan want?" he demanded as his powers were sucked back into his body. Their sudden absence made me feel chilled, as if a damp cold had found its way into my bones.

"Her heart." The words drifted down to us from the dark window, edged with a slight echo as they bounded briefly around the empty building before escaping into the night air. The tone held no menace, but sounded like the soft caress of a concerned lover wondering why his beloved companion was walking in the fading moonlight with another man.

Danaus stepped away from me and looked up at the building, his right hand unconsciously reaching for a knife at his hip, only to find that it wasn't there. After our audience with the Coven, neither of us had thought to go back into the hotel room to get our weapons. I had been too distracted by what happened on San Clemente to think about such a little thing as self-defense. The hunter pressed his lips into a hard thin line and let his hand drop back to his side, his fingers flexing in their irritation.

"What's going on?" he bit out.

"Mr. Gromenko has been sent to kill me," I calmly replied, lowering my hand to my side. The key was still tightly gripped in my fingers. I was beginning to get the feeling that Danaus wasn't going to leave. I didn't want him hanging around when Nicolai attacked. I didn't trust Danaus to keep his nose out of my business. The gods knew I couldn't.

Danaus jerked his gaze back to my face, his beautiful blues widened in surprise and confusion. I knew what he was thinking. We had eaten dinner with this man an hour earlier. We smiled, laughed, and traded worried looks about the dark days that lay beyond the horizon. And now he had come to collect my heart.

"Jabari wants me dead," I said with a shrug, as if that could explain everything. And in my world, it did. If an Ancient wanted something, it happened, regardless of what a person had to do to get it done.

Danaus opened his mouth to say something, maybe argue with what to me was a very logical statement, but before he could speak, Nicolai jumped down from his perch and lightly landed a few feet away. Danaus tensed and took a step closer, attempting to get between me and the lycan, but I laid a restraining hand on his arm. Beneath my cool fingers I could feel his muscles jump at my touch, and his energy arced through me, looking for a new home. He was tense and wasn't exactly trying to keep his powers under a tight wrap.

"Danaus!" I snapped. My fingernails bit into his warm flesh, while at the same time a part of me struggled to keep his powers from burrowing within me. "This is not your fight. I don't need your protection."

The two men stared at each other. Danaus's features were hard and unyielding, his jaw muscles tensed as he clenched his teeth. Nicolai's face was emotionless, as if a veil had come down between his mind and his emotions. I didn't know what he was thinking, and there were few ways more effective at starting a fight than rummaging around the mind of another creature who could sense it. Most humans wouldn't know, but magical creatures could, the same way a wolf could sense a coming storm.

"Can he kill you?" Danaus demanded, still refusing to back off.

"He can try," I replied, ignoring the shifter.

"Will you kill him?"

"Not if I can avoid it," I admitted. I had no desire to kill Nicolai. He seemed like a nice guy and I honestly had nothing against him. This whole hunting-me-down thing was Jabari's fault, not his. Of course, if killing him was the only way to save myself, I wouldn't hesitate.

Danaus's frowned deepened and he arched one thick eyebrow at me in question without his gaze wavering from Nicolai. Clenching my teeth, I shoved Danaus back a step. "I'm not some mindless killing machine," I snarled.

The hunter snorted, making it clear he didn't believe that bit of logic either. "Regardless, I can't just walk away. The naturi are trying to break free. We can't afford to risk your life needlessly."

"Your concern warms my cold blood." I thoughtlessly shoved the boat key back into my left pocket, irritated beyond rational thought.

"Mira—"

I didn't let Danaus get any further. Grabbing a handful of his shirt, I jerked him around and slammed his back into the nearby building, earning a grunt from him. "I did not survive more than six centuries because I had some human with a chip on his shoulder watching my back. I will handle this without your assistance."

"I'm not leaving. We promised to leave Venice together," he murmured.

That was when it finally dawned on me. Sometimes it's amazing how slow I can be to pick up on some of the little things in life. While we were flying to Venice, we promised that we would both get out of the city alive. I had taken that as an agreement on my behalf to keep him alive. It never occurred to me that he would attempt to protect my existence as well.

My grip in his shirt loosened and I took a half step away from him in surprise. Thoughts of Nicolai, the naturi, the Coven—they all slipped away for a couple of seconds. The air grew heavy with a strange silence that was broken only by Danaus's heartbeat. It was faster than usual; faster than during our fights and faster than during our arguments. The beat was hypnotic, trying to tell me another of his great secrets, but I couldn't understand what it was whispering to me.

"Fine," the lycanthrope said nonchalantly, jolting me back from our own private world. "You stay." The blond Adonis filled with rippling muscles reached around me and grabbed a handful of Danaus's black locks. Pulling his head forward slightly, Nicolai slammed the back of Danaus's head against the brick wall behind him before either of us could react. The hunter made no sound as he slid to the ground in a heap, pulling out of my grip.

I looked up at Nicolai, a smile wavering on my lips. "You better hope I kill you, because he's going to be seriously pissed when he wakes up."

"Then I guess we better get this done quickly," he replied, stepping away from Danaus's unconscious form. His dark brown eyes swept over the area, searching for something. His large, muscular frame was tensed, waiting for me to attack him. He would have been moving before I could flinch. But I wasn't going to start this fight.

"There," he said, with a jerk of his head. "The *campo*." My eyes followed his gaze to the overgrown square with the crumbling pillars and broken sidewalk. It was beyond the church Danaus and I had been in. It appeared as if the three sides of the square were surrounded by small, empty buildings, while the fourth side looked out onto the Lagoon.

I walked in that direction and paused at the edge of the square beside a tall pillar, my hands resting on my narrow hips as I looked over the proposed battlefield. My only warning was a slight shifting in the air just half a breath before Nicolai threw his body into mine. A grunt jumped from my throat as he crushed me against the column. The cool, rough stone scraped and scratched against my bare arms and back like coarse sandpaper, threatening to remove a layer of skin. Snarling, I pushed him off me before he could get his feet planted again, pitching him halfway across the square. Like a cat, he easily landed on his feet, sliding a bit on the rubble that littered the area.

With one hand braced on the ground and his feet spaced apart, the lycan was poised to jump at me again. His eyes glowed with power, a strange copperish light, as a low growl rumbled in his chest. He wouldn't risk changing. The process took too long and would leave him vulnerable to my attack.

A breeze stirred, pushing against the heavy wall of summer heat and thick moisture. The scent of the Lagoon teased my nose along with the musky scent of Nicolai. He was coated in the scent of fear, the scent of frustration.

With a sharp inhalation of air, he launched himself across the square at me. He was a dark blur, more wind than man as he moved. I darted to my right, only attempting to sidestep him, but I misjudged his speed. Pain exploded in my left forearm and I looked down to find three long, ragged cuts across my pale skin. Blood welled up and streaked down my arm before finally dripping to the ground. My eyes darted back to Nicolai, to find that his fingers were elongated and tipped with long black claws.

Frowning, I bit back a curse and slowly took a couple steps away, circling him. He could partially shift. That meant he was either a lot older than I initially thought or a lot more powerful. Shifting specific body parts was very difficult, demanding a great deal of energy and control. I had seen Alex do it only once, and it left her shaking and sweating afterward. I knew I could stretch out the fight in an attempt to wear him down, but I think we both preferred to have this done before Danaus woke up from his catnap.

Nicolai lunged for me again, but this time I remained still, my feet planted and legs braced. Ducking under massive arms that reached out to grab me, I punched him hard in the side, under his ribs. Air exploded from his lungs in a harsh grunt. His right heel scraped against the ground as he struggled to regain his balance against the unexpected blow. Before he could draw in a fresh lungful of air, I slammed my left fist into his jaw, wincing at the impact. I didn't want to hurt Nicolai, but I needed to knock him out so I could finally end this contest.

The punch knocked him on his ass. I immediately backpedaled a few steps as he rolled back to his feet, sucking in a couple ragged breaths.

"What are your orders?" I demanded. We circled each other, only a few feet of empty air separating us.

"Kill you," Nicolai evenly replied. The werewolf stepped

forward in a blur, swinging his right fist at my stomach. I jumped backward, dodging the blow and landing balanced on the tips of my toes. He dipped down before I could land flatfooted again and swung one leg around. His foot and ankle connected with my toes, knocking me back.

Instead of landing flat on my back, I caught myself on my fingertips, continuing the flip over. It wasn't pretty, but I managed to land on one foot and a knee, ready to lunge at him.

Nicolai backed off a couple steps when he realized his attempt to knock me on my back had failed. Fists raised, he waited for me to rise to my feet again.

"Just kill me?" I continued. "What about Danaus? Or Tristan?" I needed to understand this game Jabari was playing. I knew the Ancient would send Nicolai after me, but what was his rationale for doing it? Did he want me to rid him of this pet? Or was Nicolai a greater threat than I was giving him credit for? My death here would put both Tristan and Danaus at great risk. And with the appearance of the naturi in the main hall, I was beginning to seriously wonder if Jabari truly needed me alive any longer. I knew my nights were numbered, but I now felt as if I had fewer of them than I had previously believed.

"He named only you," Nicolai stated. His heavy breathing and his fast heartbeat were the only sounds in the empty *campo*. No sound came from his footsteps as we started to circle each other again.

"Alex?" I swung at him, but he dodged it. Unfortunately, I had overextended, positive that the blow would connect. Off-balance and moving too slow, I swallowed a curse when I felt Nicolai's large hands wrap around my shoulders. White light exploded before my eyes when he slammed his head against mine. The pain was immediately followed by a second swelling of pain as his fist hit my chin, snapping my head around.

Somehow, I remained standing, though I had yet to open my eyes. I didn't need to see him. I could hear him. I could smell him. I could feel the heat pulsing off his massive frame. Gritting my teeth, I drilled my right fist into his side. The sound of at least two ribs breaking was unmistakable.

"Just you," he grunted.

Taking a couple unsteady steps backward, I blinked my eyes a couple times to clear my vision. Good grief, that man had a freaking hard head! Nicolai stood a couple feet away, still upright, but one hand was now pressed against his wounded rib cage.

I snorted softly. "I'm a lucky girl."

"Sorry." The single word escaped him in a nearly breathless whisper, causing a frown to tug at the corners of my mouth. We were all trapped in this collection of islands one way or another.

Nicolai came at me again, his talonlike nails aimed to remove more than one layer of flesh from my body. I didn't try to dodge him this time. Grabbing his upper arms, I used his momentum to help me throw him away from me. Unfortunately, the lycan was smart enough to wrap his long fingers around my wrists and pull me to the ground with him.

We landed in a heap with him beneath me. Both of us grunting, we slammed into the hard, stone-covered ground. Rolling several feet as we struggled for supremacy, our legs tangled in each other. When we finally settled in one spot, Nicolai was on top of me, his knees resting on either side of my hips as he struggled to keep my arms pinned on either side of my head.

A little golden flash of light caught my eye, and my gaze drifted down to find a gold cross dangling from his neck on a thick gold chain. The little piece of metal had caught a sliver of moonlight and winked at me. It didn't glow or heat up like so many of the movies liked to show. But I could feel

it throbbing with power, beating against me as it fought to
keep me back away from the werewolf. Nicolai's faith was
strong. Without uttering a word, I knew he believed very
deeply that God and the heavenly host would keep him safe
from me.

A hiss escaped my clenched teeth and I pressed back into
the cool, broken stone in an attempt to put some distance
between me and the cross. Touching it would burn me, and
since it was a spell-induced burn, I would never completely
heal from it. And I preferred not to have a cross-shaped scar
somewhere on my face.

"Thought of everything, didn't you?" I taunted. The words
pushed past my lips in a harsh whisper since I couldn't unclench my teeth. Nicolai remained silent, focused on keeping me pinned, but even that was faltering. He was strong,
but I was still stronger. I managed to lift my arms a couple
inches off the ground, beginning to push him off me. With
one last groan, he relaxed the pressure he was using to hold
me down for less than a breath before slamming my arms
back down to the ground. The sound of bones breaking shattered the silence.

I screamed, my back arching off the ground a little. He
had brought my right forearm down on a rock, snapping the
bones in half. My vision swam in the pain for a couple seconds. The thought of defeating him without killing him van-
ished. Instinctively, I brought my knees up between his legs.
The surprise and pain was enough to finally push him off.

Before he hit the ground, a circle of fire sprang up around
him, stretching more than six feet into the air. Scrambling
to my feet, I cradled my broken arm against my chest as I
darted off to the darkest niches of the *campo*. One of the far
corners held a type of two-walled arbor, thick with vines.
The shadows were deep, affording me some cover.

Mira!

I flinched at Danaus's sudden presence in my head. The touch was tentative and distant, making me think he was still leaning against the wall where I left him.

Go away! I mentally snarled at him. *I'm busy trying not to get killed.*

You're hurt.

Go away! I wasn't surprised that he could tell I was injured, since the pain seemed to fill my entire frame. Yet I stiffened when I suddenly felt the small wave of power sweeping through me. Danaus and his warm touch were slowly moving over my body, searching for the injury. *It's my right arm. It's broken.* Even the thoughts sounded shaky and frightened in my head. Nightwalkers couldn't do this. We could read one another's thoughts and emotions, but we could not reach out and touch each other like this.

I'm coming. The thought was firm and resolute in my head. I could feel him moving, drawing closer.

No, it's healing. Stay where you are. I—

I quickly ended the thought when I saw Nicolai leap through the fire, his arms raised to protect his face. A nightwalker would never have taken such a chance. We caught fire far too easily. When he landed on his feet, I immediately extinguished the fire, plunging the square back into utter darkness. I knew that the fire would have destroyed the lycan's night vision, and I had only a couple of seconds before he could pierce the gloom again.

Grabbing a rock the size of my left fist, I darted across the square to his side in silence. My goal had been to hit him on the back of the head. If it worked for Danaus, it would work for Nicolai. But the werewolf sensed me at the last second, whether by a stir in the air or the sound of my clothes as I moved, I don't know. He turned to face me and I ended up hitting him in the temple. He crumpled at my feet like a sack of wet noodles.

A scrape on the concrete snapped my gaze to the edge of the square, and I raised my left hand with the rock, ready to throw it at the intruder. Danaus stood in the shadows, his arms raised in surrender, a smirk on his lips.

"You're a mess," he murmured, earning a glare from me.

"Have a nice nap?" I sneered, dropping the rock.

The smirk dissolved from his lips, turning into a matching glare. I hurt too much to trade barbs with the hunter. There were more pressing concerns as the night continued to age.

I knelt down beside Nicolai but didn't touch him. His chest rose in deep, even breaths and I could hear the strong, steady rhythm of his heartbeat. He would recover. Blood leaked from his temple, but I was sure that would stop soon enough. When I stood again, Danaus was on the other side of the unconscious lycan. "Check to make sure he's still wearing his cross," I said.

Danaus furrowed his brows at me but knelt wordlessly and pulled the man's shirt collar away from his throat with one finger to reveal a gold chain and cross against tan skin.

"I don't want someone else picking up the scent of his blood and making a snack of him," I muttered as I turned and walked away. I once again cradled my arm against my stomach, the pain beginning to ease. The bone was mending, but the process was slower than healing a flesh wound.

"Why did Jabari send him?" Danaus asked, following behind me.

"I don't know."

"But the naturi—"

"I don't know, Danaus. I don't know what they're planning, but I'm beginning to wonder if Jabari has something else in store for me," I softly admitted. If I was needed to protect and make the seal that bound the naturi, it meant the Coven couldn't have me killed. But after Nicolai's attempt, it meant that either Jabari had finally made his replacement or the Coven no longer wanted to protect the seal. Or Jabari had plans for me that didn't include the Coven or the naturi.

Standing on the pavement beside the boat, I looked across the Lagoon toward the bright lights of San Marco. *Welcome back to Venice, Mira.* In this dying city, pain and horror skulked in every shadow and around each corner, all held beneath a veneer of elegant, Old World beauty and civilization.

Danaus stood behind me and unexpectedly laid his hand on my right shoulder. My head darted over to look at the large hand as his warmth seeped through my cold flesh. At the same time, he dipped two fingers from his free hand into my front left pocket. I tried to jerk away from him in shock but was effectively trapped between his larger body and the open canal. My narrowed gaze snapped to his face. Danaus smirked again and dangled the key before my face.

"You're in no shape to drive," he said, then stepped into the boat. Frowning, I said nothing as I hopped into the little speedboat and settled into one of the seats. My arm was mostly healed, but I didn't care. I was feeling ragged and worn from the encounter.

The engine roared to life as Danaus pulled us away from the island and back into the Lagoon, headed for Guidecca and our hotel. The sound of the wind and waves was relaxing, wiping the tension from my shoulders. I thought of Nicolai for a moment, wondering what it was that Jabari held over the werewolf.

I shook my head, not caring that no one was around to see it, lost to my own thoughts. Jabari was playing a game. I just didn't understand his goal. Mine was unmistakable. Protect the peace. And the only way to do that was to destroy the Coven's bargain with the naturi. I just had to figure out how.

Twelve

Any reprieve I thought I might have earned after nights of running and fighting to stay alive had been adequately crushed. Now I just wanted a few minutes of quiet in which to think and try to anticipate Jabari's next move. A sigh knocked against the back of my teeth but never managed to escape as Danaus and I stepped into our suite at the Cipriani. Instead of being faced with the sweet, cuddly scene of Sadira and Tristan, the rooms were empty. I hadn't left explicit orders for them to remain in the rooms, but I didn't sense them out hunting in the streets when I scanned the hotel area before leaving Torcello.

A heavy tension hung bloated and ugly in the air, pressing against my chest. Standing in the middle of the black and gray parlor, I struggled to keep from clenching my fists. The beautiful room with its elegant furniture and shiny marble floors was untouched—indicating that they walked out on their own.

I started slowly, hesitant. My powers spread from my body in a circle, reaching outward until I had covered the main islands of Venice. There was no Tristan or Sadira. Reluctantly, I pushed out across the Lagoon to San Clemente, where I found Sadira in the Great Hall. She wasn't alone.

Her emotions were clear. She was calm, but sad. I still

didn't sense Tristan, but I knew he was there too. Someone was blocking my ability to sense him, and there was only one person who could do that: Tristan's beloved maker, Sadira. A nightwalker could keep other nightwalkers from sensing him and his children as a type of defense mechanism. Only the older ones like Jabari could keep it up for nights on end. At best, Sadira could maintain the barrier for a couple of nights, but she didn't need to hide him for long. She was only buying the others some time. And maybe so had Nicolai. Jabari might not have truly believed that the werewolf could kill me, but he knew that Nicolai could stall me for a time.

"Can you go inside a church? A still functioning church?" I asked Danaus. My low voice crept through the tense silence that filled the suite. Standing next to the sofa, I leaned down so my right hand tightly gripped the corner of one of the dark end tables, causing my newly mended forearm to ache. Danaus stood behind my left shoulder near the double doors to the suite. I didn't bother to try to hide my frustration and anger. What was the point? He could sense my emotions if he wanted to.

"Yes," he said. "What's going on?" His heavy footsteps crossed the room to stop before his bag of weapons, which sat near the sofa. Placing the worn duffel bag on the coffee table, he unzipped it without looking up at me and started rummaging around for the one appropriate item that would destroy his enemy

My lips parted but my voice couldn't quite push past the lump in my throat. I licked my lips and tried again, forcing my fingers to loosen their death grip on the table because they were starting to throb and I didn't want to shatter the wood. "There's something I need to take care of." The words came out flat and emotionless despite the turmoil in my chest. I had to go back to San Clemente.

Looking over my shoulder at my dark companion, I found

that his hard gaze never wavered from the flash of steel and leather as he dug through his bag of goodies. "Where's Sadira and Tristan?"

I ignored the question and stood erect again as I finally pried my fingers loose from the table. Silently, I removed the necklace and earrings I had been wearing, shoving them into my front pockets. They would only get in the way. "There's a small church just a couple blocks south of here. Go there and stay inside until dawn," I directed, staring straight ahead instead of at him.

"I'm going with you."

I spun around to face Danaus, standing a few feet away now. His black brows were drawn together over his nose, and his jaw muscles hardened as he clenched his teeth. His fingers deftly attached his leather knife sheath over his belt as he prepared for the coming fight. He had made his decision to follow me into whatever battle I now faced. My own frown eased from my lips and something light swelled in my chest, pushing aside the anger and fear that had been weighing me down during the past few nights. He didn't know what we faced or how bad our odds, but he was willing to follow me.

Unfortunately, he could not come with me this time. "That's not an option," I said with a slight shake of my head. "Our business is getting rid of the naturi." My voice had grown as cold and unyielding as the Russian tundra. I couldn't let him accompany me; both for Tristan's sake and my own. "This is nightwalker business. You're not going. Go to a church. I don't want to worry about someone coming after you while I'm gone."

He refused to be put off by my tone, and roughly grabbed my wrist when I tried to walk away from him. "What's going on, Mira? First Nicolai, and now this. Where are Tristan and Sadira?"

My gaze met his narrow blue eyes and for a moment I

longed to sink into their cool depths. I wanted to forget about it all and go back to playing cat and mouse with him through the historical district of Savannah. I knew he would willingly walk in the main hall and protect me with his last breath.

Of course, his protection of me had nothing to do with me per se, but with the protection of the human race. I was the key—the weapon that would beat back the naturi. For half a breath I wondered if he hated me all the more for it. A creature he perceived as completely evil, now the savior of mankind. A vampire hunter forced to protect his chosen prey.

"Sadira has taken Tristan to the Coven," I whispered.

"Why?" His deep voice had also dropped to hushed tones, as if we were sharing secrets. But we had already done that tonight, and most of what we'd said shouted at the top of our lungs for all the heavens to hear.

"Punishment," I murmured, forcing the word past a clog in my throat. "I stole Tristan from her, so she must strike back at me." My gaze wavered and darted across the room to stare out the windows that overlooked San Marco Piazza. The warm yellow light glowed in the square, beckoning the late night revelers.

"Will they kill him?"

"Yes, but not until I get there." My voice hardened and my hands balled into fists as I stared blindly out the bank of windows. "She'll want me to see it; to know that I failed to protect him."

Danaus's thumb rubbed the inside of my wrist in a light caress, drawing my gaze back to his face. "Will they try to kill you?"

A half smirk tweaked the right corner of my mouth, pushing aside the concern that had undoubtedly drifted across my features. "They can try, but I doubt it. It's time for the Coven to bring me to heel. They will try to break me and remind me that I serve them."

"I can't go," Danaus whispered, releasing my wrist. His hand fell limp back at his side. He finally understood that I had to prove my strength. It was a test. If he walked in and guarded my back, it would be taken as a sign of weakness on my part. Any help he gave me would cause more damage than good.

"No." I walked toward the door, refusing to look back at my partner in crime. They were going to hurt me. They were going to make me wish I was dead, but they wouldn't kill me. Tonight was just a bit of fun. If I somehow managed to survive the next few nights and stop Rowe's plan to free the naturi, then it would be open season on my head.

With one hand on the open door, I looked over at my shoulder into the room, suddenly hating its opulence. My eyes still refused to find his face. "It'll be over before dawn."

I wasn't exactly sure what "it" was, but I was sure that before the dawn came, someone was going to be dead. I had known Sadira would strike back at me. Beyond the fact that it was her way, it was the way of all nightwalkers. I had stolen something that belonged to her in front of a member of the court. It would have been no different if I'd walked up to her and spat in her face. Of course, word of my theft spread like wildfire through the nightwalker legions.

But, stupidly, I had thought I would have more time. Sadira was usually an extremely patient creature. She toyed with her prey over decades if time permitted, letting them dangle on a thin strand of hope for years before finally crushing them. I thought she would wait until after we finally defeated Rowe. Apparently she didn't think she'd get another shot at me so she rushed things. That, or someone else was pulling the strings.

I shot across the Lagoon in record time. I knew these waters. Maybe not as well as the streets of my beloved Savannah, but enough that I could push the little boat to her limits as I sped to the island. Circling around to a small, attractive stone landing closer to the main hall, I eased the tiny speed boat to the dock. It was crowded with boats of different shapes and sizes, but there was still one spot open. They were waiting for me.

Still in the boat, before stepping onto the stone pier I scanned the island one last time. Everyone was pulled back to the Great Hall of the Coven. I could vaguely pick out Elizabeth in the lower levels that served as the daylight chambers. Macaire was also there, but he was moving, heading for the lower levels. Jabari, of course, was nowhere to be found. It had been years since I was last able to sense him. He kept his protective cloak up constantly now, hiding from something.

As I was pulling back, a scream of pain tore through my brain, sending me to my knees. Searing pain ripped along my flesh as if the claws of a thousand cats were using me as a scratching post. Muscles trembled and my stomach clenched and unclenched, quivering under the onslaught of pain with no source. I tightly clutched the steering wheel, trying to regain my balance as the last wave of pain and terror swept through me. I had found Tristan.

A knot of fear twisted in my chest, but it was melting under the heat of the rage building in my veins. Sadira had pulled back the veil blocking Tristan from my senses. They had been torturing him, waiting for my eminent arrival. I could feel the pain as it coursed through his lean frame and the crippling exhaustion as his body strained to heal the assortment of wounds that had been inflicted. I hopped off the boat and walked briskly up to the main hall. There was no need to rush. The assembled vampires had stopped their amusements as they waited for me.

The same pair of humans from earlier in the evening pulled the massive front doors open, their muscles jumping under the effort it required to move the thick combination of wood and iron. A nervous look danced in their dark eyes, which darted only briefly to me before returning to intently stare at the ground. They knew something was happening inside, something gruesome. They had heard Tristan's screams even through the thick doors and were simply grateful they weren't the focus of these grim activities. Yet, there were still several hours before the night finally withered away, plenty of time for them to fill in.

The chandeliers dangling overhead had been extinguished, the long hallway sparsely lit with a scattering of iron candelabras holding thick yellow candles. Even after living in the glory of the electronic age, there were certain things that would not be shed, particularly in the Great Hall. The little flames danced on their precarious perches, throwing long shadows that congregated in the deep corners, plotting their own secret schemes.

Before me the doors to the main audience chamber swung soundlessly open, pushed from the inside. I couldn't see who had opened them, but it didn't matter. My gaze didn't stray from Tristan, who knelt in the middle of the room. Naked and bleeding, he had a large manacle clamped around his neck, with a heavy chain running from it to a thick iron ring in the floor. His arms and legs were not chained, so he could fight back, but the chain running to his neck was so short that he could not fully stand up.

Tristan raised his head when he heard my footsteps echoing heavily across the marble floor, his body cringing at the sound as if the vibrations added to his pain. His beautiful face was covered in blood and his nose was broken. I could see the bite marks on his neck and on the inside of one of his arms. They had taken the time to drain him before beating him so his body wouldn't be able to heal from the wounds.

However, it was his eyes that finally drew an angry hiss out of me. Those haunted blue orbs would chase me for the rest of my existence. He wasn't pleading to be saved, but for me to finally end his pain. The physical pain was minor compared to what they most likely had done to his mind. I had a feeling Macaire had had some fun with him before he handed the young nightwalker over to the rest of the court.

Movement finally drew my eyes from Tristan and I caught sight of Sadira. She was sitting on the stairs before the chair Macaire had sat in earlier in the evening. Her face was expressionless and still, as if she carved out of white marble. Gritting my teeth, I dragged my eyes from her slender form and looked around the room. Nearly a dozen other nightwalkers were gathered. High-back wooden chairs and a couple chaise lounges now lined the walls; a little comfort while they watched the show.

Tristan was the warm-up act, and I was the main attraction. Turning my attention back to Tristan, I forced the anger to coil up in the pit of my stomach as I stood before him. I would deal with them. I would teach them to fear me. My days of facing the members of the court for my survival were centuries ago during my time with Sadira. Most of these vampires had not been reborn yet. To them I was a myth, a fanciful tale based on very little fact. I would remind them that I was a nightmare.

With my hands resting limply on my hips, I stared down at Tristan. The cold marble floor around him was smeared with his blood. I somehow swallowed my rage and revulsion, lightening my voice to one of irritated boredom. "What are you doing here?"

"I was told to come," he rasped. His beautiful voice was raw from his screams.

"By whom?"

"Sadira."

"I am your mistress now," I said, amazed at how steady my voice sounded. On the inside, my muscles were trembling and my throat had constricted. I had been half his age when I made my first appearance as the evening entertainment and I'd had to be carried out. Sleep dominated my nights for more than a week as my body struggled to recover. I never forgave Sadira for my time with the Coven. Many believed playing the part of the court's entertainment was supposed to be a rite of passage. It was not only supposed to make a nightwalker stronger, but it also taught obedience. It had taught me to hate.

Looking at Tristan, I knew he was just chum. He wasn't meant to live a long existence and grow to be strong. Sadira had made him weak and kept him weak by chaining him to her side. I had slaughtered those stronger than him because they'd grown careless and could not take care of themselves. Without Sadira, he would become one of those nightwalkers, and it would be me hounding his steps one night like some dark angel of death. But I wouldn't let it happen to Tristan. He belonged to me now.

Maybe it was because there was something in his eyes that reminded me of Michael. It might have been the fact that in two nights I had failed to protect both Thorne and Michael. Or maybe it was that I saw too much of myself in those pain-filled eyes. I knew the horrors he had faced and the pain that still awaited him. But reasons why weren't important.

For once, I wanted to save someone instead of destroying them. I wasn't going to let these monsters have Tristan. But, unfortunately, we all had a part to play, a little pretense to portray before we could all go our separate ways. And I had to be sure I had Tristan's absolute obedience.

"I told you not to come here," I said. My hands slid from my hips to hang limp at my sides, even as tension hummed like an electric current through my taut body. "I should leave you here as punishment for your disobedience."

"Please, no! Mira, please! She's my maker. I had to obey," he pleaded. His soft voice barely jumped above a whisper. He lurched forward, grabbing my legs, a cry escaping his parted lips. When he leaned forward, I saw that his back was a bloody mess of tissue. They had peeled the skin from his body.

I leaned down and placed my hand gently under his chin, forcing him to look up at me. "After tonight, she is nothing to you. After tonight, I am your whole world," I said coldly.

"Yes, Mistress," he choked out past the throb of pain.

Cupping his face with both of my hands, I wiped the bloody tears away with my thumbs as they streaked down his cheeks. "Now tell me who touched you."

I slowly raised my eyes to sweep over the assembled masses as Tristan remained silent. No names left Tristan's cracked and trembling lips, but I hadn't expected him to tell me who his tormentors were. We all knew that I could pick the faces from his memories at any time. But I wouldn't even need to do that.

I didn't bother to look at Sadira. She hadn't touched him. It didn't matter if she had. It was enough that she handed him over to the court for its fun. Skimming over the faces, I noticed Valerio slumping in one of the high-backed chairs, his long pale fingers laced together over his stomach. One corner of his handsome mouth lifted in a smirk, daring me to challenge him, but his clothes were spotless, unlike some of his companions. He had watched the show. It was a neutral stance, not challenging, but he also wasn't on my side. It was the best I was going to get at the moment.

"I thought he was quite delicious," Gwen announced, rising gracefully from one of the chairs off to my left, near the dais at the end of the room. Her pale blue shirt and little white shorts were splattered with Tristan's blood. She would have looked like a tourist on vacation if not for the blood stains and the glow in her narrowed eyes.

"I was so hoping you would say that," I said, the words held in the embrace of a dark laugh. I stepped around Tristan so I was between him and Gwen. "I believe I said that he was not to be touched."

"The Elders promised him to us," she said. Her smile was triumphant, lighting up her blood-smeared face.

"I warned you," I carefully enunciated in Italian. The Italian came without thought as my mind slipped easily back into seemingly ancient memories of fights fought as the Elders watched. The violence, the brutality, the feral need to rend and shred had built in the air until it became a living, breathing creature.

As I spoke, candles around the room flared to life. The little teardrops of fire popped into existence, sending the shadows scrambling to the far corners.

"The Coven's word is law!" Gwen shouted, her gaze darting away from me as she noted the increased firelight. Lines of strain stretched from the corners of her mouth as she struggled to keep from frowning. "You're not above them, Fire Starter."

"A mistress has the right to deny the use of her pets if she so chooses," I said, quoting old law.

"His maker handed him over," Gwen argued, pointing at Sadira. Her smile had faded somewhat and there was no mistaking the trembling in her extended index finger. No one ever denied the use of his or her pet when an Elder wanted to use the poor soul as entertainment. If a master did, he would have to defend him against all comers. In all my years, I had heard of it being done only once. Jabari had denied Macaire when he made the request of me, driving the wedge even further between them. It also didn't help that during that time I was neither a Companion of Jabari nor was he technically recognized as my master.

"I am his mistress. I warned you," I repeated. My words were low and even, deceiving in their calm, but Gwen was not fooled.

"You're nothing!" she screamed, her hands balled into fists at her sides.

I chuckled, my voice sinking into lower, sultry depths. The sound stretched strangely across the room, echoing off the walls as I darted toward her. My fist collided with her jaw before I even stopped moving. She tried to dodge it but her reactions were a hair slower. I felt bone breaking beneath my hand as her head snapped back, the force of the blow throwing her backward into the wall.

Gwen tried to quickly push back to her feet, blood spilling from the corner of her mouth, but I was already there. Grabbing her by the throat, I lifted her off her feet. It was easy considering that she was several inches shorter than me. Her long nails clawed at my hand and down my arms as she struggled to get loose. Little rivers of blood rose to the surface and briefly streaked down my white skin. I smiled at her, pulling back my lips enough to expose my fangs before tossing her across the large room.

With a bone-crunching thud, she landed not far from the center of the room, near the foot of the dais. The sound of her collarbone shattering when she landed split the air, followed by the low squeal of her skin sliding a couple feet across the shiny marble floor.

I paused and looked down the line of vampires who stood watching the struggle. They had risen from their chairs and were eyeing me intently, trying to decide whether I would jump at them next or finish off my current prey. I growled low in the back of my throat, warning them to stay back. A couple hissed in return but backed off a few steps, giving me ample room. Valerio watched me with intent questioning eyes from his chair.

"Elizabeth will destroy you!" Gwen shrieked hysterically. Her jaw had healed enough for her to curse me.

"Where is she, Gwen?" I inquired, strolling back toward her as she struggled to sit up. The pain in her left shoulder from where she had hit the floor slowed her movements.

Nightwalkers had the ability to heal with amazing speed, but that didn't mean we didn't feel excruciating pain just like every other creature. "She must know by now that you're in pain. I'll wait while you call to her."

I stood over her and pretended to inspect my nails. With a howl of pure rage, she pushed off the floor with her right hand, launching herself into me. She moved faster than I'd anticipated, knocking me to the floor with her on top. Her long nails raked down my face and tore a large hunk of flesh from my throat. I backhanded her with my right fist, throwing her off so I could roll to my knees.

"She's abandoned you to your fate," I taunted, easily rising to my feet as she struggled. She had fed on Tristan, but his blood wasn't strong enough to heal her. She should have fed on a human or two before facing me, not wasted her night with him. Broken bones slowed her down, and I'd dislocated her jaw when I backhanded her.

I kept my left hand pressed to my neck as I walked back to her side. The blood seeped through my fingers and trickled down my chest to soak into my shirt. "I warned you."

With no hesitation, I knelt before her and punched her in the chest. My hand tore through skin and muscle, shattering her sternum. It took only a second to open my hand in her chest and wrap my fingers around her motionless heart. She had enough time to mouth the word *No* before I yanked it from her chest. Her body slumped lifeless to the floor, the remnants of her soul brushing against me as it floated into the ether.

Clutching her heart tightly in my right hand, her blood ran down my arm and dripped from my elbow. The lukewarm muscle squished in my fist, pushing between my fingers. A wide smile split my pale face as I laid the heart on Elizabeth's chair, a gift from me to the Coven.

Thirteen

The monster roared in my chest, the sound causing my soul to tremble in the frail casing of my body. The same feeling that gripped me in the London alley tightened the muscles in my slim frame, screaming for release. I wasn't hungry, but the air was thick with the scent of blood. My limbs were splattered with it and the only sound in the vast room was the soft patter of blood dripping from my fingertips to the shining black marble floor.

But it was more than that. Killing Gwen awakened something within me, and it wanted more. An unexpected warmth rushed through me as if I were still alive and basking naked in the summer sun. My fangs throbbed, needing to be embedded in soft, tender flesh.

My head fell back and a laugh bubbled up from my chest. When it hit the air, the sound was frosted with ice and completely void of all humor. The world slipped away and time eased to a crippled limp. There were only the nightwalkers left within the hall and myself. My eyes lazily fell on the scattering off to my left. Several pairs of glowing eyes met mine and smiled. They were swept up in the same primal wave of blood and violence. I was more than happy to oblige. Tonight, the monster was unleashed.

We were in motion at the same time. Three nightwalkers lunged forward from the far wall as I took my first steps toward them. I was only vaguely aware of the others as they slipped off toward the exits. The wave had washed through these younger nightwalkers, and now they wisely backed off, willing to get their blood and violence from a safer source than me.

The dance was graceful, full of fluid movements, but a blur to any human who would have seen us. There was no thought anymore. Just the need to kill. Or be killed. The first was young, barely through his first century. His wide green eyes glowed at me like sparkling emeralds a second before I ripped his heart from his chest. The second followed in much the same manner, but I earned a set of claw marks across my stomach for my trouble.

I turned to locate the remaining third when I was slammed to the hard floor, stars exploding before my eyes. Wincing and clenching my teeth against the pain that threatened to steal consciousness away from me, I rolled to the right. Half a breath later a heavy oak chair crashed to the exact spot I'd been, cracking the marble floor. The high-backed chair shattered, sending shards darting through the air under the force of it being thrown to the floor. Instinctively, I shielded my heart from the flying debris, though none of it had enough force to penetrate my sternum.

Rolling onto my back, I gazed up at my attacker. Standing barely over five feet, the nightwalker with the sandy blond hair and glowing blue eyes was holding one of the broken legs of the chair. I smiled up at her and the wooden leg burst into flames. All the wood from the chair scattered about the floor was instantly consumed with dancing flames. The nightwalker yelped in surprise, dropping the leg and stumbling a couple steps away from me.

The fire and pain cleansed me, washing away the blood lust and the need to kill. The monster had grown silent, pleased with my offering. My vision was blurred and my back protested any movement, begging me to lie still, but I couldn't. One remained. Pushing off the ground with my left hand, I bonelessly rose to my feet. The nightwalker paused, watching me, waiting for my next move.

Slowly, I waved my right hand, swallowing back the whimper of pain that slashed through my back. Chest-high flames sprung up around the nightwalker, completely encircling her. Her blue eyes widened, losing their unnatural glow. Frowning, I easily stepped through the flames and grabbed her by the throat, but she barely noticed me despite the fact that my long nails were digging into her cool flesh. Her eyes were locked on the fire that danced less than a foot away from her body. It was only after I gave her a rough shake that she finally met my hard gaze.

"Who am I?" I snarled, tightening my grip on the short nightwalker. Her wide eyes stared up at me, confused and terrified. There was a smear of blood on her small chin. She had fed on Tristan as well. She deserved to die, consumed in the flames that surrounded her, and she knew it.

"The Fire Starter," she whimpered in a strangled voice.

My frown hardened into a cold smile. "Tell them what I have done," I commanded in a low, grating whisper. "Tell them that if anyone touches what belongs to me, I shall hunt them down and collect their hearts for display in my domain. Remind them of who I am."

Still smiling, I shoved her away from me toward the far door on the left side of the room. A terrified scream escaped her as she threw up her arms to protect her face, fully expecting to be engulfed in the fire. But as she reached the ring of fire, I extinguished it so she would pass through untouched. She stumbled and fell to her ass. Quickly realizing she had escaped without being singed, she pushed back to her feet and disappeared through the side door.

My gaze slowly tripped around the room as my eyes adjusted to the lower levels of light. My brain took in the broken bodies and growing pools of blood as they spread about the room like small black lakes. After nearly a full minute, my eyes reached the far dais. Sadira remained on the stairs before Macaire's seat, never moving from the spot she'd occupied when I entered the main hall.

My face was void of all emotion and my thoughts a blank slate. I wasn't even aware that I was approaching her until I heard Tristan scream.

"No, Mistress!" he cried, twisting painfully so he could watch me, the chain still around his neck. His bleeding had stopped, for the most part, but he was weak. "She's our mother."

"My mother died centuries ago. She is nothing to me!" I shouted. Anger suddenly blossomed within chest and flowed through my veins like magma searching for an opening. I walked over to her, once again facing her soaked in the blood of others.

"You can't touch me," Sadira confidently announced. "I am part of the triad."

I licked my lips as a grim smile graced my features, still edging closer. "If I've learned anything during the past few nights, it's that you're replaceable. I'll find another."

The triad had been the ones to create the seal that kept the naturi locked away. And with the naturi threatening to break free, we needed to reform the triad, considering that Tabor had been destroyed nearly fifty years ago. While no one seemed pleased with the choice, Danaus had become Tabor's replacement. Maker or not, I had no doubt I could find a replacement for Sadira as well, if necessary.

"There's not enough time." Confidence still filled her voice, but she rose to her feet. "The new moon and the harvest holiday are in four nights, and they will use it to break the seal. You can't destroy me if you hope to stop the naturi."

"Please, Mistress!" Tristan begged. "It's my fault. I shouldn't have left the room. Punish me."

I paused, my teeth clenched in frustration. She was right that there wasn't enough time to find a replacement. And with my luck, it would turn out to be another Thorne fiasco. I couldn't risk it, no matter how much I loathed her.

"Why?" The single word came out strangled and fractured from the back of my throat.

"He's weak. He has to be taught what it means to be a nightwalker." Her shoulders straightened as she spoke, confident in her reasons for torturing one of her own precious children.

"Is this what it means to be a nightwalker?" I demanded, holding my bloody hands out to her.

"Yes," she hissed, her composure cracking. Her thin, bony hands clenched into fists before her stomach. An unhealthy glow rose from her wide brown eyes. "It's about power and not bowing to those weaker than you. I love Tristan, but he had to learn that."

I snorted, my fingers trembling, sending drops of blood to the black marble floor. "If you think that is what tonight was about, you're a fool. He was an appetizer and you let it happen. He relied on you for protection and you betrayed him. Tonight was about revenge. It was about striking back at me because you were too much of a coward to stand up to the court."

"They would have killed me," she argued, her voice wavering.

"Not yet. Like you said, you're part of the triad. They would have toyed with you, but you would have survived. Unfortunately, Tristan wasn't worth it for you. It was easier to hand him over."

Turning sharply on a heel, I stalked back over to Tristan,

who had been silently watching the petite tête-à-tête between mother and daughter. I wanted her to attack my back. I longed for one more small reason to lash out at her, just so the tiny voice of my battered conscience could use the excuse of self-defense when I ripped her head off. But Sadira never moved.

"Don't come back to the suite," I called back to her without turning around. "If I ever see you again after Rowe is defeated, I will kill you. And trust me, I will be looking forward to that day."

"You're not free of me, my Mira," Sadira called, her sweet lilting voice burrowing its way under my skin: *You belong to me. Tristan belongs to me. I am your maker.* It was almost hypnotic, the way it drifted through my brain. There were no protective walls I could put up to guard against her intrusion into my mind. She was my maker; she would have access as long as she survived.

I spun on my heel to snarl at her, but as I turned, the Great Hall disappeared from around me. The massive stone walls and black marble floor were replaced by a worn wooden floor and uneven stone walls. Sadira had done the same trick before when I was severely wounded. She had mentally taken me to the dungeon I was reborn in. But this time I wasn't in the dungeon. I was in the small farmhouse I had inhabited briefly back in Greece before Sadira kidnapped me.

A small whimper escaped me as I looked around the crude house that had given me such joy for an extremely short period of time. For a few years I'd lived in a home, was loved by my husband and adored by my sweet daughter Calla.

"Stop this, Sadira," I commanded in the firmest voice I could muster. I struggled to hold onto the rage and violence that had driven me through my earlier fight.

"This is where it all started, my daughter," she patiently replied. She stood before me in the open doorway, though I wasn't sure if it was truly her or simply part of the illusion.

Behind her, black night stretched in all directions. "This place was simply a dream. You were hiding. I set you free."

"You kidnapped me!" I shouted. "I had no choice." I took a step forward and swore I heard the floor creak beneath my feet.

"Mama," cried a low, sleepy voice.

"No," I gasped, taking another step toward Sadira, my arms wrapped tightly around my stomach. I moved away from the soft patter of little footsteps from the next room. "Don't do this, Sadira. She's not real. She's dead. She's been dead for centuries."

"I know that, Mira, but you refuse to let her go," Sadira gently said. Her voice was light, a caress, a soft touch on my cheek. This is your chance to say good-bye and then you can start over with me and Tristan. We will be your family. You won't have this horrible weight hanging on you."

I tried to close my eyes but it was all in my head. There was no escaping the images she wanted me to see. "It's not real. It's not real. It's not—" but my words became lodged in my throat when a girl about three years old entered the room. She wore a long white shirt that just missed covering her small bare feet. A wealth of sleep-tangled black hair fell down her back. She stared up at me with her father's brown eyes. But then, she got most of her looks from her father, and I was grateful about that. I didn't want my daughter to be cursed like me, but perfectly normal like her father.

"Mama," she repeated, stretching her arms up, her eyes pleading with me to pick her up and hold her close. My arms ached to hold her, finally filling the void that had haunted me for centuries. I wanted to feel her warmth against my body and to breathe her scent in so I could hold it forever in my lungs. I wanted to hold my daughter one last time.

Painfully, I took another step backward, trying to find a middle ground between Sadira's image and the image of

Calla. I wanted to grab up my daughter, wrap her tightly in my arms, and run from this place. I wanted to run from Sadira, the Coven, and all nightwalkers. I wanted to run back to the life I could have had centuries ago in the sunlight.

But that chance was gone forever. It was shredding me on the inside, leaving me trembling. My legs shook and my knees threatened to buckle. I refused to give in to Sadira. She would not have me again.

"I won't go with you," I growled, tensing the muscles in my legs and clenching my teeth. "Calla is dead. That life I had is dead because of you. You and Jabari. I won't go back to you."

"You will or I will kill Tristan now," she calmly said, switching tactics when images of Calla couldn't make me cave.

"Ridiculous. You won't."

Sadira laughed lightly, reminding me faintly of a bird's song. "Of course I will. You are far more valuable to me than he could ever be."

"Mira?" The voice was soft and fragile, reaching me from beyond the nightmare I was trapped in. It was Tristan. I had forgotten about him. We were really in the Great Hall, and for now Tristan was alive and still mine.

It suddenly dawned on me to fully open my mind instead of closing everything down in an effort to block out Sadira. Tristan's pain and fear instantly flooded in. It was more than Sadira could effectively block out. The image of my home in Greece disintegrated. Calla faded away to only a ghostly memory.

I knelt on the ground beside Tristan, who was still chained to the floor. Reaching across, I took his hand and gently squeezed it as I slowly reduced our mental connection. His pain was draining me and I needed to be sharp against Sadira.

The rage from my earlier fight pumped in my veins again, and a new anger filled my trembling frame. I had packed my past away and left it to collect dust in the corner of my mind, but Sadira trotted it out as a way of controlling me. She had defiled the memory of my daughter; she sullied those precious few moments in my life when I'd felt human and whole and happy. I didn't need the monster dwelling inside of me to fire my need for violence. Sadira had already done that.

"I'm free now," I said, pushing back to my feet. "And Tristan belongs to me."

You can't have him, she snarled in my mind. I felt her pulling another veil over my mind, so I opened my thoughts to Tristan again. Trapping my mind between two realities, it stole away my sense of balance. I had no idea where Sadira was. Desperate, I threw up a ring of fire around Tristan and me.

Sadira's screams rang through the hall. She had been approaching and got trapped in the fire. With her out of my mind, I extinguished the flames, but she was already blackened to a crisp.

With a little effort, I broke the lock on the manacle around Tristan's neck and dropped it with a loud clang. Tristan leaned heavily on me as we moved away, his fingers digging into my forearm as he struggled to stay on his feet.

The smell of burning flesh filled the room, overpowering the scent of the Lagoon and lush gardens that wafted in through the open front doors. Tristan struggled against my hold on him, trying to look back at the creature that had spawned us both, but I wouldn't let him stop moving forward.

Sadira didn't die that night, but every nightwalker in Venice could feel her pain. At dawn she would fall into her deep sleep wrapped in that pain, and tomorrow when she awoke would still be drowning in it. Even if she gorged herself on blood, it would still take several nights to recover from those burns. I only needed to keep her alive until we defeated Rowe. No one had ever said anything about the condition she had to be in.

Tristan and I paused at the front doors long enough for him to feed off the two doormen. I knew they would come in handy sooner or later. Borrowing a pair of pants off one of the unconscious men, we slowly walked back to the boat. My back ached and my head throbbed from where I'd been hit with the chair. From the way my vision still blurred from time to time, it seemed that the nightwalker with the chair had cracked my skull. I needed to feed and sleep for a couple days, but I doubted I would get such a luxury.

Tristan moved more easily as his body healed with the fresh infusion of blood, but our progress was slow. We were several yards from the docks when I saw Nicolai walking toward us up the path. I pulled Tristan to a stop, my whole body tensed. If the werewolf attacked now, I knew I would kill him. My body hummed with pent-up energy from the fight. I might not intend to, but I would still kill him.

"Walk away, Nicolai," I called to him. Now was not the time to resume our fight. Jabari had ordered him to kill me, and I could only assume that Nicolai would pursue that task until he finally completed it or was dead. The golden shifter had stopped in the middle of the path more than twenty feet away, watching me. "Turn around, get back in a boat, and drive off."

"Why didn't you kill me?" The question was soft and reached me on the back of the breeze crossing the island.

"My fight isn't with you," I said. Beside me, Tristan tightened his grip on my arm. He wasn't so much looking for support as he was questioning me, seeking assurance. I placed my right hand over his and gently squeezed it. He had been through enough for one night.

Nicolai caught the movement and frowned at our hands. "He's the reason I was sent to kill you," he said, the words barely pushing past his clenched teeth. "A distraction?"

"Possibly."

Nicolai jerked his eyes away from us as a string of Russian curses rumbled from his chest like a freight train across the desert. His fists were clenched at his sides, trembling. He had been used so another could be tortured, and now he knew it.

"Please, Nico," I started again, hoping a nickname would get him to acquiesce to my request. "Walk away. I need to get him somewhere he can rest and recover."

Frowning, Nicolai walked toward us. I stepped forward, putting myself between the werewolf and Tristan. His expression instantly softened when saw my aggressive stance and he halted a few feet away from us.

"I only want to help you to the boat," he said, holding up his hands in surrender.

Nodding, I turned and put Tristan's hand back on my left arm. Nicolai took Tristan's other hand and placed it on his right arm. The werewolf got a glimpse of Tristan's back and swore softly, his jaw clenched in boiling anger.

"This has nothing to do with you," I murmured a while later, breaking the tense silence.

"But I didn't help matters. I held you up when you could have rescued him sooner," he grumbled.

I said nothing because it was true. He didn't know how he was being used. He didn't know he was aiding in the torture of another. I wondered if he would have followed orders if he'd known what the plan was. By the pained anger that filled his copper-brown eyes, I doubted it.

We didn't speak again until we reached the little speedboat. Nicolai helped me lower Tristan in. The nightwalker sighed deeply as he lay across the bench on his stomach.

"I could have killed you," Nicolai abruptly said, pulling my gaze back up to his handsome face. He stood on the dock with his hands shoved into the pockets of his dirty slacks.

His left cheek was smudged with dirt, and a shadow of blond stubble outlined his hard jaw. A smear of blood stained his temple where I had hit him with the rock, but there was no lump or other discoloration. His stare was intense, holding me silent for a moment, unable to read the emotions that lay just below the surface.

"You have the ability," I conceded, a smile lurking on my lips. "But you couldn't have killed me tonight. You don't have a good enough reason, and you need a reason to kill." It was a guess, but I doubted that I was far from the mark.

Nicolai snorted and opened his mouth to argue, but I held up my hand and continued before he could speak. "Don't go back to the hall until after daybreak. I didn't leave its occupants in a good mood."

"Thanks for the warning," he said with a half smile.

With a nod, I turned on the engine and pulled away from the stone dock, eager to get Tristan back to the relative safety of our suite. By the time we reentered the Lagoon, the worst of his wounds had healed and he was beginning to relax.

My muscles were battered and the wind was chilling the blood that covered my body. We crossed those dark waters in silence, lost in our own thoughts. Even now I could still hear Sadira's screams, feel Gwen's warm heart squishing between my fingers. The soft touch of each soul as it left the bodies of the nightwalkers I had killed this evening pranced through my mind, and I smiled. I felt more alive with every existence I'd extinguished, and I loved it.

Maybe I'd been wrong about what I told Danaus. Maybe I *was* evil. I could argue that I had killed those nightwalkers of the Coven court to stop them from hurting another vampire. I could argue that I'd done it to protect Tristan. But that would have been a lie. I did it to prove my own power and exert my control over them. I killed them simply because I could.

FOURTEEN

The night closed in around me, warm and wet like a lover's lips on the hollow of my throat. But I wanted to shove the feeling away. I didn't want to be touched. I didn't want to hear another heartbeat or feel heat radiating from another human body. I didn't want to look up and meet Tristan's haunted gaze, asking questions I couldn't bring myself to answer.

For the first time in what seemed an eternity, I was alone. Gabriel, my guardian angel, was hundreds of miles away, and Danaus remained safely ensconced in a church—protected from me and my kind. Tristan had been left curled up on the bed. After a quick shower to remove the fresh coating of blood, I slipped down to the landing.

As I flew across the Lagoon, a roar rose up from the engine of the tiny speedboat and I could feel it rumbling through my bones. Waves slapped against the sides of the boat and the wind pulled at my hair, tangling it. The darkness crowded close as I headed away from the lights and sputtering heart of Venice.

I needed to be away from the pulse of humanity so I could think. Yet, something in me was afraid to plumb the dark depths of my feelings too deeply. I didn't regret the destruction I had brought at the hall. I didn't regret the lives that I took or the joy I felt in doing so. And it wasn't the act that was gnawing away at me—it was my complete lack of remorse. I don't know whether it was some wrinkled remnant of my humanity or if I truly believed it, but something was screaming inside of me that I should be horrified by the bloodbath I had created. But I wasn't.

Beyond the screaming, another, more insidious voice mocked me. Nearly two centuries ago Valerio had warned me there was no escaping what we were—heartless, cruel, and violent. I had left Europe professing that I could be different, I could avoid what he believed was fated. Less than twenty-four hours back in Venice and I was covered in the blood of my compatriots, basking in their terror, and laughing like a madwoman struck by the moon.

As I neared the dark island, I cut the engine and let the small boat glide into the dock. I had gone to the one island where I knew I would be completely alone. No human lived here, and no vampire would dare find rest here due to the constant traffic of people during the daylight hours. I had come to San Michele—the cemetery island.

The entire island was ringed with an enormous red-brick wall, and a pair of graceful white stairs and gates led into the sanctuary. The shadows were deeper on the island, thrown down by the countless cypress trees that reached up past the walls. Most of the island was thickly lined with graves, marked with headstones of varying size and decoration, from the traditional white cross to the more elaborate family crypts. The lanes were laid out in a neat grid, but due to the need for space, they were narrow, forcing visitors to walk single file in most places.

With my head down, I wove my way to the east. It had been a while since I last visited, but I remembered a small section that was left as a park. The scent of jasmine and roses drifted to my nose. The air, thick and humid, left me feeling I was pushing through wet cotton. As I turned the last corner, I allowed myself to release a soft sigh as my gaze fell on a small patch of earth that had yet to be turned into a resting place for the dead. The park had shrunk in size, but it was enough for me to sit in silence, surrounded by cypress and what appeared to be a pair of hybrid poplar trees.

Yet, something was wrong. I felt as if I wasn't alone, though I knew I was. No human lived here and nightwalkers had no reason to visit this place. Despite my logic, I still scanned the entire island with my powers, but I sensed no one. Shoving my fingers through my hair, I shook my head and forced myself to walk into the clearing. I was frazzled from the long night and the seemingly endless battles with the naturi.

I sat on the ground and threaded my fingers through the cool grass, wishing the silence of the island would seep into my soul and wipe away the pain caused by Calla's sweet memory. Behind the great stone walls, I could no longer hear the waves of the Lagoon and the clang of the buoy bells were faint. There was just me and the wind and the dead.

"I have grown very weary of you, little princess," someone above me announced.

Rolling over to balance on my hands and toes, I looked up into the poplar tree that had been at my back. But I didn't need to see him. Frustrated tears welled up in my eyes at the sound of Rowe's taunting voice. I was too tired both in body and spirit to fight the naturi now.

"Leave here," I snarled, the muscles in my calves starting to tremble from the awkward position I remained in. "I didn't come here looking for you."

He snorted and stood easily on the branch he had been sitting on. His large black wings brushed and scraped against leaves and branches as he resettled them. "You leave. I was here first."

Was it that simple? I wasn't surprised to find him in Venice after seeing the female naturi in the Great Hall. Hell, I was sure there were several other naturi wandering around the city or even swimming in the Lagoon. But he didn't honestly seem to be there for me, since his best weapon was the element of surprise.

Letting my knees fall so I was kneeling in the grass, I quickly glanced over my shoulder in the direction Rowe was facing. By my best guess, he was looking out toward San Clemente and the Great Hall.

I had to get off the island and find some way to alert Jabari or Macaire. Stopping the naturi meant stopping Rowe, but I couldn't accomplish that alone. I had no idea what the wind clan was capable of, but I was willing to bet there was more to it than just a nice pair of wings. Unfortunately, I had succeeded in pissing off everyone in the Coven, as well as angering and/or scaring the shit out of all the flunkies. I couldn't reach Jabari, Elizabeth would rather see me dead at the hands of Rowe after what I did to Gwen, and Macaire . . . well, the only way I could reach Macaire was through the flunkies, and that wasn't going to happen. My only potential contact inside the Great Hall was Sadira. I could have screamed. No matter what I did, I kept wading deeper and deeper into the mire until there was simply no escape.

With a shrug, I made a show of dusting off my hands as I rose to my feet. I was on my own. "Fine. You can have the island. I'm sure this is the only way you can tolerate being surrounded by humans."

"I have to know, Mira," Rowe began, halting me before I could take my first step. "Do you regret your decision?"

"No," I said, far too quickly to be convincing.

A low chuckle rippled from Rowe as he shook his head at me.

There was no question about what decision he was refer-

ring to. He had given me a chance to change sides, to help
the naturi in exchange for their protection. I chose my kind
without hesitation, but within minutes questioned whether it
had truly been the wisest choice. If anything, I realized that
I should be searching for a third option instead of trying to
figure out which was the lesser of the two evils.

"No? You're pleased, yet you run away to the one place in
this wretched city where there's not a single vampire to be
found?" he said. Rowe threaded a loose stand of hair behind
his ear, keeping it from blocking his one good eye. Between
his long black hair and the leather eye patch, he still reminded me of a pirate straight from a romance novel.

A smirk twisted on my lips as I looked up into the tree at
my enemy. "I like the view of the city from here."

His head snapped up to look out across the island. Another low laugh drifted down from the tree to me. From the
ground, the only thing that could be seen in all directions
was the massive brick wall that edged the island like a piece
of industrial strength lace. I wanted to keep him laughing. It
meant that he wasn't trying to kill me. Rowe's laughter was
better than Nerian's. My old tormentor's laughter haunted
me, skipping back from memories that were sealed away
under blocks of steel and concrete. Nerian's laughter was the
sound of madness and pain.

"I made a mistake with you," Rowe unexpectedly announced, again stopping me from walking back toward the
gate I'd used to enter the cemetery.

"What? When you helped Nerian torture me? Or when
you tried to grab me in Egypt?" My indifferent, easygoing
tone withered. "No, wait! You mean when you threatened to
poison me in London."

"No, none of that was a mistake," he replied with a wave
of his hand. "I mean when we first met."

"Machu Picchu," I supplied. I honestly didn't remember

him being there, but he'd said on more than one occasion that he had. And maybe it was true. There were a lot of things that were blurry about my two-week captivity on that mountain. I might have blocked him out.

Rowe dropped down from the tree branch he had been standing on, landing only a few feet from where I stood. I immediately darted backward, putting more than twenty feet between us, and even that still felt too close. Surprisingly, he lifted both hands, palms out, giving the international sign that "It's all good." Of course, I was hoping that was what the gesture meant in naturi.

"You honestly don't remember me," he said softly, staring at me with a strange intensity. His large black wings were hidden now and he vaguely reminded me of a somewhat muscular elf, without the pointed ears, of course.

"No, I don't remember you," I snapped, pacing to my left then back again. The ground was sloped and the grass was slick under my feet. Not the best location for a fight. "There's a lot about Machu Picchu I don't care to remember."

"We met in Spain," Rowe corrected.

I jerked to a halt, my lips parting at this sudden bit of unexpected news. Had he been among those who kidnapped me from Spain and took me to Peru?

"It's been more than six centuries," he continued. "I looked different, but you haven't changed much. Your hair seemed longer, and you were human. Sort of."

"You're lying," I whispered, shaken to my very soul. He knew me when I was human. That didn't seem possible. Was I a magnet for these twisted creatures? Sadira had found me living on a small farm in Greece, the nearest village almost a day's walk away. And now Rowe claimed to have known me during my brief human years.

"It was four hours from sunset and you were sitting near the edge of a lake," Rowe stated. His voice grew harder and colder with each new detail. His hands fell limp back at his sides. "You sat in the sun wearing a green dress. A strand of black pearls was woven through your hair."

While my memory of that day had faded during the long stretch of years, his memory remained crisp and fresh. But there was no question of the day he was recalling. I had worn that dress just once and then burned it, destroying the last bits of my human life. Rowe had met me on the last day that I was human.

A fine trembling started in my fingers and a knot jerked tight in the pit of my stomach. I started to shake my head, denying what he was saying, when the fog around my own memory started to clear. A man had walked up out of the nearby woods. He was tall and lean, with bright green eyes, the same shade as wet grass after a summer storm. His shoulder-length hair was a pale blond almost like milky sunlight.

"I warned you . . . that the landowner didn't—"

"Like trespassers," Rowe finished. He leaned against the tree he had been perched in only moments ago. A soft laugh escaped him as he tilted his head back, staring up at the canopy. "I would never have guessed you were talking about a flock of vampires."

"I was only trying to keep you from being dinner," I replied. I couldn't raise my voice above a whisper as my mind struggled to comprehend this information.

"And I let you slip through my fingers," he muttered, looking at me again. "I came out of the woods because I sensed you. Something strange sitting on the edge of the lake. Not naturi. And yet, not quite human. A little bundle of energy as warm and sweet as a zephyr."

"Human," I firmly said. "I was human."

Rowe shrugged his broad shoulders at my comment. "Maybe." His eyes then narrowed on me and a frown pulled at his lips. "You managed to convince me back then. 'I wanted to see the sun one last time,'" he mimicked in a high falsetto voice that sounded nothing like me.

"It was the last time I ever saw the sun," I confirmed.

"I thought you were dying," he barked, pushing off the tree, but he didn't approach me. He stared at me, his fists clenched at his sides. "Humans were dropping dead all over the land. I thought you would too."

That was part of the reason Sadira offered to change me. The Black Plague had swept through Europe for several years, and she began to fear that I wouldn't be able to escape it. If I caught the illness, she could not heal me and would have had to watch me die. So she offered to change me into a nightwalker. I'd recently discovered that there was much more to it than that, of course, but none of that was a part of my own memories, so to me Sadira remained my maker alone.

"No, I had another kind of death in mind," I murmured.

"Aarrgh!" Rowe shouted, shoving both of his hands angrily through his hair as he took one step toward me then back over to the tree. "If I'd done something that day— anything—so much could have been different. If I had just killed you then, or taken you away from those vampires, everything would have been different," he ranted.

It was an interesting viewpoint that I had not considered. If I had not been at Machu Picchu, the naturi would have most likely opened the door and returned to the earth. Things would have been vastly different if I had not lived. After looking back on so many of my seemingly harmless decisions that had gone horribly wrong during the past several days, it was nice to be faced with someone dealing with the same horror. Six hundred years ago, if Rowe had killed a somewhat strange human, his wife-queen would be walking the earth beside him along with the rest of the naturi horde.

They would not be facing the battle that was looming now. A broad smile danced across my lips and brightened my eyes. I wasn't the only one to royally screw up without realizing it until it was far too late to fix.

"We would be free," he said in a low voice full of wistful longing.

My smile withered. "And I would be dead. Countless humans and nightwalkers and lycans would be dead. The bori would be free. The old war would start again," I said, my voice gaining strength for the first time since I had seen Rowe.

"You think the bori would be free if the naturi returned?" he countered, leaning against the tree again. He seemed to have gotten over his moment of frustration, but then, he'd been dealing with that little bit of truth for more than five hundred years.

"Of course. It's the only option any non-naturi would have left." I took a couple steps closer to him, shoving my fingers into the front pockets of my leather pants. "When the nightwalkers discover that we have no way of defeating you, we would find a way to set the bori free, your one and only equal in power."

"It's a sad future you paint," Rowe said with a shake of his head.

"It doesn't have to be that way," I said, a wide grin returning to my face. "You could walk away now. Give up these plans to break the seal forever and let the naturi return to obscurity."

To my surprise, Rowe snorted again and folded his arms over his chest. "You would protect me from my kind?"

I smiled. It was the same offer he had made to me nights ago. Change sides. Betray your own people. "Of course."

"I was serious, Mira. You don't belong with them."

"I am nightwalker, Rowe. It's the only place I belong."

He sighed, then frowned at me as if disappointed. "Regardless, getting rid of me won't solve your problems." I noticed that as he spoke, his eyes darted back toward the wall over my shoulder. Toward the Coven and the female naturi within the Great Hall.

"Probably not, but it would be a great starting point," I conceded. "Of course, I'm getting the feeling that I should start with the female on that island you keep looking at. A friend of yours? Or maybe she keeps you warm at night, considering the little woman is stuck on the other side."

There was no mistaking the snarl that jumped from the back of Rowe's throat. The light banter we had enjoyed early was over and it was now time to get down to business. I just hoped I survived the next few minutes. While I could comfortably contend that killing him would halt the naturi's attempts to break the seal, my death would also ensure that nightwalkers had no way of reforming the seal or closing the door again if the naturi actually succeeded.

"You know of her?" he demanded, to which my grin only grew. Rowe took a couple steps toward me, and I matched him by stepping backward. The air seemed to swell with energy. The wind picked up, causing the trees to violently sway. I chanced a glance up at the night sky to see the clouds churning and bubbling like witch's brew. The stars had been blotted out and a low roll of thunder growled in the distance.

"I can sense her on the island, yet I cannot reach her," he admitted, and it was more than a little reassuring to discover that at least the naturi couldn't break through our protective barriers. "Nightwalkers control that island."

"Venice belongs to us," I said. "It has belonged to us for centuries and it will remain ours. Are you surprised there are places in this world that you cannot go?" I was playing with fire when it came to taunting Rowe, but playing with fire was what I did best.

"Who do you hold on that island?" he demanded, ignoring my remarks. "She's a captive."

Something in his voice gave me pause. A slight hesitation or a breathless pause that could be easily overlooked. He had intended it to sound like a statement, but it didn't. Not only was he unsure of who was on the island, but he was also unsure whether she was actually a hostage.

"Now that is an interesting question," I slowly said. "Unfortunately, you're the only living naturi I know. The rest tend to die quickly upon meeting me."

Thunder rumbled again, louder this time, the storm drawing closer. Rowe growled as his arm shot up into the air. Less than a second later a bolt of lightning plummeted to the ground, striking no more than three feet from where I stood. I jumped away, landing in a heap before rolling back to my feet. The air still tingled with the electricity hanging in the atmosphere along with the scent of burnt ozone.

Rowe's hand shook slightly as he lowered it back to his side. There was no missing the intent look on his face as he watched me. I was getting a firsthand look at the powers of the wind naturi. Not only could they fly, but apparently they could also control the weather. I would never survive a lightning strike, and I knew he could kill me before I could incinerate him.

"Hmmm," I mocked, desperately trying to hide my mounting fear behind sarcasm. "Killing me may solve some of your problems, but it won't help you discover the identity of the little naturi hiding on the island."

"Hiding? What do you mean 'hiding'?"

I laughed at him, but swallowed the sound when Rowe started to raise his arm again. Lightning darted among the rolling clouds, illuminating each black giant for a blink of an eye before plunging all back into darkness again. Gritting my teeth, I took a desperate chance. I ran straight at Rowe.

The air tingled and the ground shook as another lightning bolt struck the ground directly behind me.

Slamming his back into the tree, I wrapped my fists in his red shirt and leaned in so my nose nearly touched his. "You may be able to control the lightning, but I am willing to bet you can't survive a lightning strike. So the question becomes, how badly do you want to see me dead?"

"That's an interesting wager," he replied. His green eyes narrowed on mine and a smirk twisted his lips.

There was no mistaking the surge of energy that crackled and snapped around us. He was pulling the energy from the earth and I could sense it; something that should not be happening. Nightwalkers lost all connection with the earth when we were reborn.

The sensation from the building power was both amazing and painful, biting at my flesh and gnawing on my bones. The energy was trying to find a way into my body, but it was at odds with what I was. Nightwalkers were creatures of blood magic. We couldn't do earth magic. Or at least that's what I had always been led to believe.

"Of course, we both know that killing me won't get you any closer to finding out about your missing female," I said, just trying to buy a few seconds. "And we've both seen what a joke kidnapping me is."

"I'm sure I can come up with some other options."

"While you're at it, why not try thinking of a reason as to why a naturi may be ensconced on an island filled with nightwalkers and not be threatened?" I pulled my face away from his so I could clearly look into his eyes without going cross-eyed myself. Some of the anger had slipped from his features as he thoughtfully stared at me. Standing so close, I could see the scars that snaked across the right side of his face and disappeared behind his eye patch. I remembered that when we met years ago, there were only a couple faint scars along his neck but nothing else. Once, he was pale and blond and nearly perfect, but now he stood before me dark and scarred. What had he been through that could possibly scar a naturi like this?

"I think you've got bigger problems than just me," I said, slowly releasing my grip on his shirt. I knew that the naturi on San Clemente was not a hostage, but part of some bargain the Coven was working out. Meanwhile, Rowe knew there was a naturi on the island but had no idea who it was or why she was there, which indicated that he had not sent her. He was not a part of whatever this other naturi and the Coven were cooking up. I wasn't the only one who was being betrayed in Venice.

I winked at him one last time as I backed away, hoping I had finally given him enough to think about so I could escape to a more populated location. "Just a word of advice," I said. "I'd get all your ducks in a row before trying again in four nights."

Before I could slip away, Rowe roughly grabbed both of my shoulders, holding me just inches from his body. A wicked grin split his mouth and laughter danced in his one good eye. "You say you don't remember me being at Machu Picchu," he murmured. "Let me see if I can jog your memory."

To my utter shock, he jerked me close and pressed his lips against mine. I stood frozen, my brain completely locked up in a mix of disbelief and revulsion. And something even worse happened. I realized that his touch, his smell, his taste were all too familiar. I pushed against him violently, pulling out of his grasp as I stumbled backward. His mocking laughter followed me, but I was only vaguely aware of it as my thoughts flew back to my time at Machu Picchu.

"You were in the cave," I choked out past the lump in my throat.

"You still thought I was human," Rowe taunted.

I had been exhausted, weighed down by pain and star-vation after being tortured for more than a week. An hour before sunrise, they returned me to the caves that made up the Temple of the Moon. Only this time there was a pale blond human in there already. I didn't think about how or why. Through the fog of pain, I only saw the human I had met by the lake.

"You said they'd kill you," I whimpered, bringing a dark laugh from my companion. Rowe had told me they would kill him if I didn't do as the naturi ordered. He pleaded with me to save his life, but I couldn't betray my people to save the life of one human. When they came for him, I pulled on the chains that bound my hands behind my back. I tried to set them on fire, but I was too weak. All I could do was shout and kick as the naturi approached, tears streaming down my dirty face.

As they grabbed my blond-haired companion, he had leaned down and kissed me. I remembered the softness of his lips, the taste of sweetness in his mouth like ripe ber-ries. I could smell him, a mix of earth and desperation. He pleaded with me one last time to save him, but all I could do was weep for him as they dragged him out, the words lodged behind the lump in my throat.

I stared horrified at Rowe now, all the memories rushing back with startling clarity. I had wept endless tears for him, guilt eating away at me like acid. I had forced myself to forget about him because his memory nearly destroyed me. I thought I had sacrificed an innocent man to save my own kind from extermination.

"You may have forgotten me, but I never forgot the taste of the tears you cried for me," he said in a low voice.

I wrapped my arms around my middle, nearly hunched over in pain. They had nearly destroyed me with a trick, nearly broken me. Even now, after so many centuries, the pain felt so fresh.

Rowe simply smiled at me, making no move to stop me as I backed away from him. "It was the will of the fates you survived our first two encounters so many years ago. Your life will benefit me one day."

Shaking my head, there was nothing I could say. I blinked back tears of humiliation as I slowly walked back toward the entrance. That night at Machu Picchu replayed in my head over and over again with each step, increasing my endless hatred for the entire race.

A low rumble of thunder followed me back to the boat, but the lightning remained locked within the clouds. Rowe was still laughing at me.

Fifteen

The sun slid back beneath the earth, its long rays of light clawing at the sky in a desperate attempt to find some last second purchase. The world sighed and shuddered, shaking off the day's tight grasp like shedding a skin it had outgrown. I didn't see the sun's steady descent into darkness, but I could feel the birth of a new night. The subtle shift of the nocturnal world as it yawned and stretched, ready for a night of hunting, rippled through me.

Tristan lay silent last night in the bed after returning from the Coven, lost somewhere between Sadira's betrayal and my failure to protect him. I'm sure his mind had replayed his time with the court in all its gory detail. He'd come so close to dying in that place of permanent night and horrors.

I should never have left him alone with Sadira, completely underestimating her need to strike out at me. The court could have easily destroyed him, and Sadira had already proven that he was dispensable if it meant breaking me. Protecting Tristan was going to be harder than I'd anticipated, and he had paid the price for my foolishness and ego. His encounter in the Great Hall was my fault. We both knew now that neither of us would ever be completely free until Sadira was dead and gone. But at the moment, he slept deeply beside me on the bed, curled up in the fetal position, the blankets twisted around his naked body.

Hesitantly, I reached over and smoothed some of the soft locks from his face. Full dark was still more than an hour away, and he was immersed in the deep, healing sleep of our people. Blissful darkness consumed his thoughts, and for a time the memory of Sadira's betrayal and my failure were no doubt wiped away. He would have to face those memories again all too soon, but for now there was only nothingness.

I stared down at his beautiful form, cool and limp. A knot lodged in my throat and I blinked back a swell of tears that blurred my vision. My sweet, beautiful Tristan with the fragile, playful smile. In him, I saw both a child and a brother. Brought into the darkness by the same nightwalker, we were of the same bloodline. Yet, he was so much younger and weaker. His very existence seemed so tenuous.

Jabari had saved me five hundred years ago from Sadira, bringing me out of the shadow of pain and despair. Was it my job to save Tristan now? How could I when I could barely protect myself? Both Michael and Thorne had died while I watched. Would the young nightwalker be next despite my best efforts?

Touching his hair again, I wished his peace would last. I wished for his wounds to heal, on the outside as well as the scars on the inside, but I feared it would all be for nothing. Just nights ago I had professed to James that nightwalkers were more than monsters. I told him that we felt joy and that we loved. Yet hadn't the bloody mess that they'd made of Tristan's back when they peeled the skin from his body proven that wrong? Hadn't the fact that I reveled in the bloodbath I created proven that wrong? How could one monster ever succeed in protecting another monster?

Sparing a glance to find that his back had healed from last night's debacle, I pushed off the bed. Never in my long existence had I risen so early. I had been called. I could feel Valerio in my head the second consciousness came flooding into my brain, and then he pulled away, leaving behind a faint impression on my lips, as if he'd kissed me. Standing in the silent room, I inhaled deeply, half expecting to catch a faint whiff of his scent, and my brain even told me for a second that I did, but I knew he had never been in the room. His presence in my thoughts had been so strong that it left a mark on all of my senses.

But that was Valerio, as silent as a shade and as ubiquitous as the wind. He was a ghost from my past that I could never quite shake off. But then, there was the question of whether I truly wanted to shed his long-reaching touch.

The sound of the door to the hotel room closing jerked me from my thoughts. I grabbed the ankle-length silk robe from where I'd tossed it over a chair and quickly pulled it on. I was still tying the sash of the hotel robe when I stepped into the main salon. Danaus was pushing in a cart covered with a white cloth, laden with dishes hidden under silver covers. A dozen scents of rich sauces, cooked meat, and hot coffee suddenly filled the air. It was time for dinner or breakfast. By the smell of it, I was convinced that the hunter was indulging in both.

Danaus abruptly halted, his eyes darting from me to the bay of windows that revealed the distant sunset. The sky was painted deep shades of red, orange, and a heavy purple. It had been centuries since I last looked on such colors in the sky.

"Did you have any problems last night?" I stiffly inquired. With my arms folded over my stomach, I walked over to the windows, ignoring the silent question resting in his narrowed eyes. The fading sunlight made my eyes burn, and I blinked back bloody tears but didn't move. I wasn't sure if I would ever see the sunset again, and I wanted to soak in the colors while I could.

"No. You?"

"Nothing important." I tried to sound nonchalant and indifferent about last night, but failed. Those two words came out sounding weary and ragged. My encounter with Rowe and the slaughter at the Great Hall had left me torn in two.

"Mira?" I hadn't heard him move, but he sounded closer now. Just a few feet away, standing directly behind me. The scent of him was strong, a soothing mix of soap and the sun, with a hint of spice from his cologne or aftershave. A part of me wanted to lean back and rest my shoulders against his strong chest as we shared the sunset in comfortable silence.

"Everything is well," I said, pushing aside the silly urge.

"It would be easier to protect each other if I understood what was happening," he firmly said. "Who took Sadira and Tristan?"

I opened my mouth to say that it was none of his business and that I had it all under control, but another set of words came tumbling out. "Sadira took Tristan to the court of the Coven to punish me. He was tortured until I arrived."

"Did you destroy Sadira?" The words escaped his throat, sounding matter-of-fact, his question holding no emotion or inflection. I couldn't decide whether he would condemn or praise me for my actions.

"She still exists, though I'm sure she wishes she didn't," I finally replied.

"And the Coven?"

"Who knows what they think? They weren't present at the time. They will only act when it is to their benefit." Biting back a sigh, I turned on my bare right heel to face him. I needed to get moving. Valerio had woken me for a reason. He wanted something, and I didn't want him showing up there. "I have another meeting tonight."

"Alone?"

"Naturally," I said with a little smirk, which faded almost as quickly as it appeared.

"What about the Coven and their arrangement with the naturi?" Danaus inquired.

"I haven't forgotten. We have to stop it, or it could mean war among all of the races, along with fighting a war against the naturi. No one would survive such a thing."

"Don't you find it odd that Jabari demanded we come here, risking us discovering their grand plot?"

A smile brightened my features and exposed my fangs briefly. "Yes, I do," I said, almost chuckling. "I'm beginning to think that not everyone is of one mind on the Coven."

"And it's our job to destroy the bargain," Danaus finished with a nod.

"Destroy the naturi trying to break the seal. Destroy the Coven's bargain with the naturi."

"It's what we do best," Danaus said. A fleeting smile slipped across his face.

"True, but we may need some help, hence the meeting." I glanced over my shoulder one last time as the colors in the sky continued to fade. "Stay close to Tristan while I'm gone. Don't let him out of your sight," I commanded, not caring how the hunter felt about my issuing orders to a creature more than three times my age.

"Do you think they'll come after him again?"

I cocked my head to the side as an odd thought skipped through my brain. "Would you protect him if they did?" I softly asked, my eyes drifting over his hard features. Danaus's eyes darted across the room and his frown deepened as he paced a few steps away from me. I doubt either one of us knew the answer to that question. I opened my mouth to push on when he suddenly spoke, his voice like a distant rumble of thunder in the quiet room. "I would protect him against the creatures that hurt him last night."

I wouldn't go into detail about what happened to the young nightwalker last night. That was Tristan's choice. But

I had no doubt that Danaus felt my pain and rage. I had not attempted to shield him.

A slow smile grew on my lips, and my eyes glowed dark lavender with the memory of the bloodbath. "Those creatures no longer exist," I purred.

Danaus nodded, the frown disintegrating from his face. I was surprised. There was no disgust or disappointment in his eyes when he looked at me. All I could feel from him was a sense of peace and calm.

I blinked and the glow disappeared from my eyes, the swell of power slipping from my form as if caught up by a light breeze. "No, that is not why I want you to stay with Tristan. I fear the court may come after you next."

"And you expect him to protect me?" he asked incredulously.

"No," I said, a smile trembling on my lips. "Tristan and I are connected. I can feel his emotions and see through his eyes. I will know if you are troubled."

"Unlike our connection?" he asked, arching one thick brow at me.

"Our connection weakens with time and distance," I replied sharply. "It is also a connection I do not wish to cultivate, and would prefer it to die completely." I was still unnerved by the way his mind had touched mine last night, slowly scanning my body for the injury I'd sustained. But now the contact had dissipated, and I was only vaguely aware of his emotions, much like most humans.

Danaus simply nodded, wisely refraining from commenting on the fact that I hadn't known Tristan was in trouble last night until it was too late. But then again, I had taken care of that problem last night. Sadira wouldn't cause any problems for a long time.

As I turned to go back into the bedroom to throw on some clothes, Danaus pointed out a large box that had been delivered to the room a couple hours earlier. I shook my head as I carried it into the bedroom with me, knowing without opening it who had sent it. Valerio believed that appearance was everything in keeping up a facade.

Placing the large, white garment box on the bed, I pulled off the lid. Inside I found a black silk camisole and a white wrap made of antique lace. The straight, black skirt fell to my calves and was slit up the back. And of course, a pair of heels that had wide black ribbons that wrapped around my ankles. Quickly dressing, I decided at the last minute to leave my hair down. I took one last glance in the mirror and couldn't quite fight back the small smile that rose on my lips. The outfit was elegant and appropriately conservative. Yet, it still somehow managed to be sexy and alluring with its tiny flashes of pale skin. If Valerio could divert his attention long enough from fashion and keeping up appearances, he could be a truly dangerous figure.

I was still smiling when I strode out of the suite and rode the elevator down to the lobby. It had been on the tip of my tongue to warn Danaus that Rowe was in the area as I slipped from the room, but I knew if I mentioned the naturi's name, I would never be able to attend this meeting without his dark shadow. Besides, Danaus could at least sense the naturi, making him better protected. He didn't need my warning.

When I entered the large marble lobby to the hotel, the sun had finished its descent in the horizon and the night took over. My footsteps nearly stumbled at the sudden surge of power that rippled through the air. For a brief moment my body felt more awake and alive, connected to something larger than myself. But just as suddenly the feeling faded, leaving me aware and calm. I was back in my element.

A soft chuckle drew my gaze across the nearly empty room. Valerio folded the newspaper he was pretending to read and laid it aside as he pushed out of his chair.

Valerio was the classical image of a vampire. Not the rotting, shambling corpse with breath that smelled like death, but the Hollywood version with brown hair and pale blue eyes like a glacier kissed by the sea. His cadaverous white skin was stretched over lean muscle, created by a human life spent at hard manual labor and an undead existence filled with constant physical activity. He was shorter than me, but not by much. It was not something easily noticed either. When the nightwalker entered a room, his presence filled it in such an overwhelming way that you couldn't be aware of anyone or anything else. He became everything and was everywhere.

Handsome was an inadequate word to describe him. He was beautiful in the same fashion Michelangelo's David was beautiful or the Venus de Milo. He possessed the same type of beauty as a summer sunset on the Mediterranean with a full moon rising in the distance. Awe-inspiring. Breathtaking. The type of peaceful, exquisite beauty that made you want to believe in a God or that there was good left in the world. It was the kind of beauty that convinced you to hold on for just one more day.

But it was more than his appearance that fulfilled the image humans now clung to when it came to vampires. It was also his manner. Calm, unshakable confidence oozed from every pore and controlled the muscles in his lean frame. It was in his walk and the way he stood, poised and always aware of his surroundings. He possessed the same seductive beauty as a sleeping jaguar. Beautiful and infinitely deadly when awakened.

Sadira taught me concepts like power and control when dealing in the world of nightwalkers. Jabari gave me the concepts of loyalty and honor, instilling within me a sense of history for my kind. But Valerio taught me how to live as a nightwalker and how to live with myself. He opened my eyes to the world of pleasure and joy. I learned to laugh again. Valerio gave my kind a new reason to fear me. I learned how to play games with my prey, both physical and mental, to induce equal parts happiness and fear.

When I left both Sadira and Jabari, I had never looked back. I stepped from their shadow and pursued my own life, in a fashion. But I had yet to completely shed Valerio. Years withered away and I found myself once again seated in an elegant parlor or strolling down a rat-infested alley with Valerio smiling at my side. I'd leave him with unspoken words like "Never again" balanced on the tip of my tongue, but knew better than to say it. Our paths always found a way to cross.

I had no idea how old he was. Old enough. He had such a quiet, unobtrusive way about him that I couldn't begin to guess the extent of his powers, but none dared to cross him, and he gave few reason to do so. Was he born chum, or was he a First Blood? I couldn't even begin to guess.

I didn't fear him, and I knew that it might prove to be my greatest mistake. I didn't trust him and was extremely cautious around him, but my lack of fear could prove to be the end of me. If anything, Valerio had taught me to fear myself.

Walking over to where I stood, a patronizing smile lifted his full lips, revealing a hint of white teeth. "*Cara* Mira," he chuckled, an Italian accent faintly lacing his words. "I had forgotten you usually sleep late, missing out on the birth of the night."

"What is it you wanted to see me about?" I demanded, overcoming my momentary surprise that he had chosen to speak in English. It was a struggle to keep from crossing my arms over my chest. I didn't want him to see how tense I was, but I had no doubt he could read it in the stiffness of my shoulders and the frown that pulled at the corners of my lips.

"Where is your companion? The hunter?" he asked, shoving his hands in his pockets.

"In the suite. I assumed you wanted a private meeting."

"Oh, I do," he said, his smile widening. Valerio took one last step forward, the lapels of his jacket briefly brushing against my breasts. His left hand snatched up my right hand from where it dangled limp at my side and he placed his right hand on my waist as he forced me into a quick waltz around the lobby. If we hadn't been cloaked from the gaze of the people who lingered in the expansive entrance, I'm sure we would have earned more than a few strange stares. "I've been waiting to discuss a few things with you, sweet Mira."

Tilting my head down slightly so I could look him in the eye, Valerio took advantage of our closeness to press his lips to mine. My body reacted to the familiar contact before my brain had a chance to step in. We stopped moving and I leaned into his hard frame, relaxing at his touch as my eyes drifted shut. His right hand slid from my waist to my back, pulling me tightly against his frame. His familiar touch eased the tension from my shoulders and it drained from the muscles in my limbs. His scent teased my nose as if trying to call up some of the good memories I had packed away of him. For some strange reason, the nightwalker smelled of cinnamon.

But it was wrong. My thoughts finally surfaced above the sensations vibrating in my frame. Valerio was trouble. He was another manipulator and killer. And the kiss was no different than the one I had received from Rowe, leaving me feeling used and dirty. More of my nights with Valerio had been washed in blood than all my years with Sadira and Jabari. The only difference being that Valerio had made it fun, where his predecessors had turned it into a nightmare.

Breaking off the kiss, I pushed against his chest. The nightwalker didn't fight me, allowing me to take a few steps out of his embrace. Rubbing my eyes, I shook my head, marveling at how quickly I had been swept up in him. "Don't touch me," I said in a cold, hard voice.

"I've missed you, Mira," he murmured, drawing my gaze back to his face.

I snorted, stifling the bitter laugh that nearly escaped. "And last night you were calling me a traitor. I'm no fool, Valerio."

"Foolish, sometimes, but never a fool," he said. His smile widened to reveal a pair of perfect white fangs.

Waving my hand dismissively at him, I turned to pace away from him when the sound of my muffled footsteps caught my attention. I looked down at the thick white carpet that covered the floor. The hotel lobby was entirely filled with marble. My gaze jerked up to find that I was no longer standing in the lobby of the Cipriani, but in a salon with antique furniture.

"Damn it, Valerio!" I growled, stalking over to one of the curtained windows on the far wall. "Where the hell am I?" The decor was unlike anything I had seen in the Cipriani. In fact, it didn't remind me of anything I'd seen in Venice.

"Somewhere private," he replied.

Ignoring him, I grabbed the curtains in my fists and jerked them open to reveal concrete where the canals had once been. I glanced up and down the street but didn't immediately recognize any of the buildings. A knot of panic tightened in my stomach and I forced myself to release my hold on the curtains before I sent them up in flames. "Where the hell am I?" I snarled, turning back to face the nightwalker. He still stood in the center of the room, his hands in his pockets again. My flare of temper had no effect on his mien of perfect calm.

"In my private apartment in Vienna," he said with a slight shrug.

"Vienna, Austria?" I shouted. "Send me back now." I was furious with him and myself. He had kissed me so I wouldn't notice the push through space, and I let it happen, hoping for a moment to erase the memory of Rowe's kiss. I wanted to ask when he had gained the ability to disappear and reappear across vast distances like Jabari. It was a skill I had never seen him display before, and it made me more than a little nervous. Only the Ancients had such a skill, and Valerio never admitted to being more than one thousand years old.

"We need to talk Mira and we cannot do that in Venice," he calmly said.

"I will not let the court hurt Tristan again or threaten Danaus. Send me back now," I said through clenched teeth, closing in on him. "First Nicolai, and now you. I always thought the role of distraction was beneath you."

"I am not acting on behalf of the Coven or its pets," he continued, unmoved by my rage. "I left the island last night shortly before you did and have not returned to San Clemente. I do not know what the Coven plans for you today, but I promise that my bringing you here is not an attempt to threaten those that belong to you."

"Then send me back," I stubbornly repeated. My anger was ebbing, but frustration was still evident in my voice. I was afraid Jabari or anyone else on the Coven would sense that I was no longer in Venice. They would jump at the opportunity to attack Danaus and Tristan. I had to protect them, but I couldn't do that when I was several countries away.

"I cannot. We must talk and I do not feel safe doing so in Venice," he finally admitted. I paused, noticing for the first time a tension around the corners of his eyes and an unusual brittleness in his smile. "Reach out and touch Tristan's mind. See that he is safe. Touch the hunter's mind."

I frowned but said nothing. Touching Danaus's mind

was tricky and I doubted if I could do it from that distance. However, I did reach out and touch Tristan's thoughts. He was just awakening from his daylight slumber. His thoughts were sluggish and confused, but he was calm.

When I met Valerio's gaze again, my frown eased a bit. The nightwalker's shoulders slumped slightly as some of the tension flowed from his body. "So now you believe me?" he gently asked, a soft smile haunting his lips again.

"For the moment," I snorted, walking away from him. The door between my mind and Tristan's was left open a crack. I wasn't in his mind reading his thoughts because I wanted to give him some privacy, but the constant connection would allow me to know the second anything was wrong.

I returned to the far wall and pulled open the curtains on the three windows there, giving me the opportunity to look out on the grand old city. It had been a long time since I last visited Vienna, and my reason for leaving then had been grim. Yet, the long, endless years had dulled the pain and muted the memories. I was more disturbed now by the fact that the pain I thought I should be feeling was little more than a hollow ache.

"I haven't lied to you, Mira," Valerio continued. There was a whisper of cloth rubbing as he walked over to me. "I have missed you."

"You were never one to lie, Valerio. You just preferred to omit crucial information," I said, not bothering to turn to look at him, but continued to stare out the window. My hands rested on the smooth wooden windowsill, letting the tips of my fingers absently trace the fine lines created when the white paint dried.

Laying his hands on my shoulders, his strong fingers kneaded my tense muscles, rubbing away the several days' worth of tension. Slowly, he let his hands slide down my arms, pulling away the lace wrap to bare my shoulders. "We were so good together," he whispered, gently pressing a kiss to my right shoulder. "Remember our fun in Morocco? I don't think we stirred from that apartment for nearly two weeks."

"Or the bars after the bullfights in Pamplona," I volunteered with a little laugh. "It was a shame about the matador. I don't think he ever properly recovered."

"What's that American saying? He could have been a contender," he chuckled, pressing another kiss to my bare skin, only this time a slight whisper of teeth grazed my flesh. Only after his chuckles died did he speak again. His voice was heartwrenchingly soft, like an ex-lover's touch on my cheek. "Since traveling to the New World, you have not returned to visit."

"You could have come to the United States," I countered, twisting around slightly so I could look him in the eye. "You obviously have the ability to make it a quick trip."

"You never invited me."

My brows furrowed and my eyes narrowed at his strange comment. "My domain is a single city within the country. That's all. You don't need me to invite you into the country should you wish to visit."

"Most would question such a statement from you. It is well known that nightwalkers within that country defer to your judgment in most matters, particularly if they wish to continue their existence. Don't lie to me or yourself. You know your reach extends far beyond the boundaries of your quaint city."

Turning completely around to face Valerio, I stepped away from his touch. The fresh smile on my lips wilted and died in a breath. "I know the question without reading your mind: Do I plan to take the empty seat on the Coven? I'll tell you what I've told everyone else. No. I don't want the seat. I don't want anything to do with the Coven."

Valerio threw his head back and laughed. The noise seemed to echo and skip as he sped to the opposite end of the room and plopped down in a comfortable chair.

"Mira, my little firefly, maybe you should wonder why so many are asking you that question," he suggested with a chuckle. "You've set up your own little kingdom in the New World."

"My domain is only the city of Savannah," I interrupted.

"But you've hunted and destroyed nightwalkers who were a threat to the secret from one coast to the other in that darling country," Valerio countered. He folded his hands over his stomach as he rested his left ankle on his right knee.

"At the request of the Coven."

"A group you've never hidden your lack of respect for. And now you're back in Venice after being absent for more than fifty years—"

"Again, at the request of the Coven," I interjected, but my voice was losing strength and my fingers were shaking. I was beginning to see all my actions in a new, horrible light.

"Maybe so, but you walk in with your head held high and a nightwalker killer in tow, making no secret that he is under your protection." I had no argument to make against his words, so he continued, laughter filling his voice. "Then, as if to top it all off, the pièce de résistance, you steal one of your own maker's children from her and stage a bloodbath in the Great Hall I've not seen the likes of in more than a few centuries. Hell, probably not since you appeared before the court the last time."

"Valerio," I whispered, his words crushing my throat. "I don't want a seat on the Coven. I'm just trying to survive."

"Survive?" he gasped, sending him into new peaks of incredulous laughter. "Surviving would be keeping your head down and your mouth shut. Surviving would be allowing the court to have its fun with Tristan and the hunter. Surviving is not pissing off both your maker and members of the Coven."

He pushed out of his chair and was at my side in a flash. His large hands cupped my cheeks and his thumbs wiped away tears I hadn't realized were falling. "I have always marveled at the cautious way you've lived your life," he softly began again, his sweet voice a gentle caress on my frayed nerves and fractured thoughts. "But recently you've acted in such an impulsive fashion. I can't begin to fathom why you've acted with such a suicidal fervor unless you truly wish to die."

Lifting my haunted eyes to meet his confused gaze, I wet my lips and forced the two words past the lump in my throat. "The naturi."

I could feel the jerk in his muscles as he flinched at my whispered words, but his hands didn't fall from my cheeks as his gaze narrowed into cold blue slits of ice.

"The naturi are coming," I continued.

"What are you talking about, dearest?" he demanded. His deep voice was firm, but not as steady as I would have preferred, as his hands dropped from my face.

Closing my eyes, I drew in a deep breath, catching the hint of cinnamon mixed with the scent of roses in a crystal vase on the other side of the room. When I looked at Valerio again, I launched into my tale, starting with Nerian in my own domain and stretching through the attacks in Egypt and London. I told him of the massacre at Themis and the discovery that not only would Danaus be a part of the triad that would push back the naturi, but that I was also the weapon they would wield. I even told him of the female naturi that appeared to walk freely in the Great Hall. I talked until my throat was raw and choked with tears I was no longer willing to shed. I spoke of fear and blinding pain and night after night of death until I was sure that the grim reaper himself now hounded my every step.

I talked until there were no more words and I was on my knees, shaking and exhausted by just the memory of everything that had happened and the horror still to come. Looking up, I found Valerio standing on the opposite side of the room, one hand resting on the wall as if to steady himself. His beautiful face was blank except for the look of horror he could not push from his eyes. The distance between us made me feel as if my very presence carried with it a pestilence that would destroy all of our kind, and maybe it did. Those around me didn't seem to live long lives.

It suddenly dawned on me that he probably didn't believe me. If I hadn't lived through it, I would have claimed it all was madness. The naturi hadn't been seen in centuries, seeming content to fade into oblivion.

"Doors," he suddenly said, the word coming out ragged and breathless. Valerio turned his eyes to finally meet mine and he slowly pushed away from the wall. He took a couple steps closer to me but maintained a large distance. "In the lower levels beneath the hall, great iron doors were placed before the rooms where we sleep during the daylight hours. Another iron door was placed before one of the rooms, and guards stand at it during at all hours of the day and night. No one dared to ask the Coven why the doors were added, but everyone knows that iron affects only one creature. I spent one day at the Great Hall. At sunrise I no longer find rest within the shelter offered by the Coven. If the Coven does not feel safe on San Clemente, then none of us will be."

"The naturi are coming. The next new moon is in three nights, as well as an old pagan holiday. I think the naturi will try again to break the seal then," I explained. Placing my left hand flat on the floor, I tried to find the will to push back to my feet but couldn't. "I cannot begin to guess at what the Coven plans. You're older than most. I assumed that you might know more."

"I know nothing," he admitted with a shake of his head. "Most of the court is a witless bunch, prone to gossip. If any of them knew what was going on, I believe I would have heard by now."

"Macaire will try soon to meet with me privately," I murmured, dragging my gaze back up to his face. A new frown pulled at his full lips, drawing deep lines of worry in his cheeks. It somehow added to the distinguished age of his features.

"More games," he muttered, absently pacing the room. I had a feeling he was talking to himself more than to me.

"Jabari and I have had . . . a falling out," I said, fumbling for some phrasing to encompass my hatred for a creature I had once loved and respected. Everything fell short of what I needed, but it wasn't important.

"More games," Valerio repeated, sounding more confident.

"I will not be a pawn for the Coven," I firmly stated.

Valerio stopped pacing and looked down at me. A small sad smile slipped across his mouth and glittered in his eyes. "Firefly, that is all you have ever been."

"Even for you?"

His smile grew larger and more sheepish at my question. Extending his hand to me, I ignored it until he finally spoke. "I have never used you as such, but that doesn't mean I wouldn't or won't if the opportunity presented itself."

I hated his answer, but it was the truth, which was more than I was getting from anyone else. Struggling to keep from gritting my teeth, I placed my left hand in his so he could help me to my feet. Yet he paused unexpectedly, staring down at my hand. It was only when I felt his thumb run over my ring finger that I realized he was looking at the ring he had given me a few centuries ago. It was a silver band with ocean waves inscribed in it in an old Grecian style.

"You still have it," he whispered, not trying to keep the surprise from his voice.

"I like the memories," I admitted as he finally pulled me to my feet.

"And the creature those memories are tied to?"

"He's tolerable some nights," I teased, brushing a kiss across his cheek near his ear.

"I believe you found me more than tolerable some nights," he reminded me, his voice dipping down to a husky tone. He still held my hand in his, increasing the pressure slightly. I was being drawn back into him, his allure, his promise of happiness away from all the chaos that seemed to currently rule my life.

"Valerio . . . " I started, but paused when my voice threatened to fracture. When I could finally speak again, the words would drift no higher than a whisper. "What games are you playing?"

The nightwalker looked up at me, a smile back on his lips, but it somehow failed to reach his eyes. "I'm just trying to survive."

He tilted his head back and pressed a kiss to my jaw just below my ear. "We do not have to go back," he whispered, his lips skimming across my cool flesh. "Stay with me. Away from the naturi."

"And keep running from the Coven?" I asked, letting my eyes fall shut. For a moment the idea was truly tempting; more tempting than the fantasy Sadira had dangled before me last night because this one was real. To go back to my nights of hunting and pleasure with Valerio at my side. No more naturi. No more Coven Elders. No more worrying about whether a nightwalker could protect himself without me. No more horrid weight of responsibility dragging me down.

"In time, they will forget about you."

With a sigh, I took a step away from him and blinked back some unexpected tears. "No, they won't. And the naturi won't go away because I go into hiding with you."

"I blame Jabari for this silly noble streak in you. It certainly didn't come from me," Valerio teased before brushing his lips across mine. "But the offer still stands."

"I can't spend the rest of my existence running from Jabari."

"Facing him will only shorten your existence."

"I—"

Mira!

The sudden, unexpected shout from Tristan in my head nearly put me back on my knees. I was beginning to wonder if I would ever get adjusted to so many creatures stomping around in my brain.

No shouting, please. I briefly wondered if the sarcasm would translate this way. I never spent a great deal of time speaking with other nightwalkers that way. I never felt confident that they could see or hear only what I wanted them to, and I liked my privacy.

The naturi. They're here!

I didn't question him. At any other time I would have laughed and called him crazy, but not now. A naturi was already lounging in the catacombs of the Great Hall and Rowe was sulking on San Michele. Why couldn't more be strolling down the fractured sidewalks of Venice?

"We have to go back," I said, turning my attention to Valerio again.

"What's wrong?"

"The naturi are in Venice." Those words actually caused the vampire to backpedal a couple steps away from me, and I honestly couldn't blame him. A nightwalker did not go marching into any area where the naturi were known to be. It's why you never heard tales of vampires wandering the woods alone on a moonless night.

"No," I snapped, instantly closing the distance between us. I wrapped my fists in the lapels of his jacket, holding him close to me. "You and I are going back to Venice now or I will give you a nasty sunburn. You have to see them. You need to understand."

"Mira—"

"Now, Valerio!"

I didn't have a chance to make another argument when I felt the push of magic as it ran its hands through my body. There was only time to blink when I found us standing in my suite at the Hotel Cipriani. I opened my mouth to thank him when Valerio wrapped his arms around me, pressing my body tightly against his as he leaned forward. A second later there was the telltale thunk of a knife hitting wood.

Valerio stood, pulling me back into an upright position. We both looked around to find a silver knife with a black handle embedded in the door frame of one of the bedrooms. Our eyes then traveled over to Danaus, who stood frowning at us.

"Does he always try to kill you when you enter a room?" Valerio teased, slowly releasing his hold on me.

"We have a special relationship." I stepped away from the nightwalker. I didn't have to say anything to Danaus. The hunter had been startled by our sudden appearance and reacted. It was that kind of speed that had kept him alive for so long. I was even particularly pleased with the fact that Valerio obviously had the ability to come and go where he wanted. I'd always thought there were more rules and limitations to that type of travel. Unfortunately, asking Valerio directly was a waste of time. That wasn't the kind of information he would volunteer.

"Mira." Tristan's fragile voice pulled me back to why I had raced to the Venice in the first place. The young nightwalker was standing before the bay of windows dressed only in a pair of jeans that were too big for him. His heels were resting on the bottom of the pant legs and the waist hung low on his hips. I briefly wondered if they belonged to Danaus, considering he and I were the only ones to bring a change of clothes, but decided not to ask. My eyes briefly skimmed over Tristan's back to find only a few faint red marks.

Frowning, I joined him at the window, with Valerio standing behind me. I didn't need to follow where Tristan was pointing. The three black shapes were easy to make out despite the dark sky as they headed toward the island of San Clemente. The creatures flew like bats, with quick movements of their wings instead of gliding on the air. However, they were too big to be anything that humans were accustomed to seeing. These nightmarish figures were naturi.

"What are they?" I asked, unable to tear my eyes away from them as they drew closer to the distant island. The three figures circled once then finally descended into a pocket of trees. They were headed for the Great Hall. I placed my hand on Tristan's shoulder, meaning for the gesture to be reassuring, but removed it when I felt him flinch at the contact. His fear rippled through me, sapping my own reserve of strength, which had kept me going during the past few nights. We were all running low and this dance was far from over.

"Not sure," Danaus admitted, drawing my gaze to his face. He was standing a couple feet away from me, his features tight and drawn. After a couple of seconds he looked down at me. "But this isn't good."

"I agree. We need to get out of Venice soon. If they're going to make another attempt at breaking the seal, they'll try to do it during the harvest holiday and the new moon. That's only a few nights away, and we have no idea where the sacrifice is going to be. Delays aren't good."

A part of me wanted to know where the next sacrifice was now so we could grab my private jet and head off to that distant locale. We could stop whatever naturi were in that hot spot, but that wouldn't keep more from arriving from other parts of the world. It would be a nonstop battle for the next three nights. If one or both of us were killed before the new moon rose, there would be no way to stop the naturi from making the sacrifice.

"But . . . " A slow smile dawned on my face as I looked up at the hunter. "We could stop by the Coven and see what's happening." Jabari had brought us there for a reason, and I refused to believe it was because he wanted the naturi to destroy us. He wouldn't give up the opportunity to kill me himself if he was so desperate to have me dead. Danaus and I needed to be on the island to disrupt whatever plans the Coven and the naturi were cooking up.

A rare smile trembled on Danaus's full lips and jumped in his deep blue eyes, laughing at me. "Risky, don't you think?"

"Oh, it's definitely risky, but not as much as you would think. Besides, it could also be fun." I laughed.

"More risky than going after nearly a dozen naturi in the forest?" Danaus asked, raising one thick eyebrow at me.

"No," I said, my smile dwindling at the memory. Looking back on the hastily launched assault in the woods not far from Stonehenge, I realized that the plan had been stupid and highly flawed. I'd reacted out of fear and anger. I knew better than to launch an attack on the naturi in the woods with an inexperienced nightwalker at my side. The fact that all three of us hadn't been destroyed was a miracle in itself.

I shook my head, pushing away the memory and the need to berate myself for my impulsive stupidity. It would do no good now, and I assured myself that this time would be different. "The Coven still needs us both alive. That's our ace in the hole. You in?"

"Definitely. Weapons?" he asked, his right hand sliding down to the knife that was still strapped to his waist.

"Load up." My gaze slid over to find Tristan watching me with a blank expression. He was waiting to see if I would command him to accompany Danaus and me. And he would if I demanded it, regardless of the fear still trembling within him. "You're not coming along. Not old enough," I teased.

"Mira, I can—"

"No," I interrupted before he could continue, my hand tightening on his shoulder. "Danaus and I are the only ones going in. Makes it easier to get out again."

"Do you actually think they won't kill you for this?" Valerio demanded. I had forgotten that the nightwalker was still in the room. Looking over my shoulder at him, I was surprised to see his handsome features looking haggard. His full lips were pressed into a hard, thin line and shallow furrows now stretched from the corners of his eyes and criss-crossed his brow.

The naturi had become a garish ghost story we told all the new, little nightwalkers to give them chills, but now we were all waking up to discover that this nearly dead species was suddenly fighting back. Our nightmares were threatening to become real and expose us to the sun. Again.

"That's another question I'm hoping to answer," I admitted with a smirk. "Exactly how irreplaceable am I? Would they be willing to risk the door opening by killing me or Danaus? Would they damn all nightwalkers just to protect their schemes? Or is that their plan in the first place?"

"You're not that important, Mira," Valerio chided, his frown deepening.

That was probably true but I wasn't planning on being killed that easily. I still had an ace or two up my sleeve in the form of Danaus. Of course, this plan could just as easily slit my own throat as save it if I was reading Jabari's intentions wrong.

"I need your help," I started, turning to Valerio. I quickly grabbed the sleeve of his blazer, even though I couldn't hold him here if I wanted to.

"I'm not going with you to the Coven. They need me alive even less than they need you."

"True, but I need you alive," I countered. I took his left hand in both of mine. "Go east. Find others who are older than me. Tell them everything I told you. If the Coven succeeds with whatever it's planning with the naturi, our people have to be prepared."

"You want me to raise your army," Valerio said, trying to pull his hand free.

"No, if the Coven and the naturi succeed, it will be your army. Someone needs to protect the nightwalkers from the Coven."

"Mira, I'm not a leader."

"Bullshit. You just never wanted the responsibility. Fine. Then find someone else to give the job. Don't let the information stop with you."

Frowning, Valerio squeezed my hand. "You may not want a seat, but you're the only one that deserves to be on the Coven."

"For our sakes, I hope you're wrong."

Sixteen

Once I was back in a pair of leather pants and one of the few cotton tops that had survived my travels, Danaus and I quickly snatched up a speedboat and rushed out to the island. The hunter drove the boat, his large hands tightly gripping the steering wheel. His black hair danced in the wind, revealing his clenched jaw and narrowed eyes. Tension hummed through his muscular body and energy snapped silently around him. I wanted to remain in the far corner of the boat away from him, but it wasn't an option. We had to talk, come to some kind of understanding before we waltzed into the Great Hall.

Lounging in the other chair beside him, my eyes locked on the island as we approached. "Do you have any guesses as to what flew to the island?" I asked.

"Big bats," he muttered.

"Great. Are they the only ones?"

There was a pause as his powers jumped from his body and spread out toward the far reaches of the area. They washed through me like a warm wave. It was a feeling I wasn't sure I would ever become accustomed to, and always left me wishing I could wrap myself up for a minute longer before facing the cold reality of what loomed ahead of us.

"I won't be able to sense what is on the island until I reach it, but they're not the only naturi," he announced. His voice had a distant, dreamy quality, as if his attention was focused on a faraway point. I resisted the urge to take the steering wheel from him and remained seated. "There are another six naturi on the mainland, not far from Venice. It's hard to pinpoint. Maybe somewhere around Padua or Verona. And there's one alone in Venice. But I don't know the area, I can't tell you which island."

A chill slipped down my arms. "Rowe," I whispered, talking to myself, but I knew that Danaus heard the name the moment it left my lips. I occasionally forgot about his stronger than normal hearing.

"You think he's here?" Danaus demanded. The hunter turned his head briefly to look at me before returning his gaze back to the open waters before us.

"I know it," I admitted. "I ran into him last night after I got Tristan settled in the hotel. He knows there's a naturi on San Clemente, but he doesn't know who it is or why she's there."

"Doesn't he think she's a captive?"

"I may have disabused him of that idea," I said with a little smirk as I recalled his stunned expression last night. "At the very least, we know that he's not in on whatever the Coven is planning."

Danaus slowed up as we drew closer to the island. "How does that help us?"

"It creates turmoil within his own kind. Possibly a distraction, a weakness we can later exploit." I said, pushing some hair back from my face. "I think the other six on the mainland are to serve as backup in case something goes wrong. Together with the three we saw from the hotel window, these nine were either sent by Rowe to reclaim the missing naturi or are outside of Rowe's plans and aligned with the naturi already on San Clemente."

"Should I ask if you even have a plan?"

"Get out alive," I replied dryly, folding my hands over my stomach. The statement earned me a fresh frown as Danaus concentrated on pulling the speedboat into the dock. It wasn't the most difficult of tasks, considering there was only one other boat tied to the little stone structure. Apparently, the house had been emptied of the court before the Coven's guests arrived. The hunter had also chosen the dock the farthest from the Great Hall. With the court gone, we could quickly travel to the hall and still give me enough time to lay down a couple of ground rules. I wasn't sure Danaus was going to go for it, but I had to try.

Of course, I'd promised to keep him alive while in Venice, so I had to protect him no matter what happened with the Coven. Yet, nowhere in that agreement did I state in what condition he had to be in. If he became too much of a risk, I'd drain his stubborn ass in a heartbeat and keep him unconscious until we were out of Venice.

"We need information," I said. "We need to know what the Coven is planning, why the naturi are appearing in Venice, and what in the world they have agreed to. To get any of this information, it means no killing."

Danaus shut off the engine and stared at me as if I'd been babbling in ancient Celtic. "Your so-called leaders are making deals with the enemy and you don't want to kill them? After you were so eager to finish them just last night?" he demanded, shoving the keys into his pocket. His hands absently swept over the pair of knives attached to his belt at various locations and the sword strapped across his back. As a seeming last resort, a handgun was in a holster at the small of his back.

"You misunderstand me," I chuckled, rising bonelessly to my feet. Unfortunately, the motion wasn't as graceful as I had hoped—my sudden shift in weight made the boat rock, and I hadn't accounted for it. I wasn't meant to be on a boat for extended periods of time. Steadying myself with a hand on the back of the chair I had been sitting in, I continued, "I want each of them writhing in unbearable agony, their flesh slowly stripped from their dusty old bones, their eyeballs melting and oozing from their sockets as they beg for death. I want the Coven and the naturi dead in the worst way, but now is not the time. If the Coven is destroyed, their secrets die with them, and that does not help our plans."

"That didn't stop you from trying last night," Danaus tartly reminded me again as he stepped from the boat and onto the dock.

"That was a mistake," I conceded, jumping onto the dock beside him. "I wasn't thinking clearly and let my anger get the better of me. This time is different. I will need your help, but I need you to promise not to try to wipe out the Coven and the naturi without my agreement."

"Mira—"

"No, I'm serious," I quickly said when he sounded as if he would argue. "Do you think killing the Coven tonight will actually stop the naturi from entering our world? Will killing these winged monsters stop the sacrifices? If we're killed tonight, do you honestly think Ryan will be able to stop the naturi in three nights?"

"Then what's to keep them from killing us the second we walk into the Great Hall?" he asked.

"Fear." The hunter snorted and started to walk up the dock toward the path that wound its way through the tiny forest to the Coven. I jogged up to him and stood in his path, stopping him again. "They're scared, or at the very least wary of me, and they're terrified of you."

Danaus scoffed again and tried to step around me, but I quickly moved to block him, putting a hand on his broad chest. Beneath my fingertips I could feel his heartbeat pounding a mile a minute. It was a bit surprising to find him so anxious when none of it leaked out into his voice or expression. "You've killed countless nightwalkers, and I'm sure more than one of them was an Ancient. Jabari has also seen firsthand what we can accomplish together. By now the naturi would have heard what happened in England. Both sides may be willing to give us a little space."

"You're not afraid of me," Danaus said, catching me off-guard with the comment.

I stared into his intense crystalline eyes, forcing a smile onto my lips. "That's because I know you're a big pussycat at heart. Wouldn't hurt a fly," I teased, then turned and walked down the path before he could answer. Good thing I wore my boots, because it was getting deep. Afraid of Danaus? I was terrified. I tried not to surround myself with creatures that could destroy me with a thought. Or worse, destroy my whole kind with a thought while using me as a weapon.

The walk to the Great Hall was uneventful, but we were prepared the whole time with weapons in hand. I gripped the little dagger I had worn so tightly that my knuckles ached when the huge double doors finally came into view. Holding up my hand, I motioned for Danaus to follow me over to the tree line. The two human guards who stood at the front doors were missing, and I could sense only a handful of nightwalkers on the whole island. While we were by no means hidden, I felt a little better knowing we weren't standing out in the open.

"Who is on the island?" I asked, peering around a large oak to look up at the oppressive stone building.

"Five vampires," he began before I even felt him reach out with his powers. "A scattering of humans and four members of the naturi. Wait! The lycan is here too."

"Nicolai?" I demanded, my eyes swinging around to look at the hunter as I searched the grounds again with my powers. I had checked only moments before asking him, and picked up on the vampires and humans, but Nicolai was there now. A little faint, but definitely present. Damn Jabari!

What was the point of having this ability if you couldn't get an accurate count when you really needed one?

"Why would he still be here?" Danaus asked, staring at the building.

"Oooh," I said as the pieces started to slowly fit together in my brain. "You think he might be the next sacrifice?" I suggested, pulling Danaus's eyes back to my face. One brow arched in question as he turned over the idea. "The new moon certainly isn't going to be working in their favor when they need to perform this sacrifice under a full moon. But I bet you would probably get a nice burst of energy from killing a lycan. Enough to bust through a magic seal that's holding shut a door between two worlds."

"Possible."

"And wouldn't it be a crying shame if they lost their sacrifice to me?"

A wide grin grew on my face as he turned over the idea. "You plan to steal another pet?" he asked, reminding me of how I neatly purloined Tristan while Sadira watched. If I stole Nicolai, it could turn into a full-time job keeping the werewolf alive, but that was more of a long-term worry. Right now my main concern was just getting off the island alive. Nicolai was the key to whatever bargain the Coven had set up. It explained why Jabari had sent him after me in the first place. I had the opportunity to disrupt the plan.

"Let's go get my prize," I announced, stepping out from behind the tree and starting up the path.

"They know we're here," Danaus stated, but I had a feeling that it was meant to sound more like a question.

"Without a doubt."

"We're never going to get through the door."

"Getting in won't be the problem." I forced myself to put my foot on the first step leading up to the double doors. Getting out alive was going to be the real trick.

Seventeen

There was no one waiting to rip our heads off when we shoved open the double doors to the Great Hall. I tried to take that as a good sign. Leaving the heavy wood and iron doors open, we turned our attention to the other set of doors that barred the way into the throne room. The candles in the iron candelabras sputtered and danced in the light breeze, with a few snapping out with a wisp of gray smoke. Absently waving my hand in their general direction, I caused the teardrop flames to steady and grow brighter as I scanned the deep, shadowy corners for potential attackers. We might have sensed only five vampires and a scattering of humans, but I wasn't taking any chances.

We were about to proceed to the main audience chamber when one of the doors opened and Elizabeth slipped through the slim crack. She quickly shut the door behind her again before either of us could sneak a peek into the room. Her pale yellow dress with a high empire waist made her look like a spring tulip. She reminded me vaguely of Napoleon's Josephine, composed and regal, with her long dark hair artfully piled on her head and diamonds sparkling around her neck.

I halted, resisting the urge to reach for the dagger I had

put back in its sheath at my waist. This was the first time I'd seen Elizabeth since I slaughtered Gwen and left her heart on the Elder's chair. Acts like that didn't particularly endear you to the Ancients, and I hadn't exactly counted on a direct confrontation with the nightwalker.

"You have no business here," she crisply said in English with a faint accent I couldn't quite place. French possibly, but older. She was a tiny figure, touching five feet only when her hair was piled high on her head in a series of twists and curls. Her hands were closed at her sides but not yet clenched into fists. It was on the tip of my tongue to make some comment that she had been sent like a messenger to stop me from entering the room, but I had enough trouble planned. Why go looking for a small, petty fight like that when I could thumb my nose at the whole Coven at once?

I gave her a slight bow of my head. Not quite the usual subservience I'm sure she'd grown accustomed to, but at least I didn't try to ignore her. "I have business with Jabari," I announced.

"And I still have business with you," she said, lifting her chin so she could look me in the eye. "You destroyed my property."

"Your property was warned to stay away from my property," I bit out, taking a step closer so I loomed over her. "Your property was warned of the consequences. If you didn't want your property damaged, you should have reined it in." With my heels, I had close to ten inches on this woman, and regardless of the power I knew she wielded, my physical presence and maybe even my reputation were enough to make her take one step backward. Around us, I let the candlelight flicker a bit, with some of the candles going out, breathing new life into the shadows. I hated talking about Gwen like a piece of chattel. I may have despised the creature, but she had been a "living," sentient creature.

"You owe me, Fire Starter," Elizabeth continued. Each word escaped her lips sharp and tight, as if she ground them between her teeth before releasing them.

"Then I suggest you start a tab, because it's going to get worse before I leave here tonight," I replied, enjoying the smirk that lifted the left corner of my mouth.

As I tried to step around her, I saw her swing her left hand toward my back from the corner of my eye. Spinning on my right heel, I slipped the dagger from its sheath on my hip and sliced at her throat. I hadn't expected her to directly attack me. It wasn't the typical style of the Elders. They had flunkies around to do their dirty work. Of course, I knew absolutely nothing about Elizabeth, which made her as dangerous as Macaire and Jabari.

However, Danaus had already stepped in, grabbing the nightwalker's wrist and holding it immobile above her head before I could even touch my blade to the Ancient's smooth skin.

"Should I kill her now?" he asked simply, his face blank. I looked down at Elizabeth, whose wide eyes were darting between me and Danaus. If she flinched, Danaus would snap her wrist without a thought. And if I said the word, he'd boil what blood filled her veins until it blackened her skin and turned her organs into a pool of stinking goo.

I slipped the knife back into its sheath. "Later," I said with a faint frown. If she thought we'd spared her life now, we might be able to buy her assistance later. Besides, I wasn't convinced that Danaus could destroy her that easily.

He nodded once and released her, giving the nightwalker a slight shove to precede us toward the doors that led to the Great Hall. The Elder said nothing, but stiffly walked toward the doors, which were pulled invisibly open when she approached. It was one of the abilities I envied the most. Nightwalkers didn't generally attain the ability of telekinesis until close to the thousand-year mark. I hoped to get it a little earlier. At the moment the best I could do was rattle a teacup and saucer—not exactly useful or intimidating.

The enormous three-story room was ablaze with candle-light, as if someone was afraid of the monsters that lurked in the dark corners. Along the east and west walls, close to twenty floor candelabras flickered, with more than a dozen large yellow candles in each. The chandeliers overhead also glowed with life, illuminating the various flags and banners that hung from the ceiling. Even the black marble floor reflected the light.

Only the dais, with the seats for the Coven and Our Liege, remained blanketed with shadows. Elizabeth returned to her seat on the dais next to Macaire. Jabari sat in the third Coven seat, and the fourth was still vacant, along with the seat of Our Liege. The three nightwalkers appeared to be alone, but Danaus sensed the presence of the naturi so they had to be lurking around somewhere. Had they left the hall when we appeared?

"I do not recall summoning your presence," Macaire declared when Danaus and I reached the center of the room. We stopped walking, preferring to maintain a little distance between us and the Coven, not that it would keep us any safer. I was just hoping to buy an extra second or two to react.

"I came to claim something that belongs to me," I replied, shoving my fingers into the back pockets of my pants, affecting a casual stance. I didn't know if it worked, because I was sure everyone in the room could smell my fear.

"A vampire is here we didn't agree on," said a hypnotic voice from somewhere near the ceiling. The melodious sound was like a dream in the way it bounced off the walls before finally drifting down to me. "A stranger who carries no value here. Should we return with the threat of dawn when we will find no unwelcome ears?"

"The werewolf we came for is near," countered a second voice, not far from the location of the first. This one was significantly softer, but just as seductive as its companion. "You know leaving isn't something we'd enjoy until they speak the words we must hear, and then back home we can take the wolf boy."

"Oh, forgive me," I quickly replied, giving a large sweeping bow to the three members of the Coven before me. "I had no idea you had guests. I'll be happy to leave once Jabari hands over Nicolai."

"Why would I do such a thing?" Jabari slowly inquired, his dark eyes narrowing on me while his long fingers tightened on the arms of his throne. I half expected to hear the wood cracking and groaning under the force of his grip.

"Do you deny you sent him with the order to kill me?" I asked, my tone sweeter than sugar. My head cocked to the left and I flashed him a toothy smile. I knew when he'd figured out exactly what I was doing there because at least one of the wooden arms made a large cracking sound. Some small part of me prayed it was all an act for the rest of the Coven, or I was in serious trouble.

"He was sent for your heart," Jabari admitted. His growing anger was causing his accent to thicken, pushing him closer to his traditional Egyptian. Sliding forward, he sat perched on his seat as if preparing to leap at me.

It was a fight for me to keep from taking a step back. The hairs on the back of my neck stood on end. Confronting Jabari was like baiting a tiger—I'd be lucky if he didn't rip my face off if I was wrong.

"Then I have come to claim the spoils of the fight. I spared his life, so it now belongs to me," I said, forcing a smile. It was a very old tradition of my kind and not one frequently enforced simply because we typically killed whoever attacked us.

"You can't have him," Jabari snarled.

"What is the meaning of this?" Macaire demanded. A frown marred his distinguished features while his eyes darted between me and the Elder.

"He sent the lycanthrope to kill Mira," Danaus replied, stepping forward so he was directly beside me. In no way attempting to hide his antagonism for the whole group, his right hand rested casually on the handle of one of the knives at his waist.

"Mira?" cried one of the female voices above my head. There was a sudden scrape of movement along the ceiling as if claws were scratching the stones overhead. There was a whisper of voices, words I couldn't quite make out despite my keen hearing. I took a step backward and craned my head up in an attempt to see the creatures that lurked on the ceiling, but they remained hidden behind the scattering of flags and banners. Taking another step back, I intentionally bumped my shoulder into the hunter's.

What the hell is up there? I sent the question directly into his brain, struggling to keep from sounding as terrified as I felt.

No idea.

I quickly stepped away from him at the sound of wings and a blur of shadow. One of the creatures swooped down from the ceiling and landed lightly on the floor directly between me and the Coven. I had to clamp down on my tongue to keep the scream from escaping when my eyes clearly took in the monster for the first time.

At close to five feet tall, the creature looked almost like a woman, though only by a stretch of the imagination. And that's if you erased the batlike wings that stretched from the inside of her thin arms and down along her body. At the end of the wings were three long bony fingers, tipped with black claws. Her skin was flesh-colored and appeared paper-

thin since it sagged on her spindly body. However, it was
her crowlike feet with their long talons clicking ominously
on the marble floor that finally triggered a memory in my
mind. This creature was the source of the ancient harpy
mythology.

After encountering the two female naturi from the wind
clan in the woods in England, I had assumed they were all
the fairy-tale type, with elfin features and butterfly wings.
Sure, Rowe looked different, but then everything about
Rowe was different, from his black hair to his scars to his
black wings. I never expected to find a naturi so horrifying
to look upon.

"This is the monster who tamed the flame and reduced us
to dusty ash," the naturi said, taking a hesitant step closer to
me. She wrapped her wings around herself so that her hands
lightly gripped her bony shoulders, concealing her naked
body. "Once again fulfilling her birth name. Yet, behind her
lurks a bit of trash." The creature's narrowed yellow eyes
turned to Danaus and closely inspected him, creeping yet
another step closer.

"What is he? Please, tell me," demanded a third voice
from the ceiling. This one sounded younger, almost child-
like in its pitch and impatient urgency. "He smells of sweat
and weak human flesh, but carries behind him no shade of
death. Not human born."

"Nor vampire made," chimed in a second from
overhead.

"Nor wolf by moonlight torn," finished the other naturi
standing a few feet away.

"And he's not for sale, so don't get too attached," I snapped,
their strange rhyming grating on my nerves. I took a step
sideways, to stand between Danaus and the naturi. The creature glared at me and retreated a step, keeping a comfortable
distance between us. I was surprised they couldn't identify

the origin of the hunter's powers. The naturi and bori were archenemies seemingly since the birth of time. You'd think they'd have recognized the presence of a bori no matter how faint. Then again, it had been more centuries than anyone could count since the last bori wandered the earth. Maybe they forgot what one felt like.

Struggling to tear my eyes off the creature with the stringy gray hair, I looked up at the Coven and said, "Just send out Nicolai, and we'll be on our way."

"We cannot," Macaire said. "We have other plans for him."

"Time to change your plans." I smiled, slipping my dagger from my waist. I reached my free left hand behind me to the hunter, who took it. "Or Danaus and I turn anything that stinks of naturi into ash. Send out the wolf."

Chaos erupted. The first harpy launched herself into the air with amazing speed and grace, disappearing among the flags hanging above. Again their voices swelled as they discussed something in their own language that I couldn't quite make out. They either didn't care for being threatened or had just figured out that the wolf I demanded was their soon-to-be sacrifice.

As I lifted my eyes to try to locate the three naturi that clung to the ceiling like overgrown bats, my brain filled with pain. At first Jabari had been the only presence pushing against my thoughts, but Danaus quickly shoved his way inside. Energy from both creatures surged through my frame, battling for dominance. The hunter was winning the battle, but I had a feeling it was only because he actually had physical contact with me, gripping my hand, while Jabari still sat several feet away on the dais. My scream shattered the air as the pain buckled my knees beneath me. I was only vaguely aware of the sound of my knife hitting the marble floor at the same time my knees came in contact with the cool stone.

My bones felt as if they were being ground into dust as Jabari and Danaus fought for control. Danaus still held my hand, and I tried to pull it free in a blind effort to stop the pain. Of course, if he released me, there was a chance that Jabari would win control and the hunter would die. There were no voices in my head this time. Just raw, angry power. I screamed again, wishing there was a way I could push them both out of my head, but there was nothing to grab onto, nothing to push against. They were both everywhere at once, separate but nearly indistinguishable in the various shades of pain they caused.

When I was sure I could take no more, Danaus finally won the battle, ejecting Jabari from my thoughts. Unfortunately, there was too much energy flowing in my painfully tense frame. I couldn't let it go. A ring of fire nearly twelve feet in diameter instantly burst into existence. The flames crackled for a second in bright yellow and orange before settling into a silent pale blue. No one had put the need to create fire in my brain, it just happened.

But the ring of eight-foot flames wasn't all that ignited. Candlelight around the room flared, the little tongues of fire stretching and elongating until they seemed to take on a life of their own. Two of the flags burst into flames overhead, shoving aside more of the darkness that cowered in the room. One of the chairs that survived last night's fight also burst into flames, crackling and popping with a growl that seemed to mimic the same anger burning through my soul. The flames were soothing despite the fact that Danaus skulked around in my brain as if he owned it, seeming to wait for Jabari to attack again.

Instead the attack came from above. I heard the near-silent flap of leathery wings only seconds before I was jerked backward. Danaus's hand was pulled from my grip as he was lifted from his feet. Twisting from where I sat on the floor, I saw two of the harpies lift him into the air, their taloned feet digging into his broad shoulders. The closer he moved to the ceiling, the weaker his presence grew in my thoughts, allowing Jabari to muscle his way in again.

Desperate, I tried to throw up mental barriers, not caring who was being pushed out. With both hands planted on the floor in front of me, I gritted my teeth and pushed against anything I was sure wasn't my own thought, but even that distinction was growing fuzzy. A snarl rippled up from my throat as I barely suppressed the urge to hurl fireballs at the harpies, but I couldn't risk it. There was a good chance I would hit Danaus as well.

Mira . . . Jabari's voice in my head was light and taunting as I kneeled on the floor. It wasn't strong yet, but he had the power to wear me down.

Give me Nicolai and call off the harpies. My demand sounded ragged and breathless even to me as I shoved the thought back at Jabari, wishing I could make him choke on it.

Let them have their fun. I could easily envision the shrug of his narrow shoulders as he sent me that thought. There was laughter woven around every word that danced through my brain. *Besides, don't you think you've collected enough pets you cannot protect?*

It dawned on me then that his thoughts were devoid of the anger or frustration he had shown just moments ago when we were speaking. Damn him! He had manipulated me. He knew I would come for Nicolai, but what was his goal? Danaus's death? Mine? Or was he manipulating me into killing the naturi for him? I didn't understand his game.

This deal with the naturi can't be allowed, I told him.

Stealing Nicolai won't stop it, he admitted

Will it help? I waited for his answer. After everything that had happened, I felt as if I was extending a desperate hand to him, begging for his help after he had manipulated me into this position in the first place. I hated what he could do to me, and I hated him more because I needed him.

They will fear you more, he finally said.

Overhead, a woman's voice sliced through the silence in a heart-shattering scream. Another voice was raised in pain a second later, followed by the sound of ripping cloth. I looked up in time to see Danaus fall to the floor. He landed as lightly as a cat, his knife in hand, stained with black-looking blood. One of the flags fluttered to the ground behind him, torn from where he had grabbed it in an attempt to slow his fall.

If you fight with Danaus for control over me again, it will destroy what little is left of my mind and potentially my body. That cannot help your goal. I sent the thought lashing out at Jabari as Danaus approached. *Hand over Nicolai and we will leave.* I had only seconds to get Jabari to acquiesce. The ring of fire wouldn't stop Danaus from returning to my side. If the hunter touched me again, I knew I wouldn't survive it. My arms were trembling and my stomach felt as if it had been flipped inside out and dipped in acid.

We're close.

I wanted to asked what he meant by that, but there wasn't time. In truth, it didn't matter if I understood. I was just the weapon, not the warrior.

"Enough!" Jabari roared, surging to his feet. What seemed like a child crying in pain was the only sound in the room. Apparently, Danaus had done some serious damage to one of the harpies. There was a brief scraping and clacking of claws on stone and then the crying grew softer and fainter.

I hesitantly lowered the flames so they were only a couple feet high and surrounded me more tightly, in a circle with a diameter of only a few feet. Danaus stopped a couple feet away from me outside the flames, his knife still in hand, as we waited to hear what Jabari had to say.

"Kill her, Jabari," Macaire ordered. His arms shook from where he tightly held the arms of the chair, barely managing to keep his seat. A horrid green light glowed in his eyes, burrowing into me through the flickering flames.

A deep chuckle rumbled from Jabari and a cold smile slithered across his lean, hard features. I had seen that expression once before. The warm, compassionate veneer had been stripped away at the Themis Compound when he told me I was the weapon wielded by the triad to stop the naturi. At least this time his icy amusement was directed at Macaire and not at me.

"You've cried for her death since the second she was reborn."

Jabari's words slithered like a poisonous snake into my ears and through the cells of my brain, sending an uncontrollable shiver through my exhausted body. He had switched to our language; the first language spoken by nightwalkers, which was written in our very blood. There was no learning it. A vampire was reborn fluent and afraid. No one spoke it without a good reason. Jabari most likely had something to say he didn't want the naturi to understand.

"If you wish her dead, you must dirty your hands, because I'm not through with her," Jabari continued, gracefully sitting back down in his chair. "But remember last night's bloodbath. She's not without her own skills. And beside her stands an experienced hunter of our kind."

"It sounds as if you are afraid to attack her," Macaire taunted, also using the same language. It didn't roll from his tongue with the same elegance, and I wondered if it was because he was afraid of me and Jabari.

"No."

And that was all he had to say. Jabari could destroy me

without raising a finger and we all knew it. There was no fear, no hesitance. He would kill me when he was done using me.

"But she means to take your pet from you," Macaire said. There was no missing the desperation that colored each word. He wouldn't be able to convince Jabari to do anything he didn't want to do. If Macaire wanted me dead, he was going to have to do something about it himself.

"He was lost to me regardless of the outcome," Jabari said with an indifferent shrug. He had sent Nicolai knowing I would either kill him or claim him. Damn Jabari. After living with me for roughly a century, he had come to know me far too well.

With a wave of his hand, one of the side doors slammed open, banging against the wall. Nicolai stepped into the room, his eyes quickly taking in all the players. The handsome werewolf was wary, but exhaustion was starting to take its toll on him. His copperish-brown eyes were underlined with dark shadows and there was a day's growth of whiskers on his jaw and chin. He stood near the dais, not far from Jabari, struggling to stare blankly straight ahead. However, he could either sense or hear the harpies overhead, his eyes occasionally darting toward the dark shadows near the ceiling.

There was only the soft drip of blood leaking from one of the harpies as it hit the marble floor. Nicolai's and Danaus's heartbeats thundered in my head as I suddenly became aware of my growing hunger. My fight with Jabari and the other nightwalkers during the past two nights had pushed me too far and I needed to feed again.

Reluctantly, I doused the last of the flames, but remained kneeling on the floor, conserving the last of my energy should I need it to escape this nightmare.

"If you can protect him, you may have him," Jabari conceded. There was no missing the condescension in his tone.

I'd already failed to protect Tristan and he certainly didn't believe I would be able to protect Nicolai when the Elder chose to attack him.

Pushing to my feet, I was surprised when I didn't sway once I was standing again, despite the fact that my thoughts were coated in a thick layer of fog and pain and my body screamed at every movement. If there had been an ounce of blood left within my frame, it seemed I would have heaved it onto the floor. I wanted to curl into a little ball and pray for the dawn to wipe away my mind. Instead I squared my shoulders and nodded. We both knew that without rising from his chair, Jabari had beaten me because he had the ability to control me. I was getting Nicolai because it was what Jabari wanted, not because I had won.

He smiled widely at me, revealing a glimpse of white fangs, and motioned with a couple of fingers for Nicolai to walk over to me. The lycan's eyes darted from the Elder to me in confusion and shock before taking a couple slow, hesitant steps toward me. My muscles tensed, waiting for one of the Coven to lurch forward and attack the werewolf, but none of the three even flinched. However, understanding finally dawned on the naturi that clung to the ceiling. There was a quick flap of damp, fleshy wings as they watched Nicolai stand near me.

"What is this, nightwalker?" exclaimed one of the harpies in melodious outrage.

"The lycan was not part of the original agreement," Jabari said in a harsh voice that made me flinch.

"No!" The screech reverberated through the room as one of the harpies swooped down from the ceiling, her taloned feet extended to grab the werewolf up by the shoulders. Without hesitation, I launched a fireball at the attacking monster at the same time an invisible hand slammed into the creature, crushing it against the far wall. The harpy screamed and pushed off from the wall, returning to the relative safety of the shadows that huddled in the corners of the ceiling. I didn't have to look up at the dais to know that Jabari had protected Nicolai. He hadn't been sure I had the energy to do it after my scuffle with him.

Turning to look at a scratched and bloody Danaus, I bit out an order, "Get him out of here." The hunter was smart enough not to argue with me. He knew I was running on empty. I couldn't keep fighting off the harpies all night and still hold my own against the Coven. Danaus grabbed a stunned Nicolai by the shoulder and pulled him out the door, his eyes continuously moving from the dais to the ceiling, expecting another attack.

If anything, the fact that Danaus and I were walking out with Nicolai indicated that the Coven still needed us alive for whatever dark plan they had in mind. So far I had not stepped too far out of line. Furthermore, I had potentially completed a task that Jabari always meant for me to accomplish. *Bastard.* I would have preferred to find out what the Coven was planning with the naturi, but felt lucky to be walking out at all. There was still a little time left to discover the Elders' plans.

My gaze returned to the dais and the Elders, who were each plotting my demise in their own special way, I was sure. Macaire was expressionless as he stared at me, but there was no hiding his white knuckles or tensed frame. He was less than pleased with both me and Jabari. Only at this point he wasn't sure which of us would be easiest to kill. Besides, I was still willing to bet that he wanted to meet with me. Macaire was the type to mentally manipulate you; try to win you over with "logic" and lots of seductive promises. He wasn't willing to get his hands dirty the same way Jabari was.

Elizabeth had been silent through this whole affair, which made me more nervous than when I considered Macaire. I could guess Macaire's and Jabari's motive, but I didn't know whose side she was on or if she had her own goal. All in all, I had no doubt she would rather see me staked out in the sun than standing in the Great Hall again.

At last my gaze settled on Jabari, who was watching me with amusement dancing in his dark eyes. I bowed my head to him, no longer wishing to know his schemes that involved me and no little amount of pain. I was about to turn and stride out of the room when my eyes caught on the empty chair at Jabari's right hand. Tabor's chair. A seat on the Coven. But to be a member of the Coven would mean being Jabari's puppet. At one time I would have followed the Elder's wishes simply because I believed in him. Now I would do it because I had no choice.

My gaze stumbled back to Jabari, to find him grinning broadly at me, guessing my thoughts. He would welcome me onto the Coven with open arms, as it solidified his power over the other two members. I smiled back at him before turning on my left heel and stiffly leaving the Great Hall. My heart would be in the hunter's hand before I took a seat on the Coven.

Eighteen

Pulling the heavy doors closed behind me, I paused at the top of the old granite stairs and tipped my head up toward the stars that winked at me as if enjoying some great cosmic joke. The air was warm and moist, and the wind had begun to stir, whispering dark promises of a summer squall that would leave San Marco Piazza under a foot of water. The flood was usually reserved for later in the season, but was not unheard of during late July.

It was only standing in the summer air that I realized I was cold. The chill that had bit at my limbs finally began to permeate the aches and throbbing pains that dominated my consciousness. I couldn't remember the last time I'd fed. Had it been while I was in London? It seemed all so long ago, but only a couple of nights had passed. Despite that, I needed to feed again, and soon.

With a frown, I started to descend the stairs when my knees decided to no longer obey my wishes. My legs were made of seaweed and completely useless. I reached out to catch myself, briefly wondering if my arms would even work, when I found myself in Danaus's strong arms. I didn't see him move. In fact I hadn't been aware of him being so close, but I didn't care. I had enough to worry about.

Danaus carefully wrapped my left arm around his shoulders then swept me wordlessly up in his arms. His stride was steady and unhurried as he headed back to the boat. My eyes drifted closed as his warmth wrapped around me, helping to erase some of the aches and pains that filled my body. Beside us I heard Nicolai walking to Danaus's right.

"My hero," I murmured in a low voice, resting my head against Danaus's shoulder. He snorted in disgust, earning a breathless chuckle from me. I had no doubt he would have loved to drop me on my ass right there and let me crawl to the boat, but it wouldn't get us off this wretched island any faster.

"Was it worth it?" he asked. I could feel his turmoil and worry beating against me as if they were my own emotions. Our connection was still strong from earlier and I didn't have the spare energy to try to put up any mental walls to keep him out, not that it would have done me much good. Danaus and Jabari could waltz in whenever they pleased.

"Yes," I sighed. My right hand slid down from his shoulder to his chest, and I could feel his heartbeat beneath my palm. "We know the Coven is not of one mind about its plans and that Our Liege knows nothing of the Elders' plans. We also know that Jabari will keep us alive until after we've destroyed whatever they're cooking up with the naturi. At least he wants to keep the door closed."

"Unless you're wrong about Jabari," Danaus interjected.

"Thank you for that happy thought," I grumbled, cracking open one eye to look up at him. It wouldn't be the first time I had been horribly wrong about Jabari and paid a high price for it.

"What about him?" the hunter asked, jerking his head toward Nicolai. "He wasn't the sacrifice."

"Maybe he was, in a last minute change," I suggested.

"Sacrifice?" Nicolai finally chimed in. "What the hell are you talking about?"

"Did you know you were to be handed over to the harpies?" I inquired, letting my eyes drift shut again. Nicolai's agitation had caused his own powers to swell and brush against my skin. They weren't as soothing as Danaus's, and I found myself trying to huddle closer to the hunter.

"Harpies?" Nicolai's voice jumped from its usually deep, rough tones. "That's what was in the room with us? No, I didn't know anything about it."

"Why tell him when he might put up a fight ahead of their arrival?" Danaus said to me. "The naturi might not have been interested in damaged goods."

I fought back a snicker by biting my lower lip. It was a cold and heartless way of putting it, but it was also probably very accurate. "I think what Jabari said was true. Nicolai wasn't part of their original agreement. Maybe it was decided later that he would act as a deposit against any damage done to the female in the Coven's custody. Maybe he was a gift. I don't know. In the end the important thing was our appearance and us walking out with Nicolai. It implied that the Coven couldn't stop us. The naturi now have a new reason to fear us. Nicolai was just a pawn."

"Thanks," the wolf grumbled.

"Look at it this way," I countered, turning my head so I could look at him. "If you had been truly important to the Coven's plans, I would have never gotten you out of there. And don't worry. Once this naturi uprising has been put down, Jabari will come to claim your head the first chance he gets."

It was a grim and ugly truth. At best I extended Nicolai's life by a matter of days. If he was good at hiding, maybe I gave him a few months. But in the end we both knew that Jabari would eventually hunt us down.

Turning my head back to Danaus's chest, I was suddenly overwhelmed by the scent of his blood. It wasn't only the smell of it pulsing beneath his skin, but it was dried on his skin and soaked into his shirt from where the harpies had gouged his shoulders with their claws. Clenching my teeth, his warmth and blood beat against me, tempting me. The beast inside my chest shifted and pushed my soul down into the dark shadows of my body, fighting for dominance. The need for blood swelled within me until it nearly blotted out all thought. My head fell back, my lips parted so I could feel a brush of air across my tongue. It was only then I realized I was losing the struggle to stay in control.

I violently shoved against Danaus's chest, tumbling out of his strong arms. I hit the ground with a bone-jarring thud, which helped clear my thoughts. Huddled in the grass beside the sidewalk that led to the Coven, I dug my fingers in the dirt and clenched my eyes shut. I wouldn't bite Danaus. I wouldn't drink from him if he was the last creature that walked this earth. Wasn't it enough that he and Jabari had control of me? I wouldn't be controlled by the hunger as well.

"Don't touch me!" I shrieked when I heard the two men draw closer to me. "I—I just need a couple seconds." With my eyes clenched shut, I drew my sore and protesting body into a tighter ball. "Go to the boat. I'll be there in a minute."

"I'm not leaving you," Danaus firmly replied. "It's too dangerous."

"What's wrong?" Nicolai asked. I could feel the were-wolf a couple feet away off to my right.

"She's starved," Danaus answered before I could open my mouth. "She needs to feed." His words stunned me into silence. I forgot that he could sense my emotions. I read his so clearly, but forgot that mine poured into his mind just as easily. He knew I was fighting back the hunger and had taken a chance carrying me anyway. Was he testing me?

I had no doubt that he would have cleaned my clock if I'd taken a nip at him.

Pushing down the hunger to more controllable levels, Danaus's emotions crept back into my brain. I could hear his heart pounding in his chest as if he had run a marathon, his emotions a chaotic mix of fear and . . . something else. Adrenaline? Hunger? His overriding fear and frustration were crushing the other emotion, so I couldn't clearly make it out. And in truth I don't think either of us wanted to know just yet the other emotion Danaus was feeling.

"Mira, can you drink from lycans?" Nicolai asked, kneeling beside me in the grass. Some nightwalkers could drink from lycanthropes. Most could not. I could. I had some guesses as to why I could, but the implications were not the sort of thing that would help extend my life span; not that much could at this point.

"Go away, Nicolai," I muttered, slowly untensing the muscles in my arms so I could move away from him quickly if he reached for me. I was in better control than a couple minutes ago, but it would be too easy to go back over that edge. "I didn't risk my neck saving your worthless butt just to drain you a few hundred yards from the hall."

"The offer stands," Nicolai said, and then returned to his feet without touching me.

Shuddering, I unclenched my fingers and pushed to my feet as well. The hunger still throbbed in my chest, but I was in control again. As long as I could keep a physical distance from the two men, I could fight back the urge to feed until we reached the main islands of Venice. There, I could blend into the crowd and choose my prey from the hordes that filled the city.

The trip back to the hotel was quick and silent, with Nicolai and Danaus keeping as much distance between me and themselves as humanly possible. I nearly sighed with relief when we landed at the docks next to the Cipriani, but Nicolai didn't give me a chance. The wolf stood in front of me as I tried to exit the boat, grabbing both of my arms in his large hands. My body instantly came alive with his energy and physical contact. I was holding on by a thread, only vaguely aware of what he was saying.

"Can you honestly hunt tonight without killing your prey?" he demanded, his voice like granite. His large hands loosened their grip on me when I didn't try to pull out of his grasp.

"Yes," I hissed, gritting my teeth. It was all I could do to keep from sinking my fangs in his neck right there. He was so warm, with his life and essence beating against me in endless waves. Danaus and Nicolai were slowly driving me insane. I needed to feed before I did something truly stupid.

"You've saved my life twice," he said tightly. "The least I can do is offer my services." Before I could come up with some witty reply, the lycan bent down and tossed me over his shoulder. I don't remember passing Danaus, going through the lobby, or even riding the elevator up to our suite. My mind was occupied with his tight rear end and wondering if it was worth trying to sink my fangs into one of his cheeks. I decided it wasn't—his blue jeans would probably absorb most of his blood before I could get it down my throat.

"Mira!" Tristan's shocked voice tore me from my preoccupation long enough to look up at the young nightwalker through thick strands of my red hair as we entered my suite.

"I'm fine," I called as Nicolai headed for one of the bedrooms. "Go play with Danaus. We'll talk before dawn." My last word was cut off by the door slamming shut.

Nicolai tried to dump me on the bed and take a step away, but I didn't let him. The second my back hit the bed,

I reached out and grabbed a fistful of his dark burgundy T-shirt. I barely scooted out of the way in time before he fell backward onto the bed with a bounce. In the blink of an eye I was straddling his hips, one hand entangled in his long blond locks, pulling his head to one side to expose his beautiful neck.

I wanted to ask him one last time if this was what he wanted. I wanted to give him a chance to back out, but I couldn't. There was only the red haze of hunger filling my brain. Enough of me was left to be aware of the fact that I was in a safe location with a source of blood. Willing or not was no longer important. I would console myself later with the thought that having brought me up there, he supposedly knew what he was getting into.

The second his warm blood hit my tongue, the world faded away. There was nothing beyond the warm body lying beneath me and his beating heart. All the aches and pains subsided and the beast inside my chest sighed with relief. I relaxed against him, gentling my hold on his head. One of us moaned as he wrapped his arms around my body, pressing me against his hard length. Drinking his blood, I slipped into his mind, sending a hundred feelings of pleasure through his body. This time I was sure it was Nicolai who moaned, his fingers sliding down my back as they searched for the edge of my shirt.

The first touch of his hands on my skin sent me scrambling off his body. Crawling to the top of the bed, I sat with my back pressed against the wood headboard. With my head tilted back, I ran my tongue over my teeth, taking in the taste of him. His heartbeat and heavy breathing were the only sounds in the room. I hadn't taken much blood from him, nowhere near as much as I needed. I would have to feed again later, but his blood took the edge off my hunger and gave me back a measure of control.

Nicolai shifted on the bed, and I opened my eyes to find him lying on his stomach looking up at me, a wide grin playing on his lips. My eyes drifted to his neck to find that the wound was already healing on its own. That was one of the nice things about feeding on lycans—they healed so fast there was little chance of leaving behind any evidence you were ever there.

"You've not fed enough," he said, his voice a low, husky rumble.

Shoving my right hand through my hair, pushing it back from where it fell around my face, I smiled at my companion. "I've had enough to get me to my next meal," I murmured, feeling a little more relaxed for the first time in several nights. "I'll not drain you to satisfy my cravings."

Nicolai chuckled. "I'm not offering all of my blood," he said, a smile lightening his features, easing back some of the worry lurking around his eyes since I'd first met him. He slid his right hand up to lightly wrap around one of my ankles. "But I can take more than that little snack."

"For some reason, I get the impression you're offering more than just a meal," I hedged, my eyes pointedly slipping down to look at the long fingers wrapped around my ankle. This hadn't been a part of my plan when I sank my teeth into his neck.

"And you're opposed to the offer?" he inquired, making no effort to keep the sarcasm from his voice. Pushing to his knees, Nicolai sat up and pulled his shirt over his head, revealing acres of tanned skin and muscles pulsing with warmth and life. I think he dropped the shirt over the side of the bed, but I honestly couldn't drag my eyes from his chest or his arms.

I'd been with my share of handsome men during my extended lifetime; human, lycan, and nightwalker. I'd been with enough to think that my head couldn't be turned by a nice body or a handsome face. But Nicolai was putting my resolve to the test. He didn't have the same, almost frightening beauty that Valerio possessed. Nicolai had his flaws. There was a long white scar on his chest, stretching above his heart. His stomach seemed almost too thin for his frame, making me wonder if his meals recently had been too sparse or infrequent. But it was this perfect combination of frailty and strength that was intoxicating.

With considerable effort I closed my eyes, but the image of his chest seemed to have already been burned into the insides of my eyelids. "I don't want your body in exchange for your life." I had to force the words from my mouth because something in me simply ached to run my tongue over his chest.

His laugh caused my eyes to open my eyes and focus on his handsome face again. Slowly, he reached down and took both of my ankles in his hands, making me feel very small. With a quick jerk I slid down the bed toward him so I was laying flat on my back with my knees brushing against his hips. Planting his hands on either side of my head, he leaned down until his lips were inches from mine.

"The blood was in gratitude for my life," he whispered, his lips brushing against mine with each word. He moved his head, running his lips along my jaw as he spoke. "The sex is as much for me as it is for you. We've both had enough death and violence during the past few days to last a lifetime. And it's not over, is it?"

His question gave me pause, waking me up from the spell his husky voice was weaving. I met his eyes and found those large copper-brown orbs asking me the same question I had seen in the eyes of Tristan, Sadira, James, Alexandra, and, for even a fleeting moment, Danaus. Were we going to survive? Was I going to protect them? Was there a hope to cling to? And for some reason, they all looked to me to be their savior. A pariah among my own kind. The Coven's anathema.

Threading the fingers of my left hand through the golden wave of hair that cascaded down to frame his face, I pulled him closer so that my lips brushed against his. "It doesn't matter. There is only now," I whispered. Nicolai smiled against my lips as he leaned in to kiss me.

My eyes fell shut and there was only the feeling of his lips and his warmth wrapping around me like a wonderful cocoon, smothering all thoughts of the rest of the world. My tongue easily slid between his parted lips, and the taste of him reminded me of honey and fresh bread, memories of a home I was forced to leave years too early. My fingers left his hair to slide down along his massive shoulders, taking in skin that seemed impossibly soft. I turned my head and trailed kisses along his neck as I ran my hands down his back, lightly scratching him with my nails as I dragged my hands back up to his shoulders.

"Still looking for a bite?" he chuckled, nuzzling my neck before his lips finally settled on my earlobe. A sigh escaped me as the tip of his tongue ran along the edge of the sensitive piece of flesh. Tension that had hummed throughout my body for so many endless nights was beginning to unravel from each one of my muscles.

"Hmmmm . . . There are far more interesting places for me to snack," I teased. Planting my heels in the bed and wrapping my arms around his waist, I rolled us over so he was lying on his back and I was straddling his hips.

Surprise lit his eyes, but he quickly recovered. He didn't seem willing to relinquish control that easily. His hand shot out to snake around the back of my neck, pulling me back down so his mouth could reclaim mine in a long, deep kiss. His tongue slid along one of my fangs until finally pricking it. There was no fighting the moan that swelled up in my throat at the taste of his blood. Stretching out my legs on either side of him, I pressed the length of my body into his as I sucked blood from his tongue until the tiny wound finally healed on its own.

As a shiver ran through me, I broke off the kiss and slid my mouth down along his jaw near his ear. "You've done this before," I purred.

"Been with a vampire?" he asked, running his hands down my back to cup my rear end. As he pressed my body closer to his, he arched his hips, grinding his hardened body into mine. "Oh, yeah. Surprised?"

"No," I laughed, pushing up with my hands braced each side of his head so I could look down at him. But the laughter died when I thought about it. He had been held to Jabari's side while at the court. I knew the horrors the Coven's court were capable of. "While you were here?"

Nicolai cupped my cheeks with both of his hands and tried to pull me back down to him, but every muscle in my body had stiffened and he couldn't move me. "No," he said in a firm but gentle voice. "No one's touched me while I've been here. My experience came well before Jabari."

I sucked in a cleansing breath of air, trying to wipe away the moment of tension. I agreed that we both needed to heal, and sex would at least give us a moment of that. But doing something that mirrored anything he may have been forced to do with another nightwalker would not help him.

Nicolai pulled me back down and we got lost in another series of drugging kisses that only left us needing more, needing to be closer. The scent of his blood just below his warm skin beckoned to me. His blood was wonderful, better than pure human. It was richer and more potent, but my hunger for his blood was steadily being overpowered with the need to know every inch of his long body.

Nicolai had no problem with my intentions, and was already pulling my plain cotton shirt up and over my head as I sat up. Once again straddling his hips, I reached back to unfasten my lacy black bra. He snatched the opportunity and, sitting up, pulled the bra down to free my breasts.

My eyelids fell shut as his tongue slowly circled the left nipple before taking it into his mouth. The fingers of my right hand fumbled with the clasp twice before I finally used both hands to undo the bra. The wonderful moist heat on my left breast and his strong, kneading fingers on my right had successfully scattered my thoughts to the wind. My hands fell to his shoulders, then of their own will slid into his hair, holding his head gently imprisoned as I arched my back, pressing closer to him. Lifting his mouth from my breast, his breath skimmed over the damp flesh, sending a chill dancing over my whole body before he shifted to the other breast, his tongue briefly dipping into the valley between them.

A soft sigh whispered past my parted lips. There was only Nicolai and his gentle hands and seeking mouth. How long had it been since I had last been touched like this? Weeks? Months? For a heartbeat the memory of the last time I'd had a moment like this drifted through my brain, but I quickly pushed it aside. So many mistakes made. So many lies and denials that only ended in death. I needed this now, a break from the ghosts that haunted me, to escape the pain that waited for me. To bask in gentle hands that didn't want to hit, stab, or tear.

Forcing his head up, I kissed him deeply as I pushed him back to the bed. "I need another snack," I murmured when I finally lifted my mouth from his. Inching my way lower, I kissed and licked a long trail down his chest to the waistband of his pants. I kissed the hard bulge at his groin as my fingers pulled at the button of his jeans. I kissed him again, but this time my teeth lightly scraped against the thick fabric. I wouldn't dare bite a man there. Any sane man would faint dead away in a heartbeat, but the tease had been enough to increase Nicolai's heart rate again.

"Mira," he said in a husky voice edged with warning.

"I wouldn't dream of it," I whispered, unzipping his pants. "I've got another place staked out."

Slipping my fingers inside the waistband of his pants and boxers, I slowly pulled them down, climbing down the bed as I went. I paused long enough to strip off his shoes and socks before letting my eyes travel back up his body. Nicolai now lay stretched out before me, all golden skin and hard muscle. Little blond hairs curled along his legs, and I ran my hands up his calves as I settled between his thighs. I kissed his right inner thigh, drawing an infinity sign with the tip of my tongue.

"Mira." My name escaped him in a breathless whisper, holding an almost pleading tone. He knew what I was looking for; the large vein that ran along his inner thigh, pulsing with life. As my fangs pierced his skin, I wrapped my fingers around his hard length, stroking him as he arched against my hand, keeping him rock hard as I took a quick drink.

Closing the wound after a couple of seconds, I moved higher. I kissed the inside of his hip, running my tongue over the soft tender flesh there. I was drunk on the power I had over him. For once, it wasn't about physical strength or the power I had gained as a nightwalker. It was solely about being female and Nicolai wanting me as a female the same way I wanted every inch of him, because he was a very handsome male.

He allowed me to run my tongue along his engorged penis before entwining his fingers in my hair and hauling me back up to his mouth. Clamping his mouth on mine, he rolled me onto my back so he could more easily kiss me while pulling off my pants. I had no clear memory of it, just his tongue thrusting into my mouth as he fumbled with the button. In the next second, I simply wasn't wearing pants any longer. There was only his hot soft skin rubbing against mine, his hard body nudging against the entrance to mine.

"Mira?"

I blinked and forced myself to look into his eyes, which were now more copper than brown. His voice was thick and husky, but I didn't miss the question there. He was holding himself perfectly still, waiting for me. I wasn't sure if he was giving me one last chance to back out or if he needed to know if I was ready. It didn't matter. I was well beyond such thoughts.

"Please. Now," were the only words I could manage, and they escaped me as a shaken, desperate plea. It was enough.

Nicolai thrust into me, tearing a cry from my throat. He was larger than I expected, and my body hadn't been as ready as I thought, drowning me in equal parts pleasure and pain. It didn't matter. By his next thrust I was arching my hips to meet him, taking every inch of him I could get. We were beyond soft touches and gentle caresses. Now it was rough and fast, with strong, hard hands pushing and pulling us closer to that oblivion of pleasure that lay beyond the horizon.

My mind was overloaded with sensations. His heartbeat was pounding in my brain, mixing with the sound of his heavy breathing and a so-soft grunt as he thrust into me. I breathed him in, drawing his unique scent along with the smell of his sweat and sex into my lungs to hold him there as well. I leaned up and ran my tongue along his neck and up to his ear, needing the taste of him imprinted on me.

Nicolai reached down and cupped my bottom with both of his large hands, changing the angle slightly, grinding his body into mine. Pleasure finally edged ahead of pain in their battle for my body. One last scream was torn from my lips as my body imploded with the force of the orgasm that tightened every muscle. For a moment there was only blinding starlight and an intense pleasure that filled all of my pores. *Dear God, never let this end . . .*

It was minutes later when my brain started to function enough that I realized Nicolai was lying on top of me, his body still shivering inside me with the aftershocks of his orgasm. A silly grin lifted my lips as I briefly wondered if it was possible to destroy brain cells with a really good orgasm. Probably not, but I certainly didn't feel all that intelligent as my brain struggled to pull together a string of coherent thoughts.

Slowly, he began to stir, burrowing his face in my neck. He nipped at my earlobe, earning a chuckle from me before he finally lifted his head. His large eyes had returned to their normal shade of brown, with only a faint hint of copper. Staring at the shadows clinging to his smiling face, I realized neither one of us had bothered to flip on a light. Of course, we both had the night vision of cats, so why bother?

"Feeling better?" he inquired, a cute smugness filling his tone.

"Much." I smiled, pressing a gentle kiss to his lips. "Thank you."

"Thank you," he replied, kissing me back. "We make a good pair."

"You mean when you're not trying to kill me," I teased.

The easygoing smile slipped from his full lips. "I didn't have a choice," he firmly said before rolling off me. Then he lay on his back in silence, roughly running his hands over his face a couple times, as if it could help clear his thoughts. He finally dropped his hands back to his sides, staring up at the ceiling. "Besides, I'm apparently not the first murderous stalker you've tamed."

"Don't misunderstand my truce with Danaus," I said, turning onto my side. Leaning on one elbow, I brushed a lock of hair behind my ear. "If he gets the chance, he means to kill me when this is all over. That hasn't changed."

"Despite the fact that you've protected him?"

"It's a special relationship we have." I flashed him a wide smile, letting my fangs poke out from beneath my upper lips before I rolled off the bed.

"Like this?"

I couldn't stop the laugh that bubbled up as I snatched the black silk robe that lay draped over one of the chairs in the bedroom. "No, we've just called a truce until we can find an appropriate time to kill each other." I pulled the robe on as I strolled over to the window and jerked open the heavy curtains. The window faced San Marco Piazza and the Grand Canal. The large *campo* was aglow with lights, while stars winked in and out overhead. The waves in the Lagoon had grown during the past several minutes and were beginning to whitecap as a storm blew in.

"Speaking of special relationships," I slowly began, not bothering to look over at my companion. "What hold does Jabari have over you?" I waited for his answer, but there was only silence. With a frown, I turned away from the window and walked to the end of the bed with my arms folded over my chest. Nicolai lay as still as death, his golden body gilded with starlight that leaked through the window.

"Before the Coven, I took you into my keeping. I claimed you from an Elder," I said, stressing each word. "I have promised to protect you from any and all who would harm you, including the Coven. I don't know if lycans have an equivalent of such a vow, but it is not something to be taken lightly among nightwalkers. When Jabari comes to claim your head and I sacrifice myself to stop him, I would like to know exactly why he is ripping my heart out."

When Nicolai finally spoke, his voice was low and void of emotion, but his words nearly brought me to my knees. "Members of my pack were aiding the naturi."

"No," I gasped, my voice going hoarse. My mind stumbled forward, struggling to understand the concept. Why would anyone assist the naturi? They were horrid creatures whose only goal was to destroy anything that was not of their kind. "*Willingly?* Were they willingly helping the naturi?" I asked, grasping at my last few desperate straws to understand what he was saying. Maybe they had been forced, mind-control wiping away all choice.

"Yes."

I was moving without a thought. One second I was standing at the foot of the bed, and the next I was kneeling beside him, my hands reaching for his throat, my fangs bared. Nicolai caught my wrists at the last second and was struggling to hold me back. "Were you? Were you helping the naturi?" I snarled.

"No!" he shouted. "I would never help the naturi. I know what they've done. I know what they're capable of."

"Then why did Jabari want you?" I demanded, jerking my wrists from his grasp.

Nicolai pushed up so he was leaning back on his forearms and elbows. "There were three naturi sympathizers in my pack. Somehow Jabari found out and threatened to tell the other packs. Everyone in my pack would have been killed, no questions asked. Instead he killed two of the sympathizers immediately and wanted to keep the third as a pet. I bargained with Jabari to take me instead of her."

I sat back on my heels, hating his words, despising the fact that I sympathized with him. Of course, if I had been in Jabari's place, I have no doubt that I would have destroyed the whole pack without a second thought, and not feel an ounce of remorse about the deed. In this war, it was us against the naturi. There was no room for sympathy or betrayal. But betrayal seemed to surround me when it came to the naturi. Trust was a withering corpse in the sun. Vampires and lycans were siding with the naturi. Witches and lycans were with the Daylight Coalition. And I stood alone with a bori half-breed at my back.

"Girlfriend?" I asked after a long moment of silence, pondering the "her" he had mentioned.

"She was my sister," he softly replied.

With a growl, I climbed off the bed and strode back over to the window, my arms once again folded tightly under my breasts, as if to protect myself against the very idea. There was no questioning the "was" in his statement. We both knew his former pack would have killed his sister the second Jabari departed with him. She had betrayed not only her own kind, but also the pact made by all the other creatures to fight against the naturi. When given the choice between what could be a long, painful existence in servitude to a nightwalker and a quick death, Nicolai stepped in to give her the more merciful option. Would I be so forgiving of someone I loved?

I roughly ran my right hand through my hair, pushing it away from my eyes, trying not to think about the answer that came so quickly to mind. Despite my so-called noble actions in regard to Tristan, I didn't like myself much when it came to my dealings with the naturi. The blood flowed too easily and the joy too sweet.

What was also eating away at me was the idea that Jabari had discovered this betrayal within the United States. It wasn't my domain, but it felt too close. The Elders never came to the New World, and there only a handful of Ancients in the region. The idea that Jabari had come and gone without my knowledge had left me feeling . . . violated. Maybe the others were right. Maybe I had begun to see all of the New World as mine. Or at the very least, safe from direct interference of the Coven.

"I'm sorry," I whispered. We both knew her betrayal had left her with no other fate, but that knowledge did little to ease the pain of loss. "I have to get you to my domain," I said when the silence began to grow between us again. Turning away from the window, I walked over to the nightstand by the bed and picked up my cell phone. Nicolai covered my hand with his before I could pick up the phone, dragging my eyes to his face.

"You'll still protect me?" he asked, confusion furrowing his brow.

"I promised to protect you. I keep my word," I said solemnly with a nod of my head. "But I can't do that here. I have to get you and Tristan to my domain back in the United States. As repayment for this protection, you must guard Tristan during the daylight hours as you travel to my home. You must promise to guard him with your life."

"I swear I will. No harm will come to him." Nicolai squeezed my hand as he made his vow. I tried to smile at him, reassure him, but I couldn't. I believed him. He would die before he allowed anyone to lay a hand on Tristan, and that was reassuring. Yet when I looked at him, my mind now wondered if he had known what his sister was doing. Did he try to hide her actions? Protect her the same way he protected her from Jabari?

"Get some sleep. I have to make some arrangement. You'll be flying out in the morning." Picking up my cell phone, I wordlessly walked out of the bedroom into the main living area and shut the door behind me.

It was four hours until sunrise and I needed every minute of it to make my plans. I spent nearly an hour on the phone arguing with Barrett, the Alpha of the werewolf pack in Savannah. He was less than pleased with the idea of me bringing an unknown lycan into his territory; not that I could blame him. Naturally, I couldn't tell him the real reason as to how Nicolai came to be in my care. It didn't help matters that the Savannah pack was very peculiar since most of those in it were actually related by blood or marriage, and outsiders were very rarely permitted to move into the region. I think Barrett finally caved in to my request only because I promised him that it would not be a long-term arrangement.

Other than the brief, heated argument, it felt good to talk to him. Since leaving Savannah a week ago, the naturi had disappeared completely from my domain. There were no more attacks, no more deaths. Prior to my traveling to Egypt with Danaus, the naturi had attacked a human nightclub and a private nightwalker club, resulting in several deaths— some at the hands of werewolves being controlled by the naturi. Tension was still running high, but the area was otherwise quiet.

With Barrett reassured, somewhat, it was then on to my human assistant Charlotte, who would make the arrangements for the private flight from Venice to Savannah. She had received enough bizarre phone calls like this one to know not to ask too many questions. After talking to her, I contacted my bodyguard Gabriel, still recuperating in England following our last battle with the naturi. A lump grew in my throat at the sweet sound of his familiar voice. Closing my eyes, I could see his crooked smirk. Gabriel had protected me for years, knew my secrets. He would also grab a flight tonight and be waiting in Savannah when Tristan and Nicolai arrived. My angel would see to it that Tristan was properly taken care of when he arrived in my domain.

I wanted to call Knox. While relatively young, he had proven capable and intelligent enough to manage the region when I was out of town. I wanted to hear his voice, the touch of dry humor that laced his every comment. I needed to know from him that all the nightwalkers I had left behind in my domain were still safe. But Tristan and Danaus returned as I ended my call with Gabriel and sank into the soft cushions of the sofa, forcing me to put aside my phone.

The nightwalker had been considerate enough to go hunting while I occupied myself with Nicolai. Neither said anything about how I had spent my evening because Tristan got it into his head to argue with me for the next hour over whether he would travel with me to the site of the next sacrifice and battle the naturi.

In the end I won and he agreed to travel to my domain. He had suffered enough, and I wasn't willing to lose him to the naturi. I prayed it was the start of a series of smart choices on my part.

Nineteen

If I had been human, I would have tossed and turned, twisting the smooth cotton sheets. I would have stared up at the ceiling as the minutes crawled by, imagining the hundreds of threats and dangers Tristan could potentially face while he lay helpless during the daylight hours. I would have laid there hating Danaus and Nicolai, fearing they would betray my desperate trust. Hell, if I was human, I would have accompanied Tristan's lifeless form down to the airport and personally secured him on the private jet.

But I wasn't human, and at times I wondered if I had ever been human, considering my horrid past. I was a nightwalker. When the sun finally tore at the horizon and the night gave its last shuddering breath, consciousness left me no matter how badly I wished to remain awake. There were no thoughts of Tristan, no bits of safeguard I could offer him. There was only the desolate blackness and an emptiness from which I could not pull away. In those last seconds, I hated the dawn and my weakness, not for the first time since being reborn.

Yet, my daylight hours weren't completely filled with undisturbed nothingness. In my final hour before waking, images of Tristan filled my brain, flashing in my mind like a demonic slide show. This was not like the nightmares I suffered in Egypt and England. Those grim plays had been a mix of my own memories and growing fears.

These garish images were from Macaire's memories of the night when Tristan was tortured by the court. But there was no order to the images, no linear progression. The Elder's memories flickered in my brain like a reel of film that had been badly spliced together. One moment Tristan was hunched over covered in blood, his back raw and his limbs trembling in pain. Yet, in the next moment, he was standing unharmed, surrounded by his kind as he anticipated his fate.

The only thing about the nightmare that was linear was Tristan's thoughts. They whispered through my head like a ghostly soundtrack, going from disbelief that his beloved maker would abandon him to his fate, to broken pleading for her to save him. Save him from the pain. Save him from the blackness that was swallowing up his hope. In the end his fragile, fractured mind clung to a single, unwavering word: Mira. He knew I would come and end the pain.

When I was finally released from the hellish nightmare and awoke, my body began trembling and I choked back a sob. Rolling onto my side in the bed, I curled into the fetal position as I waited for the shaking to pass. My thoughts were sluggish, as if a thick, tarlike film covered them, a disgusting residue left behind by Macaire's mental touch.

When I could finally unclench my fingers, which were twisted in the sheets, I mentally reached out for Tristan, but came up with only dead air. Instantly lurching into a sitting position on the bed, legs bent before me and eyes tightly closed, I concentrated again. All of my energy poured into the single act of touching his thoughts, being able to feel his presence. I needed to know he was safe.

When the sun had risen that morning, Tristan was laying beside me. Danaus and Nicolai had agreed to get him safely aboard the chartered jet. Either one of them had ample opportunity to stake him while he slept.

No. Shaking my head at the thought, I knew Danaus wouldn't kill a nightwalker when he or she slept. The hunter might hate my kind, but his sense of honor ran deeper than that. If he wanted Tristan dead, he'd take care of the matter while the nightwalker was awake and able to defend himself.

Nicolai, I didn't trust. He could have been lying. Maybe he was a naturi sympathizer and I'd left Tristan at his mercy. Damn it! I was an idiot.

Twisting on the bed, I snatched up my cell phone from the nightstand and pulled up Gabriel's number. My bodyguard answered after the second ring, and some of the tension in my stomach slowly unknotted at the sound of his voice.

"Do you have Tristan?" I quickly demanded, inwardly wincing at the harshness of my voice.

"Yes. Are you in trouble?" he asked.

I ignored his question. I was in all kinds of trouble, but there was nothing he or Tristan could do about it. "Let me speak to him."

"Mira," Gabriel started hesitantly, "he's still asleep. It's about two-thirty in the afternoon."

Falling back against my pillows, I gave a breathless chuckle, laughing at my own stupidity. All the chaos flying about me had scattered my thoughts. I was so worried about Tristan's safety that I forgot about the six-hour time difference.

"Sorry," I mumbled.

"He's safe," Gabriel reassured me, his voice growing soft. "Both he and Nicolai landed around one."

"Is Nicolai with you?"

"No. You didn't say anything about him staying with you, so I left him at your town house. He wasn't happy about it."

The thought brought a faint smile to my lips. Nicolai possibly didn't trust Gabriel with a vulnerable Tristan, but I had told the lycan that Gabriel was my bodyguard.

"I had to agree to have Tristan call Nicolai the second he was awake," he continued.

"Have you actually seen Tristan?"

"I opened the trunk after I pulled into the garage at your place. He's curled up with head and heart in their right places," he teased, and I couldn't blame him. My paranoia was worse than usual. "I won't leave him until he's in the house and knows how to set the alarms."

"Thank you, my angel," I sighed, letting my eyes drift shut. The security system for my house wasn't quite Fort Knox, but it would deter most humans and give Tristan enough warning if another creature was near at night. There was also a vault in the basement with a separate security system, which would keep him safe during the daylight hours. Not even Gabriel knew how to disarm the locks on the vault. I had given Tristan those codes before he fell asleep that morning.

"How bad is it?" Gabriel inquired when a comfortable silence had grown between us.

"Bad enough." I didn't want to say more. It would take too long and serve no good purpose. "Have you healed?" I asked, changing the subject. The last time I saw him, he had sustained a wound to his side and thigh, and was still nursing an injured arm from a fight in Egypt.

"Enough to be a threat." I could imagine one of his rare smiles flitting across his lips as he spoke.

As my own smile faded, I gave him instructions to contact my assistant, Charlotte, and have her arrange for a chartered jet to be ready to leave Venice that night. The new moon was in two nights. We had enough time to be at whatever location would be the site of the next sacrifice. Enough time to face the naturi for what I hoped would be the last time.

Rolling out of bed, I showered and dressed. Unfortunately, I was down to my last clean garment—a sleeveless cotton dress that hung down to my ankles. I had hoped to wear it in Egypt as I wandered around the decaying monuments, listening to the sound of the Nile splashing between its banks. The breezy, navy blue skirt would only hinder me in a fight, but I knew I wouldn't be fighting Macaire when he finally decided to appear. The Elder might be seriously pissed at me, but he also understood the value of a good weapon. And if I had proved anything during the long years, it was that I was an efficient killer.

I had hoped to slip out of the suite without being stopped, but Danaus was sitting in the living room drinking coffee. The remains of his dinner rested on a trolley brought up by room service. A ghost of a smile floated across my lips as I looked at the hunter settled comfortably on the sofa. It always amused me when I saw him doing such mundane things like eating or enjoying the warmth of a good cup of coffee. It kept my mind struggling to grasp hold of him, as he constantly shifted between ruthless killer and human in my thoughts.

He was dressed in a dark navy linen shirt with short sleeves that revealed his deeply tanned, muscled arms. His shoulder-length locks were pulled back, letting my eyes caress his strong features. The day's growth of dark stubble had been removed from his chin, but it did nothing to lessen the shadows that clung to the hollows of his cheeks. Danaus looked like a wealthy Italian gentlemen on holiday, but there was a seriousness, a dark shadow in his sapphire eyes, that no amount of expensive clothes could hide.

Had circumstances been different, I would have been content to spend the night staring at him, slowly memorizing his features. I would have happily passed the night curled in a chair, arguing philosophy, mythology, and our place in the universe with him.

"You're awake early," he said, setting his cup on the

table before him. He rose from the sofa, slipping his hands into his trouser pockets. A knife was once again attached to his waist, and he was wearing a hard leather wrist guard on his right arm. The weaponry and guard were at odds with his clothes, reminding me that there was no escaping what he was—a hunter.

"Another meeting, I believe," I said. I was dead inside after all that had happened during the past several nights. Walking over to the wall of windows, I leaned against the wall and crossed my arms loosely over my stomach.

"Like last night's?"

"No."

"Alone?"

I stared out the wall of windows, admiring the pallet of colors washing across the sky. Since becoming a night-walker, my skies had been limited to inky black and sickly shades of gray. Yet, while in Venice, I had been given two chances to add some color to my skies. Tonight, the sky was bathed in deep reds and oranges as the sun sank deeper beneath the horizon. "No," I said, a surprised smile dawning on my face. Danaus knew almost as much as I did at this point. Why should I try to hide this? He was also part of the triad. If Macaire wanted to talk to me about the naturi, then he would have to tell Danaus as well.

"We have to leave tonight," Danaus reminded me. I knew that. The new moon was in two nights. It was also Lugh-nassadh, the pagan preharvest festival. Ancient lore said the celebration was in honor of the god Lugh's wedding to Mother Earth. While I can't say that I put much stock in the old pagan tales, it would have been rather fitting if the naturi managed to break the seal on that night, erasing the one thing blocking the union of the two worlds.

"Do you know where the next sacrifice will be?" I asked, turning to look at him.

He shook his head, a grim smile lifting the corners of his mouth. "I was going to ask you the same question."

"Great," I muttered, walking over and plopping down in one of the chairs next to the sofa. "We're out of time."

"We should never have come here. We should have been looking for the next location, or at least trying to hunt down Rowe," Danaus growled, but to my surprise, he seemed as frustrated with himself as he was with me.

"I don't remember us having a lot of choice in the matter," I said, fixing my dark gaze on the hunter. "Or at least, I didn't. Jabari wanted me here. I wouldn't have been able to fight him. I'm a puppet, remember?"

Danaus sat down on the sofa again, leaning forward so he could rest his elbows on his knees. He stared off into space, lost in his own thoughts. Unfortunately, this arguing wasn't getting us anywhere.

"The naturi can't do anything for another two nights," I said with a sigh. "If we hadn't come here, we would have been jumping from place to place, chasing anything that looked suspicious. That would have been a waste of our time and extremely dangerous. Rowe could have attacked at any time during the day. At least here we were protected."

That comment finally made Danaus's head snap up, a frown pulling at his mouth. In this case, "protected" simply meant that we were safe from the naturi because this area was controlled by nightwalkers. And apparently because the Coven had struck up some kind of bargain with the naturi.

"Look at it this way, if we hadn't come, Tristan and Nicolai would most likely be dead. We wouldn't know the Coven has cooked up some scheme with the naturi, and we wouldn't know that Rowe is unaware of the alliance. Once we know what the Coven is planning, it will be easier to stop them," I argued.

"But that still leaves us with one very large problem,"

Danaus countered. The hunter picked up his coffee cup again and drank the last of its contents.

Pulling myself up using the arms of the chair, I sat up straight. "I think we have more than that, but which one are you referring to?"

"Where is the next sacrifice?"

"We should know tonight. I think Macaire will tell us," I said, causing Danaus's features to twist in confusion.

"And why do you think he will do that?"

"Call it a hunch." I shrugged my shoulders at the hunter as I smiled at him. "Have you talked to Ryan recently? Are your people looking as well?"

The warlock was the head of Themis, a research group that had spent centuries watching nightwalkers, lycanthropes, and any other creepy-crawly creatures the rest of the human race wasn't aware of. Their numbers were large enough that they could watch all twelve of the so-called holy sites and report back any kind of activity. And the one major advantage they had over nightwalkers was that they could keep an eye on things during the daylight hours. While I fully expected Macaire to tell us the site of the next sacrifice, I wanted Ryan to confirm the information for me. Macaire would tell us the location; I just wanted to be sure it was the real location.

"Ryan is looking into it," Danaus replied. "No word yet on the location."

"Gabriel is contacting Charlotte. She'll arrange for the flight out tonight," I said, pushing back to my feet. Forcing a smile onto my lips, I motioned with my head toward the door. "Ready?"

The hunter's muscular body was almost humming with energy as we headed down to the main landing. Pausing near the canal, I willed my body to relax, pushing the tension from my arms and down my legs until it flowed out of my toes. A light summer breeze stirred, dancing down the canals and threading its way between the buildings. Street lamps were popping on and the glow from Piazza San Marco was starting to swell.

"How do you like your rooms?" inquired a gentle voice from behind me in strangely accented English. I jerked around, stunned to find Macaire seated on a bench just a few feet from us. I hadn't felt him there a moment ago, hadn't even sensed his approach, but I guess that's what made him an Elder.

Danaus instinctively reached for his knife, but I gently laid my hand on his wrist, halting his movement. Macaire had done nothing yet to threaten us. I was willing to play it cool for now. No reason to start a fight. There would be plenty of time for that later.

"They're stunning, particularly the large wall of windows facing the east," I answered. His face split into a wide, almost malicious grin. "When did the Coven acquire the Cipriani?"

"A few years ago," he said, pushing to his feet and walking over to us. His English was perfect, but the accent was strange. I knew he wasn't as old as Jabari, making me doubt that his people were a dead civilization. Slavic, Eastern European, or maybe Russian? But even that seemed wrong.

Macaire wore a pale, mint green button-up shirt that contrasted nicely with his deep brown eyes. His white linen pants and supple brown loafers made him look so damn approachable and pleasant. He should have looked more predatory; something to indicate to the world that he was one of the most powerful nightwalkers on the planet.

When he was standing beside me, he offered his arm. With a great deal of effort, I managed to keep my face expressionless as I slipped my hand into the crook of his arm while I let my other hand drop from Danaus's wrist.

"The hall was receiving too many visitors, making sleeping arrangements uncomfortable," he continued, pleased to see that I was willing to play along. His eyes for a brief moment skimmed over Danaus as if weighing some thought.

"We thought it wise if we started keeping some of our guests off the island."

"It's beautiful. I've always liked the quiet of Guidecca," I said, strolling down the street next to him. In the eyes of the world, we were a trio of tourists on an evening walk along the narrow street of the island, not enemies trying to find a way to accomplish our individual goals without dying in the process.

"How is Tristan?" Macaire abruptly asked as we crossed a small bridge, heading deeper into the island of Guidecca.

"I imagine he is faring much better than Sadira." I couldn't quite stop the smile that rose to my pale lips. Her screams echoed through my memory for a brief moment, loud enough that I felt muscles twitch in Macaire's arm. I figured he was listening to some of my thoughts.

"Yes, I fear she'll be in pain for quite some time," he said, his voice hardening. "Not exactly a wise choice, considering that she must be strong to help you with the naturi."

"Nor was her choice of enemies wise," Danaus darkly interjected.

I was pleased with the hunter's comments, but I didn't want to worry about trying to separate the Elder and Danaus while I was still trying to get information. "Are you concerned?" I asked quickly, arching one brow as I looked down at him.

Macaire paused and turned his body so he was facing me. He laid one of his hands over my hand, which was lightly resting on his arm. "Of course I am."

"I had my doubts," I said with a frown. "Considering your new business partner, I was under the impression that maybe the Coven no longer wanted to keep the door closed."

"Ahhh," Macaire said, resuming our walk through the neighborhood. "You misunderstand, my young one." His condescending tone made my teeth clench, but for now I knew it had to be tolerated.

"I can't imagine why." Hidden by the material of my

dress, my free hand clenched into a fist at my side. "What is going on, Macaire? What has the Coven done?"

"We've struck a rather unique bargain."

"Has the Coven decided to destroy us all?"

Macaire stopped walking again. He reached up and placed his hands on both of my cheeks, his eyes softening to a look of sweet concern. The nightwalker looked older than many of the others. It appeared that he was in his late forties to early fifties when he was reborn. His dark brown hair was sprinkled liberally with gray, giving him a wise and distinguished look. There was a cleft in his chin and deep lines around his mouth and eyes. It was strange. He looked like he was almost twice as old as Jabari, but the Egyptian was the older of the two.

"What we have done is for the protection of our kind," he reassured me. His eyes pointedly moved from my face to stare at Danaus, who stood behind my right shoulder. "What have you done for the protection of our kind?"

I stepped backward out of his touch, my brows bunching angrily over the bridge of my nose. "I'm not a fool. You can't make deals with the naturi and expect them to live up to the agreement."

"Some would say the same about you," he ruefully stated, looking from Danaus to me again.

"Enough! What is going on?"

Smiling, Macaire lifted his arm, patiently waiting for me to place my hand back in the crook of his elbow. He liked the farce, and I knew he would say nothing until I complied with his wishes. Nearly growling in my frustration, I placed my hand back on his arm and we continued our walk.

"Several decades ago, the Coven was quietly approached by a handful of naturi," he began, sounding as if he was retelling a tale of misadventure at the office. "They told us of their queen's plans to open the door between our worlds. It seems that they had become content with the way things had gone since becoming separated from the rest of the host. They had no desire to fall back under the thumb of their illustrious ruler. This small group came to us requesting that we not only close the door, but that we also kill Aurora."

My legs stopped working as I listened to these words, as if the very idea had locked up my brain. I stood planted to the spot, blindly staring ahead at the large plaza we had entered. "Kill Aurora," I repeated dumbly.

"They wish to return to the peaceful existence they had found. Aurora will not allow that. She will continue with her plans for wiping out both humans and nightwalkers."

"I don't believe it." I shook my head, as if trying to clear the clutter of questions that had crowded in my brain. Macaire tried to continue walking, but I wouldn't move.

"You do not have to," he said patiently. "The Elders do."

"To kill Aurora, she has to come through the door, which means we have to allow them to open the door," Danaus reminded him. "It would be safer to stop them before they open it. It may be centuries before she has another chance to open the door again."

"We considered that, and there is one problem . . ." Macaire paused, moving his gaze from Danaus to my face. "You."

I lurched backward a step, putting a little distance between us. The sidewalk seemed to have narrowed, leaving me feeling trapped between Danaus and Macaire. This conversation had taken a strange, unexpected turn. "What do you mean?"

"You are needed to shut the door and form the seal. We also believe you are our best chance at destroying Aurora," he said. "Unfortunately, considering your reckless lifestyle and your unexpected alliance, the Coven doesn't feel confident that you will survive long enough to stop Aurora if she tries again a couple centuries from now."

"Best chance—don't you mean best weapon?" I snapped irritably.

"Yes," he said in a slow hiss. "You are an exquisite weapon, whether you act alone or are being wielded by another. The Coven thinks this is our best chance to stop Aurora once and for all. To finish it. And we're not sure we'll have another chance like this one."

"So we allow her to come through the door, close the door, and then kill her," I stated, frowning darkly at him. "After that, the naturi that hired us go free."

"Returning to their quiet lives," he said with a nod as he laced his stubby fingers behind his back and continued to walk along the sidewalk until it opened up into a large, open square.

"What do we get out of this?" I demanded, unable to keep the skepticism out of my voice. I folded my arms over my chest and stared hard at the Elder, but he ignored my dark looks.

"Besides the chance to destroy their queen and cripple their race?"

"Yes. We're the ones risking everything."

Macaire smiled and strolled into the center of the *campo*, his hands clasped loosely behind his back. Reluctantly, Danaus and I followed him into the center of the square. The area was mostly empty. At the far end of the *campo* a stage was being decorated by several people. They appeared to be preparing for a festival, though I wasn't sure which one. On the stage sat a row of five chairs with high backs, reminding me vaguely of the Great Hall dais. Obviously, Macaire had planned on walking to this part of the neighborhood. He had something else on his mind.

"What do you know of the Great Awakening?" he asked, his tone sounding as if he had just asked what the weather would be like tomorrow.

"A general outline of the plan. Why? It's not supposed to be for another fifty years and even that's still up for debate."

"It's the debate that has the Elders concerned," he said. His hands swung from his back and hung limp at his sides. He looked around, taking in the string of little lights overhead and the other tables that lined the edge of the square. Tomorrow they would most likely be overflowing with food while the square buzzed with conversation and laughter. "It seems Our Liege wishes to change the date of the Awakening."

"To what?"

"Next year."

"Is he mad?" Danaus blurted out, causing me to wince at his volume and tone. It was not the type of thing anyone dared to voice about Our Liege. You never knew who was listening. I had always been outspoken, but there were a few lines even I was hesitant to cross.

"That's not the word I would use," Macaire said, his grim voice a proper reprimand for my companion's unseemly outburst.

"It's too soon," I said to the Elder, resisting the urge to place my hand on Danaus's arm to steady myself. My world was spinning out of control and I desperately wanted to run away from them all. "The humans may be able to adapt, but there are still a few stages that are supposed to be implemented. It would make the transition easier. The timetable was developed to protect our kind. You can't throw it aside."

"You're not telling me anything the Coven has not already discussed." Macaire waved one hand absently at me. A frown dug deeper lines into his grim face.

I walked over to stand directly in front of him, lowering my voice. Our agitated conversation was drawing the confused gaze of those on the stage at the far aside of the square. "What about the other races? What have they said?"

"They wish to stick to the timetable."

I closed my eyes, not wanting to hear any more, but there

was one other question that had to be asked. "Will Our Liege proceed without the rest of the races?"

"It is his intention."

"Then it will be war," I said wearily. The other races would attack nightwalkers around the globe to keep us from pulling aside the veil that protected our common secret. If I survived Aurora's planned assassination, I would be headed into a war against creatures I had been at peace with for centuries. And in the end, the humans would still discover us ahead of schedule. We wouldn't be able to hide the war from them forever, and they would discover us in the worst possible way.

"So now you understand our dilemma." The Elder sounded tired, as if the weight of centuries had trickled into his voice.

"What is the Coven's plan?"

Again Macaire smiled at me, sending a shiver skittering across my skin. Nightwalkers may not have been reborn evil, but there were moments when I thought something truly evil resided in Macaire's chest. "The naturi can move about during the day. They would be able to get past bodyguards."

"You plan to—"

"Do not even breathe the words!" he sharply said. Even the powerful Macaire had his fears. I knew what they planned to do. The Coven planned to have the naturi assassinate Our Liege while he slept during the day.

"And all of the Coven has agreed on this course of action?"

"Of course."

"Even Tabor?"

The Elder's gaze darted to Danaus before he could stop himself and then he stared silently at me for a long time. I could almost see the thoughts bouncing around in his head as he weighed my question. His lips twitched. It wasn't quite a smile, but it was something. Maybe a word that he had stopped at the last second.

"That is an interesting question," he said at last. "I think he would have if he had survived longer."

"But he didn't initially," I prodded. Something still didn't feel right about this. It might have just been my survival instincts telling me not to trust a word Macaire told me. I believed there was some kernel of truth to this tale, but I also knew there were a few other important tidbits he was leaving out. I had never met Our Liege and didn't feel any particular allegiance to the nightwalker. As far as I knew, he had done nothing for me and was generally indifferent to my existence. In truth, Our Liege and the Coven had little effect on the night-to-night life of a vampire.

"He had his doubts," Macaire said. "Why do you ask?"

"Just curious," I replied with a shrug.

I strolled through the *campo* then, heading toward the stage, when I abruptly stopped, my eyes locked on the five chairs. The people who were hanging the last of the deep purple cloth to hide the wooden beams supporting the stage had finished and left the plaza. Danaus and I were alone with the Elder.

"Another question if you please?" I called into the air, trying to lighten my voice of the fear coursing through my entire body.

"What is on your mind, my dear?" Macaire said, coming to stand beside me. His voice was sweet and pleasant. He already knew what thoughts were dancing through my head.

"Supposing Our Liege meets an untimely demise at the hand of the naturi. Then our kind will find itself without a clear leader for the first time in several millennia. That cannot be in the best interest of our people."

"No, that would not be," he said with a solemn shake of his head. "But our race wouldn't be without guidance. The Coven would remain."

"So the rule of one and four would be replaced by the rule of three," I said. That did not feel like an improvement.

"Until someone rose to power to reclaim the throne, and a fourth filled the empty seat on the Coven."

I was frowning again. The Coven was not an improvement over Our Liege if one used the court as any kind of example of what the future would hold for my race. The Elders did as they wanted, but Our Liege held their collective leash. I might not have been too keen on his plan to throw away the timetable and start a war, but I wasn't thrilled with my other option either.

Thick, heavy shadows had moved into the large plaza, and the voices of the people had dulled. Night was fully born. To my surprise, Macaire hopped up on the stage. The nightwalker sat down in the chair in the center, balancing his left ankle on his right knee.

"There is a belief among our kind that you will take the open seat on the Coven," he casually began, motioning toward the seat that would have been Tabor's.

It was a fight not to clench my teeth. I was doomed to hear this question repeated until it drove me mad. "I'm not an Ancient," I said carefully.

"That is more a tradition than a law," he said with a dismissive wave of his hand. I remained silent, waiting for him to finally say what was on his mind, but I should have known it wouldn't be that easy. "The rumor has begun to pick up steam now following your return to Venice and your little display the other night with Gwen. You were never one to adopt pets. I also heard what you told Valerio the other night about choosing sides. One might think that you are starting to build a following." All this was said with a great amount of indifference and a frosting of boredom, but I wasn't fooled. There was something he wanted to hear from me, and he was hanging on my every word.

"My actions during the past several days have nothing to do with the Coven and everything to do with defeating the naturi. That is all," I said sharply, folding my arms over my stomach.

"Even Nicolai?"

A wide grin spread across my face, exposing my fangs. I was wondering when he would get around to what had happened with the harpies. "That was only a bit of fun."

"As you wish. But the question remains . . . "

"Part of being on the Coven means being able to defend your position, and I am not strong enough to do that," I hedged.

"This, coming from the one who tried to destroy all three members of the Coven at once just nights ago," he scoffed, putting his foot back on the stage with a hollow thud as he leaned forward.

"That was a stupid move on my part. I lost my temper and did not think," I conceded. My eyes fell to look at the cobblestone plaza, an appropriate stance of subservience. I wasn't sorry about the whole thing. In fact, if Danaus hadn't stopped me, I might have been able to pick off one of them before my head was ripped off.

"True, but you do have a nasty past with the naturi. It was understandable and I have forgiven you."

I wanted to tell him to choke on his forgiveness but thought it better not to antagonize Macaire, since we were currently getting along so well. I decided to wisely ignore the comment and push ahead.

"Regardless of recent events, I know that there is at least one Elder who would not support my ascension to the Coven," I cautiously hedged, curious as to his opinion. "And after Gwen's demise, I have succeeded in upsetting another. Even you called for my death last night."

Macaire sighed dramatically, shaking his head slightly as he chuckled to himself. "You do have a way with people," he murmured, sitting back in his chair. "I acted rashly last night. The development with Nicolai was unexpected. Elizabeth is not pleased with you, but you did warn Gwen. She had to fight her own fights. Elizabeth accepts that."

"And Jabari?" Danaus asked, as he came to stand beside me. He placed his hand on my shoulder, but I could not feel his presence in my thoughts. I was suddenly wary of his new interest. Could he honestly want me on the Coven? I wanted to shake my head to clear it of the thought. The only place Danaus wanted me was staked and headless. Yet the new thought stuck like a worm in an apple's core.

"No, Jabari means to have Mira's head after the door is closed," Macaire said sadly as he returned his ankle to his opposite knee.

"I can't defeat him." There was no emotion in that statement. It was a simple fact I had known for as long as I'd been a nightwalker. As long as Jabari could control me, it was impossible for me to destroy him. And even without that ability, Jabari was extremely old and powerful. I wasn't sure anyone could actually defeat him.

"I think you underestimate your powers." I opened my mouth to argue, but Macaire held up his hand, stopping the words in my throat. "If half of what Ms. Brooks described is true, I think you could easily triumph with some help from your hunter."

"But that would not be on my own."

"No one else would know that." His words escaped his thin lips as a whisper, a grin reappearing on his face.

"No one but you," I corrected. Nicely done. He had found a way to not only get rid of Our Liege, but Jabari as well. Unfortunately, for him, I wouldn't let myself be used by him. "I won't be a puppet for you."

"How is that possible? I'm sure you have guessed by now that I cannot use you the way Jabari has," Macaire said, with no small amount of bitterness.

"I won't do it."

"Loyal to the end," he sneered, his mouth twisting so that I saw a flash of fangs. "Even after all that he has done to you. Even though he means to end your life."

"If I defeat Jabari, it will be on my own. Besides, I don't want a seat on the Coven." I didn't want to have anything to do with the group. I just wanted to go home and forget about them all. Of course, if I did somehow manage to kill Jabari after we defeated the naturi, it would mean leaving two seats on the Coven open and Our Liege standing in danger. It would be all too easy for Macaire to take the throne and create his own Coven.

"If that is what you wish," he said softly. He rose from the chair and jumped back down to the ground. I turned my back to him and stepped away from Danaus as I let my gaze sweep over the square. Lights in the shops and houses threw down a mismatch of golden squares on the plaza. Within the walls I could feel the humans going about their tasks, making dinner and talking to their loved ones. Just a few yards away their lives hung in the balance, being decided by creatures they didn't even know existed.

"Are you prepared to leave?" Macaire inquired, returning my thoughts to the most urgent problem.

"A jet will be ready to leave by midnight. Where are we going?" I asked, swallowing some of the horror and anger that were still crowding in on my thoughts. This was why I had been brought to Venice. Not so much for my protection, but to make sure I understood what was at stake. To Macaire, I was being called in for one last mission on behalf of the Coven. When the time came, he expected me to kill Aurora as if she was some rogue nightwalker reeking havoc in a tiny town half forgotten by the world. However, it seemed Jabari wanted something else from me. He'd brought me there for the sole purpose of discovering the bargain, and wanted the naturi to fear me. But I had no idea what his ultimate goal was. After the horrid tale Macaire told, could Jabari truly want me to disrupt this bargain when it could stop two wars?

"Crete," Macaire replied to my question.

A bubble of laughter escaped me as I shook my head. Oh yes, it could get worse. I hadn't been to Crete since I escaped that wretched island as a young woman hoping to elude the mob screaming for my head. More than six hundred years had passed since I touched that land, and I had no desire to revisit it and the ghosts that waited for me.

Danaus stepped close. He didn't touch me, but I could feel the warm brush of his powers against my bare arms. It was like a soothing embrace. "And what exactly do you want me to accomplish?" I bit out when I finally got control of my emotions again.

"Allow the naturi to complete the sacrifice," Macaire replied. "The seal must be broken if they are going to be able to open the door."

"Then why send me?" I demanded, taking a step closer to him. His unique brand of logic was starting to drive me crazy. "Why send anyone? If we take on the naturi again, there's a good chance we're going to end up dead."

A grim smile graced his lips, and he stepped closer, in no way intimidated by me or my reputation. "Because I need you to kill Rowe. He's their leader. He has the best chance of stopping us when we attack Aurora. He also has the best chance of keeping the naturi organized. The remaining naturi will most likely scatter and die off without a strong leader like Aurora or Rowe."

"Do your new business partners know about this part of the plan?" I inquired sweetly.

"No, but they have been made aware that it is very likely many will be killed during this campaign."

I nodded and took a step backward, my shoulder bumping

into Danaus's chest. Very neatly done. I had trouble believing the Coven would agree to anything that would allow the naturi to walk away and live in peace. The hope was that if we wiped out those who comprised their monarchy, it would eventually result in the complete destruction of their race.

"Will Jabari and Sadira be joining us in Crete?"

"No."

"Are any others being sent?"

"A few others have been summoned and sent on ahead. They will be arriving tonight. They have been instructed to stay away from the site of the sacrifice and remain hidden until you have contacted them with the plan of attack. Remember, you can't act until after they complete the sacrifice," he instructed.

I frowned, staring off into the darkness. I still didn't know what I was going to do. Not that I had that much choice in the matter. I was just the weapon. While I agreed that we would all be better off with Aurora dead, it was a great risk to allow the door to open. The only other wild card in this disaster waiting to happen was Danaus, and I couldn't even begin to fathom what his thoughts would be on the situation.

"You have to bring that hunter to heel, Mira," Macaire said, not caring that Danaus was standing right behind me. He had obviously been listening in again. I wanted to laugh. Danaus wasn't controlled by anyone, least of all me.

"I'll do what I can. Danaus does as he pleases," I warned.

"We can't afford mistakes."

"I know," I whispered, but when I looked up at him, I discovered that he was gone. Bastard. I hated it when the Ancients did things like that.

As I started to shuffle out of the plaza, I paused and looked back at the stage where the five chairs loomed over the large stone square. Jabari kept the balance on the Coven, protected the calm. If I killed him, there would be no stopping Macaire, except possibly Elizabeth. Unfortunately, I knew nothing about her. In my experience, she had always been like Tabor, a silent partner who enjoyed a little entertainment from time to time but kept to the shadows for the most part. Did she actually believe this scheme would work, or was she worried that she would be crushed like Tabor?

I wished I could talk to her for a few minutes; find out if she stood with Our Liege or Macaire. But after I played doctor with Gwen, I didn't foresee that conversation being particularly productive. I also feared she wouldn't be willing to speak for fear of being heard by Macaire. After seeing Jabari's willingness to shake up the agreement with the naturi last night, I knew he wasn't too keen on this plan either. That would also explain why Jabari remained in constant hiding. It meant neither Macaire nor the naturi could find him.

Sighing softly, I folded my arms over my chest. What was I left with? Let Jabari kill me when I finally grew useless so the balance on the Coven would remain. Not exactly my first choice. If I killed Jabari, would I have to take a seat, and spend the rest my existence butting heads with Macaire until he finally had me killed? Should I try to warn Our Liege? Other than the fact that he was trying to destroy us all now, he was an improvement over Macaire. Of course, the whole story could be a lie.

To add to it all, I had never met Our Liege. I didn't know where he was or how to contact him if I wanted to warn him. Not to mention that there was no telling if he would actually believe such a ridiculous tale. As it had been pointed out on more than one occasion, I wasn't the most popular creature among my kind.

But all of that was secondary to the greater, more immediate problem: What was I going to do when I got to Crete? The command to kill Rowe wasn't a particular problem. I couldn't see any benefit to leaving him alive, since he either wanted to use me or kill me. Yet, allowing them to complete the sacrifice would allow them to open the door at a later date. If there were any mistakes when the door was opened, all of the naturi could come rushing back into the world along with Aurora. A very bad thing.

On the other hand, if the door never opened and Aurora was never killed, then the naturi would never fulfill their promise to assassinate Our Liege. While I might not want him dead, I definitely didn't want him to send us into a war with all the other races just to stop the Great Awakening from happening ahead of schedule. Another very bad thing.

It seemed I only had two choices: war with the naturi or war with creatures I had once called friends.

Shuffling back toward the hotel with a silent Danaus, my mind a jumble of thoughts, I realized that I missed my original plan. It had been a good, solid plan.

1. Kill Nerian.
2. Find Jabari or some other Elder.
3. Tell Elder of the naturi plan.
4. Return home.

Oh, and kill Danaus.

But even that had gotten fouled up along the way. To hell with plans. In less than twenty-four hours I was going to be standing in the remains of a place I had once called home, surrounded by the naturi. I doubted another one of my brilliant plans was going to see me through. May the fates forgive me, what I needed was to talk to Jabari

TWENTY

M y skin crawled. I stepped onto the tarmac of the runway at the Nikos Kazantzakis Airport in Heraklion and my stomach lurched and churned within me. Clenching my teeth, I paused at the foot of the stairs leading down from my jet and wrapped my arms around my middle as if I could protect myself from the memories that seemed to rise up from the dead in the back of my brain.

I might never have lived in this town—my family had lived in a small house to the south of Chania, a port town west of Heraklion—but I was home. After standing on the runway for less than a minute, the familiar smells were already teasing at my mind. The wind swept up from the south, running over the island before finally reaching me. The warm breeze had skimmed through the valley and over the mountain ranges that bisected the island, carrying with it the rich scents of Jerusalem sage, Cretan bee orchid, and dark Cretan ebony from where it clung to the cliffs down at Siteia. Mixed in was the heady scent of olives and lamb roasting on a spit. *Oh God, I was home.*

Since leaving Crete as a young woman, I'd never looked back, never set foot on her sandy shore. My mother died when I was twelve and my departure to the mainland left my father alone in Chania. Laying under the stars in Greece, I cursed myself more than once for leaving my father, wishing I'd had the strength and courage to convince him to come with me. I should have demanded that he leave Crete behind and join me on the mainland. There had been nothing left for either of us on this island. But he returned. He went back to the same house I'd been born in, the house he'd been born in, because it was the only place he could ever call home.

"Mira?"

"I'm fine," I snapped at Danaus before I even thought about what I was saying. Straightening my spine, I resettled my bag on my left shoulder and took a few steps away from the jet so he could finish descending the stairs. "Do we have company?"

"There's a vampire headed this way, but other than that, I don't sense anyone else in the area," Danaus replied, coming to stand beside me. His bag of clothes and weapons was slung over his right shoulder. None of his usual weapons were visible, but I knew he had something lethal within quick reach.

During the short flight, we'd discussed possible scenarios that could occur at the airport when we landed. The naturi would expect us to show up at the Palace of Knossos, after I had stopped them at Stonehenge just a few nights ago. We would continue to thwart their every move until they finally gave up or we were all dead. I wasn't in the mood to contemplate which would happen first.

The night air was surprisingly quiet. I had expected them to attack us as soon as we stepped off the plane. The flight would leave us stiff and somewhat disoriented as we struggled to acquaint ourselves with our new surrounding. It was one of their best opportunities. Of course, the prime time to attack was going to be sunrise, and I still needed to come up with a good plan for that eventuality. A part of me wished

I could climb back on the plane and fly to Greece, where I could spend my daylight hours in peace. I didn't want to sleep here. Were there stories of me in Crete? Old folklore of a demon child born with hair the color of Hell's fires? Were the children taught to fear me like other nightmarish creatures? Damn, I wanted to be gone from this island and her memories!

Forcing myself to concentrate, I scanned the area and picked up two nightwalkers, but only one was approaching us. This was not what I had expected. There were only two in the entire region. The palace was not far from the city. The whole area should have been teeming with nightwalkers. Two vampires was all the Coven had thought to send? *Bastards.* Every last one of them.

The nightwalker slowly sauntered across the tarmac from the nearby hangar, her heels clacking loudly on the hard surface. A wealth of black hair spilled over her left shoulder and down her back while a secretive smile played across her mouth. As she approached, her eyes never left Danaus. I couldn't decide what had caught her attention: his dark attractive looks or any of the rumors that had leaked from Venice.

"Who sent you?" I demanded before she could draw enough of a breath to speak. I was already on edge about being in Crete, and we still needed to come up with a plan to defeat the naturi. We were running out of time. Our flight out of Venice had been delayed, and it was now nearly 4:00 A.M. Dawn was drawing close.

"The Coven," she said, her lips twisting in a frown as she looked me over. My clothes were rumpled and wrinkled, appearing as if I had wadded them up in a tight ball before bothering to put them on. I looked like a lost vagabond next to her neat cream-colored slacks and pale blue blouse.

"My name is Penelope. Macaire requested that I meet you and aid you against the naturi."

"Where are the others?" I barely resisted the urge to run my hands over my dress in a senseless attempt to smooth out some of the wrinkles.

"Hugo waits at a distance, watching to make sure we are safe," she replied.

"And that's all?"

"Yes."

I had a few choice words to say about Macaire and the rest of the Coven. This was ridiculous. There was no way Danaus, a pair of nightwalkers, and I could defeat all of the naturi lurking on this island. With odds like these, the naturi were going to have little trouble breaking the seal, and I was going to get staked in the process. However, before I could vent my growing irritation, Danaus spoke up.

"We need to get moving." His deep voice pushed aside my anger. He was right. We were easy targets standing out in the middle of the landing strip.

Without any further discussion, Penelope led the way out of the airport and to a taxi she had waiting. At one time or another all three of us looked over our respective shoulders. It hung unspoken in the air. The naturi were out there and they were watching us. I wasn't sure why they hadn't attacked yet, and a part of me didn't want to know the answer.

Penelope took us to a small square house she was renting. The exterior was painted white and the roof was flat. It looked like there might be some kind of awning covering part of the roof, offering tenants a place to rest at the end of the day and look out over the city. Even after all the centuries, Venetian influence was still visible in most of the buildings. For a time, Crete had been controlled by the Venetians, who left behind their form of art and architecture as a pervading influence. The cities such as Heraklion and Chania still glowed with the beauty of that dying city.

The interior of the house was the typical Cretan structure, with windows along only the front wall, while the other walls were covered in colorfully woven cloths and painted plates. A rounded archway led from the main living room into the kitchen and dining room, while the bedrooms were at the back of the house, off the kitchen. A window air-conditioning unit filled one of the few windows, growling softly as it put out a steady stream of cold air. The evening air had cooled to the low seventies, but the house retained most of the balmy afternoon heat.

It was a considerably larger house than the one I'd grown up in, and obviously more modern, but there were too many similarities in the design and the use of color. My hands trembled and a knot seemed to be permanently lodged in my throat.

Dropping my bag of clothes on the floor, I once again tried to push the little reminders that I was in Crete out of my mind and focus on why I had come to the island now. "How long have you been here?" I asked, trying to sound polite despite my raw nerves and growing frustration.

"I arrived on the island a few hours after sunset," Penelope replied. She was watching me warily from the opposite side of the room. She stood underneath the tall archway, her arms folded over her chest. "I have been living in Athens for almost a century and I come to Crete during the summer season for the tourists."

"Does this Hugo belong to you or did Macaire send him too?" I walked over to sofa that faced a corner fireplace made of small stones placed in an interesting mosaic. I leaned against the back of the sofa so I could face the night-walker, crossing my left ankle over my right.

"Macaire sent him," Penelope replied. "Is it true that you stopped the naturi at Stonehenge?" She made no attempt to hide her skepticism when she fired back at me before I could continue to interrogate her.

I smiled at her and rubbed the knuckles of my right hand on the front of my dress as if shining my nails. Holding my hand out in front of me, my fingers instantly became engulfed in blue fire. "I've got a few tricks up my sleeve." As I had expected, Penelope took one step backward, but she quickly stopped herself and returned to the spot she'd been standing, determined not to be bullied.

"You're going to need it," Danaus remarked.

"How many?" I asked him, instantly extinguishing the fire. My fun was over. We needed to get back down to business. We needed to figure out exactly what we were up against and how to defeat them.

Danaus's power brushed past me as it moved out of the house and across the island. His eyes remained opened as he searched Crete, but his focus was not on anyone in the room. "A couple dozen. Less than England," he said.

I was surprised. They had staged an enormous attack on the Themis Compound, throwing more naturi at us than I thought had lived on the entire earth. Had we seriously depleted their numbers to the point that they could no longer risk such a significant assault, no matter the importance of the event? One could only hope.

"Where are they?"

Danaus's gaze focused as he leveled his blue eyes on me. "I don't know this island."

"Would a map help?" Penelope inquired in a voice so sweet it grated on my nerves.

"Yes," I snapped before Danaus could answer. "Find one."

After throwing a nasty look at me, Penelope stomped out of the room, disappearing into the kitchen as she headed toward the back of the house. A snort from Danaus caused me to look back over at him.

"What put you in such a mood?" he asked.

"I just want to get this done and get the hell out of here," I snarled, no longer even trying to control my temper.

To my surprise, his expression softened. It annoyed me. I didn't want to see sympathy or pity from the hunter. I wanted him angry or annoyed or any of the other moods I had grown accustomed to seeing on his face. A moment later I felt a faint touch in my brain, like a hand feeling blindly about in the darkness.

Maybe it's time you faced your past. The sound of Danaus's thoughts echoed in my mind. He was getting too good at speaking to me telepathically. Just over twenty-four hours had passed since he had last pushed his powers into me, but our connection grew stronger each time he did it.

To hell with my past. This isn't the time to go all Freudian on me. We find the naturi and stop them. That's it, I mentally flung back at him.

Danaus didn't reply, but I could feel him laughing at me, some silent chuckle rumbling through his mind and slipping into mine.

But the feeling ceased at the sound of the front doorknob turning. A knife seemed to magically appear in Danaus's hand as he twisted around to face whoever was entering the house. I stood, my knees slightly bent, ready for anything. We both scanned the house at the same time to find the other nightwalker. However, neither of us relaxed when he stepped into the room with hands up and palms out and open.

Hugo was built like a freaking refrigerator. The nightwalker could have caused a lunar eclipse if he happened to step in front of the moon. His shoulders were wide, tapering down to a narrow waist and hips before splitting into legs that resembled tree trunks. He could have easily palmed a basketball with one large hand. I would have taken a step backward if my left thigh wasn't already pressed against the back of the pale yellow sofa. I'd never seen a vampire as big as Hugo. The only relief I felt was the fact that he wasn't very old; less than a century.

"Hugo?" I asked in a hard voice.

"Ja," he grunted, lowering his hands.

A curse rose up the back of my throat but I swallowed it down again. I spoke only a sprinkling of German and it had been a long time since I had last tried. *"Sprechen Sie Englisch?"*

"Ja," he replied, to my immediate relief. "Mira?"

"Ja," I said, trying to match his low growl and not quite pulling it off. I guess I needed a set.

"Hunter." Hugo's mouth twisted into a sneer as he looked over at Danaus.

"I'm glad we've got the introductions out of the way. Now, if we can get back to business, we—"

The sound of Penelope's heels clicking across the floor as she returned to the kitchen halted me. She opened what appeared to be a travel guide for the island of Crete and unfolded a colorful map from the back.

"Have either of you seen or encountered the naturi since coming to the island?" I asked as I walked over to where she'd spread the map out on the table.

"No, but neither of us has been on the island that long," Penelope said, shaking her head, her black hair flowing down around her face, nearly blocking her eyes. For the first time since meeting her, I saw a flicker of fear cross her face.

"Danaus," I called, looking over my shoulder at the hunter so I didn't have to look at Penelope any longer. I put my finger over Heraklion, which was on the northeastern part of the island. "This is where we are. Where are the naturi hiding? In the city or farther away?"

He moved behind me so he could see the map, but at the same time he didn't have his back completely turned toward Hugo. I didn't particularly want to turn my back to the enormous vampire either, but if Hugo knew that I was unnerved by his great hulking mass, he'd never follow my orders. And right now I needed him to follow me without question.

Once again Danaus's powers flowed out of his body, passing through me like a warm wind, threatening to sweep my soul out of my body and drag it across the entire island. "Farther away," he murmured. "None are in the city right now."

"He—He can sense them?" Penelope asked, her voice wavering.

"Mmmm . . . he knows all kinds of nifty tricks." A dark smile lifted the corners of my mouth. The nightwalker took a step back from the table, the fingers of her left hand curling into a fist. She glanced over her shoulder at Hugo, but I didn't catch his expression. Danaus had lifted his right hand, moving it from Heraklion toward the west.

"They're all gathered in one place," he continued, his hand hovering over a relatively broad part of the island.

I leaned in close to read the tiny print on the map. "Can you get a sense of the region? Does it have a green feel? Mountainous?"

"Mira, my powers aren't that exact," he bit out as his hand moved back a little, toward the west. "I don't sense the earth, just the naturi."

"What about humans?" Penelope inquired, taking a tentative step closer again. "If they are in the Amari Valley, there are other villages there. People would be close to the naturi."

"No, there are no humans. Not for a good distance."

"Then they are on Mount Idi," I said, straightening from where I was bent over the table. I looked up at Penelope as she straightened as well, a frown flattening her full lips into a thin line.

"That entire area is dotted with caves," she stated, waving

one hand over that part of the map. "The naturi could be hiding anywhere, and it would take us several nights to flush them all out."

"We won't need to flush them out," I said. "They'll be at the Palace of Knossos in two nights."

"You want us to wait for two nights and then take on all the naturi at once?" Hugo asked from where he was still standing in the living room. "I was told that I was to kill a naturi called Rowe. How am I to get to him if he is surrounded by his brethren? There are only four of us."

Hugo's German accent was incredibly thick and it wasn't helped by his growing anger. It had actually taken me a couple seconds to figure out what he was saying.

"Wait! You mean, this is it? No one else is coming?" Penelope shouted, slamming both her open palms on the table. "I never agreed to a suicide mission. The tales of the battle at Machu Picchu told of hundreds of nightwalkers. Why are we the only ones?"

"Don't know. You piss off Macaire or the rest of the Coven recently?" I asked. I was about to say more but my cell phone started ringing, stunning everyone into silence. Stepping away from the rest of the group and walking into the living room, I hiked up my dress and got my phone from where it was strapped to my leg. No pockets.

The little LCD screen revealed that it was my home phone number back in Savannah. There were only a couple of people who could be calling me from that number. "Who is it?" I demanded.

"Gabriel said you wanted me to call," replied a soft voice that instantly made my hands begin to tremble in relief. It was Tristan. He was awake and safe. For once, something had gone right.

I turned my back to the group and hunched my shoulders as if I could disappear from their view. I even went so far as to lower my voice, though I knew they could all clearly hear me. It didn't matter. I needed this private moment with Tristan to settle my own nerves.

"Are you okay? Did Gabriel show you around?" I asked, cringing at my own questions. I sounded like a worried, overprotective mother. I sounded like Sadira.

"He said he would after I called you. Are you still in Venice? What about the naturi? I can still—"

"No, I'm in Crete," I interrupted, and instantly wished I hadn't used such a harsh tone. "We should have this all cleaned up in a few nights. I'll be home in three or four nights, and then we can . . . find a more . . . permanent arrangement for you."

A heavy silence filled the air. I couldn't guess at what he was thinking. He either doubted that I would be back at all or was insulted by the idea that I was already looking to unload him like a pile of unwanted baggage. I had never wanted a family for this very reason. I didn't want anyone underfoot and didn't know what to do with someone once he was in my life.

"I should let you go," Tristan murmured.

"Wait! I . . . If you don't hear from me within the next week, I . . . I want to you seek out a nightwalker called Knox. He . . . sort of helps me out and . . . " I stumbled awkwardly. It was like telling my next of kin where to find my will. I had no provisions set aside, no preparations made for Tristan should something happen to me. He would be on his own in a foreign country. But at least for now he'd be away from Sadira and the Coven.

"I understand. I'll be fine. Take care of Rowe," he said, then hung up before I could say anything truly idiotic.

After returning the phone to its place on my leg, I turned back around to find everyone staring at me. Hugo looked a little stunned, while Penelope was outright smug. On the other hand, Danaus's expression was blank. But then, he knew who had called. He knew why Tristan was half a world away.

"As I was saying," I stated, trying to ignore the blush that I was sure stained my cheekbones, "we don't need anyone else. The naturi numbers are fewer. We're chipping away at their ranks and we'll continue to do so until we finally get to Rowe."

"But—"

"We'll plan a series of incursions for tomorrow night based on their location," I pressed on, cutting off Hugo before he could argue. "We can try to wipe them out before the new moon."

"I can do some scouting during the day," Danaus offered. I opened my mouth to argue when my phone rang again.

"By the gods, Mira," sneered Penelope. "Hire a babysitter."

I turned my back to her, refusing to comment as I grabbed my phone. However, the number was different this time, not one I remembered seeing before. Few had my number, and those who did knew to only call in an emergency.

"Who is this?" I demanded.

"Mira?" answered a startled voice. "This is James. James Parker. We met a few days . . . er . . . nights ago. I'm with Themis."

"Yes, I remember you, James," I said as I turned to look at the only other Themis member in the room. I didn't have to ask how James had gotten my number. Danaus had used my phone to call him days ago. "I'm a little busy right now."

"Actually, I'm looking for Danaus. You see, we're here and we need to know where—"

"What?" I exclaimed, my thoughts coming to a screeching halt. "What do you mean 'here'? Where's 'here'? And who's this 'we'?" That's when I felt it. The first tear in the night. We had less than an hour before sunrise and I still needed a safe place against the daylight and the humans. "Never mind." Stalking across the room, I slapped the phone into Danaus's open hand.

Leaning against the wall with my arms crossed over my chest, I watched as he slowly paced away from us. The hunter quickly gave his assistant instructions to get settled in a hotel and told him he would go there after sunrise. We were all eavesdropping on the conversation. There was no such thing as privacy when a nightwalker was in the room.

I was shocked to hear that James had traveled to Heraklion with the intention of helping Danaus. We had contacted him before leaving Venice, wanting Themis to confirm that Crete would be the next location of the sacrifice, since I didn't trust the Coven to tell the truth. It was part of the reason we had delayed our flight, waiting for the little research society to hear from all its field operatives at the twelve locations.

But I was speechless when James revealed that Ryan had come to Crete as well. The gold-eyed warlock was trouble. I might have temporarily escaped the scheming and torture of the Coven, but I was now faced with an extremely powerful human with an agenda I had yet to understand.

"What's this Themis?" Penelope asked softly, taking a couple steps closer to me.

"The help you were looking for." My gaze returned to Danaus as he ended the call. I'd been with the hunter every moment since we had spoken with Macaire, heard both of his conversations with James. He had not yet spoken of the Coven's pact with the naturi. But he was now planning to meet with Ryan without me.

Will you tell him? I asked when his fingers brushed against my hand as he returned my phone.

I have to.

Don't. Not yet. Telling him will only start a war.

And if I don't, we could all be in danger, he argued, frowning at me. However, the look in his eyes told me a different story. He was worried and unsure. I could see it, and feel the emotions beating between us.

Just give me one more night.

Why?

I need more time to think. There has to be a better way. Please.

Postponing won't help us.

It buys us one more night without war among all the races. Isn't it enough that we're fighting the naturi?

After a moment, Danaus softly grunted and walked away from me. I had bought one more night. I trusted him to keep his word, even though he had not actually spoken at all. Chaos was swirling around us and we needed to tread carefully if we had any hope of protecting what we had all come to value in this world. And I had a dark suspicion that I would get only one shot at this.

Twenty-One

No one was happy the next night when we finally left
Ryan's hotel. Danaus didn't want me alone with Ryan;
Ryan didn't want Danaus paired with Penelope; Penelope
didn't want to be left alone with the hunter; and James didn't
want to be left behind at the hotel. Only Hugo wasn't ver-
bally complaining, but by his expression, I could tell he
didn't want to go at all. By the time the bickering stopped, I
was ready to leave them all behind. However, I wasn't that
insane just yet.

After waiting for Ryan to change from his dress slacks
into a pair of worn blue jeans, the warlock and I set out in
a tiny taxi to the Palace of Knossos. Danaus had already
confirmed that the naturi left the mountains and were approaching the city. However, due to his lack of familiarity
with the area, he couldn't tell whether they had arrived yet
at the Minoan ruins.

I rubbed my eyes, trying to push aside some of the tension humming through me. I didn't feel rested. Crete was
eating away at my peace of mind. My sleep had been filled
with nightmares of running from an angry mob, my father
fighting to save me, only to be killed himself. To add to it,
I knew very little about the warlock who sat beside me. We

had met only a few nights earlier at the Themis Compound back in England. Sure, we were technically on the same side now, but he'd ordered Danaus to kill me some time ago. I wasn't completely confident that the order had merely been put on hold until this little naturi mess was cleaned up.

I was more than a little curious to discover why Ryan had come to Heraklion himself. Of course, from what I'd gathered during my brief visit to the Compound, Themis wasn't exactly crawling with magic users. He might have been the only one with enough power and skill to be of real aid—not that this made me feel any better. But for now I had a more pressing questions beating against the back of my brain.

"What possessed you to bring James along?" I asked him, trying not to sound too snide.

"Whatever do you mean?" Ryan asked, positively oozing faux innocence. His perpetual smile grew on his lips, mocking me.

"He's not like us. You're putting his life in danger," I bit out in a low voice. There was no doubt that the taxi driver could hear us; I was just hoping his English wasn't that good. Or at the very least, that he thought we were a pair of crazy tourists. "He doesn't need to be here."

"That's surprisingly sweet of you, Mira," Ryan said, his facade of innocence never wavering. "I wouldn't have expected that."

"Oh, shove it, Ryan!" I snarled, flashing my clenched teeth at him. "You're not this dense."

The smile remained on his lean, ageless face, but it faded from his golden eyes as they danced over my features. He watched me with a frightening intensity before he finally drew in a breath to speak. "I brought him for three different reasons. First, he is the assistant to both Danaus and me. He will be aiding us in any matters that we are unable to address while we are looking into our current problem."

It was a reason. I didn't think it was a particularly good reason. Charlotte Godwin was my human assistant back in Savannah and she took care of the day-to-day problems of managing my financial interests and seeing to my travel arrangements—things that generally needed to be addressed during the daylight hours.

"Second, James has been with Themis for several years," Ryan continued, "but he has had very little field experience. I thought this would be a good opportunity."

"You could have started him out on something a little less dangerous," I criticized, shaking my head at him. As we stopped at an intersection, I scooted forward in my seat so I could address the taxi driver. "How far to Knossos?" I inquired in broken Cretan Greek. Despite all the years I'd been gone, my knowledge of the language hadn't faded from my brain, as I would have expected. However, my dialect was archaic. It was unlikely anyone would be able to understand me. After listening to others, however, I'd picked up enough to get by. Undoubtedly, I sounded like a tourist.

"Less than a kilometer," he said, glancing over his shoulder at me. He was an older gentleman with white hair and a lined face weathered by time and the sun.

"Let us out here," I said, pulling a few euros out of the front pocket of my leather pants. I had converted the last of my Egyptian pounds into euros at the Cipriani before Danaus and I flew out. I didn't have much on me but figured it would get me through the next couple of nights. Beyond that, I had to survive our next encounter with the naturi before I worried about my cash flow.

The driver seemed about to argue, but swallowed his comment when he heard Ryan already getting out of the car. He hadn't been too sure about us heading to the palace at this late hour, but with a slight mental push, I managed to convince him to take us anyway.

We had left the city of Heraklion behind and entered into the hilly countryside filled with vineyards and olive orchards. From a quick scan of the region, I was relieved to find very few humans in the area. I didn't have to worry too much about being discovered or anyone stumbling into a deadly battle. The problem with many of the so-called holy sites was that they were now major tourist attractions, leaving the area thickly surrounded by shops, restaurants, and hotels for weary travelers burdened with far too much cash.

Ryan and I silently waited in the darkness until we saw the taxi driver head back toward Heraklion and the relative safety of the city before we turned and headed down the empty lane toward the Minoan ruins. Danaus and Penelope had taken a taxi ten minutes before us, to head south of the palace before getting out and walking back toward the ruins. Hugo took a separate cab and would be arriving at the palace from the east. If we couldn't stop them, our goal was to at least herd the naturi back toward the caves of Mount Idi and away from any of the large cities and towns in the immediate area. It was a temporary solution at best if we couldn't destroy them all.

For the first time since I'd become a nightwalker, the darkness felt like a physical weight pressing on my shoulders, rather than the soothing presence it had always been, Dark violent memories of fear and hatred lurked behind every tree. My mother's death, the men I killed—all ghosts waiting for a moment of weakness before they would strike. With my fists clenched at my side, I struggled to stay focused on the task that loomed before me and the potential adversary beside me.

"You said there were three reasons for bringing James," I said to Ryan, resuming our earlier conversation from the car after we'd walked in the dark for a few minutes. "What was the third reason?"

He remained silent for a long time, until I was sure he wasn't going to tell me at all. He drew in a deep breath and his hands stopped swinging loosely at his sides. "Something has happened, and James—being the responsible fellow that he is—feels he should be the one to tell you."

"Why do I get the feeling that you don't want him to tell me?"

"At the very least, I'd rather he not tell you in person. I fear that you're the type to shoot the messenger," Ryan stated, cocking his head to the side as he looked down at me.

"I didn't kill Danaus when he told me of the naturi. I would think that would be proof enough." I shoved my hands in my back pockets, my eyes sweeping away from the warlock beside me to the rows of trees and hills that rose up around the winding road. I had the Browning that Danaus had given me in a holster at my lower back, and I was ready if anything so much as twitched. The only one in the immediate area who I could sense was Ryan, and it was driving me crazy. The air was still, redolent of the earth and wildflowers. It felt as if the world was holding its breath in anticipation of the inevitable battle.

"You needed Danaus alive," Ryan countered. "Besides, I'm not entirely sure you could kill him."

I bit back the first sharp comment that rose to mind and pushed on. He was trying to distract me, but there was no reason to jump at the bait. "Are you going to tell me or do I have to drag it out of James later tonight?"

"Michael is missing," Ryan softly said.

I sighed softly, the sound barely rising above the scuff of my boots along some loose gravel on the road. "Michael isn't missing. He's dead."

"Yes, I know. Gabriel told us." Ryan stopped walking and I looked up at him. The tall man's white hair framed his narrow face, creating a strange outline to the shadows that filled the hollows of his cheeks. "We can't find his body."

My temper instantly flared and I took a step toward him. It was a struggle to keep my hands from closing around his throat, but I succeeded. There was a tingle of magic in the air coming from my powerful companion, and I had no doubt that he could send my flying across the road without blinking an eye.

But this horrible news diminished the danger of the warlock. Michael had been one of my guardian angels for several years. He'd been an able, dedicated bodyguard; a sweet, gentle man; and a considerate lover. He had watched over me during my daylight hours and stood with me against the naturi, who physically took his life. Recently, I realized that I'd been slowly stealing his life on another level, and the naturi had stolen away my chance to ever make it up to him.

But now this? Lost? A dead body lost?

"What do you mean? The night of the attack, I left him in the front hall. What did you do with him?" I shouted, not caring if I caught the attention of every naturi in the area. Michael deserved better than this. I needed to take him home where he could finally rest.

"We couldn't find him. I met him. James knew him. Gabriel was there. We searched every inch of the manor and all the area surrounding the Compound. He's not there," Ryan calmly said. He laid his large hands over my shoulders, squeezing lightly. The small comfort eased some of the tension from them, but I couldn't unclench my jaw.

"Who?" I whispered in a choked voice. "Who has him?"

"Mira . . . " Ryan paused again and licked his dry lips. "The naturi were all over the first floor of the manor—"

"No!" I jerked away from him, walking to the other side of the road while shaking my head in denial. My hands were shaking. The very idea of any naturi touching Michael's lifeless body fueled a mindless, irrational fire within me. "Absolutely not! No! They don't need his body. Why would they do it?"

"To get at you."

"No, I don't believe you. You have him."

"Why? So I can point the finger at the naturi and get you to hate them more?" he argued, his voice growing firmer. "That's impossible. According to Danaus, your hatred of the naturi is boundless and eternal. There's nothing I could do to increase that."

I paced back across the road toward Ryan, my fingers clenched into shaking fists. The urge to set the surrounding fields on fire was overwhelming, like a boiling kettle of water begging to blow off some of the steam before it overflows. "Why?" I growled.

"I don't know who has Michael, but it doesn't matter. As you said, he's dead. There's nothing they can do to him now."

Yes, logic said that Michael was in a better place and that his empty body was not important. But I needed this. I needed to bury him in the plot of land that had been put aside for my bodyguards. During my century in the United States, I had survived a few other bodyguards and seen to their burial since they had no other family. Michael belonged with them and me, back home in Savannah. In the one place where I could watch over him.

Turning away from Ryan, I resumed our walk toward the palace. He fell into step beside me after a couple seconds. I didn't know whether I believed him. To me, it didn't make sense for either Themis or the naturi to take Michael, but I knew it would come back to haunt me someday.

We had been walking uphill and could now see the valley spread out around us, dotted with farms and vineyards off in the distance. As the road curved to the left, the line of trees parted before us, revealing the first glimpse of the ruins of the palace. From what I could see, it was enormous, as if a city unto itself.

But something felt off. A few minutes later my steps slowed as we approached the Minoan ruins. I held my right hand out before me with my palm open. There was an energy growing in the air, unlike the tingling electric feel coming off of Ryan. This was different; hot and thick, as if it were a living thing growing in stature and substance.

"Can you feel that?" I whispered, my dragging feet finally drawing to a stop. I held up both hands before my body, feeling the air as if pressing against a solid creature, though the area was empty before me.

"Yes, an energy," he replied. He stood beside me, his left hand slowly waving through the air before him. "Did you feel this at Stonehenge?"

Did I feel this at Stonehenge? When I'd arrived at the ancient location, my body was still wracked with pain from Danaus stealing away my abilities and body for his own purposes. I couldn't stand and every inch of me had screamed in agony. There had been a layer of pain in the air, but my senses were so clouded that I wasn't sure which of the feelings was related to Stonehenge and the swell of power from the earth.

"I'm not sure. I think so," I hedged, finally forcing my feet to resume their steady approach. My hand fell back to my side, where I anxiously flexed my fingers a few times as if to loosen the muscles. The power in the air was building. "Can you tell if the energy will peak tonight or tomorrow night?" I asked, glancing over at him.

"No idea." He shrugged his wide, narrow shoulders before looking down at me. "I'm not an earth user."

Frowning, I paused before a set of cracked and crumbling stairs that led up to the palace. There were essentially two types of magic: earth and soul, which was also referred to as blood magic. Most magic users dabbled in both, but eventually everyone specialized in one side or the other. Both sides could do the same things, but each magic style had its own requirements and limitations.

And then there was Rowe. As a naturi, he was naturally a strong earth magic user, but he seemed equally adept at weaving blood magic, given that he'd gone to the trouble of arranging a harvest in Egypt less than a week ago. It would have been so much easier if the naturi stuck to earth magic and the bori stuck to blood magic. Then a person would know exactly where she stood when the shit hit the fan.

With one foot on the stairs, I reached out and scanned the area. Danaus and Penelope were roughly south of us, slowly approaching, while Hugo was in position to the east. Unfortunately, out of the five of us, only Danaus could sense the naturi. We were waiting for him to fire a shot to signal that they were here if no one else reacted first.

Creeping to the top of the staircase, I paused, squatting down, pressing my hands against the worn stones. The palace was mostly raised above the hill upon which it stood. If I walked onto the ruins, I would stand out as an easy target for any of the naturi. Despite the darkness of the night, I could easily see within the thick shadows. The only forms I could pick out were columns and bits of broken stone. The area appeared deserted, but I knew better.

I rolled my shoulders once and clenched my teeth. The push of the power in the area had grown a little stronger as I climbed the stairs. A throbbing had started in my temples and I could feel pressure building at the base of my skull. For a whole new reason, I had begun to hope that this battle wouldn't take too long. The pain was starting to become a distraction, and I wasn't sure how it would affect my ability to control my powers.

Ryan eased down so he was sitting opposite me on the stairs, his body held low to the ground. I wasn't sure how good his eyesight was in the pitch-black, but I assumed he knew a spell or two to make it better than the average human.

"Has Danaus told you about Rowe?" I whispered, drawing the white-haired warlock's attention back to my face. He nodded, so I continued to pick away at the thought that was nagging at me. How often would I find myself in the company of an ancient warlock with oodles of magic information crammed into his brain? "He's different. Scarred. Dark hair, dark eyes. Unlike the other naturi. It's from the magic?"

Ryan seemed to hesitate a moment before he nodded. "He's tainting the magic so it's tainting him," he finally replied in a low voice. "He's using the power of the earth to fuel blood spells."

I stared at him for a long minute in silence, taking in his snow white hair and gold eyes, features I'd never seen on another human being in all my six hundred years, before finally voicing the thought we both knew was floating through my head. "The opposite of what you've done. You've tainted earth spells by fueling them with blood magic."

The perpetual smile that seemed to haunt Ryan's face melted away and his expression became completely unreadable. There were no laws against what he and Rowe were doing. However, it was my understanding that the mixing of styles was dangerous and frowned upon.

"This isn't the time for this conversation," Ryan stated in chilled tones.

"Actually, it is," I corrected, smiling broadly at him. I leaned closer and lightly laid my hand over his wrist. "You know earth spells. You've got an abundance of power flowing up from the earth here. Use it. Cast something here and now. Anything."

He pulled back, his mouth finally slipping into a frown. "The earth spells I know aren't to be used lightly, and my strength isn't in using power from the earth. It would be too dangerous."

"More dangerous than allowing the naturi to complete their sacrifice here tomorrow night?" I demanded, my voice briefly spiking higher. "If you cast something here now, won't it siphon off some of the power? Couldn't it disrupt their ability to break the seal?"

The warlock looked away from me, staring off across the ruins. His brow was furrowed in thought as he turned over my argument. My understanding of how magic worked was pretty rudimentary, but the logic seemed to fit. If we used the magic here before the naturi, the power from the earth would dissipate and move on to the next location. It was extremely unlikely that the naturi would be able to find the next location before the new moon tomorrow night. They would have to wait until the Fall equinox more than a month away. That would give us ample time to hunt down Rowe and destroy him.

"There's another problem," Ryan stated after a couple minutes. "Regardless of which earth spell I cast, I'd have to start it with blood magic and then switch to earth magic."

"Can you do that?" I asked, earning a very smug smile as laughter danced in his narrowed eyes. I rolled my own eyes in response. "So what's the problem?"

"I don't use my own soul to fuel my magic," he admitted, his smile never wavering.

Of course not. That kind of nonsense was for the novices. Why waste the energy from your own soul when you could drain anyone else's energy that happened to be near you? No wonder he was so comfortable as the head of Themis. Not only was he tapped into an excellent source of information regarding all the other races, but he was constantly surrounded by an ample source of energy. Much like night-walkers, blood warlocks always stuck close to cities, while the few earth witches in the world preferred wooded regions. You have to stick close to your food source. Or in the case of magic users, your fuel source.

"I repeat: What's the problem?"

"No humans nearby."

It was on the tip of my tongue to remind him that Danaus was not far, but I swallowed the hunter's name. We both knew that Danaus wasn't entirely human, though I wondered if Ryan was aware that Danaus had some kind of bori connection. Obviously, the hunter was off limits, which was probably best for everyone involved.

"Can you use a nightwalker?" I asked. I wasn't exactly comfortable with the idea of Ryan highjacking some of the energy that kept me alive, but I was more afraid of facing the naturi here in another battle to protect the seal.

"I can't. You don't have a s—"

"That's bullshit and you know it," I hissed, tightening my grip on his wrist. "Nightwalkers have souls. Besides, we're pure blood magic. It's how we stay alive."

He moved his arm, twisting it so I would release him. "I can try. I've never done this so I can't be sure—"

"I'll be fine," I said, cutting him off. Turning my attention back to the ruins, I looked over the area, searching for any sign of the naturi. It remained quiet, with only the sound of the wind lightly rustling the leaves in the surrounding trees. Before we moved, I mentally reached out and told Penelope and Hugo what our plans were. They would keep us covered while Ryan cast his spell.

I pushed off the ground with both hands, climbed the last couple stairs, and walked across the stone floor, heading deeper into the ruins. Since Danaus had yet to fire a single shot, Ryan and I assumed there wasn't a naturi in the actual ruins. Of course, I checked more than once to make sure that Danaus was still alive and conscious. Not that I thought Penelope could kill Danaus, but I definitely didn't trust her. I needed the hunter alive much more than I needed her at that moment.

"Where are we going?" Ryan whispered, leaning close to me as he spoke. It seemed silly to me. We were completely out in the open, easy targets. If the naturi couldn't see us, I certainly wasn't going to worry about them hearing us. Of course, when I replied, I whispered too. Some things defy logic when fear is twisting like a knot in your stomach.

"There's a large courtyard in the center of the palace. I'm willing to bet the magic is strongest there," I replied. Danaus and I had spent most of the flight to Crete studying maps of the Palace of Knossos. There was more than one place the naturi could use for the site of the sacrifice, which might be problematic with only five of us there. It would be better if we just got rid of the magic now and ruined their plans.

Pausing to edge around the corner of one of the few walls that was still standing, I saw Ryan closely examining the faint mural that had survived the centuries. Even in the darkness I could tell that the colors were relatively crisp despite the wear of the ages. I wished I could have taken the time to wander the ruins and marvel at what had obviously been an amazing structure. But for now the naturi dominated my thoughts.

"Mira," he said, laying his hand on my shoulder before I could walk away from the wall. "Those old myths about the labyrinth . . . "

"The labyrinth was supposedly found under the palace."

"And the minotaur?"

One of my eyebrows popped up in surprise at his question. I honestly couldn't tell if he was serious or joking. The minotaur? The half-man, half-bull creature that was supposed to be held captive in the center of the maze.

"They made the lycanthropes," Ryan reminded me when the silence had stretched for longer than he was comfortable.

"That has never been proven," I murmured, shaking my head. I had trouble accepting that supposed myth surrounding the lycans and the naturi because there was a second half to it that I found even more distasteful, which had to do with the origins of my own race. "There's no such thing as the minotaur. Just a fanciful human tale."

We continued on for another couple minutes before we came to a large clearing in the center of the palace. The space was rectangular, its edges marked off by broken rocks from what had been the walls, columns, and roof of the building centuries ago. I had heard old tales of the Palace of Knossos when I was growing up in Chania, but we never traveled far from our home.

"Do you have a spell in mind?" I asked, turning my back to Ryan as he stood in the center of the clearing. The power in the air was incredible, pushing against me as if it could force its way through my skin and into my organs. But at the same time, the energy felt thick and heavy. The very molecules felt too large to sink into me, but it didn't keep them from trying.

"Yes," he replied. Even his voice seemed more muffled here, as if the sound was fighting its way through energy. "I'm going to create a storm."

I suddenly spun around to face the warlock, my mouth falling open at his announcement. "Isn't that a rather big spell? With this much power in the air, you could destroy half the island, not to mention us."

"Actually, if I'm not extremely careful, I could destroy not only this island, but several others in the area," he said. His voice was calm and even, as if the notion of ending countless lives didn't ruffle his feathers in the least. "This is what you wanted."

"I want you to cast a spell, not cause mass destruction. Why such a big spell?" I might not have known much about magic, but I did know that weather spells were extremely complicated and took a great deal of energy. Very few could even cast them, and of those that could, even fewer had the ability to control them once they were started.

"I told you, I'm not an earth user. I don't know a lot of earth spells and the few I do know are very dangerous. Do you want me to do this?" he demanded. Both his hands were raised out to his sides, his palms facing out. It was as if he were about to grab the air around him and pull it in toward his body.

To my surprise, I hesitated only a moment. This was stupid. This was dangerous. And this might be our only chance to stop the naturi in Crete. If we could stop them tonight, I thought, we could spend the next few weeks hunting down Rowe, our main target.

"Do it."

Ryan drew in a deep, cleansing breath while his eyes fell shut. I was turning my back toward him again when a gunshot rang out. Damn it. We had company. The warlock was of no use to me now. He couldn't be distracted from the complicated spell he had committed himself to, and I needed to protect him no matter what.

Pulling the gun from the holster at the small of my back, I turned slowly around, holding the weapon before me with both hands as I scanned the area. I didn't see or hear anything yet. A second shot was fired, the bullet pinging off a stone behind me.

My stomach lurched and I spun around in time to see a naturi running toward me with a short sword raised above his head. I squeezed off three rounds before I finally managed to lodge a bullet in his chest. The naturi jerked at the impact before stumbling over some broken rocks, sending him to his hands and knees. With a loud clatter, the sword hit the ground while the naturi softly groaned.

A smile drifted across my lips, and then I was unexpectedly knocked to my knees. My arms fell and the gun almost slipped from my numb fingers. Nothing had hit me. From my back came a tugging sensation, as if something within me had been snagged or caught. My vision blurred and fatigue weighed on my shoulders.

Ryan had succeeded in tapping into my energy. I doubted that most humans would have even detected it, maybe only paused and yawned at the sudden wave of fatigue and then gone on with their day. However, my existence was pure soul energy, I could no longer generate my own, which was why I had to feed on the blood of others. If Ryan didn't release me soon, I would need to either feed or sleep. Not an option at the moment. As much as I wanted to drain the moaning naturi dry, their blood was poisonous to all nightwalkers.

A scrape of stone and a new voice jerked my attention back from my own fatigue. A second naturi knelt next to the one I had shot only seconds ago. With her right hand, she was helping him to sit up, while still holding a sword in her left.

I pushed to my feet at the same time she rose to hers. Gritting my teeth, I prepared to attack when I saw Danaus and Penelope appear out of the shadows to my right. They had finally come to join in the fun. I realized then that the naturi were attacking from the east. They had circled around to surprise us. But that also meant they had either slipped by Hugo undetected or silently killed the nightwalker before reaching the palace. Unfortunately, we couldn't go looking for him until the naturi were taken care of.

Turning back to Ryan, I found the warlock standing where I'd left him. His hands were stretched above his head, reaching toward the heavens he sought to control. His lips were moving quickly but I couldn't hear anything he was saying. The wind had picked up, dropping the temperature in the area several degrees. Overhead, dark thick clouds churned in the formerly clear sky, blotting out the stars. A massive storm was forming.

The weight on my shoulders suddenly lifted and the fatigue slipped away like a wave pulling back out to sea. Ryan had released my energy and started to use the earth energy that was rising up from beneath our feet. The war-lock grunted, drawing my gaze back to him. Lines of strain deepened in his face. Above him, his long fingers trembled. I wanted to ask him if he was okay but knew better than to distract him. Regardless of what his answer would have been, there was no turning back now.

A whisper of cloth, a prickling of the hairs on the back of my neck—they were my only warning. Turning on my left heel, I spun around, raising the gun in both hands at the same time. I unloaded four shots in the naturi before he finally fell to the ground dead. Clenching my teeth, I hurried over and picked up the short sword he'd dropped.

Standing over the dead naturi, I took an extra moment to cut off its head. No reason to take silly chances. I wasn't a very good shot with a gun. Strangely, this naturi had been from the earth clan. From my experience, they weren't melee fighters. That was left to members of the animal clan. The earth clan preferred to use magic, letting the earth and plants do the fighting for them.

The naturi weren't using magic. Was it for fear of tap-ping into the earth magic that permeated the area? A smile lifted my lips as I turned back around to where Danaus and Penelope were battling four naturi. My guess could prove to be right.

Large drops of ice cold rain started to fall from the sky, landing on my head like small pebbles and instantly soaking into my T-shirt. A flash of lightning forked through the sky, darting from one black mass to the next before being followed by a loud bang of thunder. The storm was still building.

The wind gusted, blowing my hair in front of my face, momentarily blinding me. I pushed it back in time to see another earth naturi running toward Ryan and me, sword raised. Returning the gun to the holster at my back, I beat the creature back with the short sword in my right hand. I didn't think the worsening weather would help my aim, and I needed to save the last few bullets I had for an emergency.

It was a struggle to fight back the naturi as the storm continued to build. The wind roared while the rain fell in relentless sheets, blinding us. Lightning lashed at the sky, lighting up the area like a strobe light in a smoky night-club. After finally dispatching my opponent by plunging my sword through his heart, I turned back to Ryan, pressing my left hand to my left thigh in an effort to stem the bleeding. The naturi had gotten in a lucky strike before I killed him. The pain was only a dull throbbing in the back of my mind.

The rain was coming down so hard I could no longer see Danaus and Penelope. All sounds of the battle had been drowned out by the rain and thunder. I couldn't see Ryan either. He had been only a few feet behind me. I took a few frantic steps forward, sucking in a lungful of air to shout his name when I nearly tripped over his foot. The warlock was seated on the ground, his arms resting on his bent knees before him.

Kneeling before him, I grabbed his slumped shoulder. Ryan jumped, his head snapping up. The tension instantly eased from his shoulder when he realized it was me. "It's done," he announced, wiping some of the water from his eyes. His clothes were plastered to his lean frame and he was trembling, either from the cold or exhaustion.

I glanced up at the sky. The storm was still building around us. The lightning that had been content to jump from cloud to cloud was now slamming to the earth with increasing frequency. A couple of trees had already exploded in a shower of sparks and wooden shards as they were struck.

"What do you mean it's done?" I shouted over the pounding rain. Water blurred my vision and dripped off the end of my nose. If I still breathed, I would have been afraid of drowning. "The storm is getting worse."

"The storm is getting its energy from this spot. It will continue to build until the energy runs out," Ryan shouted back.

I instantly released him and nearly lost my balance, as if the world had shifted beneath me. The storm was drawing its power from the well of the earth. It wouldn't run dry. "Are you insane?" I screamed. "You have to stop it!" If this storm left Crete, it would sweep up through the Aegean Sea, crushing one island after another before slamming into the mainland. Thousands of people were going to be killed.

He stared at me, his mouth soundlessly opening and closing a couple of times. "I can't," he finally said when he could use his voice again. "I released this spell. I can't call it back or control it."

"Are you insane?" I repeated. It was all I could think to say. Terror had locked up my thoughts.

"You said you wanted to use up the energy," he shouted angrily back at me.

"Yeah, but not destroy all of southern Europe in the process." I tightly gripped both of his shoulders and shook him. "You have to stop this." By the weight still in the air, the spell hadn't made a dent in the power swelling up from the earth. Ryan had to stop it before it got any worse.

Pain exploded in my cheek and jaw as I was thrown backward, Ryan's shoulders wretched out of my hands. I slid back across the broken rock until I slammed into a bigger, immovable rock. The sharp edge dug into my back, trying to insert itself between the vertebrae of my spine.

With a groan, I looked up to find Rowe standing next to a confused Ryan. Drenched, but entirely unfazed by the growing storm, the naturi smiled at me as he shoved the warlock aside. Planting his feet wide apart, Rowe casually raised his left hand above his head, his eyes never wavering from me as I pushed to my feet again.

Overhead, the storm calmed. The pounding rain lightened to a steady downpour and the wind stopped trying to push me across the clearing. Rowe had taken control of the storm with little effort and strain.

I shouldn't have been surprised. He had demonstrated his ability to manipulate the weather when we met in Venice. I just didn't expect it to be so easy for him. No struggle. No strain. He simply lifted his hand and the fury of the gods slipped into his palm.

While the naturi calmed the raging storm, I quickly looked around. There were still no humans, which meant they couldn't complete the sacrifice. And then my gaze stumbled back to the warlock, who had also pushed to his feet. They couldn't complete the sacrifice unless they grabbed Ryan. I needed to get him out of there. I didn't think Rowe would try to break the seal tonight, but I didn't want to take my chances and be proven wrong.

"Fancy meeting you here," I called, brushing my scraped-up hands on the legs of my leather pants. My body was battered, bruised, and thoroughly chilled. What I needed was a good soak in a tub of hot, sudsy water. Instead I got a naturi with an attitude.

"Ancient ruins. Middle of the night. It's where all the lovers meet," he taunted, his smile widening to a malicious grin.

I slowly stepped to my left, edging closer to Ryan. I wanted to get between him and Rowe, but the naturi guessed my plan. With a slight twitch of his fingers, a lightning bolt slammed into the ground between Ryan and me. We both dove in the opposite direction, the air around us crackling with energy.

When I looked back at Rowe as I regained my feet, he was closely watching Ryan. The warlock was preparing to cast something; I didn't have a clue what. I was just worried that he would draw the energy from me, leaving me weak and vulnerable.

"Stupid humans," Rowe growled, letting his arm fall back to his side. "You'll never gain the ability to control the weather. The earth is beyond your comprehension."

"Wow!" I mocked, luring his stare back to me. "I would never have guessed you to be an elitist prick." Gathering up my energy before Ryan could tap it, I created a fireball in each hand. Because of the ceaseless rain, I put a little more energy behind it.

But something unexpected happened. The energy that had been pressing against me finally found a way into my body. The softball-size fireballs I had attempted to create appeared in my hands larger than basketballs, crackling and spitting in horrific fury. I hurled both of them at Rowe before I could contemplate it any further. However, once the energy found a way into my system, I had no way of stopping it. The power continued to flow in, hot and biting.

I blinked, struggling to rise above the flow of power, watching as Rowe darted away from the fireballs. With the energy filling me, I had no choice but to continue to pitch fireballs at the dark naturi in hopes of setting the bastard on fire. Not the easiest of tasks even with the free flow of energy. I had an amazing source of power, but I didn't have the same level of control I had perfected over the long centuries.

As Rowe hit the ground, he swung one arm at me. A bolt of lightning plunged from the sky, striking a few feet from where I stood. I lurched backward, my onslaught of fire halted. Rowe took advantage of the pause to cause the storm to build again. Lightning bolt after lightning bolt hammered the earth, each striking closer and closer to me. He was driving me back, farther from him and the center of the clearing.

Keeping me on the run was also stopping me from using the power building within my body. I couldn't force it out. I couldn't stop it. The only relief I could find was to use the energy, but I couldn't concentrate on using my ability if I was dodging lightning bolts.

Mira.

The relief I felt at the sound of Danaus's voice within my mind was instantaneous. I had been so centered on taking out Rowe, I forgot that the hunter was lurking somewhere about.

What do you need me to do?

Get Ryan out of here. They could use him, I ordered in a brief respite between strikes. I quickly threw another fireball at Rowe, but it went wide of its mark and struck another naturi, bathing him in liquid orange flames. I hadn't had enough time to concentrate and aim.

Another lightning bolt. It hit far too close. I jumped but didn't look at where I would land. My right foot came down on a large chunk of rock and I fell backward, landing heavily on my back. I cried out as the pain shot through my spine and ribs. My control slipped on the energy that was vibrating through my body. A wall of fire whooshed up around me with an angry roar.

Laying on my back, I looked up to find a circle of fire surrounding me, reaching up more than ten feet into the heavens. The snapping orange and yellow flames encased me like an oven, drying my clothes and hair, sucking away cold that had chilled me to my bones. I hadn't thought of the wall of flames. After more than six hundred years, it was a reflexive move, like raising my hand to protect my eyes from a bright light.

Mira! The frantic shout in my head was my only warning. Danaus was there. More than just a presence in my head, he was inside me, his power burrowing down into me until I could no longer separate myself from him. Pain exploded in my frame. I thought my bones were going to splinter under the force of the energy he was pushing into me.

I nearly shouted at him to release me when I realized that as his energy filled me, the energy flowing into me from the earth was being pushed out. The circle of fire was shrinking back down into the earth. I lay still, letting my eyes fall shut as I concentrated on the war being fought within me, but without my influence.

"Mira!" Danaus shouted. He was still within me, but he was calling now. He was close.

"I'm fine," I muttered, but that was questionable. My body hurt in a hundred different ways, making me wish I'd let Rowe hit me with a lightning bolt. I couldn't imagine a nightwalker surviving such a thing. Of course, it would be just my luck that I would.

Release me, I said to Danaus, using our private connection. No reason to let everyone in on our little secret. We had enough problems. Slowly, I felt him pull his powers out of my body, leaving me feeling cooler, emptier. I immediately noticed that the power I had felt pouring from the earth into me didn't return, but went back to pushing against my skin.

A light rain splattered on my face and a grumble of thunder rolled in the distance, pulling me back to the present. I lurched back into an upright position, wincing at the pain in my back and in my head. Rowe had been firing lightning bolts at me only moments ago. But now he was gone. All the naturi were gone.

"Where?" I whispered in confusion, pushing back some hair that had fallen around my face.

"They left," Penelope answered as she hesitantly stepped closer. "When the wall of fire went up, they ran." I briefly wondered if this new cautious attitude was the result of the havoc Danaus and I had created when we destroyed so many naturi near Stonehenge.

"Should we follow?" Danaus asked. The hunter extended one hand to me, offering to help me back to my feet. I hesitated only a second, frowning at his hand. Before when he had pushed his powers into me, he needed to be touching me. But, much like Jabari, Danaus had learned to do it without touching me. I didn't want to know how far away he'd been at the time.

"No," I said, shaking my head as I regained my feet with his help. I had a feeling we had a new problem. "We need to find out what happened to Hugo first."

Twenty-Two

Penelope and I stumbled across the clearing, weaving through the crumbling remains of the ruins until we reached the far eastern edge of the Palace of Knossos. We could still sense the nightwalker's soul, but it was weak and thready. He wasn't going to last much longer if he didn't receive help very soon. The rain had slowed to a light drizzle, more annoying than anything, as it added a chill to the air we shouldn't have felt for a late summer evening.

Slipping in a patch of mud, I finally located Hugo lying under a couple of trees, covered in blood. I hadn't liked leaving him alone to face the naturi, but I was short on help. I had hoped that his enormous size would add some menace to his figure and deter the naturi without him needing to raise a sword or gun. Instead they had taken advantage of the fact that he was alone and overwhelmed him.

I knelt beside the wounded nightwalker. His eyelids fluttered as he attempted to open his eyes. I hadn't made a noise in my approach, but he could sense me. I laid a hand on his barrel chest and he flinched at my touch. There was a long cut on his throat and another across his middle. Shallow cuts covered his arms and legs. His face was bruised, with his left eye nearly swollen shut. Hugo was lucky they hadn't cut off his head or carved out his heart. They had left him to suffer as pints of blood slowly poured from his body. He was losing blood too fast for his body to heal the wounds and hold in the blood.

Looking over my shoulder at Penelope, who was staring white-faced down at Hugo, I ordered her to fetch a car. We needed to move the giant vampire. If we were going to be lucky enough to save him, we couldn't do it here.

"What should we do?" Ryan inquired, taking Penelope's place behind me.

I gritted my teeth, catching a whiff of his blood on the slight breeze. It wouldn't help Hugo. Ryan wasn't a candidate for a donation. Warlock blood didn't always go well with every nightwalker, and I didn't see Danaus allowing it even if Ryan agreed.

"Go gather up all the dead naturi," I said, putting my hand over the wound on Hugo's stomach in a desperate attempt to slow some of the bleeding. He let out a low moan as I applied pressure, sending a fresh wave of pain through his body. "Put them in one spot. I have to dispose of them before we leave."

I waited until the sound of Danaus's and Ryan's footsteps faded in the distance before turning my attention entirely back to Hugo. His body was ice cold to the touch, and if I hadn't felt the actual presence of his soul in the large body before me, I would have assumed he was dead.

I dipped into his mind and immediately got sucked into a swirling maelstrom of pain. Not that I could actually feel his pain. It came through to me as black chaos that permeated every thought and memory. It was difficult to locate Hugo within the chaos, and it didn't help that everything was coming through in German.

Can you tell me what happened? I asked, finally finding Hugo within the haze of pain and hunger.

Naturi . . . everywhere. There was a long pause and I could feel him pushing against the pain, fighting to focus his thoughts. *I heard something. Rocks shifting. I turned and they were beside me. Too many. Too close.*

It's okay, I murmured in his head, wishing I could lend him some of my strength.

They came from . . . southwest . . . I thought they killed you before reaching me.

No. We didn't see them. I closed my eyes, trying to ignore the scent of his blood. It was everywhere, coating my hands, filling the air with its oh-so-sweet smell. I was still achy and tired from our encounter with the naturi. I needed to feed myself, but it would have to wait.

My mind drifted. I didn't know how I was going to save Hugo. We needed to get him some blood, lots of it. We would need to keep pumping it into him until the wounds finally closed and he could hold it within his body. The wounds had to close before the sun rose or the blood would drain out of him during the day and he wouldn't reawaken with the setting of the sun.

The sound of a car motor approaching the ruins jerked me from my thoughts. A quick check revealed that it was Penelope and she wasn't alone. She was bringing two humans with her. I hadn't thought to ask her to round up a quick bite for Hugo, just something to buy him a little more time. Of course, no matter what my condition, I tended to be somewhat selective in my meals. Looking back down at Hugo and his gray pallor, I doubted I'd be picky if I was in the same state as he was.

Penelope parked the car not far from Hugo's location and made her way toward us as quickly as possible. A dark frown tugged at the corners of my lips when I saw the elderly couple preceding her to the site. They wouldn't survive a substantial blood loss, but I was willing to bet she'd simply grabbed the owners of the car. There was no time to go hunting down a pair of strapping young men who could stand to lose a couple pints of blood each.

The hiss of a sword being pulled from its scabbard sent

a chill up my spine. With my hand still pressed to Hugo's stomach, I twisted around to see Danaus pointing the sword at Penelope, who had taken a step in front of the two humans as if to protect them from the hunter.

"Mira!" Danaus's hard voice landed heavy on my shoulders.

"Danaus, wait!"

"Hugo needs blood," Penelope argued, lifting her upper lip in a snarl that revealed a pair of perfect fangs. It was a warning.

"Hugo won't last much longer if we don't get some blood back into his system," I said, trying to keep my voice calm and even. The sound of Danaus's and Ryan's hearts pounding seemed to echo through the tree-lined area, rising above the rustling of the leaves. Everyone was tense from the fight with the naturi and tempers were short. I couldn't afford to have someone snap.

"She means for him to kill the humans," Danaus said, taking a step closer. The hunter lifted the point of his sword to the level of Penelope's throat. "Release the humans."

"No! Hugo needs them!" Penelope shouted. "Mira, control him! Hugo needs blood."

"Danaus! Stand down!"

"I won't let you kill humans," Danaus said. His grip on the sword shifted, tightening. It was my last warning.

Time slowed down and I sat on the ground, one hand on Hugo, frozen. Danaus swung his sword twice; first plunging it into Penelope's chest, then removing it and swinging it in a wide arc, slicing off her head. I watched it happen, unable to bring a single word of protest from my throat as he moved in a flawless, fluid swing. Shock halted any useful thoughts. In a span of just a few seconds everything had spiraled completely out of control.

The spray of Penelope's blood washed over all of us. With her death, the humans woke up from the trance she had been holding them under to keep them calm and quiet. Their screams rang through the valley, bouncing off the nearby mountains and waking me from my own morbid thoughts. The old man and woman stared down at their blood-covered hands and clothes, screaming and shaking. They had woken up to find themselves standing outside with two blood-covered bodies on the ground and three soaked, scary figures looming before them. Looking into their wide, horrified eyes, I briefly wondered what Our Liege was thinking when he decided to move up the Great Awakening. It was madness.

"Ryan!" I shouted, my voice shaking. Hugo was stirring, a new moaning rumbling through his brain. Danaus was denying him his only chance at survival. Fear had gripped the nightwalker, and I didn't want him to try to move, reopening wounds that had begun to heal.

"I've got it." The warlock's voice was remarkably calm despite the insanity reigning around us. With a wave of his hand, the two humans grew instantly silent. A dull, unfocused stare returned to their faces. They were no longer aware of where they were or what was going on. I had thought Ryan would know such a trick. We all had to learn to hide in the open and control the minds of others if we were going to survive in a world that demanded we keep such a big secret.

With a growl, I finally turned my attention to Danaus, who was putting his sword back to the scabbard on his back. "What the hell were you thinking? She was only trying to save Hugo. How could you kill her, you heartless bastard?" My voice was choked and broken, struggling to push past the lump in my throat.

"She was going to let him kill both the humans," Danaus said. "You know she was. She was going to sacrifice two humans in hopes of saving him." I looked up again to find him staring down at me, his blue eyes narrowed on my face. "I won't let you kill humans to save yourself."

"Yes she was! But did you ask me what I was planning? Did you ever wonder if I would allow such a thing to happen?" I had to close my eyes to keep the tears from falling. I felt so betrayed. Not until that moment did I realize how much I'd come to depend on Danaus. I had wrongly thought that he'd started to trust me, that he believed in me to do the right thing.

But even the idea of the right thing had begun to blur. Was sacrificing two humans such a bad thing when it came to trying to save the entire human race from the naturi? Keeping Hugo alive would give us one more fighter against the naturi. As it stood now, Penelope was dead and it was highly unlikely that Hugo would last the rest of the night. Any other nightwalker wouldn't have thought twice about draining those two humans dry, but I'd hesitated. No longer sure.

"I don't kill humans when feeding," I said in a voice that sounded broken and beaten. "And I won't allow those around me to do it either. I thought you knew that. You didn't think and you've damned us all." Shaking my head, I looked up at Ryan, who was standing next to the humans. "You and Danaus take the humans. Wipe their memories and send them home. Leave me the car. I'll take care of Hugo."

"But—"

"Just go," I interrupted Ryan before he could argue further. "I'll clean up here."

I sat still on the ground next to Hugo, my hand still pressed to his stomach as if it was my only anchor to sanity in this world. For the first time since becoming a nightwalker, I could feel the night pull in around me and a deep emptiness filled my chest. Even when I was being held captive by the naturi, I didn't give up hope that Sadira or another nightwalker would come to my rescue. But with one nightwalker dead by the hand of a man I had come to rely on, and another dying in my arms, I couldn't find any hope to cling to. The naturi would crush us all.

Twenty-Three

I sat with my back pressed against the stone wall of the mausoleum I hid in during the daylight hours. Exhaustion had settled deep within my bones, making it hard to even move, let alone crawl into the crypt so I could hide from the approaching dawn. Too much had happened in the past few hours, which left me struggling to find some good to cling to in the end.

When I moved Hugo to the car, I discovered that he had also been stabbed in the back, puncturing his heart, which explained why he was so weak. Stopping at the edge of Heraklion, I summoned a dozen inhabitants from their warm, comfortable beds. Hugo fed briefly from each of them before I sent them blindly back to bed again. The drain on my powers was enormous, forcing me to feed as well before I could deposit a sleeping Hugo in a dark crypt in a cemetery between Heraklion and Knossos. When I dropped him off, only the worst of his wounds was slowly seeping blood. I hoped he would last the day.

After leaving him, I returned to the palace ruins, where I burned the bodies of the naturi and Penelope. Guilt gnawed at me for burning her with the naturi, but I no longer had the strength to maintain several fires, and I didn't want to take any chances being so close to the swell of energy rising up from the earth. I'd been burned once; I couldn't afford for it to happen again. What bones I couldn't destroy were buried in a shallow grave. It was the best I could do. Daylight was approaching.

With all evidence of our existence eliminated from Knossos, I cleaned the blood and fingerprints off the car and left it in the heart of Heraklion. I checked on Hugo one final time before finding my own crypt, not far from his.

Now as I sat in the dark, my mind numb, I felt someone approaching me. I pulled the Browning from the holster at the base of my spine and laid it on the ground beside me, partially hidden in the shadows cast by my body. A quick scan revealed that my visitor was Danaus, but I was surprised when I found that I didn't want to put the gun away. I didn't trust him any longer. If push came to shove, I knew I wouldn't try to kill him with a gun. I'd just try to slow him down enough so I could rip his heart out with my bare hands.

"You shouldn't be here," I murmured wearily when the hunter finally came into view. He was still several yards off, but his hearing was nearly as good as mine. He heard me.

"I came to talk," he said in a low voice, as if he was afraid of waking some other graveyard occupant.

I snorted, but still loosened my grip on the gun at my side. My fingers didn't completely uncurl from around the butt, but stayed close just in case. "I can't image we have much to talk about. Everything has been cleanly laid out."

Danaus walked around the last tree separating us in the cross-dotted garden, coming into full view. From what I could see, he was completely unarmed. Both his guns were missing, along with the sword on his back and the two knives usually attached to his leg and waist. Even his leather wrist guards were missing. He stood before me as vulnerable as it was possible for him to be. Could he still kill me in a heart-beat? Without a doubt. He could boil my blood as quickly as I could set him on fire, but he was trying to come before me without weapons.

"I—I came to apologize," he admitted.

I sat in stunned silence for a moment before finally shaking my head to clear it. "I'm not the one you should be apologizing to. You should be apologizing to Penelope for taking her head off. You should be apologizing to Hugo for stealing away his one chance at survival," I bitterly snapped.

"I'm apologizing to you because I should have trusted you," he corrected, standing before me with his legs spread wide, his hands shoved in his pockets. I gazed up, my frown matching his. "I know you. You wouldn't have let Hugo kill those two people. But Penelope would have. Hugo would have. They wouldn't have thought twice about it, and I can't forgive them for that."

"You can't forgive them for wanting to survive?" I demanded, my hand reflexively tightening around the gun as my other hand balled into a fist in the dirt.

"I can't forgive them for killing innocent people," he said. What sympathy and compassion he may have felt drained from his voice, leaving it cold and hard like Siberian permafrost.

"But you have no problem with him dying for these people that you protect," I said, gritting my teeth as I sat up. "We're allowed to fight for them and die for them, but we're not allowed to do anything that might save our own lives."

"It's not like that," he said, hesitant. He took an unsteady step backward with one foot then shifted it forward again.

"Yes, it is." I rose to my feet in a boneless manner, using my powers instead of my muscles for the sole purpose of unnerving him and underscoring my otherness. I did nothing to hide the act of putting the gun back in the holster at my lower back. "You and I work great together so long as you forget what I am. When it's just you and me against the world with sword in hand, we work great together. But if I need to feed or give you some other small reminder that I'm a nightwalker, then you freak out. You can't understand that I'm something beyond *what* I am."

"Forget?" he said in a louder voice. "How could I ever possibly forget what you are? I sense you more clearly than I have ever sensed any vampire. When you're hungry, the feeling burns through me like a fire in my veins. When you use your powers, it's like a cool breeze on a hot summer day. You're in my head and I'm in yours. Do you think I didn't feel your horror and disappointment tonight? What am I supposed to do? I'm a hunter! I'm supposed to protect humanity from threats like nightwalkers."

"Maybe it's time to get a new job," I said, feeling myself softening toward him. I hadn't realized how strong our connection had been for him. I didn't want to forgive him. I didn't want to understand his point of view. I wanted to hold onto the anger so I could easily walk away from him when we finally finished our business with the naturi.

"Enough, Mira," he said in disgust. I had given him similar advice in the past, but this time I was serious.

"Do you believe in fate?"

"What?"

"Fate. That great cosmic force that leads us down particular paths during our existence to—"

"Yes, I know what fate is. No, I don't believe in it."

"Maybe you should," I suggested, sliding my hands into the back pockets of my leather pants. "I'm beginning to wonder myself. Maybe fate brought you to this point not to be a nightwalker hunter but a hunter of naturi. You have the strength, the speed, and the ability to sense them. You have an edge over every nightwalker in existence. Maybe it's time to stop saving humanity from my kind and start saving them for the naturi."

"And who will protect mankind from you?" he demanded, shaking his head at me.

A weak smile twisted one corner of my mouth as I looked up at him. His hair fell forward around his face, hiding his features in dark shadows. "Nightwalkers? No one will need to. It looks like we're on the path to extinction without your help at all."

In fact, my people were on the fast track to extinction. Just on the off chance that we did succeed in stopping the naturi from opening the door and flooding the world with their kind so they could start a massive war, there was still Our Liege's plan. Pushing the Great Awakening ahead of schedule was going to start a war with every lycanthrope, warlock, and witch on the planet. The war would leak out and humans would discover us ahead of schedule in the darkest light. They would join Danaus in the hunt for nightwalkers. Our nights were numbered.

Danaus shocked me when he reached up and gently moved some hair from where it had fallen in front of my face. I looked up to find him faintly smiling down at me as two of his fingers rubbed a lock of my hair as if memorizing the feel. "Rowe won't get you. Remember, we still have to finish our dance. I won't let some dirty naturi kill you when I've promised myself that honor."

"We're overdue for that dance," I said, smiling back up at him.

He shrugged his large shoulders and dropped my hair, letting his hand fall limply back at his side. "Things have gotten in the way. There's still time."

"Is there? What have you told Ryan about the bargain?" I asked, abruptly changing topics. I knew this might have been my only chance to question the hunter while we were completely alone. I had to know if the warlock was looking for a way to stick a knife in my back at the first opportunity.

"Against my better judgment, I've said nothing to him."

"Really?" There was no hiding my surprise. I couldn't begin to fathom Danaus. He did trust me in some strange fashion, just not when it came to controlling the baser needs of my kind. I was beginning to wonder exactly what he felt when he sensed my hunger.

Danaus shoved both of his hands through his hair as he paced a few steps away from me. "I thought you might have a plan to stop this from turning into a war among the races. Ryan is viewed very highly among the warlocks. If he says one word about what is going on in Venice, there will be no stopping the war."

"I have been thinking about it, and no matter what we do, we're screwed. If we let the door open, so we can get our shot at Aurora, the naturi will spill out. There's going to be no hiding them or the war they start. The Great Awakening will happen regardless of anyone's wishes." I leaned back against the small crypt, folding my arms over my chest.

"And if we break the bargain?"

"Assuming we can, we stop the sacrifice and kill Rowe. Once that's done, I imagine that Macaire will hunt me down and cut my head off after he's done torturing me. The Great Awakening will happen within the next year and there will be war among the races, but then, I think we're building toward that already, considering we saw a witch and a lycan traveling with a Coalition member."

"One war or two. That's what we face. Fighting a war on one front or on two."

My head snapped up and I stared silently at him. I didn't need to read his mind to know that he was thinking of the same thing I was. At some point that war was going to put us on opposite sides. He would fight with my kind against the naturi, but he would fight against nightwalkers if it meant protecting humans from us.

We had gotten accustomed to being on the same side. We fought well together, like two dancers in an intricate tango.

"We break the bargain," I said at last, shattering the growing silence. "No bargain should be made with the naturi. We may still find a way to stop Our Liege from pulling back the veil so early. The only problem is, how do we convince the naturi faction that the bargain has been broken?"

"Besides stopping them from breaking the seal?" Danaus said, walking back toward me.

I shook my head, shifting from one foot to the other. Night was wasting away and I was exhausted. I had fed enough, but I needed my rest. Unfortunately, we needed to have this settled before we went into battle tomorrow. "It needs to be more than that. There has to be no doubt in their mind that we are the enemy and they are not going to be permitted to open the door for any reason. They need to know that we won't allow anything to happen to Our Liege."

"You could kill the naturi we saw in Venice," Danaus suggested. "That could be pretty convincing."

"A little late for that now that we're in Crete. I can't go running back—"

"She's here," Danaus interrupted. "I saw her tonight and I noticed that she wasn't among the dead. She's here with Rowe. Apparently, she's making sure everything goes according to plan."

"Sounds like a good plan to me." I nodded, then moved my head to one side, cracking my neck. "Now get out of here so I can get some rest. We'll come up with a more definite plan tomorrow when we have Ryan with us."

"Hugo?" he asked hesitantly.

"Resting for now. If he's lucky, he'll make it through the day, but he won't be with us tomorrow."

Danaus nodded but didn't move from where he stood staring at me. "I can stay."

And a part of me desperately wished he would stay. While trapped at Themis, he'd sat outside the room where I slept helplessly throughout the day while surrounded by his brethren. He had hovered close on so many occasions while I slept that I now hated the idea of him not being there when the sun broke above the horizon. Danaus was my only sense of security in this world that was changing too fast. He threatened to destroy everything that I believed in and everything that I protected. But at the same time, he seemed to be the only one left trying to protect me.

"Get out of here. You'll attract too much attention. I'll be fine," I said, waving him off.

He hesitated a moment before turning around and wandering out of the cemetery back the way he had come in. I concentrated on him with my powers until I felt him just on the edge of the city, well away from the graveyard.

My whole body ached and felt like a giant bruise. I needed some rest, but even now with the approaching dawn, I wasn't tired. In fact, I was wide-awake with a new frightening thought. Killing the naturi wasn't going to be enough to convince the faction that some rogue nightwalker had the power to break a promise made by the Coven. I knew what had to be done. The only problem was, I needed either Jabari or Macaire's help to accomplish it.

Twenty-Four

I didn't want the sun to set. The dawn had finally brought on a blissful peace, sweeping me away from death, Danaus's betrayal, and the wars that were brewing. By the time I had settled into the windowless crypt, I was trembling from exhaustion that reached down to my very core.

Lying in the stone crypt at nightfall, ignoring the sound of bugs crawling around me, I tried to focus my thoughts. I needed to know how old the night was. I needed a plan for how to deal with the naturi. But instead I got the feeling I wasn't alone in my tiny mausoleum. I scanned the immediate area but didn't sense anyone—not human, vampire, or warlock. Regardless, I still couldn't shake the feeling.

My right hand tightened around the gun I'd left on my stomach while I slept. With the other hand, I pushed back the heavy stone lid to the crypt that had protected me from the sun. It was not the first time I'd slept in a cemetery, and no matter how distasteful I found it, I doubted that it would be the last. When desperate, it proved to be one of the safest places to hide without fear of being exposed to the sun.

Sitting up, I pointed the gun directly in front of me, swinging it back and forth, trying to find the creature my instincts were screaming was close. Fear and anger swelled in my stomach and I clenched my teeth. The sight of the gun wavered when my gaze fell on Jabari leaning against the wall near the door. I still couldn't sense him, but I had known he was there. All I could figure was that he had appeared the moment I awoke for the night, and I sensed the shift of energy in the air.

"You can lower the weapon now," he said, his dark eyes locked onto my face.

"Really? That doesn't seem like such a good idea to me," I sneered, more irritated with the fact that I couldn't get my hand to stop trembling than with him.

Jabari arched one eyebrow at me in mocking question as his gaze shifted to the gun. He didn't have to say anything. We both knew he could make me drop the gun at any time. Or if he was feeling particularly evil, he could make me raise the gun to my temple and pull the trigger.

With a growl I couldn't stop, I returned the gun to the holster at my lower back and climbed out of the crypt. "What are you doing here? I thought no one else was coming."

"I came to check on your progress," he said. "Things don't seem to be going so well. Hugo is barely clinging to life."

"He made it through the day?" I demanded before I could stop myself. Jabari's presence surprised me so much that I had forgotten to scan the cemetery to see if I could still sense the big nightwalker.

"Yes, but he will be of no use to you tonight. He will need to feed and sleep for a couple more nights and days before he will be of use to anyone." He paused as I slid the lid of the crypt back into place and leaned against the stone coffin. "And I can no longer sense the other nightwalker that was sent with you . . ."

"Penelope," I murmured. My head fell and I shoved one hand through my hair. I still had to face the nightmare that played through my head like a broken record. "She was killed. Danaus killed her. To stop her from killing two humans."

I waited for the Ancient to strike me, to break me in some horrible, painful way because I had failed to control the hunter. But it never came. After a few seconds I looked up to find him still watching me from where he stood near the door.

"I can't control him," I started, talking simply to fill the growing silence. "I never claimed to be able to control him, but we need him alive. Regardless of how we all feel about him, we need him."

"But you feel betrayed by him," Jabari said, taking a step forward. I took a quick step back, my spine slamming into the stone crypt that ran horizontally along the back wall of the mausoleum. Only a few feet of open, thick blackness separated Jabari and me. The Elder closed the distance as I remained trapped. "I can feel the pain rolling off you. He betrayed you. You trusted him and you thought he trusted you."

A bitter smile twisted my lips as I looked up at one of my three makers. "You'd think I would have learned not to trust powerful creatures."

Jabari leaned close, his eyes glowing faintly in the absolute darkness like a cat's eyes catching a car's headlights. There was no hiding my fear from him. My stomach clenched and my hands trembled despite tightly gripping the edge of the crypt. He might need me alive, but he could cause me severe amounts of pain.

"You still trust me," he whispered, his voice low and hypnotic.

I closed my eyes for a second, trying to quell the shaking that had gone from my hands to encompass my entire body. He couldn't be right. I wouldn't let him be. Clenching that thought between my gritted teeth, I opened my eyes to find him standing by the door on the opposite side of the tiny room. I hadn't even heard him move.

"Why are you here?" I demanded, summoning up my anger again. I knew better than to believe his line that he was just checking up on us. I was surprised by his appearance, but I shouldn't have been. The last time he had randomly appeared was at the Themis Compound, the night of the attack and the sacrifice at Stonehenge. "Afraid of missing out on another sacrifice?"

Jabari smiled this time, a dark and evil thing. "Just missed the last one." The smile slithered from his face and he turned serious again. "You know why I'm here. It's the same reason I commanded you to appear in Venice. The one place in the world where you could prove to be the greatest nuisance."

"Because of the naturi in the Great Hall," I said.

Jabari simply nodded, the smile returning to his lips.

My hands fell back to my sides and I leaned against the tomb that had served as my daytime bed. "Honestly, old friend, is what Macaire told me the truth? Just between you and me and the spiders."

"I do not know, but I have found that it's very rare for Macaire to speak the truth," Jabari replied, matching my mocking tone.

"Has the Coven truly made a bargain with the naturi?"

"A small group within the naturi, yes," Jabari corrected.

I bit on my lower lip for a second, trying to hold back a smile, as he carefully hedged. "They want us to kill Aurora."

"That is correct."

"And the Coven wants them to kill Our Liege."

To this, Jabari said nothing, but he did nod once.

Yeah, I was the only nightwalker insane enough to actually say those words out loud. But then again, I had lots of people trying to kill me, what was one more? "And this is because he's trying to move up the Great Awakening."

Again Jabari nodded.

"This is ridiculous!" I shouted, barely resisting the urge to start pacing in the tiny crypt. "This is nothing more than Macaire's power play. He has to know that allowing the door to open will bring about the Great Awakening. There will be no hiding a war with the naturi from the humans."

"That is true, but it is proving to be effective. Tabor was vocally against the plan, threatening to go to Our Liege."

"And he ended up dead," I said, finishing the thought. "I'm assuming this is the reason no one has been able to sense you for the past several years."

"I prefer my privacy, yes," Jabari murmured, as if this was all a lighthearted game. He leaned against the wall opposite me, crossing one leg in front of the other. His dark skin allowed him to nearly blend into the darkness, giving the night an almost velvety texture where he stood.

"But I don't understand." I shoved one hand through my knotted and dirty hair in frustration. "Why drag me into this? Kill Macaire and end the bargain. You didn't need me in Venice for that."

"I needed you causing chaos in Venice, threatening to spread our secret and disrupting our meetings with the naturi. It strikes fear in them, and we need them to fear us. Besides, you should never underestimate Macaire. He has been on the Coven longer than me. He is harder to kill than you would think."

"So I was brought to Venice to discover the secret?"

"With the hunter at your side, it was inevitable."

"And Nicolai?"

"We offered him as a sacrifice."

"So I was supposed to save him . . . "

"No, you were supposed to kill him, but everything still worked out in the end," Jabari admitted with a shrug of his broad shoulders.

"What's the next step in your master plan?" I demanded, my temper flaring. I had been used and manipulated since the moment I stepped off the plane in Venice. Jabari didn't have to use his powers to control me. He could do just fine with me running around on my own, creating chaos wherever I went.

"The same plan that I am sure you have already cooked up with the hunter," Jabari said, pushing off the wall. He slowly walked over to stand before me. Only a slender column of air separated us when he spoke again. "Kill the naturi called Rowe. Stop the sacrifice and protect the seal. We must make it clear to them that there is going to be no bargain between nightwalkers and naturi."

"The naturi from Venice. The one in the hall. She's here with Rowe," I said, trying to swallow back my fear. My anger had slipped away and now there was just the cold chill of the crypt as I stood alone with one of my makers, and one of my greatest betrayers. Once again we found each other as allies when I knew it was only a matter of time before we would find ourselves on opposite sides of the battlefield.

"Then we kill her. If the harpies appear, we kill them as well."

"Jabari, I—I . . . " I hesitated. I had some fears about our plan, but I didn't want to volunteer my solution unless it was absolutely necessary. "Do you still mean to kill me?"

Lifting one hand, he cupped my cheek as he leaned forward and brushed his lips against my other cheek. His lips strayed down my jaw to my bare neck, sending a chill sweeping through my entire body. "My fragile desert blossom," he murmured in my ear. "I want you dead in the worst way. But for now I have a use for you, so you live."

That's what I thought. I was trapped, surrounded by creatures that wanted me dead, but for now all seemed to have a use for me as some kind of weapon against the naturi. Except for Rowe. He wanted to use me as a weapon against the nightwalkers.

I bit back a sigh as Jabari stepped away from me. Our course was set. The big bad Ancient could make it sound easy all he wanted, but I knew the truth. When we walked back into the Minoan ruins that night, the naturi were going to throw everything they had at us to ensure that they completed the sacrifice. There was no way they were going to let us stop them a second time.

Twenty-Five

R yan and Danaus were waiting for us along the road to the Palace of Knossos. Both of them looked surprised to find Jabari walking beside me, but neither one asked about Hugo, which was probably the smartest course of action. His absence indicated that he either hadn't made it through the day or was too weak to aid us tonight.

After last night's freak storm, summer had returned to the island, leaving the air thick and heavy like a sweat-soaked blanket. The wind was silent, allowing any noise we made to travel easily to our intended prey. But I didn't actually have much hope of sneaking up on them anyway.

As we walked along the side of the road, bits of gravel crunching beneath my feet, I completed my weapons check for the second time. The weapons Danaus gave me when we flew into Venice had been reorganized due to the unexpected arrival of James and Ryan. One of my guns now rested with James, whom I suspected was once again pouting alone in the hotel room. My sword had also been replaced with a pair of knives that rested in holsters strapped around my legs. I had more experience with close, hand-to-hand fighting, and my speed made me more lethal with a knife. The sword had been handed off to Danaus.

However, I still had one of the detested guns the hunter had given me. I pulled the Browning from where it rested at my lower back and ejected the magazine from the butt of the gun. The magazine wasn't fully loaded.

"Here," Danaus said, walking up beside me.

I looked down at the spare magazine he extended toward me. With a grunt, I accepted it, sliding it into my back left pocket. I hadn't forgiven him. I wanted to spend several nights beating him senseless for what he'd done. A part of me also wanted to curl up into a ball and weep. But the naturi were gathering and I didn't have time for either, so I accepted the bullets and kept walking.

"What's the plan?" Ryan inquired from the rear of the line.

"Jabari," I quickly said, hoping the nightwalker would happily step up into the lead. He was, after all, an Ancient and an Elder member of the Coven.

"This is your dance, Mira. You may lead. I am here only to fill in for the fallen nightwalkers," Jabari called from behind me. I could almost hear his mocking laughter with each syllable. *Rat bastard.*

I hesitated, resisting the urge to look over at Danaus. Had he told Ryan about the Coven deal with the naturi?

"We have to face the fact that it is very unlikely the human they have selected for the sacrifice will survive," I slowly began. My stomach churned with each ugly word I uttered. "Even if we rescue this person, as long as he or she in the area of the palace, they can be used as the sacrifice. The only way to eliminate the risk is to eliminate all humans from the area."

"You're saying kill the human before the naturi get the chance?" Ryan said. There was no surprise or disgust in his tone. He had asked matter-of-factly, as if simply confirming what I'd said.

"Our main focus needs to be eliminating the naturi threat," I replied, aware of Danaus and evading a direct response. "Jabari and I will focus on Rowe. We will need you and Danaus to keep the naturi off our backs."

If anyone was planning to comment on my ultracrappy planning skills, they lost out on the opportunity because we had reached the edge of the palace. With the gun clenched in my right hand and a knife in my left, I moved onto the first step leading up to the palace and paused. There was no time for fear or anger now. It was time to just worry about killing Rowe and surviving the next hour or so.

The energy I had felt last night was nothing compared to what I felt beating against me now. Ryan had created a storm with the force to not only destroy all of Crete but also wipe out several of other islands in the region, and it hadn't even dented the energy I now felt vibrating in the air. It pushed against my skin, determined to once again find entrance into my body. I couldn't use my powers tonight. This energy would shred me.

"They're here," Danaus murmured.

My head jerked toward the hunter, forcing me from my dark thoughts. "How many?"

"About two dozen. Most are centered in the main clearing, but there are a few hanging back toward the south. Two more are in the air."

Before shifting my weight to take the next step, I scanned the area as well, looking for the exact location where the human was being held. The naturi would wait until the night was near its peak, but they would be preparing the human. I was willing to guess that Rowe was hovering close to the human as well. But the naturi managed to surprise me again.

"Damn it," I snarled in a low whisper. I stepped backward and lowered my gun.

"There are three," Jabari said from behind me, stating what I'd just discovered. I walked a few feet away from the entrance to the ruins, flipping the safety of the gun back on in an effort to keep from putting a bullet in my foot in a moment of frustration. There were three humans at the center of the ruins. Not one. Three.

"Decoys?" Danaus asked, drawing my gaze to his face for a flash.

I looked away just as quickly, my eyes darting from Danaus to Ryan before finally settling on Jabari. "Yeah, maybe," I softly said, holding the Elder's eyes.

"And one of those decoys is James," Ryan announced.

"What? How?" I gasped, feeling the need to point my gun at the warlock. Bringing the human along had always felt like packing live bait to me, and now the young man was caught.

"He was grabbed during the middle of the day," Danaus answered. "He ran down to the corner store and never returned."

I wanted to smack them both for letting James out of their sight. Hadn't my own mistake with allowing Michael to get involved in a fight against the naturi taught them anything? Humans only ended up dead when the naturi and nightwalkers were involved.

We needed to hurry now. It had been night for more than an hour already. They could have started the process. While they might not complete the sacrifice until the peak of the night, the naturi could spend several hours in the ritual, removing the human's various organs and burning them. They would keep James alive and conscious right up until the end. But we wouldn't have any hope of saving him if they had already cut him open.

"New plan," I announced, insanely hoping I could convince Danaus and Ryan to go along with my newest bout of insanity. "There are three humans but only one is the true sacrifice. I will go after Rowe and keep the bastard occupied. Danaus will focus on freeing James and getting him over to Ryan. Once Ryan has James, the two of them will return to Heraklion."

"Mira, I think I can—" Ryan started, but I quickly cut him off.

"No, you can't. You're still a human, Mr. Warlock, and can be used as a sacrifice. Both you and James have to be away from the site. Jabari will focus on the other sacrifices. Ryan, I need you to hang back until James has been freed. If Rowe or any of the other naturi tap into the weather again, I need you to stop it."

"Mira, that's earth magic. Not my strong suit," he argued.

"You have to try." I flipped the safety off the gun again and took a step toward the entrance. "Do whatever you can to interfere with the spell. We'll try to keep them away from you so you can work."

Turning, I walked toward the entrance and up the stairs without looking back at anyone. I knew that none of the humans were decoys. Rowe wasn't taking any chances. We had stopped him once, and now he was betting we wouldn't be able to stop all three sacrifices.

As I reached the top of the stairs, a high-pitched screech rent the silence of the night. I cringed, lowering my head as if I expected the wrath of the heavens to fall on me at that second. Not quite. Two of the harpies from Venice had come to Knossos to help Rowe with the sacrifice. And we had obviously been spotted.

Sneaking around one of the remaining walls, a smile lifted my lips. The idea was to let me protect the seal and kill Rowe. The positive aspect to the plan was that I could kill every naturi that stood between him and me. I knew I would find a bright side somewhere within this nightmare.

We edged closer to the central courtyard. Only a handful of naturi stepped forward to harry us. With Jabari tagging along, they were quickly dispatched with little trouble before any of them could fire up their special powers. I wasn't surprised. The main force of the naturi was pulled back to defend the sacrifices.

The wind suddenly picked up, shifting twice before it blew at my back, pushing me forward. Climbing over a low, broken wall that surrounded the courtyard, I tightened my grip on the knife and gun. Rowe stood a few yards away, legs spread and hands on his hips. He smiled at me. Behind him more than a dozen torches flickered and danced in the wind. Spread before us across the wide courtyard were the three humans; two men and one small child. They had been tied down, their bodies stretched out from east to west. Just like at Stonehenge not so long ago.

"Is this all you brought?" Rowe demanded, arching the eyebrow over his one good eye. "I thought last night was a little scouting party. But this is it?"

"Why waste the manpower when four is all we need?" I mocked. "We're ending this tonight."

"I agree."

A duet of screams filled the air above me. Reluctant to take my eyes off Rowe, I looked up in time to see the two harpies plunging toward me, their fleshy wings pulling in close to their bodies to increase the speed of their fall. I lunged forward, slamming against the rock floor while Danaus and Jabari dove in opposite directions. Pain exploded in my ribs as I hit the ground, but I pushed it aside and kept moving. Rolling onto my back, I lifted my gun, searching the black skies for the mythical nightmares. But they were gone.

Rolling to my knees, my head snapped back as pain exploded in my jaw and I cried out, falling to my back. Rowe was on me in a second. His fist connected with my cheek-bone, both sides of my face now throbbing in pain. The naturi straddled me, his knees pressed against my hips.

"You should have taken my offer," he growled, and slammed his fist into my stomach. "We would be on the same side now."

I swung my right hand up, trying to aim the gun at him. "Never," I grunted.

Rowe easily knocked my hand away, but I was counting on it. I swung my left hand up, burying my knife up to its hilt in his side. He screamed, backhanding me as he pulled away. His blood covered my hand, causing the knife to slip out of my grip as he stumbled off.

I pushed back to my feet, the pain in my face beginning to subside. I tried to get my bearings as Rowe hurried away to heal the latest wound I had inflicted on him. But I didn't have a chance. They attacked silently this time and I wasn't watching the skies.

The winged naturi swooped down in a rush of wind, blotting out the meager starlight. I'd taken half a step back when impossibly long talons dug into my arms and shoulders. A scream was ripped from my throat as my feet left the ground, matched by the sweet sounds of their laughter as they carried me off.

I tried to twist from their taloned grasp, but the claws only dug deeper into my flesh and muscles until I could feel them scraping against bone. Blood streamed from my shoulders, soaking into my cotton shirt, still stained from last night's battle. Lifting the hand that held the gun, I tried aiming it at either of my two captors as we rose higher into the night sky. I managed to get off only two shots before the gun was ripped out of my hand, and looked down in time to see it plummeting to the earth, which was steadily receding farther and farther away. The ruins were drifting away too

as the pair of wind naturi carried me to the north, toward
Heraklion and the sea.

With each flap of their massive wings, a gust of wind hit
me. A chill flashed across my body, cooling the blood that
crawled across my stomach in a growing stream. A reflexive
shiver shook me, causing their talons to dig deeper. I had to
get free. Danaus and the others were outnumbered. James
had to be saved. Rowe would complete the sacrifice soon,
and the power . . . I couldn't feel the power any longer. The
harpylike naturi had carried me far enough away.

My head fell back and a bubble of laughter jumped from
my throat a second before both of the naturi holding me
erupted into flames. Their screams echoed across the skies
as their clawed feet opened, releasing me. I moved quickly,
grabbing an ankle of each naturi before I could fall back
to the earth. Pain burned in my shoulders, threatening to
loosen my grip, but I held tight. If I lost sight of them or lost
contact, I wouldn't be able to keep the fire going.

The flames ate at their flesh, burning holes in their fleshy
wings until we were all plunging to the ground in a hideous heap of burning, melting flesh. The naturi in my grip
twisted and screamed, not so much fighting me, but simply
trying to escape the pain. I finally released my hold on their
legs as the ground approached with surprising speed. I had
made this mistake before, not paying attention to where I
was falling. The last time it happened, I'd been impaled on
a tree limb and barely survived the encounter. And Sadira
wasn't around now to save my sorry ass.

Plummeting to the ground, I looked down to discover I
was falling into an orchard. Damn it. Ready-made stakes. I
lost sight of the two naturi, so the fire I had created instantly
went out. Crossing my arms over my chest in a desperate
attempt to shield my heart, I crashed through the smaller
upper branches. My feet hit a larger branch, but I just as

quickly slid off so that I landed across it. Something cracked. Whether it was my ribs or the branch, I don't know, but only a moment later both the large branch and I were laying on the soggy ground.

I wanted to stay there awhile. Pain throbbed in my body in half a dozen places, and I wanted to collect my thoughts before adding to the network of cuts and wounds that crisscrossed me. But a pair of low moans pulled me back. The two wind naturi had crashed through a tree right behind me.

Using the trunk of the tree I'd fallen through to help me to my feet, I hobbled over to where the naturi were writhing on the ground. Their pale pink skin was now black and flaking off in bits of ash. Their wings had burned straight through, leaving them grounded. But then, we all knew they would never fly again even if I hadn't destroyed their wings.

Their screams lasted for less than a minute as I once again encased them in bright orange flames. I felt no remorse, no regret, no doubt. The naturi intended to do the same to every other creature soon enough.

When they were destroyed, their ashes left to dance in the wind, I summoned up my powers again and searched the island for Danaus. I had a vague idea where I was but couldn't waste time wandering around in the darkness. I located the hunter with ease. He was my beacon in the night.

Cutting across the open farmland, I ran as quickly as my wounded body would permit. I had lost blood and my body was trying to repair itself, but it wasn't an easy job, as I refused to stop and rest. Reaching the road again, I picked up speed, and returned to the ruins in a matter of minutes.

At the main courtyard, I found Jabari at the westernmost sacrifice. He was easily tearing through one naturi after another as each one bravely approached the Ancient. Danaus was to the east, holding his own with a sword in his hand while naturi formed a semicircle around the hunter. James was still staked to the ground, though one of his hands was loose and he was struggling to free his other hand.

Ryan was my greatest concern. The warlock stood opposite Rowe. As I approached them, I paused long enough to pick up a short sword from the ground. A lost weapon from a dead naturi. It wasn't my first choice, but I'd lost one of my knives in Rowe earlier and the harpies had stolen my gun. I had one knife left, and I was going to need that if Rowe pinned me again.

Overhead, the sky had begun to churn and the wind gusted, whipping my hair in front of my face. Rowe was calling up another storm. The ground around Ryan glowed a strange pale blue. The warlock had created some sort of protective circle to keep the naturi physically at bay. But I knew it wouldn't protect him from a bolt of lightning. At least, not for long.

"We're not finished!" I shouted across the courtyard. Rowe's head snapped up, and for a breath he actually looked surprised. Then the shock melted away, the fleeting emotion replaced with a grin that reminded me of my old tormentor, Nerian.

"Good to see you in one piece," Rowe replied. His one good eye jumped from me to Ryan and back again as he struggled to watch the warlock and me at the same time.

I was about to lunge at him when someone far more interesting captured my attention. "Rowe, you once said there was some great reason why I was left alive that day. Some role I had yet to play," I shouted over the gusting wind. "Call this me returning the favor."

Rowe genuinely looked confused as I sidled past him and moved toward the female naturi who stood nearby. She was the one who'd appeared within the Great Hall. She was the one with whom the bargain had been made. She held a sword in one hand and her lips were pressed into a thin line of worry. She knew I recognized her despite the fact that she now wore a pair of jeans and a black tank top.

"I see you got your playmate back," I taunted. "Did she enjoy her stay within the hall?"

The tip of Rowe's sword dipped as he looked from me to the other naturi at his side.

"She's insane," the female quickly said, shaking her head. "She's lying. I don't know what she's talking about."

"Hmmm . . . " Rowe said, taking a step away from her. "Maybe. But then, Mira's not one to lie."

"Jabari! Is this her?" I shouted across the courtyard, hoping to snag the attention of the Ancient as he tore apart another naturi. The Elder turned, his robes soaked in blood. He casually paused for a moment and looked at the naturi I had indicated.

"Yes," he said with a nod. "Kill her. The bargain is off."

"You can't call off the bargain!" she screamed without thinking. "A single member of the Coven can't call off the bargain. You promised us!"

I didn't think she would go for it so easily. I wasn't sure how many of the remaining naturi in the region were a part of this faction that wanted Aurora dead. I needed to not only convince Rowe that there was a deal, but those faction members also had to believe that the bargain was dead. I had dreaded this moment, but now that it was here, I didn't feel the panic I'd anticipated. Adrenaline pumped through my body and my hand tightened on the hilt of the short sword I held. I was ready to finally take matters into my own hands, ready to take back a measure of control of my life.

"I claim the open seat on the Coven," I announced, straightening my stance. "Jabari, do you recognize my claim?"

The smile grew across his face and I could feel him laughing in triumph. "I recognize your claim," he solemnly replied with a bow of his head. And then his voice changed to something darker, more insidious, as he finished, "Welcome to the Coven."

"Now, as we were saying," I continued, turning my attention back to the naturi, who stood before me with her face growing redder with anger. "The bargain is off. If you want Aurora dead, you can do it yourself. The door is staying closed."

"No!" she screamed. She came running at me with her sword raised above her head.

Grabbing a knife from my side with my free hand, I knelt down and threw it directly at her chest. The small knife buried itself in her heart. She paused, still standing, long enough for me to rise to my feet and remove her head with a single, fluid swing.

Her blood sprayed everywhere, pelting me in the face. I wiped it off with the back of my hand as I turned my full attention back to Rowe. "Obviously, you didn't have all your ducks in a row, but you do now."

"The same could be said about you and your young man," Rowe countered, motioning with his sword toward Danaus.

James was sitting up now, but the naturi were getting closer. Danaus was painfully outnumbered, while Jabari was trying to defend the two other humans at the same time. The bargain was dead, but we were stretched too thin to try to stop the sacrifice. Besides, there would be no combining our powers this time. Danaus and I were desperate, but what we'd done last time was too ugly to repeat. There had to be another way.

"I—"

Whatever Rowe meant to say was cut off when another naturi called to him. His whole body stiffened at the sound of her voice. He quickly stepped backward, putting some distance between himself and Ryan. But I also noticed he carefully positioned himself between me and the newcomer.

It drew my attention to her. She was shorter than me and her body was incredibly slender, as if she were only an animated skeleton in soft gray clothes. A mass of straight black hair hung down her back. She watched me with enormous eyes that seemed to be the same shade of pale gray as her clothes. In fact, the only thing that didn't seem to be monotone in this slim creature was her ruby red mouth, which at the moment held neither a smile nor a frown. I watched her until Rowe stepped into my line of sight, thinking insanely that she looked familiar.

Rowe shouted something at her and she responded. They spoke in their own language, which I couldn't understand. But Rowe's body language and tone spoke volumes. He pointed his sword at me with his right hand and waved his left hand at her, motioning her to stay back. Eyes narrowed and body bent forward, he was ready to attack me if I took a single step toward her.

Again he shouted some direction at her that I couldn't understand. Just over his shoulder, I saw her gaze up at the sky once. There was no moon to see, but I knew what she was doing. She wasn't looking for some celestial body or even a fresh wave of winged naturi to aid them. I knew her expression—she was gauging the night. We were out of time.

Something clenched in my stomach and my hands started to shake. Now was the moment, and I felt trapped. I was afraid to use my powers. I could kill us all. There was too much energy in the air and I wouldn't be able to control it.

"Danaus!" I screamed. I hoped the hunter heard me. I hoped he understood by the desperate plea in my voice what I was asking, because there was no more time for plans and explanations. "Kill the female! Stop her!" My voice rang out over the fighting, echoing across the valley. Jabari, Danaus, and Ryan heard me. They would stop her if I could not.

Rowe's face twisted in rage at my words, turning his whole body to face me. He raised his sword and came at me. I countered him, and his sword clashed with mine again and again, the impact sending sparks flying around him. We were both desperate, but Rowe was also afraid of something, which made him sloppy. Dodging a blow meant to remove my head, I punched him in the face, knocking him back a few steps. To my surprise, he fell backward over a piece of broken rock and didn't get back up.

Chaos surrounded me. Dropping the short sword, I reached inside of myself and tapped my own abilities. I was ready to summon up all the fires of Hell. No one would leave the ruins alive. The sacrifices had to be stopped. The seal had to be protected.

With the first flicker of fire, the energy came rushing into me, alive and crackling. For the first time in my life, I was fully in touch with the powers of the earth. There was no calm, sweet peace. No sound of babbling brooks or whispering winds. There was only crackling rage and the fury of a power long unused. Mother Earth was fucking pissed and I was now her outlet.

Each naturi that approached me burst into flames instantly, but it wasn't enough to relieve the pressure building in my body. The torches became engulfed in flames while giant basketball-size balls of fire hovered in the air, lighting the courtyard so it appeared as if daybreak had finally arrived. I located Danaus and James and quickly encircled them in a protective wall of fire. I did the same with Jabari, but it wasn't enough.

The power was building. It was going to destroy me, and I couldn't find the gray female Rowe had been so intent on protecting. The power was going to kill me before I could stop her.

Danaus. I reached out. My voice in my head seemed like

a small whisper compared to the roar of power within me. I couldn't concentrate anymore. The fires were getting larger, brighter, stronger. I was going to kill the very people I was trying to protect.

I'm here. His voice in my brain was a cool balm against the burning inside me.

Can't concentrate. Can't find her. Don't know which sacrifice she's going after.

She's here.

"No!" I screamed. *James!*

Pain exploded within me. I didn't even have a chance to react. My whole body was thrown backward. I flew what felt like yards through the air in a terrifying blur of motion before my spine slammed into the hard stone ground. An incoherent scream of pain erupted from my throat as I writhed. Something was being torn deep within me, as if someone or something was attacking the fragile shreds of my soul, trying to pull them from my body. I curled into the fetal position, desperate to hold my soul within my battered frame. The pain burned within me. Nerve endings trembled and twisted. Organs sizzled. Agonizing pain ripped through my brain until there wasn't a single thought.

And then the blackness seeped in. It consumed everything, the pain, the tearing sensation in my chest, the outside world. The blackness blotted out everything and then it stole me away.

Twenty-Six

I jerked upright and gasped, which sent razor blades down my throat and through my lungs before the first clear thought rang through my brain. I didn't need to breathe, but there were some instincts that even death couldn't kill. When I awoke each night from a nightmare, my first reaction was always to gasp for air. But this wasn't a nightmare.

Blinking as I tried to clear my blurred vision, I felt a hand at my back and on my shoulder as someone eased me back to the ground. I coughed and tried to roll back onto my side as I pushed the unnecessary air out of my body. Something inside of me ached. My thoughts were fuzzy as I tried to remember what had happened. No one had touched me, but pain had exploded inside of me, frying every organ and brain cell.

"Rest, Mira." Jabari's deep voice swept over me from my right. I lay on my back and unclenched my eyes. Ryan was kneeling beside me on my left, one of his hands holding mine. Jabari was kneeling too. His clothes were torn and he was covered in blood, but a soft smile hovered on his lips. He had won. I was on the Coven, which only benefited him because he was able to control me.

"James?" I asked, fearing the answer when I looked up at

Ryan. The warlock nodded over past Jabari. Twisting, I saw the young man seated against the wall, bloodied, bruised, and swollen, but still breathing.

"But Danaus—" I started, then slowly shook my head as I tried to clear the fog from my thoughts. "He said the naturi was by him. Is the seal still safe?"

"The seal was broken," Jabari confirmed, his smile falling into a dark frown.

"How?" I demanded in a raspy voice.

"The human male I freed. He jumped through the ring of fire you created and into the waiting arms of the naturi. It took them only a second to subdue him and complete the task."

"And the child?" I whispered.

"He sleeps," Ryan said. "He'll be returned to town to-night and will remember none of this."

I pressed my right hand to the center of my chest. Was the seal breaking what I had felt? Had the seal been tied to my soul? The pain had been excruciating, as if something were being torn from me. Even now there was a hollow, ragged sensation throbbing within me.

"I . . . felt . . . pain," I said. My voice wavered and sounded rough to my own ears.

Jabari nodded. His large hand swept over my forehead and down as he moved some hair from my face in a surprisingly comforting gesture. "You created the seal. It's natural that you felt its destruction."

Ryan's hand tightened at Jabari's words. "You created the original seal?"

I pulled my hand out of his grasp and rolled away from him. I couldn't look at the warlock. Getting my knees beneath me, I slowly sat up. However, all thoughts of standing left me when I looked around the area. The carnage was gut-wrenching. Blood and bodies were strewn everywhere, bringing back images of the battle at the Themis Compound less than a week earlier. There was nowhere I could go. Destruction seemed to hound my every step. Chaos followed in my wake.

And now the seal was broken. The naturi would soon determine a time to open the door between our two worlds, and the war would officially begin. What lay before me was simply a minor skirmish.

"I'm a monster," I whispered, shaking my head as tears slipped unchecked down my scratched and dirty face. Burned corpses filled the area, with smoke still rising from their bodies. "I'm a monster with this kind of power and yet still I fail."

"The bargain has been broken. Our Liege is safe," Jabari patiently reminded me. "We succeeded."

"No, the seal was broken," I moaned.

Kneeling before me, he placed his hands on either side of my face and forced me to meet his dark gaze. "We failed because we didn't work together. We separated when our greatest strength is to work together through you. This will be for the best. This is the only way to end this permanently. We will kill Aurora and destroy the naturi for all time. No more seals and no more gateways to other worlds. We end it for all time."

"But—"

"To protect our way of life, to protect the humans, we have to destroy the naturi. And the only way to do that is to destroy their queen."

I wanted to believe Jabari. I couldn't remember ever wanting anything more. And he might have been right—the only way to destroy the naturi could be through Aurora. But all I could see was this black shadow of death stretching across the earth. To get to Aurora, so many would have to die; vampire, lycanthrope, and human.

But at least now we had some time. We had time to plan. We had time to hunt.

I pulled back, removing my face from his grasp. "You had better be right."

Painfully, I pushed to my feet. The sound of Jabari and Ryan rising as well drifted to my ears, but my attention was on the carnage around me. Danaus was slowly approaching. He was covered in blood and scrapes. A long cut ran along the right side of his face, blood dripping from the end of his chin. His deep blue eyes glittered in the fading torchlight.

"Rowe?" I asked.

"Unknown," Danaus said with a slight shake of his head. "He was badly wounded. They carried him out of here."

I knew better than to hope. Centuries ago I had left Nerian for dead at the top of Machu Picchu, confident the naturi would never be able to pull his intestines back into his body before he bled to death. I had been wrong. I wouldn't believe that Rowe was actually dead until I saw his cold, lifeless body lying on the ground before me. And even then I'd incinerate him to white hot ashes just to be on the safe side.

But for now I wanted Rowe alive. He knew there was a faction within his happy family that wanted his wife-queen dead. That division within the naturi could work to our advantage in the coming nights. Rowe would be forced to conduct a witch hunt within his own people to find out who wanted Aurora dead. It would create chaos, and creating chaos was what I did best.

Turning, I looked over at one of the nightwalkers who was rumored to have created me. Something deep inside of me hated Jabari for using me, for making me his own powerful plaything. But I didn't have the memories of those horrible moments to keep the fires of hatred burning brightly. All the memories I had of him were of loving companionship and trust. Even now, knowing the truth about my creation and past, some part of me still trusted him, needed to believe that what he'd told me was the truth.

Regardless of my feelings for Jabari, I didn't want to be on the Coven, but for now, my presence struck a balance against Macaire and maybe even Elizabeth. And until Macaire was either broken or dead, Jabari would be content to leave me alive. I had bought myself and Our Liege some time.

"I'm leaving," I announced.

"You're to go back to the Coven," Jabari ordered. "You belong with the Coven."

I smiled at him. "No," I simply said. "I'm going where I am needed. I'm going home. When the time comes to fight Aurora and the naturi, you know where to find me."

I walked toward the northern entrance, but stopped after only a few feet. Looking over my shoulder, I stared at Danaus for a few seconds in silence. So many unanswered questions, confused emotions, and ugly mistakes. A bori wrapped in human trappings. A hunter who was no longer sure who the enemy really was. And a nightwalker who was no longer sure where her loyalties lay. There was only one thing I knew for sure when it came to Danaus: We weren't finished yet.

"Are you coming?" I called.

He arched one thick black brow at me. His lips twisted and one corner of his mouth quirked in a mocking smile.

"It'll be easier to kill you if I don't have to hunt you down," I said, answering his unspoken question, *Why?*

Without a word, Danaus slid his blood-smeared sword back into the sheath on his back and followed me out of the Minoan ruins. For now, we could both say to hell with the Coven, Themis, and the naturi. I was headed home, where Danaus and I could focus on more important things. Like to get back to the business of killing each other.